Joseph Goodwin Terrill

The Life of Rev. John Wesley Redfield, M.D.

Joseph Goodwin Terrill

The Life of Rev. John Wesley Redfield, M.D.

ISBN/EAN: 9783337333249

Printed in Europe, USA, Canada, Australia, Japan

Cover: Foto ©Raphael Reischuk / pixelio.de

More available books at **www.hansebooks.com**

THE LIFE

— OF —

Rev. John Wesley Redfield, M. D.

—BY—

REV. JOSEPH GOODWIN TERRILL.

"Whose Faith Follow."

CHICAGO, ILL.

Published by the Author, 104 Franklin Street,

1889.

TO ALL THOSE,

who, with evangelical faith,

and fervent love,

by their prayers, means and personal efforts,

are engaged in the glorious work

of leading souls from sin and the world

to partake of the

peace and joy that springs from that

"HOLINESS
WITHOUT WHICH NO MAN CAN SEE THE LORD,"

these pages are inscribed by the

AUTHOR.

CONTENTS.

CHAPTER XIX.

CHAPTER XX.

CHAPTER XXI.

CHAPTER XXII.

CHAPTER XLII.

CHAPTER XLIII.

CHAPTER XLIV.

INTRODUCTION.

BY REV. B. T. ROBERTS.

DEAD trees can be made into blocks, or boards, of the same length, and breadth, and thickness. But plant two seeds from the same tree, in the same soil, exposed to the same influences, and they will grow up resembling and yet unlike each other. You can easily tell them apart. *Life abhors uniformity.*

In a dead church, ministers may be essentially alike. They may all go through with the same routine duties, in the same manner, and with the same results. But let spiritual life get into a church, and men are raised up to do ministerial work outside of the regular ministerial channels. The church itself may recognize but one class of ministers—it may insist upon their absolute equality, and require of all the same service; but when life divine comes thrilling through its members, some will break through all their regulations, and exercise the functions of an office which the church does not recognize. And thus in face of all human provisions to the contrary, the Scriptures are fulfilled, "And God hath set some in the church, first apostles, secondarily prophets, thirdly teachers, after that miracles, then gifts of healings, helps, governments, diversities of tongues."—1 Cor. xii. 28. The phrase *hath set* denotes a permanent arrangement. In the original it is a word frequently translated "ordained." It does not refer to a short-lived plan that was to last for but a single generation. So the error is apparent, of the assumption that there were but twelve apostles, and that the apostleship ceased with these. In fact the New Testament speaks expressly of other apostles besides the twelve. The Church of England has an order of ministers which it calls "priests," for which order the gospel of Christ makes no provision. Not once in the New Testament are any of the ministers of the gospel called *priests*. They are called by a great variety of names, but this is not found among them. A priest is one that offers sacrifices; and in Christ, the High Priest of our profession, the priesthood *as a ministerial* order ceased. James is nowhere in the New Testament called a priest, nor is Peter, nor Paul, nor any other minister of the gospel. The term priest is applied in the New Testament to all of God's people. "Ye also, as lively stones, are built up a spiritual house, an holy priesthood, to offer up spiritual sacrifices, acceptable to God by Jesus Christ."—1 Peter ii. 5. "But ye are a chosen generation, a royal priesthood." —v. 9. So Christians are required as priests to present their bodies a living sacrifice. (Romans xii. 1.) To present to God broken hearts and contrite spirits,—for these are sacrifices which he will not despise. (Psalm li. 17.) To abound in good works. "But to do good and to communicate forget not, for with such sacrifices God is well pleased." (See also Phil. iv. 18.) To offer praise to God. "By him therefore let us offer the sacrifice of praise to God continually, that is, the fruit of our lips, giving thanks to his name."—Hebrews xiii. 15. But none of these things can we do by proxy. No priest can step between us and God to do them for us. If not done in our own proper person, and from our own free will, they are not done at all. Others may persuade us; but any other sacrifice than that which Christ has made for us once for all, we ourselves must make. So those who would be real Christians must reject all assumptions of priestly authority.

Though the Church of England does not recognize the order of apostles as still in existence; yet from the ranks of its ministry, John Wesley stood forth before the world an apostle sent of God.

The Methodist Church of to-day acknowledges no apostles, yet William Taylor has shown himself to be as truly an apostle, as was St. Paul or John Wesley.

Among Independents, Dwight L. Moody has shown himself to be an evangelist, though the Independent churches know no ministers but pastors.

So John Wesley Redfield stood forth in the Methodist Episcopal Church, the most wonderful evangelist of his day, though that church makes no provision for evangelists among its ministers.

He went into the work, because of an overwhelming conviction from God that this was his calling. Like Paul, his "own hands ministered to his necessities"; and when he felt called of God to go to a place to hold meetings for the salvation of souls, he never stipulated that he should receive anything for his services, or even that his traveling expenses should be paid. But where he went without the promise of purse or scrip he never lacked-anything. The Lord, in one way or another, provided for his wants.

I first became acquainted with Dr. Redfield when I was a student at Middletown, Connecticut. He held a protracted meeting in the Methodist Episcopal Church. There was a large society, but a low state of religious experience. He preached in the afternoon to the church, in the evening to sinners. A great excitement was soon stirred up. Such preaching and such praying had never before been heard in that city. Many of the most prominent members of the church went forward for prayers, and obtained a new experience of entire sanctification. A spirit of opposition was manifested, and it seemed doubtful for a time how the tide would turn; but Dr. Stephen Olin, president of the University, who was suffering from a general nervous prostration, got up from his bed and went out to hear him. He gave the work his strongest endorsement, saying in substance, "Brethren, this is the work of God and you must stand by it."

The college faculty, and the church generally, did stand by it, and a revival remarkable for its depth, and for the number of its converts, was the result. Some twenty-five young men who afterwards became preachers were converted. The whole city was in commotion and the country for miles around. The influence of that revival is still felt, not only in this country, but also in Europe, and Asia and Africa. No mortal can tell where a mighty wave of salvation once set in motion will end.

The following pages, written by one who was converted under Dr. Redfield's labors, will give the reader a correct idea of the wonderful work which God carried on through the instrumentality of his devoted servant.

We have heard many able, distinguished preachers, but we never heard another who would stir the human conscience to its depths like Dr. Redfield. His statements were clear, his descriptions vivid and eloquent; but his appeals to the conscience were overwhelming. He made those who would not obey God feel that they were utterly without excuse.

Those who were justified or sanctified wholly under his labors were not easily drawn away unto the gospel of expediency. They were governed by principle rather than by policy. Time-serving preachers did not like his converts. They had no relish for religious theatricals or church festivals. They were hard to manage. Hence, Dr. Redfield generally encountered, wherever he labored, fierce opposition from ecclesiastics. A whole city would be moved by his preaching, while the presiding elder, and such as he could influence, were doing all they could to destroy his influence. But when once started the work went so deep and so strong, that no degree of violence permitted under our laws could kill it out. All through the land are still to be found those who were saved through his instrumentality, and they are generally characterized by their uncompromising opposition to sin in all its popular forms; by their firm belief in the power of the Holy Ghost, and by their clear, strong, definite testimony.

We trust that this book will be extensively read, and that it will carry a saving influence into thousands of families.

3

AUTHOR'S INTRODUCTION.

In the month of January, 1858, a rumor reached the neighborhood in which the writer lived, four miles west of Elgin, Illinois, that a remarkable preacher was holding revival meetings in the Methodist church in town. Their curiosity being greatly excited, a wagon load of young people, myself among the number, started out one evening for the place of meeting to hear the great preacher for themselves.

Though we arrived at an early hour, we found the house then partly filled, and long before the time for the service to begin, it was filled to its utmost capacity. Our company found seats well forward, and my own was where I could see every one who came in at the door. A few minutes before the appointed time of service, a man entered, whose personal appearance instantly commanded my attention. He was small of stature, with a massive head, pale, delicate countenance, and lustrous eyes. Softly and quietly he moved along the aisle toward the pulpit which he reverently entered. He laid aside his wraps, and as though shrinking from the gaze of the assembled multitude, he knelt for a few moments in silent prayer. His presence and manner thrilled me though he had not yet spoken a word. The congregation had been hushed into perfect silence by the same subtile influence. At this time I was unconverted, and I had not time, nor did I care, to analyze my impressions of the man; but from that moment, however, I was ready to listen to him with the profoundest attention.

He arose and gave out a hymn with clear and distinct enunciation. The reading of the hymn was peculiarly impressive. Though a familiar one, each line of it took on a fullness of meaning which it never seemed to me to have before. He expressed its meaning, not only by the intonations and modulations of a remarkably sweet voice, but by his countenance, which seemed quietly, but forcibly, to utter the same sentiment.

The prayer which followed was more impressive still. The deep reverence with which he uttered the names of the divine Being, the clearness and simplicity of the language he used, the definiteness of his petitions, and the humble confidence of his manner, completely charmed me.

The text for the occasion was, Mark viii. 36: "What shall it profit a man if he shall gain the whole world and lose his own soul?"

At this point the preacher's manner entirely changed. His style became abrupt, startling, and was characterized by great clearness and strength. He chose the most forceful and expressive words. His sentences were short and crisp. His dialect, that of the common people. His method, declarative and descriptive.

His first few sentences were the following:

"There are persons in this congregation who will sell their immortal souls for two-and-sixpence. Before they will lay aside a galvanized pewter ring they will run the risk of losing heaven. There are others here who will sell their immortal souls for some picayunish office, and they'll never get as high as constable."

There seemed to be two general divisions to his discourse —the value of the soul as estimated (1) by what it can be purchased for; (2) by what it cost. About half of the time was spent in elaborating each point. On the first he gradually rose higher and higher in the estimate; but when he reached the second, his eloquence became overwhelming. One of the closing passages in this part of his discourse was as follows:

"The angels of heaven were grouped together, endeavoring to estimate what would be the cost to redeem a human soul; but all in vain. The red-fingered lightning played around the rocks of Mt. Calvary, endeavoring to trace it in letters of fire there; but all in vain. Only one thing could express it, and that was the dying groans of the Son of God."

My most vivid recollections of the man are as he appeared in the pulpit that evening. In one of his most impassioned utterances, he stood, with both hands raised above his head, his face shining as with a halo of light, and his whole soul thrown into the eloquent thoughts that came like a torrent from his lips.

The preacher to whom I listened that evening, and whose eloquent words and impressive appearance I still recall as vividly as though what I have described occurred but yesterday was the

Rev. John Wesley Redfield,

whose biography is recorded in the following pages.

The impression produced upon me that evening made this man of God, to me, an interesting study during the few years of my personal acquaintance with him, and while preparing these pages for publication.

His mental characteristics were peculiar. The intuitive faculties predominated. He did not reason to conclusions like most men. He saw, instantly, what many strong minds would require much time to reason out. This, doubtless, was an element of his strength and success as an evangelist. Difficulties had not time to develop and ripen before he was prepared to meet them.

He read men. He knew what were the determining influences upon them. This gave character to his style of preaching. His first sermon in a place was with the confident positiveness of long acquaintanceship. This thrilled men. They knew that he knew them. When this is as-

sumed by the weak, it is repulsive and disgusting, and men
will not listen to it; but when one speaks from this intuitive
knowledge, with the unction of the Holy One, their respect
is challenged. This is because they recognize the message
to be truth.

Another element of his character was that of experimental conformity to the divine will. He utterly abandoned himself to the known will of God. There was no reserve in his
consecration. Whether in the light or in the dark, favored
or frowned upon by men, to his advantage or disadvantage,
in peril or in safety, he aimed to do exactly what he thought
God wanted him to do. One of his peculiar phrases was,
"the exact right." He dealt with men, from the pulpit, in
the altar, and in private, on that principle. *"Calling things
by their right names,"* was another of his peculiar phrases.
He did not

> "Smooth down the stubborn text to ears polite,
> And snugly keep damnation out of sight."

With him, there was no seeking for "honeyed phrase."
He used but few large words, and those such as were in common use. He aimed to be understood.

Whether naturally or acquired, he had all the elements of
the orator. His imagination was fervid, quick, broad, and
accurate; this made his mental pictures vivid and true to nature. He never lacked for the right word; this helped him
to express himself clearly. His elocution was perfect. The
framing of his sentences, the order of his thoughts, his gestures, the modulations of his voice, the expression of his face,
and his manner, all, were in harmony. All these made it
possible for him to transfer his thoughts to the minds of others with accuracy and power. So complete was this, that
sometimes his audiences forgot themselves, the place and the
speaker, in the vividness of the truths to which they were
listening. This was the result of his naturalness. He felt
what he thought, and expressed what he thought and felt.

It will be noticed where he is quoted in the following narrative, that he often says, "I felt," where others would have said, "I thought."

Another element in his character was his implicit faith in God. No doubts respecting God's word made their appearance in his discourses. With him there was no apologizing for the facts or the truths of the Bible. Like Abraham of old he "believed God." In his public addresses he seemed to take it for granted that all men believed God. Such faith begot faith; and the discouraged became hopeful, and the weak became strong in his presence. A minister, while severely criticising his methods and labors, admitted that he would rather trust his own child under Mr. Redfield's preaching than under that of any minister he knew. ·

Another element of his character was his great sympathy. Suffering in others he could not witness, unless he could assist in relieving it. When visiting among the farmers, the killing of animals, though for food, greatly distressed him. He would walk his room in agony until informed that it was over. He shrank from inflicting mental pain, and only from a sense of duty could he bring himself to do it.

One of the hardest things for him to do was to bid farewell to his friends. He has been known to take a night train to avoid this. This trait made him apparently a coward. It was only when convinced that duty demanded it, that he could do the severe and faithful work that he sometimes performed. This accounts for many strange passages in his life which are recorded in these pages. Those who knew him only as he appeared in public, supposed him brave to a fault.

· Doctrinally he was in accord with the standards of Methodism. He often called upon his enemies in the church to show wherein he was unsound in the faith. Only once was this attempted, and the result was in his favor, and against his opposers. In his work as an evangelist, he recognized the

office of the truth.   He believed that men were born again
by the word of God; that they were sanctified by the truth.
He was careful as to his teachings, especially so with seekers
for salvation.   In altar services he often took more time to
explain the way than he did for the season of prayer.   He
held his prayer services to definite work.   The nature and
fruits of repentance were kept clearly before the minds of
those seeking pardon.   The nature and the details of entire consecration were kept clearly before those seeking for perfect
love.   He believed in, and taught, an itemized dedication of
all the seeker possessed, or hoped to have, to the service of
God.   Before he attempted to present the way of faith, he
would, in individual cases, carefully test the purposes, and
motives, and desires of the seeker. All these he would bring
to the standard of God's word.   That standard, he taught,
is the absolute and unconditional surrender of the soul to
God.   He taught that there is no hope of reconciliation with
God without perfect renunciation of sin, and acceptance of
Christ.   He taught that there is no hope of attaining perfect
love while there is the least reserve in the aims, or desires,
or affections from the will of God.   This thoroughness with
the seekers often caused them great mental suffering.   There
was no attempt to shield them from feelings of despair
while there was rebellion existing in the heart, or any doubt
of surrendering all to God.   This was what made those who
were saved through his instrumentality so definite and clear,
and, consequently, strong.   The transition from the agony
of surrendering to the peace of believing, was usually so
marked that it thrilled all who were looking on.   This encouraged even the impenitent to believe that if they started to
seek Christ they would succeed. It was not unusual for seekers
to make that transition before they reached the altar of prayer.
One result of this was that the many were saved soon, and but
few came to the altar more than once.   In his preaching, he
was careful in his enunciation that every word and syllable

should be heard and understood. If there was the least disturbance in the congregation, by the moving of persons, the
crying of children, or the shouts of the saints, he would wait
in silence until all was quiet before proceeding. He aimed
to present the truth which the people mostly needed. He
had no time to spend in idle speculations or fanciful interpretations of the word of God. He waited before the Lord, in
prayer, until he felt satisfied that he knew the mind of the
Lord. The consciousness that he had made a mistake in
this gave him intense pain, and caused him to humble himself before the Lord. When duty became clear, whether
the truth to be preached was popular or unpopular, acceptable or unacceptable, he went boldly forward, trusting God
with the results. This was not unattended with suffering,
for his shrinking, sensitive nature was often put upon the
rack by it. Coarse natures who have no care how they
make others feel can have no appreciation of his feelings at
such times.

But while he gave the truth its proper place, in his work,
he did not ignore the offices of the Holy Spirit. He believed
it the work of the Spirit to make the truth effectual. He
believed the Christian minister might have his immediate
presence and aid. He gave him free course in his meetings.
He would not labor, nor dared he to try, where this was not
allowed. He was more particular about that preparation for
his pulpit efforts than he was about the sermon. The Spirit's
dispensation was illustrated in his labors. Many and varied
were the manifestations of this. There were often mixed
with these that which was merely human, springing from
the weakness of human nature, and which called forth the
tenderest sympathy for the subjects of them, and the most
careful dealing with them. There were often, also, those
which seemed to be Satanic. He believed in a personal,
intelligent, powerful devil. He expected every possible
resistance to the truth and the Spirit of God. But he

believed himself too weak to contend against the devil. When such manifestations appeared, instead of warring against them, he prayed for more of the Holy Spirit's presence. He believed in the all-conquering power of the truth and the Spirit; and that where victory for Jesus is complete, poor human nature will act properly, and Satan's power is broken.

Because of this recognition of the Holy Spirit, the spiritual among God's people were greatly enlightened, strengthened, and often wonderfully moved under his preaching. Such people understood him when others did not, and were among his best and firmest friends. His enemies were among the worldly and time-serving. He was accused of dividing the church in his later years, but it was because he left no middle ground. The spiritual became more so, and they who would not yield wholly to the Lord went to the other extreme. No matter what the opposition or prejudice in the way, where the church authorities gave him freedom, almost invariably, he was victorious; for the truth and the Holy Spirit conquered all.

He was developed by the circumstances and experiences of his life. The rebellion of his early days, the providential difficulties which grew out of this, and the mental struggles through which he passed, were used by God to prepare him for his great work. In the following narrative it will be interesting to trace the process by which this was effected.

The most of the matter for this volume is from his own recollections, as penned by himself, in the last days of his life, after having been disabled for active labor by the palsy. He knew he was rapidly approaching eternity. With the most solemn feelings, he carefully reviewed his life and labors. It would have been pleasing to have given these recollections in his own words; but whether it was natural with him, or caused by the paralysis from which he was suffering, his style of writing was so unlike that of his preaching, that his friends would have doubted the genuineness of them, if they had been published as he left them. Again, for some reason, he omitted dates, and all but the initials of proper names. It has, for this reason, been very difficult to verify some of the most interesting details of his labors. I have been greatly assisted in this by his friends, who have contributed much that is valuable, which had been overlooked by Mr. Redfield, and who have also loaned me the use of many letters written by himself during the later years of his active ministry. This has made it necessary to change the style from the *autobiographical* to the biographical. I am much indebted to the assistance of these friends, and especially to Mrs. M. F. La Due, for valuable recollections of her own, and to Rev. W. T. Hogg for his assistance in the finishing touches to the work.

The beautiful steel engraving which faces the title-page is-contributed by Rev. B. T. Roberts, editor of the *Earnest Christian*, and senior-general superintendent of the Free Methodist Church. The engraving represents Mr. Redfield as he appeared in the days of his strength.

In hope that the following narrative may perpetuate the influence of this remarkable man of God, and that through it, though dead, he may still speak, I send it forth upon its mission, commending it to the kind recognition and devout perusal of the Christian public.

CHAPTER I.

JOHN WESLEY REDFIELD was born in Clarendon, New Hampshire, January 23, 1810. On the night of his birth an esteemed Christian woman dreamed that she was visited by an angel who told her to go to the home of the Redfields and she would find there a new born son; and that she must announce to the mother that he must be named John Wesley. She was also informed that this would be assented to immediately by the mother, who would respond, "That is his name." This woman did as she was bidden, and all came to pass as she had dreamed. In mentioning this in his journal, Mr. Redfield says, "By that unlucky name was I baptized and have been known through life."

So strongly was he impressed with his call to the ministry that when only eight years of age, and just able to write legibly, he attempted in secret to compose a sermon. When it was completed he borrowed a volume of Wesley's sermons that he might compare his production with them. When he saw the great difference between them, in perplexity and sadness he exclaimed: "Oh, I can never preach! I don't know anything about religion. I am sure I never can preach."

So persistently did the impression of his call to preach follow him in his childhood that, in mature years, when attempting to run away from it, he was inclined to consider it an "antenatal mark."

When about twelve or thirteen years of age he was informed of his mother's impressions concerning him, and the dream already related. So great, however, was his aversion to the work of the ministry that he studiously contended against his conviction by concealing his feelings and avoiding all conversation concerning the matter.

When between thirteen and fourteen years of age he had such alarming views of his sinful state that he feared he was past all hope of mercy. This fear became so intense at one period that he was tempted to provoke God to destroy him, that, without the guilt of self-murder, he might learn the certainty of his fate, and, by the shortening of his sinful course, render his doom less aggravated. He had been seeking the favor of God in a secret way for some time, but in vain. He now gave up hope, not knowing any other way than that which he had followed. His distress of mind continued without abatement until he overheard some Christian friends speak of a contemplated camp meeting, which they trusted would result in the conversion of sinners. At this, hope revived, and to himself he said, " If I go, I too may be converted."

He obtained permission from his parents to go, and when the time arrived he was on the campground. His attention was directed to the altar before the stand, with the remark, " There many were converted last year." Almost instantly his heart rebelled against the thought of going to such a place. Even in his last days he would express his astonishment at that manisfestation of rebellion against God.

In due time a goodly number of tents had been erected, and an old gentleman invited him to a prayer meeting about to commence in one of them. He went and was asked to kneel with the company. He did so, but soon felt greatly mortified at the thought of its being in sight of every passerby. The praying seemed childish, if not ludicrous. He made up his mind that it would be impossible to find salvation there.

In process of time the erection of tents was completed, and the congregation gathered before the stand for the first preaching service. The sainted Wilber Fisk was in charge of the meeting. The preachers were called into the stand, and the service commenced. At the close of the sermon seekers were invited into the altar, and the troubled boy was found among them. The same good old man who invited him into the prayer meeting was now by his side, and tried to instruct him in the way of salvation. There was quite a number of seekers and all were praying lustily. This completely absorbed his attention. As many others have done, he began to criticise, instead of praying. In relating this experience he says, " I thought, this cannot be the way to seek religion! Why can't they be more calm and rational about it? Certainly they will never be able to think their way through amid so much noise and confusion! At least I can do nothing without a quiet time to think." Speaking of this in his last days, he said, " How little did I understand that all reasoning or human planning was useless here!"

But he soon saw that this apparently irrational way and this vociferous manner were successful; for some of the seekers were getting saved. As every other way with him had failed, he at last thought he would try this one. So he cried aloud, " Lord, be merciful to me, a sinner." But he was shocked and mortified at the sound of his own voice. He did not find salvation in loud prayers, nor was he finally converted while praying. This effort to pray proved a good thing to him, however, in one respect; he was now fully and publicly committed to seek the Lord, his pride was humbled, and he was fast getting down where Jesus could help him. He gave up all his experimenting and reasoning, and determined to take the narrow way at every cost.

He soon left the altar and went out into the woods alone. Under a large tree he knelt and vowed to take Jesus for his only Saviour. Speaking of this experience, he says: "Instantly, as I ventured on Jesus, my burden was gone. I was filled with inexpressible delight, and before I was aware of what I was doing, I was on my feet and shouting, 'Glory to God'! Shocked at this strange and almost spontaneous utterance, I said to myself, 'What does this mean? I have heard the Methodists say, "Glory to God," but I don't know what it means!' My burden was all gone. Everything around seemed vocal with the praises of God, and as the Indian said in similar circumstances, 'The trees looked glad, and the birds sang glad, the world looked glad, and I felt glad.' All nature seemed in harmony, like a beautiful and well-tuned harp, and sang praises to the Most High. My heart could now beat time to the heavenly music I heard around, above, beneath, and within. But I had not the most distant idea that this was conversion. I thought some strange thing had happened to me. I had been sure that I would know when I was a Christian by a peculiar gloom that would settle down upon me. I had thought that a peculiar desolation of the heart and of the appearance of all things would attest that I had obtained that for which I sought. I was desirous of attaining such an uncomfortable state, that I might be saved from the doubts and despair that hung over me. Bewildered at what had now taken place, and wishing to know what to do, I returned to the campground and asked an elderly lady who professed to be a Christian, 'What do you think is the matter with me? My burden is all gone, and I can't feel bad if I try; and I love God and everybody. I don't know but I'll have to be damned after all; but I can't feel one fear.'

" 'Why,' said she, 'you are converted, and this is religion.'

" 'But I thought that religion would make me feel gloomy!'

" 'Oh no!' said she, 'it makes people feel happy.'

" 'Well,' said I to myself, 'if this is religion, the world will now soon be converted; for I shall tell it so plain that everybody will certainly believe and seek, and find it.'

"So exalted did salvation seem, and so valuable, and so ardently did I desire the salvation of those around me, that I felt I could have laid down my life to impart salvation to the world. I now found elements in my soul, which by their aspirings, and exalted perceptions, and appreciative powers, showed me to be in family alliance with the great Father. I would often say, 'I am a child, an heir of God!' How astounding was the thought! How overwhelming! When I passed along the streets, after my return home, every sound and sight seemed written all over and vocal with, 'Glory to God in the highest, forever.' "

He immediately went to work for others. Full of the hope of success, he approached a young man of his acquaintance and spoke to him on the subject of salvation. He says, " I expected to see his eye flash with hope, and to hear him exclaim, ' Where! where! where may I find it?' and to find him ready to do anything to obtain it. But he turned upon me with a look of unutterable scorn, which seemed to say, ' What! have you become a Methodist fool? Away with such stuff ! I don't want to hear a word about the silly subject.' I was taken all aback. I had expected the same kind of a reception that I would have had if I had brought to him the news of a gold mine, or that he had been selected for one of the highest officers of the state."

After the camp meeting, young Redfield started for his home. He visited some relatives on the way, told them what the Lord had done for him, and urged them to seek the same salvation. But he seemed to them like one that mocked. He obtained permission to pray with one large family, and a short time after was made happy by the news that all had been converted. On the way home he told a young man who had also been converted at the same meeting, that for a long time he had desired that he would make a start, that it might be easier for himself to do the same, and was surprised to find that this young man had experienced the same feeling with respect to him.

When he reached home he set up the family altar in his father's house. This, by some, was thought to be going too far; but the importance of the matter, and the danger in which he saw sinners, swallowed up all false propriety. In

4

a little while he had the privilege of seeing a large number of acquaintances starting out to go with him.

He now began to go from house to house and from town to town, to carry the glad news of a Saviour. While engaged in this work he learned what he had not thought of before— that the human heart hates God and dislikes those who love God; but he resolved to be the friend of God if it made every one his enemy. Referring to those labors, he says:

"I came to a house in my journey, and went in and asked of each inmate their religious state. The woman ordered me to leave. As I left, I said, 'I am clear from all further obligation, and now I shake off the dust of my feet against you. I will meet you once more, in the judgment of the great day.' I left, as I felt forbidden of God to stay. But the woman came to the door, and, until I was out of hearing, called for me to come back. But I followed my own impression and went on."

In the house of a Universalist he pressed the matter of personal and immediate salvation until the man's patience gave out and he threatened him with violence. Being only about fifteen years of age, his youthful appearance made him friends who protected him. He here learned a lesson—the people were forsaking their sins and seeking the Lord, and the Universalists were made angry by it, notwithstanding their boasted religion of love.

CHAPTER II.

DR. WILBER FISK, who was a familiar guest at the home of the Redfields now began to take a great interest in this young worker, and suggested to his parents that he be sent to the Wilbraham Academy. The young man saw that the old subject of preaching was at the bottom of this; and that the course he was even then pursuing would lead him into that work sooner or later. Then all his old abhorrence and dread of that calling revived, and he resolved to quit the field at once. He says, " I had such views of the awful responsibility of a Christian minister that I dared not undertake it without the most positive evidence of my call. If I could have had that I would not have stopped to confer with flesh and blood. I felt, as it seems to me, like a man ignorant of navigation would feel if sent to take charge of a vessel freighted with human life, and liable to run into danger, not knowing when or where. This sense of responsibility was to me overwhelming."

This feeling never left him. Even in the days of his greatest success and pulpit power, he has been known to be unable to eat his breakfast when he was to preach. in the morning; and he usually did not partake of supper until after preaching at night. The reader will see more and more how this feeling evoked his rebellion against God, and was the occasion of the most terrific mental sufferings. If his friends could have foreseen the fearful results of their anxiety and haste in reference to this matter, probably they would have taken a different course. How often is the same mistake made with the young and inexperienced !

In the state of mind which has just been described, he returned home; but his peace and power with God were

greatly diminished. He began to try to settle the question
by mere reasoning. His youth, his limited knowledge, his
want of means for acquiring knowledge, and his sense of the
weakness of all human effort, took on an importance in his
consideration of the matter which, for the time, overshad-
owed the promises of help held out in the Bible. His Christian friends still unwisely beset him with their impressions of
what his duty was. He says, " My own earlier impressions
and those of my mother and the talks I had from time to
time with Dr. Fisk, made me perfectly miserable. I think it
was these influences, at this time, more than the voice of
God, that caused it. My whole nature shrunk from occupying a position so sacred as that of the Christian ministry.
Without the sanction of God, to me it was sacrilege. I now
reasoned that my first impressions in this matter were the result of the influence of others upon me, and resolved to go
among strangers, that I might be beyond the reach of this
influence; and, further, so to commit myself by contract to
the service of another, and he a stranger, as to make it impossible for me to engage in religious work. It seemed to
me that I might, at least for a time, in this way secure a settled state of mind."

The gentleman whom he sought was an artist by profession, and noted for his proficiency. Without giving his
reasons, young Redfield obtained the consent of his father to
go, but hid the matter from his mother.

He started on his journey, and when beyond the limits of
his acquaintance was thankful to feel secure from the beset-
ments of other people's impressions. He called at the home
of a minister to leave a letter that had been committed to his
care. The minister was away, but his wife was at home.
As he handed her the letter she looked him in the face and
said: " Tell me, are you not running away from God?"

To this he replied: " I think, madam, that some one has
been writing to you concerning me."

" No," she replied, " I never saw or heard of you before; but as soon as I saw you I was impressed that you were running away from your duty." She then asked: " Will you please bring me a pail of water from the spring?" He could not well refuse to do this, but when it was done she asked him to cut her some wood. Before he was through with this an old man came into the yard, attended by a girl he had seen in the house when he first came. He was now invited into the house and introduced to the old man, who, he found, was a minister of the gospel. Now he saw that the woman had detained him purposely until this man could be brought. The minister was introduced as Father Liscomb. The old man informed young Redfield that he was holding a revival meeting in a little hamlet a short distance away, and desired him to go and see the young converts. To avoid any talk on the subject of duty he instantly said, " I will go," but he secretly determined to leave the old gentleman at the first convenient opportunity.

They soon started away together, and as they walked along he inquired the way, and the distance to W——, his place of destination. This was given him, and they walked on until they came to a house. The old man knocked at the door, and was bidden to come in. As he passed in, young Redfield turned and ran towards some woods that lay between him and the place he desired to reach. It was a beautiful afternoon in September, the sun was about two hours high, and it was only five miles to W——, by the woods road. About eighty rods brought him to the woods, and he entered them with congratulations at his nice escape. He lost his way and wandered about until night came on. His experience on this occasion is best related in his own words.

He says: "I could not tell East from West, nor North from South. Soon I was wading in mud and water, stumbling over logs and running against trees, scaring up squirrels and wild creatures until I seemed to be surrounded by ani-

mals and reptiles which I could hear, but not see. I at last
felt I was contending with a power that was stronger than
myself. My fears were so greatly aroused that I promised
God if he would lead me out of the dreadful place I would
take any course he might direct. In a moment I felt a gentle pull no stronger than a hair leading me, but I could not tell
the direction. Soon I perceived I was out of the woods. I followed that leading until I found myself against a fence. I got
over, crossing several fields and climbed as many fences, until I
perceived by the feeling of my feet that I was in a road. While
stopping to ascertain my whereabouts, I saw a light in a window
a short distance away, and it proved to be at the very house
where I met the old minister. The thought came in a moment, if I return to the house the lady will only distress
me by pressing upon me her convictions of what my duty is,
and that I cannot bear. The next thought was, this is the
direct road to W——, and it is only seven miles there. There
is now no fear of my getting lost, for the fences will guide
me, and possibly by morning I may reach the place. By going to-night I shall avoid any further annoyance from the
preacher's wife. As I turned to go I saw the woman in the
road as plainly as I had seen her the day before in the house.
I asked, 'Mrs. B——, what time of night is it?' But she
gave me no answer. Again, I asked, 'Did you feel alarmed
at my absence? and have you come out to look for me?'
Still she did not answer me. I then told her I had been lost,
and was just out of my dilemma. I also told her that I desired she would say no more to me of duty, for I was too agitated to hear it. Yet she did not speak, and I thought, she
is trying to frighten me into obedience to her opinion of what
is my duty. I then said to her, 'You will not frighten me
for I am resolved never to preach until I am positive that
God says, *Go*. I am going this night to W——; so good-
night.' As I started she stepped in front of me. I turned
to pass by her, and she stepped in front of me again. Again

I endeavored to pass by her, but again she stepped in front of me. I then said, 'Madam, I thought you were a professor of religion. What will your neighbors think when they know of your conducting yourself in this manner?' Still I got no response from her. 'You need not think to crowd me to the course you think I ought to go, by tricks of this kind,' I continued. Still she was silent. I was then seized with such fear that I turned and ran to the house; and as I entered, she sat there as if waiting for me. She immediately said, 'I expected you would come back; for I prayed God to put my image before you as the angel appeared before Balaam.' 'Well I thought it was *you*,' I said, and with this one sentence I exposed all the facts.

"On looking I found it was twelve o'clock. I asked her for a place of rest for the remainder of the night. She gave me a light and told me where to find a room. I now resolved to get up and be off for W—— before she could have a chance to annoy me in the morning. Notwithstanding the remarkable character of this experience, it seemed to me I was enduring great hardship.

" I arose early as I had determined, but when I stepped into the sitting-room, which it was necessary for me to pass through, there she sat in a chair. I spoke first, and said, 'Don't say a word to me about duty, for I am resolved that no human influence shall determine my course. I shall go to W—— to-day. I dare not allow myself to be prevailed upon to take so fearful a position as that of a gospel minister. So good morning.'

"On attempting to open the outside door, I felt the force of a hand on the latch outside. I stepped back, and when the door opened, there stood a man, who, putting his hand upon my head, said to me, ' Stop, Jonah! for you are running away from God.'

"Said I, ' You are in the secret, too! are you?'

" ' I never saw or heard of you before this moment,' he

replied. 'I live four miles from here—I am not a believer in dreams, but I had one last night, in which I was told to come to this house, and here I would find a young man who was trying to run away from God. And I was told to tell you to go and preach the gospel or you would be damned. I have come four miles to stop you.'

"But I broke away and went on my journey.

"I found the artist. He was willing to enter into a contract with me, but while I was talking with him, I was again seized with such fear, and with such a sense of guilt, that I dared not say a word more. I went out and left the place, nor dared look back until sure that I was out of sight of the town."

CHAPTER III.

RETURNING HOME, young Redfield now resolved to live religion, but to abandon all thought of preaching, unless God by unmistakable signs should reveal it to him as his will. He passed the winter and the following summer in a restless and uncomfortable state of mind. He was continually mourning over his sad condition, and wondering why he should be the victim of such impressions, and yet have no certain evidence to settle the matter. He would allow none to speak to him in regard to it, and would seek counsel from none.

Late in the fall he saw, in the western sky, an indescribable sign. The impression made upon him by it was, "That hangs over where God would have you go to labor." But this distressed him still more. The thought of following such a sign was contrary to all his ideas of propriety in matters of such great concern. He reasoned that in a matter of such importance, where there is possibility of making a mistake, and that mistake liable to be a fatal one, he had a right to expect of God a reasonable and unmistakable evidence of his will. But in spite of all, "Woe is me if I preach not the gospel," continually rang through his heart. Still, also, that sign hung in the sky, with the same impression of its import. At last he determined to ask for another to corroborate the first, but none came. His appetite and sleep forsook him, until in two months he was very much wasted. He became afraid that he might become insane. He had asked that an angel or a bird might come to him as an assurance that the sign he continually saw in that place in the sky was from God, or that an audible voice might speak to him, then he would obey it. Still the answer did not come. He at last resolved to seek for it by fasting and prayer. He set the day for the struggle, also determining to follow it by a watch-night. He expected that by twelve o'clock at night, a bird or angel, or voice would settle his doubts. The hour came, the town clock struck; he counted the strokes; it was twelve; but no bird, nor angel, nor voice came. He said to himself, "I am glad that I have gone through with my fast and watch-night. Now I can go to rest, and drop this terrible subject. The absence of the testimony I have asked for is sufficient to satisfy me that my impressions as to preaching, and that sign, are unreliable. I have been the dupe of hallucination."

An impression now came to him to open the Bible and see what light he could get from that. He says: "I opened it at random and let my finger touch without knowing where. On looking I found it on the words in Genesis 17: 3: 'Therefore, my son, obey my voice according to that which I command thee.' For a moment I was disturbed; but soon I reasoned: that was purely a happen so; I will try once more; I'll reach far enough in opening not to touch the same spot again. I next put my finger on Deuteronomy 28: 15: 'But it shall come to pass if thou wilt not hearken unto the voice of the Lord thy God to observe to do all his commandments and his statutes which I command thee this day, that all these curses shall come upon thee and overtake thee.' I reasoned this away and tried again. This time my finger fell upon Jonah 3: 2: 'Arise, go unto Nineveh, that great city, and preach unto it the preaching that I bid thee.' This shook me greatly and well nigh upset all my hopes of finding relief; but I reasoned: we are not under the Old Testament dispensation. I will venture to open in the New Testament. My finger now touched the quotation by the Saviour, 'The Spirit of the Lord is upon me, because he hath anointed me to preach the gospel,' etc. Filled with fear, I begged the Lord not to be angry with me, but to let me try once more, and I would not ask again. I opened and touched the words, ' Go ye into all the world and preach the gospel to every creature.'

" Thus five times in succession did I touch upon the words that corroborated my impressions, and the impressions of others, but which were opposed to my opinions and desires. My soul was now upon the rack worse than ever. I could not rest, I could not sleep. It was in midwinter and very cold; but I went forth into the fields and woods to try a new place, in hope that God would send me a bird or angel or voice. I knelt in the snow and pleaded with God as a man would plead for his life to grant me such an answer as I desired ; but no ·answer of that kind came. I went from place to place until I reached the top of a hill in a grove. Here I knelt once more. While pleading there I had such a sense of the awful majesty and near approach of an offended God that my agony of body and soul became extreme and I thought I could not live. Instantly I cried out, ' O God, re-move this from me and I'll go.' Immediately I was relieved; but soon my doubting heart said, ' I've seen no bird, nor angel, nor heard a voice ; how can I go?' I went to a hill-top farther on, overlooking a swamp, knelt down, and con-tinued in prayer for some time. When I tried to rise I found my clothing was frozen to the earth. So great had been my agitation that I had not thought of the cold. I pulled my knees loose, but found I could not rise until I had rubbed my limbs warm. At last, with great difficulty, I arose and started towards the house. I passed the spot where I felt the presence of God so painfully, and went down into a valley, and sat down on a log. Though still in great distress of mind, the impression came: ' Stand still and see the salva-tion of God.' The next moment a bird came and alighted on my shoulder. I shook it off, but it came again. I then thought: I may be in its way. I arose, went to the top of another hill, and knelt in prayer again, under a pine tree.

While thus engaged, a sound passed through the tree like that of a stiff breeze, but no wind seemed stirring. I listened and looked, but saw nothing. I arose and went home. It was morning, and my father, after building a fire, had gone to the barn. When I entered the room and came in contact with the warm air I became so faint that I dropped into a chair by the door, pale, haggard, and weak. My mother came into the room that moment, and seeing my distressed look, was frightened, and exclaimed, ' Why, John! what's the matter?' I made out to answer, ' Nothing, mother '; but perceiving my feelings about to betray me, I arose and went out into the cold again. When beyond hearing I gave vent to my anguish in loud sobbing and weeping.

" I now determined to spend this day also in fasting and prayer, and conclude it with a watch-night. When twelve o'clock at night came again, it was with the same results. I then thought: I will turn to the word of God again. I opened to the words, " There shall no sign be given." As this spoiled all prospect of sleep, I went out into the fields again. I said to myself: There is that sign still in the sky. Reason says: I must be under a religious hallucination; but, true or false, I cannot settle the matter of duty or shake it off. My body is worn down; my mind is almost distracted. I must either go deranged or die. There is but one thing I can do, that is, to go to the place and test the matter. I had no sooner resolved to go than, cold as it was, I was all in a glow of warmth, and as happy as I could bear.

" I could not tell any one my feelings. I returned to the house. It was now daylight. I entered the parlor and went to a bureau in which my linen was kept, and commenced to pack a small bundle to take with me. While thus engaged, my sister Mary, then living at home, came into the room and with streaming eyes handed me a Bible and hymn-book, and said: ' Brother John, the victory is gained.' I could contain no longer; I broke forth in convulsed sobbing and weeping, but said not a word. She afterwards told me that she knew at this time, all about my struggle, and was engaged in secret prayer for me all the time; and also that she knew the very moment when it was over, though she was in the house and I quite a distance away. I had supposed all the time that none but God and I knew anything about it."

CHAPTER IV.

Taking only a small bundle with him, and without saying farewell, he started out to seek the place designated by the sign. He intended to take a straight line to the place, regardless of roads. His joy was now unspeakable. When he opened the door to start, a young man stood before it, who asked, "Where are you going?" He could only say, "I am going west." Said the stranger, "Wait a minute and you can ride with me." The invitation was accepted, but with the determination to ride with him only as long as his course was toward that sign. All day they rode in a westerly direction. Just at sundown, as they reached the bottom of a hill, the driver turned to a road leading south, and the sign disappeared. Young Redfield said not a word, but thought, "The mystery is solved. I have been following a phantom." He asked the young man to stop and let him get out, as he desired to take the road to the right. That led to the west. The stranger answered: "You had better go to the top of the hill, and stop there at the house of an old minister until morning, as it will be a long way before you will find a stopping place on that road." He accepted the suggestion and went on. When they reached the house the young man knocked at the door and they were bidden to come in. The minister and his family were standing around the table and had been about to say grace over their evening repast, after the manner of that day. As the old man looked upon young Redfield the tears filled his eyes, and it was some moments before he could control his emotions. At last he said, "This young man must stop with me. God showed me in a dream

sometime ago that you were coming to help me on my circuit. I never saw you before except in my dream, and
when you came I instantly recognized you." On taking a
seat Mr. Redfield opened his hymn-book to the verse,

"Master, I own thy lawful claim,
  Thine, wholly thine, I long to be;
Thou seest at last I willing am,
  Where'er thou goest to follow thee.
Myself in all things to deny,
  Thine, wholly thine to live and die."

He says, "I now felt myself fully committed to do God's
will, although I kept and pondered these things in my heart.
The heavenly sweetness and calmness which took possession of my soul, I have no words to describe."

The old preacher took him on to a part of his circuit
where Universalism was a great obstacle in the way of the
work. He commenced his work here in the same way in
which he had previously labored, by visiting from house to
house. He met with opposition and threats of personal violence, but the more he labored the more he felt the value of
souls, and the importance of his mission. When threatened,
he would reply, "My message is from God to you, and I
shall not, I dare not, disobey him. It is at your peril if you
do not heed it," and with tears running down his face he
would insist upon a definite answer to his appeals. Sometimes amid threats he would kneel and pray, presenting the
case of each person present to God. On rising he would
take them by the hand, when they would allow it, and tell
them, "I am here in the name of the great God. I have
done my duty faithfully. Farewell, I will meet you again
in the judgment."

He would leave them in various moods. Sometimes
penitent and sometimes in a rage. "Yet," he says, "I do not
remember a single instance where they did not send for me
within twenty-four hours, to come and pray for them."

One afternoon, two Methodist ministers called and asked him to visit a Mr. B——, a Universalist, by whose influence the revival was much hindered. They had both been to see him, but could not convince him of his error. One of them said, "I have used the arguments of Fisk and Fletcher, and yet nothing shakes his confidence in Universalism." Young Redfield said, "I will ask the Lord about it."

"That night he was instructed in a dream to visit the Universalist, and also as to how to approach him, and by what method he should endeavor to draw his attention to the great importance of attending immediately to the matter of his personal salvation. The next morning early, he proceeded to the man's house, and, on entering, said to him: "I have a message from the great God to you, and that is, you must repent and seek salvation or you will be damned."

Said he, "I don't believe in your damnation doctrine."

Without attempting to reply the young man asked, "Will you obey God and shun damnation?"

Again Mr. B—— tried to avoid answering, but young Redfield said, "My message is from God; will you obey it?"

At this the man became very angry and ordered him out of his house, threatening him with a beating if he did not go.

Mr. Redfield replied: "You strike me at the peril of God's displeasure; for the God who has sent me on this errand of mercy will certainly stand by me and defend me. So touch me if you dare. I am on God's business."

The Universalist's wife now exclaimed, "Oh! will you pray for me?" with tears. He instantly knelt, and both the man and his wife knelt with him. God so far broke his opposition that his influence for evil from this time was checked.

The work of God soon broke out with power, and swept over all that section.

CHAPTER V.

AFTER a short time, the sign appeared again, directing him to another field. Yet he secretly resolved to go home. Carelessly he signified this intention to one who immediately said: "I should think you would be afraid the judgments of God would follow you." The following morning, as he was making preparations to go home, he was suddenly seized with great pain, and to find relief, he consented to obey God. As soon as the pain was gone, however, he made another attempt to return home. He finished dressing, and reached the top of the stairs, when the same agony of body again came on, and with it the impression, "If you do not consent, you will die and be lost." He says: "I then told the Lord if he would relieve me, I would go, and instantly I was free from pain, and as happy as I could be."

"After breakfast," he continues, "I started. It was very cold, and the snow was deep, but I went on, singing, 'December's as pleasant as May.' I visited every house as I went, warning the people to flee from the wrath to come. My name and manner of work had gone before me, and some were so much afraid of me that they left their houses at my approach.

"When I reached the place of my destination, I was led to go to the class leader's first. The day had been too severe for the children to attend school, and they were all at home. I asked the father and mother: 'Are you on the way to heaven?' The father replied: 'We trust we are.' Said I: 'God has sent me to tell you that you are on the road to hell, and you will certainly be lost unless you repent and seek the pardon of your sins.' I had no sooner spoken than the tears began to stream down my face; but my words aroused a turbulent spirit within him, and with vehemence he ordered

5   •   (37)

me out of the house. I told him I could not go until I had
obeyed my instructions from God. 'Then,' said he, 'I'll use
means to get you out,' and he seemed about to raise a chair
to strike me. I said to him: 'You will strike me at your
peril while I am delivering God's message to you.' I then
turned to the children and asked them: 'Do you wish to go
to hell with your father and mother?' With tears, they
said: 'No, sir.' I asked: 'Will you kneel down while I pray
for you? You need not fear that your father will hurt me,
for God will defend me.' Down they knelt, and that brought
their parents to their knees, and they began in good earnest
to seek God. When I arose, the man and his wife began to
confess their backslidings, and invited me to stay for the
night. This I did, but feeling in the morning that my work
was done in that place, I returned. The class leader went to
work for God, and was the means of reviving the work of
the. Lord in that neighborhood."

Soon after his return, he met the preacher in charge, who
informed him that it was the desire of the presiding elder
that he unite with the church, be licensed to preach and take
regular work on a circuit. To this he finally consented, and
went to the next quarterly meeting. The elder preached as
usual at the Saturday service, and held the quarterly conference immediately after. While the congregation was
passing out, and the members of the conference were waiting for it to become quiet, the elder related a ridiculous story
that produced boisterous laughter, in which he joined; and
when it was at its height, he said, "Let us pray," and immediately led in prayer. The effect of this upon young Redfield can best be given in his own words:

"This was too much for my sensitive conscience, and the
devil took the advantage of it by setting me to reasoning
thus: 'Does this man believe the Bible? Did Jesus set such
an example of trifling in the presence of a perishing world?
Is it true that sinners are now passing away, every hour, to

the judgment? Is this like Paul, who for the space of three years, night and day, with tears, labored for the salvation of sinners? Am I in a hallucination? Am I wild, or blind? Be it as it may be, all I can see from my standpoint is the Saviour of the world, staggering under a world's sin, while its masses in proud procession are on their way to eternal night. If the Bible is true, the world is on the eve of a terrible catastrophe, and about to pass into eternity unprepared. I can hardly stop to sleep lest men be lost while I am at rest. There must be a mistake somewhere, and it is quite probable I am the one that is mistaken. The elder is a man of years, and in all probability when young was as zealous and ardent as I am, but he has found that religion is a sham, and now continues to preach for the profit it is to him. I will never accept of a license until I settle the question for myself of the truth or falsity of the Christian religion.'"

He refused the license, and after the quarterly meeting went home to his father's house. In after years he could look back and see that here was the great mistake of his life. He says: "Little did I dream that I had undertaken one of the most absurd tasks imaginable. I might as well have attempted to solve a question in algebra, by the principles of music, or the science of astronomy by the rules of grammar, as to attempt to solve the problems of religion by the light of reason. However, I began the attempt. But I again found myself beset with people who would urge upon me their impressions of my duty to go into the gospel field. To get rid of this annoyance, I again resolved to go where I was not known. My motives for going I kept a secret, lest I should involve others in my perplexity."

CHAPTER VI.

In the peculiar state of mind described in the foregoing chapter, young Redfield again left home, going about a hundred miles from where he was known. In less than a fortnight after his arrival at his new destination, however, he was questioned about the duty of preaching. This caused him to leave again. This time he chose a place where he felt sure he would not be annoyed by anything of that kind, but here he found old acquaintances who raised the question, within a week. Then he left again, resolved not to profess religion at the next place, nor to have anything to say on the subject, thinking in that way to avoid the annoyance. Soon after this he found himself beset with infidel notions; and at last his faith in Christianity utterly gave way. He could now get along comparatively well in the daytime, but his nights would be filled with dreams of preaching, and so overcome in his feelings would he be, that on waking he would find his pillow wet with tears. He now began to believe that he had been the dupe of deception through all his strange course. To end the matter once and for all he finally resolved to ask God to take away the conviction of duty, even if it was from him. He had heard of a man who did that, and who was instantly relieved, never to have the feeling come back. He now experienced the same relief. In after years, when looking back with horror upon this passage in his life, he could only account for the after return of the Spirit by referring it to the prayers and intercessions of his mother. He says:

"I felt the Holy Spirit leave me as plainly as I ever felt the taking off of my coat; and yet with no greater alarm than at the loss of a penny. To me, now, infidelity was a fact, and right in its wake came downright atheism. For as soon as I resolved to settle all theological questions by my external senses, a vague uncertainty came over everything. Nature's laws were all the God I could find, and the mere notion that a given system of religion might be true was the utmost my reason could conjecture. It now seemed to me that all the phenomena of religious emotion, of mental and moral changes, were due to laws within us, and beyond our control. Now, the funereal pall of annihilation settled down upon me, and I could see nothing but darkness and desolation. Man and earth seemed orphaned. I sought in anatomy, physiology, and philosophy for testimony to clear this up, and, if possible, give me a single fact to settle my distracted mind. One favorite haunt of mine during this period was an ancient Indian burying ground. Some of the graves were entirely gone, washed away by the high waters of an adjoining stream; others were partly gone, the dark sands of which gave traces of the bodies which had been laid there to rest several hundred years before. A few sea-shells, flint arrowheads and hatchets, and beads were all that bore testimony that these bodies had ever lived. In contemplation of these things my whole soul would cry out, while the suffocation of death seemed to be upon me, 'O God, if there be a God, send me to the hell of the Bible, but don't annihilate me.' It seemed to me at such times that I could have died a hundred deaths if that would have made the Christian doctrines true, and have run my chances of heaven or hell.

"I now commenced the systematic study of anatomy, for the purpose of ascertaining whether man had a conscious, thinking, acting, soul, independent of the body, or whether a fortuitous combination of matter in conjunction with material laws might not produce the phenomena we observe; and therefore these phenomena cease with the combination. Among other works, treating upon this subject, I met with Paley's Natural Theology Illustrated, which gave a sober, common-sense, bias to my mode of reasoning. As a result of this I was cured of atheism and infidelity. I now saw the fogs of doubt all clear away, and the doctrine of the nature, operations, independence, and perpetuity, of the human soul, redeemed from all doubt, and established upon solid foundations."

While he was passing through all this, his mother, hearing of his infidelity and abandonment of religion and all thought of entering the Christian ministry, became very sad and would not be comforted. Not only were her hopes, but her faith also was involved with his. In his failure, she saw all her hopes concerning him, from his infancy, dashed to the ground. She pined away, and nearly lost her mind in mourning over him. She became so weak, that she would stop strangers as they passed her door, and ask them in plaintive tones, "Have you seen my son, John? Where is he? and what is he about?" Only as a pious mother could, she kept his case before God, and quite likely it was in answer to her prayers that he was finally brought back not only to Christ, but into the work of soul-saving, for which he became so eminent.

He says, "During the period of my infidelity, I saw and believed that human nature needed some kind of religion to restrain it from injuring society. For this reason I would attend church, read prayers with the congregation, to cultivate a moral tone. I reasoned: 'If there be a God, and the Bible proves true, it is best to be fitted for any possible emergency that may arise, even if not contemplated by the Bible. If there is no God, or only such an one as the deranged condition of nature reveals; if we have nothing to hope beyond the grave, not even the guarantee of an abstract existence, the uncertainty is terrible."

In after years, he would say, "Men may talk of annihilation as a possible fact, and regard the theory as a light affair; but let them stand where I have stood, by the graves of the long forgotten dead, and in imagination pass down the vista of coming time, and think: 'With all my longing for life, I must lie down in the dust and darkness of the tomb, and let the rusty centuries fold over my head, till ages have passed and gone, and I sleep on still as these have slept, who now lie here in a common ruin, forgotton and forever gone! Poor nameless dust, who lived, hoped, feared; made as they thought ample provision for life in the spirit land; yet all in vain!' and they will cry out, as I have cried, 'O God, spare me at least a bare existence.' No! I would know the truth, however unwelcome it may be."

His study of anatomy, under the tutorship of an eminent physician, was continued after his return to faith, and laid the foundation for his future practice of medicine. This struggle with unbelief, and the various lines of investigation that it led him to undertake, in mental and moral philosophy, as well as in the physical sciences, was a valuable training for the especial work to which he was called. Every phase of unbelief, mental and moral difficulty seems to have been reviewed by him, not simply by reading, but by personal investigation, until it seemed that no obstacle of that kind could stand before him. "Questions of magnetism, clairvoyance, and much of what now passes for spiritualism," were carefully studied by him at that early period (between 1830 and 1840). The perfect ease and simplicity with which, in the days of his power, he would remove the difficulties of doubt and solve the problems of conscience, was an astonishment to those who listened to him. From the foregoing account may be seen how these problems were worked out in the fierce struggles of his own early experience.

Concerning the period in which he was pursuing these studies he says: "During this period my former experience in the Christian life was not taken into account. It furnished me with no help whatever. And even after this struggle was over, and I began to seek my personal salvation again, at first it did not occur to me that I had once been a Christian. I commenced entirely anew. When I set about it in good earnest I purposed to do it among a people that I thought would not annoy me about preaching. But here I found myself mistaken again. Scarcely had I obtained a little light on experimental religion before the minister whose church I attended, met me in the street one day and made an appointment with me to meet him at his house at a certain time. When the time came, fearing it was the old subject that was coming up, I did not go. When I met him again, he expressed his disappointment at my failure to come, and set another time for me. When the time came I went, and my fears proved true. Said he: 'I have little confidence in impressions, but I wish to know for my own satisfaction if you have ever been called of God to preach. I wish you to give me a direct answer.' In my soul I cried out, 'My God! am I found out here also?' I then frankly answered: 'I have.' But I stated to him that there were barriers now in my way, the principal one of which was a promise to marry. This barrier I had placed in the way some time before. My object was to create an obligation that would prevent me from entering the ministry. This proved to be another great mistake of my life. I was soon made to know how surely God could confront me, how terribly he could chastise me, and how intensely I could be made to suffer."

CHAPTER VII.

THE BITTER and sorrowful experience occasioned by his rash marriage engagement will be related in Mr. Redfield's own words. Speaking of this matter, he says:

"Gladly would I suppress this chapter of my life, were it not for the fact that the cause of Christ has suffered from the misrepresentations of it that have gone forth to the world. I might have told my story long ago and saved myself much misunderstanding, but I wished not to appear as the revealer of my family sorrows. If I had spoken, my enemies would have made capital of that, as they have made capital of my silence. Now at the close of my life I feel free to speak. I shall withhold much of the worse, and only state enough to give a specimen of what I have suffered. I ask the candid reader to make the case his own, and then ask himself if he would have done better. I have not borne all this in silence and alone, refusing to accept of that relief, which making known the facts would have given me, and making them known now in order to gain sympathy. It is too late for that; my only object is to correct unjust imputations on the cause for which I have labored. I must, as a last act of my life, do this. What I now give to the world of this unfortunate affair, is all that it will ever get, unless circumstances shall compel me to give more.

"I married one whom I thought would make me a happy home. I hired me a house at the desire and with the approval of my wife, but within three weeks was compelled to abandon it. I found she was no more fit than a child to take an interest in or care for a home. I saw no other way than to board. I could find but one place where I thought it at all proper to board, and that was at her own father's home. But he soon told me I must take her away for he

(45)

could no longer endure her. I hired another house. To make it at all possible to keep house I was obliged to hire housekeepers, but it was only to have them turned away as fast as I could hire them. In one week I hired six in succession and all were turned away within that time. I next sent for my sister, who came and tried to make my home tolerable; but in a few days I was compelled to permit her to go elsewhere to board until she could arrange to go home.

"I next tried to get along by doing the housework myself and hide from the world my misfortune; but neglecting to keep my doors fastened, I was caught doing my own cooking. When asked of the whereabouts of my wife, I could not tell, for I did not know. The fact of my being alone and doing my own cooking soon reached the ears of her parents, who, mortified by their daughter's conduct, attempted to bring about a reform. I had kept all this to myself, not even telling them. Her father, learning that she often came to his home, and left me to do the work in mine, forbade her coming again without me. Of this I was ignorant for a long time.

" Late one night she told me she was going home and I must accompany her. I replied: 'It is late, and your people will be in bed. I cannot go and disturb them, as there is no urgent need.' I then locked the door, put away the key and went to bed.

" I was soon aroused by the fall of a window. I immediately arose, and saw she was out of the house, and with a light in her hand was passing through the back way, going to her father's house. I knew now there was fresh trouble for me. So, I staid up awaiting the results. I soon heard a heavy knock at the door. I went to it, opened it, and asked who was there and what was wanted. It was her father. Said he, 'I will see if you are going to turn my daughter out of doors.' I had no light, and he tried to find me in the darkness. I knew by the tone of his voice that he was

greatly exasperated, and determined to commit violence upon
me. I ran into the parlor, and he followed. 'Be quiet and
calm, until I can explain to you,' I said. But he was too excited
to hearken to reason, and only knew my whereabouts when I
spoke. I could hear his footsteps and thereby I kept out of
his way. Thus I continued to avoid him until he so far cooled
down as to pass out and go home. I then closed and fastened
the door, fully resolved that I would never submit to have
her return until the matter was fully understood and settled.
I cooked my breakfast when the morning came, and went
out to my business.

"About 10 o'clock she came and asked my forgiveness, and
desired me to give her the key to the house. I told her she
could not have the key until the last night's difficulties were
settled. 'Well,' said she, 'go down home with me and I
will confess it all.' So down we went to her parents' house.
We found them in a very unpleasant mood. I spoke to her
mother, calling her by that title. She said, 'Don't you call
me mother as long as you treat my daughter as you have.'

"I replied, 'Let your daughter tell her own story then.'

"I then asked her, 'Did I turn you out of doors?'

"She answered, 'No, sir.'

" 'Did you not leave the house when I was asleep?'

" 'Yes, sir.'

" 'Did I know you were going?'

" ' No, sir.'

" 'Did you not climb out of the window as still as possible,
so as not to awaken me?'

" 'Yes, sir.'

" 'Then', asked her parents, 'why did you say to us, that
he turned you out?'

"She answered, 'Because you told me never to come
home again unaccompanied by my husband, unless he should
turn me out of doors. I made up the story so you would let
me stay.'

"Now the whole indignation turned against her, until she called upon me to protect her. I felt sorry for her father, for if he got the right of a matter he had generosity and Christianity enough to induce him to do right. I could but feel that through this whole affair he was an honorable and right-minded man.

"I now permitted her to return. But the same state of things continued.

"Next I was suddenly called upon by a church committee to investigate matters that could not be tolerated longer. I said to them 'Go on and find out all you can, for I am ignorant of the object of your investigation.'

"I permitted her to tell her own story uncorrected. They found it entirely a matter of misrepresentation. She confessed the whole to be false. She had reported that I would not make any provision for her wants. That I had starved her by not providing the necessaries of life. When the committee found plain bread, meat, and all kinds of provisions in abundance, her mother greatly mortified, asked her how long these things had been in the house, she answered,

"'I have never been out of them.'

"'Then, what could you mean thus to report what is false?'

"'Oh!' said she, 'I wanted some oysters, and he said he could not find them, and I didn't believe him.' The committee knew it was the season when there were none in the market.

"Again, her mother, deeply mortified, upbraided her severely, when she turned to me for protection, saying, 'I wonder how you can live with me?'

"I was exonerated by the committee of course, and one of them said to me, 'No one can blame you if you leave that woman, for such conduct is past all forbearance.'

"But all I could do was to wait for deliverance in God's time. Nothing but the consciousness that I was enduring the result of my own disobedience made my case endurable. And my conscientiousness would not allow me to take legal steps to get rid of her.

"I was now taken violently sick, and was brought nigh unto death. It was the first of the cholera season, and I was the only one afflicted with the disease in that section who survived. I passed into what is called the stage of collapse; but I felt, I have not yet done my work, and I cannot die. I then felt, I shall not die. Shortly after this I was restored to health.

"Still my family trouble continued. Now and then my wife would have a religious streak. One night after making a great disturbance and giving me a terrible scolding, she suddenly turned upon me and commanded me to pray as her father prayed. To this I replied, 'I cannot think of mocking God by any mixture of prayer with such wicked and violent manifestations of temper.' I saw she took it in ill part, but I thought it best to drop the matter and go to rest, still keeping a disguised but vigilant watch of her. When she supposed me to be asleep, I saw her come near enough to me to get a clear view of me and how and where I lay. She then took the light and set it back so it would not shine in my face. I could see her movements, however, all the better. She then went to the fire-place and took up a pair of heavy brass-mounted tongs, and taking a good hold of them with both hands, she came softly within a few feet of me, and then darted upon me with great fury and began to strike with heavy blows at my head. Having seen the whole operation, I was prepared for it; and by holding the bed-clothes over my face and head, I received the blows upon my arms.

"For some time after, I felt I had reason to fear much more violence from her. I kept up a vigilant watch, but unbeknown to any one else. I could not inform even her own parents of this, much less others.

"Several times, by accident or intentionally, she burned up her dresses, and then came to me and demanded more. I think her mother must have known that she burned them; for once she came to me and asked me to furnish her with one or two cheap ones to keep peace. Then when I did this the mother made a fuss about it, and went among their relatives with a subscription to buy her daughter a more expensive suit, declaring that I refused to dress her in a becoming manner.

"When my friends came to see me she would tell them to leave for they could not be harbored there. My troubles had now become so great, and having none to whom I could tell them, I cried, 'O Lord, my punishment is greater than I can bear.' I was unfit for business, and in short was so broken in spirit that I could not attend to business as it was necessary to do, and was obliged to fail. I gave up all I had to the last chair and spoon. I had nothing left. I could not hire a room, nor would my wife stay if I did. There was only one place where I could procure shelter for the night, and that was her father's house. What to do or where to turn was more than I could tell. I might have found some employment, but no place for permanent board, as no one would board my wife. Her father would only engage to board her until we could leave town and rid them of the mortification to which they were subject on her account. I believe they felt truly sorry for me when they saw me in this distressed condition. They advised me to take up some business with which I could travel and hoped that my wife being among strangers might do better. I borrowed money enough to get out of town, and went where she was not known, and soon procured a place to board; but shortly I saw from the deportment of the people that something was amiss. I knew my only way was to keep perfectly still and wait for matters to develop. We had staid in this place about four weeks when the lady of the house informed me that we could not stay longer. I found this had come from misrepresentations of me. I had known it was going on, but I had thought it best not to attempt to correct it until I was compelled to; for I utterly despised the man who would reveal the afflictions to which he was subjected by a bad wife. When the truth came out the lady of the house expressed her sympathy for me, and said 'You are welcome to stay as long as you please, but I cannot have my house so disturbed by that woman; you must take her away.' I secured another place but could stay only one week. I then procured a team and took her some thirty or forty miles away among strangers again. I found a place in a genteel family. Here we staid twelve weeks.

" I soon saw that something was going wrong, but waited again for developments to indicate my course of action. It continually became more evident that my time was coming to a close. One day the lady said to me: 'Such has been the reports by your wife concerning you that I have believed you to be a bad man. But I have found out where the trouble lies, and though I deeply sympathize with you in your affliction, yet, we can endure her no longer.' Of course I expected this, and I could not blame them for turning me into the street. What to do I could not tell; houseless and homeless, and almost without money and no place to get board where my wife was known, I must leave town to find a place for shelter. So we took stage to a place about fifty miles away. Here we got board in a public house; but after only a few hours she positively refused to stay a day or a night. Now I did not know what to do. Finally I said to myself: 'I will try one more experiment; I will take her to my father's house; her own father will not take her, and every boarding house refuses to keep her or bear with her. I took the next stage and brought her to my father's. I went on some fifty miles farther, and here my funds were exhausted and I was in great distress of mind though I managed to hide my sufferings from others. I soon found that my good old father and mother could not endure her conduct, and they told me I should not live with such a woman. I felt this was my last experiment and if this failed the Lord knows I don't know what to do next. I saw nothing but agony and the poor-house as the final winding-up of my calamity. My spirit utterly sank within me. I was advised. to leave her and get a bill of divorcement from her; but while I was in this suspense, and wondering what to do next, all at once she resolved to go home to her father's house and demanded the money to go with. My funds were exhausted, but she insisted on going, and actually started on foot for a hundred miles through mud and snow. When I found she was fully bent on going I went after her, and promised to see if I could send her in any way. So I sold my watch to pay for the hire of a horse to carry her home. I took care not to go myself. Now I felt a little relief at being free for a short time of my trouble. Very soon, however, a letter came from her father saying she was very penitent and sorry for having left me, and would promise to change her conduct if I would take her back. I wrote back that I had suffered enough, and tried experiments enough, and I could do no more. I felt that the last bond of attachment had snapped, and that if the offense of not living with her should bring me to the state's prison I would go there.

"In the spring I started for the West. I passed through the place where her father lived, and where she then was; but I could not bear the thought of seeing her. So I passed on about three hundred miles, and located in Lockport, N. Y. After I was settled, I wrote to her father, to let him know where I was, and to inquire after the wretched woman. And now he beset me to take her back, saying he believed she would behave herself. I wrote back that I had no confidence in her reform, and could on no condition take her back. I was finally overcome by his entreaties, however, and thought it might be possible after all that she would do better, as she had professed to become religious. So I wrote him that he might bring her about half way, and I would meet him and her there, and would make one more trial. I went in due time to the place and found them there. I took her to my place of residence and to make all as favorable as possible for a successful trial we went to a first-class hotel to board. We staid one night only when she point-blank refused to stay any longer. So off I went and found a private boarding house. Before the week ended she was turned out into the street. The lady of the house forbade her returning on any terms. She said to me, 'You are an unfortunate man, and are welcome here as long as you wish to stay; but that woman must not come in at all'. A lady of the place helped us to obtain another boarding place, and we found shelter for the night. We had staid here but a few weeks when I was again warned to leave. I pleaded to be permitted to stay from day to day until I could write to her father and ask what could be done.

"The lady of the house told me she was a bad woman, for she had seen men follow her off into by-places. I could not say anything in her defense for I had found her once in the embrace of one of the boarders, and another who thought me to be away came in the night to my room. He tried to excuse himself as best he could, but I believe him to have been none too pure for the commission of great evil. I told her how improperly she was acting, in taking such liberties, when she gave me to understand that she should do as she pleased without my consent.

"Not knowing what to do or where to go, I was nearly distracted. I was again informed that she must leave the house. Suddenly she said she would go home to her father's; and I must take her to the boat, about fifteen miles away. I did so, but when we arrived at the place the boat was gone and no other would go until the next week. I

6

must take her back; but there was no place to stay for a single night, except at a public house. I thought I will at least have one more night in which to contrive what course next to take. In the morning we started back to the place we had left, and she promised to let me take a room and keep house, and she would not leave me; but just before we entered the village, she suddenly resolved she would not stay, but would go home at once, and I must take her that night to Rochester where she could take the cars. I knew it was useless to attempt to persuade her to stay even for the night. So I borrowed the money and we left that night in the stage. When we arrived at Rochester, I gave her the money to pay her fare all the way home. As soon as she had gone I felt such a sense of relief that I fainted, and could with great difficulty stagger along to a place where I could lie down. A high nervous fever set in, and for fifteen days I was not able to be moved. A physician, like a good Samaritan attended me faithfully, whom I owe a debt of gratitude which I can never pay. I sank lower and lower until I was near death. Two consulting physicians came to visit me. They told my nurse I must die, and they must make ready to bury me in two days. They also told the people where I was staying that my sickness must have been caused by some deep trouble. I knew not their decision, but I saw them leave me to my fate.

"The old subject of duty now came up, and I inwardly felt, God will not permit me to die; I shall live to preach the gospel. At once I began to mend. In a few days after they left me to die I walked into the doctor's office. They stared at me as though I had come out of the grave. They then told me the conclusion of their council."

CHAPTER VIII.

No way is so long but that it has an end, and no night is so dark but that the dawn of day at last dispels the darkness. Even so the end of some of Mr. Redfield's sorrowful experiences was drawing near, and better days were soon to dawn upon his pathway, as the sequel, related in his own words, will show. Continuing the narrative, he says:

"When I was able to ride, I returned to the place of my late residence. My long absence had induced the people to believe that I had run away, and the man with whom I boarded had taken all my possessions, with an absconded debtor's writ. When he learned the cause of my prolonged absence, however, he returned me all my property without cost. Next I was waited upon by a committee from the church to know how my moral character stood. I learned that I had been accused of keeping a bad woman in town under pretense that she was my wife; that I had never been married to her; and that I knew her to be corrupt. But I was able to convince the committee that I was indeed unfortunate but not criminal; that I was indeed married. I was at once restored to the confidence of the church.

"A lawyer learning the circumstances of my misfortune, came to me and offered to procure me a divorce free of expense. But my lacerated, timid spirit could not consent to go through all the details of litigation.

"Now that I was free from this great trouble, my former impressions of duty came upon me with redoubled force, and I longed for an abode away from the busy world of mankind, and resolved to find me a home like a hermit in the wilderness, where I might serve God, commune with nature, and at last lay my bones to rest in some lonely place unseen and unknown by man. I did go into rooms by myself, and but for neglected duty, which it seemed to me must now be forever abandoned, I should have been comparatively happy; but it seemed to me that my afflictions must prove an obstacle in my way. I thought, everybody will find out that I have had family trouble and will feel at liberty to make out of it what capital they please; and how can I preach when I am thus marked with suspicion? I could have set all things right in the eyes of the honest and well-meaning, but I could not bear to go over the facts of my sufferings for that purpose. No! I must forever abandon the idea of preaching. Yet, I must meet God at last and answer for the neglect of duty. Night and day, for a number of years, I silently brooded over my sad state, and tried all means in my power to banish the scorpion stings of a guilty conscience. 'You knew your duty but did it not,' constantly rang in my ears. A large portion of my time I spent in the grove near by weeping before God.

"I would sometimes go to the church on Sunday, but the sight of a gospel minister would make me writhe with agony, and compel me to leave. I would then resort to the woods and there weep and pray for deliverance. Yet I kept this all buried in my heart. If I saw a minister in the street my eyes would follow him as long as I could see him, and, choked with emotion, I would sigh over my own unhappy state.

"I began to be impressed at one time that I should never see my father and mother again in the flesh. So strongly did this come that I shrank from going to the post-office for fear of finding the sad tidings that they had passed away. On going and finding no letters at all, it would be with a sense of relief. I prayed that I might be permitted to see them again. An answer seemed to come, 'You shall.' The fall came and I went to the city of New York to spend the winter. I procured my winter quarters and began a course of study in the fine arts. I now felt a strong impression to go immediately to my father's home. I had felt perfectly at rest as to the health of my parents from the witness I received that I should see them again. I promised myself that I would take the steamboat the last of the week, and go home. It was about two hundred and fifty miles. But I was so urged by my impression to go that I decided to start a day earlier than I first intended. Still that did not seem to be satisfactory, and finally I resolved to take the first boat. I did so and arrived home just one day before my mother died. Her last rational word was, in effect, "I could die in peace if my son would do his duty." She was then dying of apoplexy. I watched my opportunity to go to her dying bed when we could be alone, and tried to arouse her, but I got no response. I took hold of her, and said, 'Mother, do speak to me once more.' I wanted to tell her I would obey the call of God to preach the gospel; but she was too far gone to understand me. Ten days later my dear father fell sick and passed away.

"I followed them to the tomb, but oh! how my heart did sink on leaving them in their last resting place. Memory with a thousand tongues spoke of the anguish I had caused that sainted mother. I had so often heard her prayers as she pleaded with God to spare her boy and fit him for the mission that was awaiting him. I found myself at home after father's funeral, by the desolate hearth-stone, but so sad at my loss that I have never been able to call to mind any of the circumstances.

"I went almost immediately to visit one of my sisters who lately had lost her husband. She was glad to see me, but began at once to urge me to promise that I would go and preach the gospel. She said: 'You know, brother John, that mother has gone to her grave broken-hearted over your neglect to obey God. And now this is the last time that I shall ever see you on earth, and I want you to promise me that you will do your duty, and let me carry that promise to mother.'

"'But,' said' I, 'I shall visit you again next week.'

"'No,' she said, 'this is the last time we shall meet on earth, so you must promise.'

" Her appeals in mother's name broke me down, and to get rid of her importunity, I made a promise which she con-strued to mean all that she desired, and then she said: 'Come, brother, let us get down and ratify it before God.' Of course I knelt, and she poured out her soul for me in tones and words that stung me to the quick. We arose, and I left her house expecting to visit her again the next week; but on going to the post-office I found a letter calling me to go im-mediately six hundred miles away as an important witness in court. I obeyed the summons, and my sister's words proved true. I never saw her again. I learned in about a month from the time I saw her last, that she, too, had passed away to the spirit land.

"I was very sad because of these repeated desolations in the loss of my dearest earthly friends, but conscience bade me be still and know that God was dealing with me in mercy in permitting me to live, and that in view of the pos-sibility that I might yet do my duty."

CHAPTER IX.

Mr. Redfield soon returned to his bachelor's hall again. It must have been a curiosity shop indeed. Shelves covered the walls on all sides. These shelves were loaded with geological specimens, freaks of nature in wood and stone, Indian relics and mechanism of his own invention. Two mice, bound with delicate chains of his own manufacture, which fed and sported and slept at their pleasure, were his only companions.

Here he secluded himself from the world and Christian friends lest some of them should mention the subject of preaching the gospel. Neither he nor they could let the subject alone. His presence impressed them with the subject, and his sore heart kept it upon his own mind whether sleeping or waking.

One day he met the Methodist preacher in the street, who began immediately to urge him to consent to go to work in the vineyard of the Lord. He tried to avoid it by arguing both himself and the minister to another conclusion. He had held an exhorter's license for some time, which had been crowded upon him against his will, but he had never used it. The minister now asked that he might present his case to the leader's meeting for a recommendation for a license to preach. A strong and abiding impression seized him that unless he consented he would be killed by lightning. It seemed to him utter foolishness to allow himself to be swayed by any such thing; especially in a matter of such moment. His past experiences of a similar nature helped this impression to take the firmer hold upon him. It haunted him day and night for a long time. When the terrible thunder storms which frequently passed over would arise, and especially in the night, all his peace and rest and sleep would be at an end until the storm ceased. He would resort to all the precautionary measures that his knowledge of the laws of electricity would suggest to him, as opening the windows and giving a free circulation of air through the room, setting a chair in glass tumblers and sitting in it with the feet upon the rounds, and then pray and tremble until the storm was over. The familiar acquaintances of the man can fully appreciate this.

This state of mind lasted for some weeks, when one night his fears became so great that he promised most fervently, that if God would relieve him, he would present his case himself to the leaders' meeting on the first opportunity to do so. In an instant, when the storm was at its highest, his request was granted, and he went to rest and sleep, as calmly as ever in his life.

The Friday evening after, the leaders were to meet, and he went to redeem his pledge. The meeting was held in the basement of the church. When a suitable opportunity came, he arose and stated his feelings. He was about to retire as usual in such cases, when he was stopped by one of the members and asked how he stood on the question of abolitionism. This question was then greatly agitating the Methodist Episcopal Church. He answered, "I am an abolitionist of the strongest type."

"Then I shall oppose the recommendation." said the brother.

He earnestly hoped they would not grant the recommendation, for that, he thought, would release him; and to make it doubly sure, he now said, "I wish it distinctly understood that if I am granted a license to preach, and that shall add anything to the influence I now possess, I shall certainly use it for God and the slave. So now your eyes are open and you know what I am and what to expect."

Again it was remarked, "We shall contest the matter."

He retired, and immediately the vote was taken, and the recommendation was granted. The meeting adjourned, and before they had hardly reached their homes the church was struck with lightning. This made a profound impression upon him, and when soon after, the quarterly conference convened, he was ready to be examined according to disci-, pline. The license was granted, but when it was handed to him, he felt he could not use it.

He was in constant dread of his wife's returning, for he believed he could do nothing with her. He was also in constant fear that the tongue of slander would break out upon him in regard to his family matters, and that the more certainly if he began to preach. He used the license for a few times, and was urged to go upon a circuit as a supply. He consented to this for a short time, and though pressed to continue, he refused. He also refused to accept of any compensation for his services. He not only shrank from the responsibilities of the sacred office, but also from the very name of a Christian minister, and pay for his services implied that. He finally gave up preaching altogether, and went to Cleveland, Ohio, for the winter.

CHAPTER X.

IN CLEVELAND, Mr. Redfield engaged in his chosen profession—portrait painting. He gave in his letter to the church, and was enrolled as a local preacher. Now and then, he preached as called upon by the pastor, and during the following winter assisted in a protracted meeting. His labors were owned of God in the conversion of souls.

By invitation he supplied the pulpit of the Seaman's Bethel one Sunday in the absence of the stated preacher. When the hour came he found the house full. He resolved to do his whole duty. While speaking against gambling, swearing, horse racing and drunkenness, one cried out from the congregation, "Do you mean me? Do you mean me?" He instantly replied, "If that is your case, I certainly mean you." When the services closed the deacon who had invited him to preach said to him, "That was a very sad mistake, and you have done us a great wrong." And then, as if to spare his feelings, he excused the matter thus:

"Our minister, I don't think is quite right. He knows they will do these things of which you spoke, but he never reproves them, or speaks against such conduct, and they are all bound up in him. Sometimes I think he does not go far enough, but you went entirely too far. And besides this, many of these are rough sailors and they will not bear reproof."

Shocked at this, Mr. Redfield turned away with a thankful heart that he was not more closely identified with such a state of things, and resolved that what work he did for the Lord should be faithfully done.

Soon after this his pastor asked him for his views on the slavery question. The answer was, "I am an abolitionist from head to foot."

"Then," asked he, "would you be willing to give us a lecture on the subject? Our hands are tied by a vote of the conference which forbids the preachers meddling with the question; yet the colonizationists make it a point to create all the prejudice against us they can, until some people think we are the vilest disorganizers in the land. I am not allowed to speak for the poor dumb slave under pain of conference penalties. And it does seem that those who dare should be permitted to speak the sentiments of the anti-slavery part of the church. There are a number of strong abolitionists in the city who would be glad to stand by any one who dares to take a firm stand; but they have not the courage to take a stand themselves unless some one takes the lead and meets the brunt of the opposition, which is sure to come, when an anti-slavery society is started."

Mr. Redfield promised the preacher to lecture, feeling glad that he had nothing too good to sacrifice in such a cause.

The appointment for the lecture was made. When the time came, a mob had collected, nailed up the doors of the building in which the lecture was to be given, and were waiting for the lecturer himself. He felt it was no compromise of right or conscience to avoid an infuriated mob, when by no possibility could he get a hearing.

His quiet retirement aroused the better element of society, who were not prepared to surrender the right of free speech in a free state to a mob. A demand was therefore made that the house be opened, and Mr. Redfield given an opportunity to present the views of the abolitionists. The plea was made that the colonizationists had free opportunity to misrepresent the abolitionists, and it was no more than right that the latter have an opportunity to reply. Another appointment was then made.

Before the time came round, Mr. Redfield had the opportunity to prepare himself more perfectly for the occasion. The opposition to the first meeting created a deeper and wider interest to hear him. It also aroused him to see more clearly the terrible sinfulness of the slavery feeling in this country, and to make the stronger effort against it.

Mr. Redfield's lecture gave a synopsis of the slave codes in each State; the attempts of humanitarians in these states to ameliorate the condition of the slaves; and the facts recited in the preambles of the bills presented in the different legislatures for this purpose. These referred to the taking of the lives of slaves; robbing female slaves of their virtue; and the overworking and starving of field hands. He then called attention to the extent and the manner in which these laws were disobeyed, and the advantage that masters took of their legal powers. He read extracts from Southern papers to illustrate the foregoing, one of which was as follows:

"RAN AWAY FROM THE SUBSCRIBER.

"My slave, Sally, who, without doubt, is lurking about the plantation of Mr. ———, in Georgia, as I sold her husband to that gentleman about eighteen months ago. She has been very sullen ever since. She will try to pass herself off as a white woman, as she is very white and beautiful spoken, and very capable of putting on the airs of a white lady. Fearing she might run away I took the pains to mark her by knocking out two of her front teeth and branding her on the buttocks with the letter S. She is likewise much scarred with the whip on her neck and shoulders. Her legs are torn by the dogs, done in catching her fifteen months ago. Her left thumb has the mark of a rifle ball where I shot her before she would surrender."

This was followed by recitals of cruelty, blood-curdling to read at the present day.

Mr. Redfield's audience was large and many present were members of the mob which gathered at the time of the other appointment. He observed before he was through that the opposition began to yield, and the mob spirit to quiet down. He had expected that an attack would be made upon him before he was through, but all remained quiet.

He finished the lecture with a picture in which the actors were reversed. The scene was in Algeria. The slaves were Americans. The same scenes were enacted as read from the Southern advertisements. He then appealed to their sense of justice and honor. He finished by representing himself as hazarding his reputation and life by pleading for those supposed Americans in Algeria, and asking his audience if now they thought him worthy of tar and feathers and other maltreatment. He waited for the mob to make a demonstration, inviting them to do so if they thought it right, but all remained quiet. He then said: "If you think the cause is worthy of support, we will form an anti-slavery society." Nearly all present were then enrolled as members. This was the first organization of the kind made in the city.

Soon after the lecture and the organization of the society, he was called upon to put his principles in practice. Cleveland was a point on the under-ground railroad where many fugitives from slavery took their departure from the United States, where they were unsafe, to the Dominion of Canada where they would be safe. It was a criminal act, according to the law of the land, to harbor or assist a fugitive slave.

One Sunday evening he observed in the congregation at church a tall, straight, well-built and genteel appearing man, who, with hymn-book in hand, took part in the worship. The hue of his skin and the wavy ringlets of his hair showed him to be one of the despised race which the law of the land and the unwritten creed of some of the churches had declared had no rights that white men were bound to respect.

Shortly after night-fall the same manly form came to Mr. Redfield's lodgings, and in great agitation said: "O sir, save me! I am in great trouble! Will you help me?"

"I will, if I can," answered Mr. Redfield, "but tell me first what is the matter."

O sir," said the stranger, "I am a slave. A large reward has been offered for me; and I learn that there is a man in the city looking for me to take me back into slavery."

"Come in," said Mr. Redfield, "and you will be perfectly safe. My windows are all shut, fastened and blinded, and I will fasten the door."

"But what if they break in?" the fugitive asked.

"I will do the best I can at all cost to defend you," replied Mr. Redfield; "sit down and tell me your story. Why did you run away? Were you badly treated?"

"Oh, no!" he answered. "In the first place, I belonged to a man who died some years ago. His widow married again, and before the legal heirs could put in their claim to their portion of the estate my new master desired to sell me. Of all this I knew nothing until one day while I was working in the tanyard cleaning out a vat (I had been hired out to a tanner, for I was a tanner by trade,) shoveling out the old bark and singing a Methodist hymn as I worked, I thought I heard a voice saying, 'You are sold.' I straightened up and looked around, but saw no one. I went on with my work again, still singing a favorite hymn. The same voice came again, 'You are sold.' I sprang out of the vat and looked for the author of the dreadful sound, but in vain. I went to work again, determined to banish my fears. But the same voice said again, 'You are sold.' I looked again, and at a distance I saw my master in company with a stranger walking leisurely around the tanyard. I knew then that voice was correct. The thought, I will be torn and forever separated from my wife and child, now rushed upon me, and with it a sense of the wrong about to be perpetrated on us. I instantly resolved: 'I will die first.' I kept an eye out, and went on with my work. They gradually drew nearer and nearer until they stood at my back. As I lifted a shovelful of bark one of them asked, 'Shall I not help you lift it out?' Instinctively

I knew that this meant to tie my hands while I was holding them up. Blind to all consequences, and with the nerve of a madman, I sprang out of the vat and raised my shovel in self-defense. Instantly they both drew pistols, and bade me surrender or die. I cared not a fig for death, I was so aroused by the sense of the wrong they were doing me. But the thought came, 'It is no use to contend; they have the law on their side and can do what they please with me. I must submit like my Saviour. I must resist not, but endure for his sake.' It was my conscience and not my fear that subdued me. It told me to look to the future and to God for the settlement of my troubles. I then let them tie my hands behind me with a long rope. They then gave a loud whistle which was answered by a man coming to us, to whom they gave me in charge. He took hold of the rope and commanded me to walk on. He took me to a place by the roadside where there were about fifty more slaves, tied together, preparatory to being taken down the river to be sold again. When we had got away from the two men I asked the one who had me in charge to let me go and see my wife and child before I was separated from them forever.

"'No,' said he, with a terrible oath, 'you shall not. Your wife would make a —— —— fuss, and you will feel a great deal worse. You had better make up your mind never to see them again.'

"Oh, I was so heavy with grief that my feet seemed to slump into the ground at every step. Suddenly, with all my might I gave a wrench to the rope, and so loosed my hands, and, being much stronger than he, I pulled him right up to me, and then said, 'I shall go and see my family before we are parted forever.' When he saw I had him in my power, with another oath, he said, 'Well, you may go, but it will be the worse for you.'"

While thus narrating his story, this noble specimen of man would falter, choke, and struggle with the grief which was yet rending his heart. Then again he would nerve himself to continue the narration.

"Finally," said he, "we reached the cabin of my family, and as soon as my wife saw me, with a shriek she fell upon the floor, and my poor heart seemed to break worse than before. As I was compelled to hasten, I picked up a few articles of clothing, tied them up in a bundle, and kissed my wife and boy for the last time. Oh! how my brain reeled as I turned to leave them, forever. I felt that sense of my feet sinking into the earth again, at every step, as I walked away. I was now hurried back to the coffle of slaves, and was soon bound by one of my wrists to the chain, which ran the whole length of the gang. The driver being in a hurry urged us on, to the top of our speed. My rough old shoes that I wore in the tannery soon so galled my feet that the blood ran out at every step. We reached the river that night and were taken into a tavern at the landing. We were all put up in the garret, which was made like a jail, with grated windows, for the accommodation of slave-traders.

"Soon the whole gang were asleep. Some cried themselves to sleep, some were sullen and apparently careless as to what became of them, for the last tie had been broken and the last hope had fled. Others were so gross and stupid that they fell asleep from want of energy and life to keep them awake; like beasts when out of reach of the lash, they were at rest. It was raining hard without, and the patter upon the roof and the splashing upon the ground, made it difficult to hear other sounds. When I thought all were sound asleep, I walked carefully around the room. I put my hand upon a rope, which I found to be a clothes-line, for the family used the garret to dry clothes in when not in other use. I went to a window, and with an old jack-knife which I had to use about the tanyard, I dug out of the wall one end of an iron bar, and that made a place just large enough for me to squeeze through. I then fastened one end of the clothes-line to another bar, threw out my little bundle of clothing, carefully climbed out, and ventured my weight upon that frail rope. I heard one of the strands break, and expected to fall to the ground the next moment; but it held me until I reached the end. I had not reached the ground by a number of feet, when, as I hung there, I saw a door open and some one passing in. For a moment all my fears were aroused, thinking I was discovered. But they did not see me in the darkness, and I only saw them by the light of the open door. The rain was still pouring down. I now let go my hold and dropped to the ground. I carefully felt around until I found my bundle, and then made my way to a stream of water near by, and waded it a long distance, that the hounds might be unable to follow me. The stream led me in the direction from whence I came. I followed it until about daybreak, and then hid in the woods until night, when I started again for home. The succeeding morning I came in sight of my little home again. From fear of frightening my dear wife, and arousing some slaves who slept in part of the cabin, I went cautiously to a little window, and in a low tone of voice, called:

" 'Liza!'

" With a scream she cried out, 'O my God! that's my Thomas! O Thomas! Thomas! the patrol will kill you!'

" I said, 'Hush! Liza, keep still, and we will manage some way.'

" I went into the cabin and climbed up into the little garret through a hole over a door between the two rooms. My wife put up a box on to the door casing to hide a part of the hole through which I had passed. When it was fairly daylight, the patrol, who had heard of my escape, came to the cabin and asked Liza if I had got back. She answered, 'No! I have not seen him since he left with the slave-trader.' This was literally true, for it was dark when I came. 7

" The patrol kept such a close watch that I dared not go out anywhere. So I concluded to change my place of concealment, and started in the night for my mother's, some four miles away, where she was owned. Lest I should startle her, I went to her window, and in a low voice, asked, ' Aunt, is uncle at home?' She knew my voice, and knew I had run away, and that the patrol was after me. She cried out, 'Oh! it is my poor boy, Tommy! O Tommy! Tommy! the patrol will kill you!' She let me into the cabin, and we took up a board of the floor, and I laid down on the ground, and she put the board back again. Here I could stay until the patrol would pass on to the next beat, and then I would come out and stretch myself.

" My wife's and mother's cabins were watched closely. I changed my hiding place from under the floor to the garret, which was reached by a ladder. As my mother could have my boy with her without suspicion, I had the mournful consolation of caressing him often.

" I resolved at last that I would come North as soon as I could with safety; but so closely was I watched, that I was compelled to hide under the floor and in the garret, at mother's, for thirteen months. By this time I was so completely bleached out, and my skin was so fair, that after mother got me some women's clothes, I was able boldly to take the stage as a white woman and make my escape without detection. When I had reached a section where I was not known, I got out and went into the woods and put on my men's clothing. I then traveled nights and slept daytimes until I reached a free state. I lived on corn, fruits and such other things as I could help myself to. After a long time I found myself in this state.

"I now felt so badly about my wife and child that at last I ventured to get a white man to write to my master for me, that if he would allow me to live with my family I would go back and give him my labors for the rest of my life. He wrote me in reply that he would have me any way and he would do as he pleased. When this hope failed I resolved to go myself and by some means bring my wife and child away. So I turned my face toward the land of bondage again. I traveled nights and slept daytimes in the woods, until I came in sight once more of my little cabin. When I got inside I found my little one was dead and buried. My heart was nearly broken again. With my wife I started again for the land of freedom. We passed the patrol and entered the woods. It was night; but my poor wife had become so nervous and broken by the long struggle with her wrongs that the least unusual sound or the breaking of a twig would cause her to cry out, 'The patrol is coming! the patrol is coming!' I carried her in my arms until I saw I must give up the effort, as her fears would be our betrayal, and we should both be taken back to bondage. I was obliged to let her return, while I turned my steps toward the North again. And now they have got track of me, and are in the city after me."

Mr. Redfield had the privilege of learning that this suffering man landed safely in Canada, where colored people had equal rights with white people. He knew he was making himself liable to church proscription by aiding such suffering followers of Jesus, but he told the authorities that he should stand for God and humanity. The laws of the state would have sent him to the state's prison for ten years, and made him pay a fine of five hundred dollars for sheltering and aiding that poor man if his offense had been known; but to use his own words, "What had I to do with protecting my own freedom and rights when there stood my suffering Jesus in the person of this poor outcast. I seemed to hear his voice ringing in my ears, 'Inasmuch as ye have done it unto one of the least of these my brethren ye have done it unto me.' Yes, and I would have done it again if I had known that I certainly would have had to suffer both the imprisonment and the fine."

Mr. Redfield lived during the period of the great anti-slavery conflict in this country. All the different phases of it passed before him. The Methodist Episcopal Church, of which he was a member, and within whose pale he performed nearly all his ministerial labor, and which he loved as he loved his life, he saw hesitate and cringe before the slave power, and at last become an agent of persecution against such as could not refrain from lifting up their voices against the gigantic wrong. His sensitive soul listened with horror to the accounts of proscription against such men as Orange Scott, Cyrus Prindle, Luther Lee and others of its most de-voted ministers. He lived to see a combination formed in the General conference of that body, in 1860,* that prevented the redressing of the grievances that resulted in the organi-zation of the Free Methodist Church, and that also prevented the change of the general rule on slavery until 1864, when there were no more slaves within the bounds of the United States.

He did not live to see that change of the rule. If he had, the act coming at such a time, would have appeared so ungracious to him that it could have afforded him no pleasure. If he had lived several quadrennials longer, he might have been gratified by witnessing the adoption of a resolution by the General conference of that body, removing a censure passed upon Orange Scott, by the General conference of 1836, for taking part in an anti-slavery meeting in the city of Cin-cinnati, during the session of that conference. Orange Scott had passed into the eternal world, however, long before this relief to his memory.

It is hardly possible for the present generation, though little more than a quarter of a century has since passed by, to conceive of a state of society in this country such as has

---

* Rev. William Hosmer, in the "Northern Independent," editorial.

been illustrated in this chapter; but many there are who have outlived the generation in which these cruelties were perpetrated, and who, vividly recalling those exciting times, will testify that the picture is in no wise overdrawn.

CHAPTER XI.

Mr. REDFIELD had now passed one winter in active service for God and humanity. Many had been converted, an efficient anti-slavery society had been organized, and nearly fifty fugitives from bondage had been assisted in their efforts to reach Canada. He now determined to return to Lockport, N. Y., the scene of some of his severest conflicts, and where he consented to accept a license to preach the gospel. On his return, he was urged to take the place of a preacher who had made himself unacceptable by his anti-slavery views. He accepted the position, but soon was equally as unacceptable as his predecessor, and for the same reason. He gave up the charge and returned to his bachelor's quarters. He now despaired of doing his duty acceptably to God, and satisfactorily to himself. The summer was spent in studying into the works and ways of God as seen in nature. He gave up the idea of going into the work as a traveling preacher. He thought to content himself with preaching occasionally, but giving his time mainly to business. When he did preach he refused to receive pay for his services. The hand of disease had fastened upon him, but still he endeavored to keep his conscience free from condemnation, by visiting and praying with the people, and exhorting sinners to seek Christ. In this he saw some success, but so little was he satisfied with his labors, that he was in great distress of mind.

He was under conviction for and began to seek the experience of entire sanctification.

He says: "I thought that experience would empower me to do my duties with greater success and satisfaction. In my ignorance of the true way, I wept and mourned before God, and wished to meet with some one who could instruct me. I finally became desperate, and resolved to make a business of seeking it. I began with a day of fasting and prayer. This was followed with a watch-night. I resolved never to

close my eyes or leave my knees until I could claim the blessing; but nature sank under the burden, and I fell to the floor
and went to sleep. When morning came, I awoke to find
myself exhausted and on the floor. When I remembered
the vows and resolutions I had made the night before, and
how poorly I had kept my promise, I blamed myself for
faithlessness, and in tears asked God if I must live another
day in this condition. Can I be no more like thee than this?
I could say from the depths of my heart:

"''Tis worse than death my God to love,
And not my God alone.'

"Again I fasted and kept watch-night. I resolved not
to move until I either died or gained the great pearl; but
being still more exhausted, I again sank to the floor and went
to sleep, and awoke the next morning to upbraid myself for
my broken vows. All these struggles only proved to me
how useless were human plans and will-power to gain what
I afterward learned must be obtained by faith alone. By
the Holy Spirit I was led to make a thorough search of self
and find to what extent my will was in harmony with God's
will. Now my mind was brought to face the great question with me. I said to myself, how can I think of preaching after my troubles with that unfortunate being who has
blasted every hope of my life! I cannot attempt to regulate
public opinion by a narration of my sorrows! I shall be
misunderstood, and my misfortune will be the foundation of
a large amount of slander, which will hedge up my way.
'No, Lord,' I said, 'I cannot go. I might once have gone
without impediment, but that day has passed forever. I will
do the best I can in a private way, but to devote myself to
the work of the ministry is impossible until I have an honorable discharge from the woman who has embittered my life.'

"I now resolved to spend my time in active service for
the Lord, but in a private way. I commenced visiting the
sick, praying with them, and pointing them to the Lamb of

God. I went to see a young man who was very sick, and who had been given up by the counseling physicians, who had just left him. While at prayer for him an impression came upon me that the young man would not die, and I instantly gave utterance to it. I then arose, and taking him by the hand, said to him, 'You will not die. Now give your heart to God and live for him.' This he promised to do, and I left the house. Two or three brethren who were present and heard me make this declaration were distressed at it, for fear of the consequences in case it should not prove true. I felt the same, nor was I relieved until a short time after when I saw the young man walking the street in comparatively good health.

"Soon after this I was asked to visit another man who had been given up to die by his physician, who said he could not live through the night. The man insisted that I should be called, and declared he would take no medicine from any hand but mine, or by my direction. He had heard of the case just narrated, and as soon as I approached his bed he said to me, 'Don't pray for me to get well, I prefer to die.' But the impression came to me, and I said to him, 'I can pray in no other way, for you will certainly get well.' The sequel justified this prediction, for he did get well.

"I was called upon by a class-leader to visit a member of his class, then apparently dying with the consumption. It was a cold night in March. We found the windows and doors open to give her air. The physician had just left, after declaring that she was dying. While I was praying with her, as in the other cases, the impression came that she would recover. It came this time in such power that it was with difficulty that I could repress the utterance of it. On leaving the house I said to the leader what I thought. To this he answered, 'It is a good thing you did not say so, for she is certainly dying. If you had said what you felt, the cause of religion would have been greatly injured.' To the astonishment of all she was able to walk the streets in a very few weeks, and lived for a long time after.

"Another instance, but with a different result, occurred soon after. One of the class-leaders was taken sick, and to all appearance the sickness was unto death; but the suggestion came to me with great power that the prayer of faith would save the sick. The leader was a man of great value to the church, and I felt that he could not be spared. I shut myself up in my room, determined if possible to prevail with God to raise him up to health. I continued in prayer until the same impression came with a slight shade of difference, that the leader would live, and not die. But that slight difference in the impression made me hesitate to declare that the sick man would recover. Soon after the man died."

These instances made a profound impression upon Mr. Redfield, and led him to do some very careful thinking upon the general subject. He says, "I then saw that none of these cases were restored by faith. In the first three the result was intuitively perceived as a coming fact. In the last the impression was on the imagination, prompted by strong desire. This experience has been of great benefit to me since then, as a guage by which to test the strong impressions, and to distinguish between faith, fancy, and intuition."

It is difficult to account for these peculiar manifestations and successes upon any other ground than that the Lord was preparing him for future usefulness by the study which these facts induced. He was still bent on compromising the matter of his call if he could. He resolved to pay the preachers more; he denied himself all luxuries of the table, and lived for a season on roast potatoes cooked by his own hand that he might give more.

In the midst of this two young men came to his apartments, and the three bound themselves together to pray for a revival of religion. One night when they were engaged in prayer the village band met in the adjoining room for practice. They each prayed that the music might be stopped, and held on until each felt that he had received an answer. Soon the music stopped, and they heard the members of the band pass down the stairs from the room. This encouraged them to ask for greater things. They held on until they each received an answer that God would revive his work in the place. The next day they learned that several members of the band were awakened the evening before and had been inquiring the way of salvation. Soon after the minister commenced a protracted meeting, and before it closed about two hundred professed conversion. Mr. Redfield now had his hands and heart full, in laboring in prayer meetings, and in personal effort with souls. He tried to think that he would not have to preach if he proved faithful in this manner.

He became much concerned for the gentleman with whom he boarded before he went into bachelor's hall. He was an infidel Sabbath breaker. Mr. Redfield had often recommended religion to him in a general way, but now he felt that he had not been sufficiently in earnest about it. He resolved to do his whole duty at all hazards. The man came into Mr. Redfield's room one day, and he took him by the hand and said, "I have tried to recommend religion to you by my life and gentleness, but I see and feel I have never done my duty to you as I ought, and now I will never let go of your hand, nor let you go, until you either repulse me or give your heart to God." With deep emotion he said, "The last obstacle is now removed. I was a disbeliever in religion until I became acquainted with you. I have watched you, and could find but one fault in you, and that was, if you really felt friendly to me as you seemed to, I could not see how you could believe my soul in danger and not compel me to seek religion. But this removes that obstacle. Now," said he, with tears in his eyes, "take me to some of your prayer meetings."

"There was another gentleman," says Mr. Redfield, "an

acquaintance and friend, whom I had often tried to lead to
Christ, but who, with his wife, still remained impenitent, and
whom I now resolved to visit and talk and pray with. I
sent word to them that I would come at a certain time, and
that my object was to talk with them on the subject of their
soul's salvation. When the time arrived I went to their
home and found it closed against me. To all appearances
they were not at home. Again I appointed a, time, and
and again I found the house shut against me. After this
the gentleman came to my apartments one day, and I stepped
to the door and locked it, and said, 'I will never let you leave
this room until you promise to seek salvation, or utterly refuse me.' To this he answered, 'I appreciate your motives,
but if it has come to this I must tell you distinctly, I shall
not make you any such promise.' 'Very well, Lyman, an
impression comes to me that God will now visit you with
judgments.' Shortly after this I was called to go to his
house to see his dying wife. The violence of her disease
ended in mortification while she was yet living, and had now
reached its crisis. When I reached the house groups of
neighbors were standing here and there talking in low tones,
and whose manner indicated that the subject was more than
ordinarily distressing. I passed them, approached the door,
opened it, and in the first room sat others in melancholy
mood. They were talking in the same manner as those outside. Now and then a cry of agony came through the closed
doors of the sufferer's room. The door opened, and the
eyes of the dying woman met mine. Hers flashed with a
gleam never to be forgotten.

"She cried out, 'Oh! why did you not come before?'

"I drew near her and replied, 'I have tried, but you
closed your door against me.'

"'Well, then pray for me now,' she said.

"I knelt and tried to pray, but it was in vain; I could
not get hold. She called upon her attendants to remove her

to another room. This was done by moving the cot on which she lay. When they set her down she raised her mortifying arms toward heaven and uttered the mournful cry, 'O God! for a few hours to get ready for this awful change.' Her arms fell and she ceased to breathe. I then approached her distracted husband, and asked, 'Lyman, will you now yield to God?'

"He answered, 'I cannot now as well as I could before.'

"I replied, 'Then God will come again.'

"In a very few days one of his children was called to pass away suddenly. I was called again to visit the house of mourning. The father was convulsed with grief. On being approached and asked, 'Has God done enough? Will you now yield?' he answered as before. I then said, 'Well, God will come once more.'

"In a few days I was called to visit Lyman himself. He appeared to be rapidly passing into eternity. He now seemed to have given up the controversy and professed to have yielded his heart to God. Still a doubt hung over the case that eternity alone can clear up."

CHAPTER XII.

Mr. Redfield was now conscious that disease had fastened its grasp upon his own frame. To all appearances he was rapidly sinking under that fell disease, consumption. All remedies seemed to fail. He had but one hope left, and that was to escape the rigors of winter by going to one of the Southern states. A few remedies that he still thought of using were packed with his clothing and books, and with a limited purse, he started for New York city to take a steamer for the South. On arriving at the city, and while waiting for the day of the steamer's departure, he met an old friend, who insisted upon his stopping with him during the winter. It was urged that there would be sudden changes of weather in the South that would seriously affect him; that he might have a room at the home of this friend, where he could regulate the temperature as he pleased, and he need not go out until spring. He finally accepted the kind offer, and soon went into most favorable winter quarters.

Here he wasted fast with hectic and cough. He was soon so weak and emaciated, that he was obliged to lie upon the bed most of the time. His room was opposite a Methodist Episcopal church, with a public cemetery and vault in the rear. Every day, and sometimes twice and thrice a day, funeral processions would pass in and leave the bodies of departed ones. In his morbid state of feeling these scenes had a strange fascination for him, and he would gaze upon them and think, " Thus it will be soon with me."

On bright and pleasant Sunday mornings he would wrap himself and cross over to the church and listen to the sermon. He did not give in his church letter, for that stated that he was a local preacher, and he might be called upon to preach. His disease gained rapidly and soon it was doubtful whether he would live to see the coming summer. His mar-

velous imagination would picture to him scenes of decay, as
he looked upon his colorless and emaciated hands and his
conscience goaded and upbraided him because of neglected
duty.   He often would ask himself, "What can I do to soften
this terrible punishment, or to appease this God who has
borne with me so long?"   His room often resounded with
his sobs and crying.   He appeared to himself to be too far
gone with disease to be ever able to perform the duty that lay
so heavily upon him; yet to die, he felt he could not, he dare
not.   These struggles of mind would bring on profuse sweat-
ing, and that would be followed with chills, and all seemed
to aggravate and hasten the work of disease.   Yet he was
powerless to shake off these thoughts and feelings.

One day his mind recurred to the fact that four times he
had been raised from the borders of the grave, as he thought,
that he might preach the gospel, and weak as he was, he immediately knelt and pleaded with God for his life. Days went
by in which he spent much of his time in this manner, but
all seemed in vain.   At last, despairing of help in any other
way, he vowed again to do the work God had called him to
do.   He spent the most of one night in prayer, weeping,
promising and pleading.   About three o'clock in the morning
the answer came, clear and distinct, "You may live while you
preach, but no longer."

From that hour, as we shall see, that declaration was the
inspiration of his life.   Many times, when heart and hope
had failed, that assurance nerved him to go forward in the
conflict.   He says, "This single sentence has kept me moving
for more than twenty years at my own expense to toil in the
face of all opposition, and hold my tongue and let God who
sent me settle up all in the final day of reckoning."

On the Friday evening after receiving this answer to his
prayer, he was able, by carefully wrapping himself, to attend
a love-feast in the church across the way.   He went designing to present his letter.   He had been seated but a short

time when the minister came and spoke to him; and, though they were strangers, asked, "Have you a preacher's license?"

Mr. Redfield answered, "I have."

"Well, you must preach for me in this church next Sunday morning," said the pastor.

"But, sir, you must excuse me," rejoined Mr. Redfield.

The minister would not excuse him, and Mr. Redfield found himself in trouble again. All his old questionings arose once more. Some of his wife's relatives lived in the city, and they might make him trouble. Still there was his promise made to God, and the answer, "You may live while you preach, but no longer." At last he answered, "I will try." Yet he secretly hoped that he might make so bad a failure of it that he would never be called upon again. If anything could happen to cause this, for which he would not be responsible, and the cause of God not be injured by it, he felt he would be thankful. He had yet to learn that the callings of God are without repentance.

Saturday morning came, and with it the thought that he must try and preach on the morrow. He was in a tremor accompanied by alternate sweats and chills all day. He begged of God to be released. Thus the day was passed. The night came on, with no alleviation to his feelings. In speaking of it, he says, "I have often thought I could appreciate the feelings of a man about to be executed; how the very hours were given tongues to distress his spirit with their suggestions. I went to bed, but not to sleep. Occasionally I would begin to lose myself, when it would seem to be screamed in my ear, 'Preach to-morrow,' and I would spring up in the bed, and the cold sweat would start all over me. Thus the long night passed by."

Daylight brought him no relief. Sunrise succeeded the dawn, and in due time the church bells began to ring. He looked out upon the street and saw the people gathering in large numbers to the church. All seemed to conspire to

make him as miserable as possible. The moment came for
him to walk over to the church. He started, but with his
heart crying out, "I cannot." Again the Voice said, "Live
while you preach." He reached the pulpit, in great distrac-
tion of mind, and made some mortifying blunders. He
arose to give out a hymn, but was too weak to hold up the
book. He clung to the desk to keep from falling, and had
to sit while the congregation sang. The prayer over, the
lesson read, and another hymn sung, he arose to announce
his text. An unearthly power seemed to sustain him; he
had volume of voice, readiness of thought, and freedom of
utterance. He concluded, but was ashamed of himself and
his effort, and thought, "This will put an end to invitations
to preach." To his surprise, however, the preacher said to
him, "You must preach again," naming the evening when
his services would be expected. Mr. Redfield pleaded to be
excused, but the minister was unyielding. Said he, "If you
refuse, I must lay my commands upon you." Had it not
been for falling into the hands of such a man, it is quite
probable that the church would never have been stirred by
the mighty eloquence of Dr. Redfield.

On Friday evening, he was again at church. The minister said to him, "You must preach Sunday night." Again
his soul was on the rack. Saturday night was spent in prayer. If he must preach, he must have a text and subject.
About two o'clock Sunday morning the answer came; but
with it, another of his strange impressions. The substance
of it was this: "I will be with you in awful power; but you
must open the service with the declaration that this night
there will be such a display of divine power as they have
never witnessed; and further, that eternity will reveal the
fact that the probation of one soul in the congregation ends
this night, so that it is salvation for that person now or never."
He well knew that no one who would be present could sympathize with him in making such a statement; that it would

probably shock the church, and if it proved a failure, be disastrous to the cause of Christ. He prayed to be relieved from such a duty; and was instantly thrown into great darkness and distress of mind. His text and subject seemed all confusion, as well as his own relation to Christ. This he could not endure. He now pleaded with God to show him what he would have him do, and promised to yield all his objections to the divine will. Then the answer came again as before. Again he shrank from taking a position that seemed so full of presumption; but only to be instantly overwhelmed in darkness, and distress of soul. He finally promised to obey.

He went to the Sunday morning service. The noted Dr. Luckey preached. When the congregation rose to sing the first hymn, the thought came home to him with great power, the doom of one soul will be eternally fixed to-night. Such was the intensity of his feelings he had to sit down, and hold his hand over his mouth to keep from screaming aloud. The natural impropriety of making such a declaration as he felt he must make to please God, made his entire nature shrink from the purpose of doing it. Thus he alternated between the resolve to do so, and drawing back from it through the entire day. In the afternoon Dr. P——— preached. The work of the evening was to fall upon him. These great preachers occupying the same pulpit, both the same day, did not make his cross lighter.

At the appointed hour he walked over to the church. The house, a large one, was densely packed with people, gallery, standing-room, vestibule and all. At the last moment he made up his mind to venture all, and leave the results with God. At the proper time in a firm, clear voice, he said, "You may prepare for the greatest display of God's power that you have ever witnessed in this church; besides there is one soul here whose probation ends to-night, forever. With that soul it is salvation this night or never. I may not be able to prove

8

this true, but that soul will tell me in the judgment that this Sunday night, in the year of our Lord 1841, was the last of its probation." As soon as he had uttered these words he was perfectly relieved. The members were shocked, and so great were their fears, as they afterwards confessed, that they prayed God to overrule his presumption.

He then gave out his text and began to preach. An awful sense of the divine presence pervaded the congregation. To use his own words, "An unearthly power so lifted me up that it seemed to me that my feet only touched the earth, while my whole head, heart and body were above the skies and in heaven. The thrills of heavenly power which I then felt I can never describe. It was a power given me for the occasion, and it seemed to me that it could move a nation, or shake a world."

He had not finished his sermon when, without an invitation, the congregation arose and many flocked to the altar, screaming for mercy. When all the space around and within the altar was crowded with seekers, the preacher in charge asked all in the house who desired to become Christians to arise, when it was thought that five hundred more arose for prayers. The number afterward converted justified that estimate. For many years that night was commonly referred to as *the great night.*

About a month after this an old class-leader asked Mr. Redfield if he remembered making the statement on "the great night" that the probation of one soul would end that night. On being answered in the affirmative, he went on to say that a lady converted that night, and who afterwards joined his class, had told him that six weeks previous she dreamed three times during one night that in just six weeks her probation would end. That night the six weeks were ended and she was happily converted.

Though this incident is given by Mr. Redfield himself in this connection, it is not designed to teach that probation

ends with conversion. He was the furtherest from teaching any such doctrine, as his experience herein would show.
The account is related because of the remarkable coincidence in the events described.

CHAPTER XIII.

THE great awakening with which the last chapter concluded continued without interruption for fourteen months.

Mr. Redfield was invited to preach in different churches in New York. His health rapidly improved, and he conscientiously used it for God's glory. Many remarkable incidents occurred during these labors. Great manifestations of divine power often attended his ministry. Persons under conviction would sometimes fly from the house to avoid yielding to Christ, and afterwards be found lying upon the walks, helpless. At first, the policemen would take them to the station house, and lay them side and side upon the floor, and watch them until they "came to." The first night this occurred it created no little excitement. Quite a number had thus been gathered in, and a large crowd stood around the door wondering what it meant. While they were gazing and commenting, and endeavoring to account for the strange phenomena, the head of one of the prostrate ones raised, and a shout of "Glory to God!" came from his lips. Then, another, and another, and another, did likewise, until all of them were at it at once. The station was made to resound with unaccustomed noise—the praises of God instead of cursing and blasphemy. When it was discovered that such persons were neither harmed nor harmful, the officers ceased to take them to the station, but watched them where they fell, until they "came to" and were able to care for themselves.

Singularly, this timid, shrinking man, who dreaded the responsibilities of the Christian ministry so much, was providentially thrown into the great metropolis of the nation to commence his work; where the people, gathered in such masses, made the responsibility so much the greater.

In the midst of this great victory, Mr. Redfield was not without temptation. His clear perceptions of what was meet and right, sharpened by his struggles with unbelief, the rough handlings of providence, and the rougher handling of his fellow-men, made him feel intensely his weakness and his dependence upon God. Above all, the constant dread of his wife making an evil use of the facts of his family life, and of evil-disposed persons making a worse use of what they did not understand, kept him in the dust at the foot of the cross. Now and then he seems to have had a glimpse of the benefit God was making these things to him, but generally this fact was hid from his mind. His greatest fear was concerning the harm they might work to the cause of Christ. He resolved to say nothing about his matters, except when asked, and then to be perfectly frank with all who sought for information. But he soon learned that a story once out was likely to grow into untruthful details. At last he came to the conclusion that this was to be his "thorn", and his best way was to bear it in silence and alone.

He now instinctively turned toward the mercy-seat, and asked for greater grace to meet his great responsibilities. To fit himself especially for the work before him, he once more began to seek the experience of holiness. The next chapter relates this experience in his own words.

CHAPTER XIV.

Mr. REDFIELD relates his experience in the matter of seeking holiness as follows:

"I now began to see and feel my need of entire sanctification. I had perverted views of what constituted that state of grace, and of the way to seek it, but I resolved to set about seeking it as best I knew. I inquired of a number of persons who professed to know something of the experience, what I must do to obtain it. Their instructions did not help me in the least; and all I had done to this time furnished me with no evidence that I had made any appreciable advance toward it. My resolve now was to make a business of seeking it, and to be desperate in the effort. Long before this I had earnestly sought for it, by fasting and prayer, and watch-nights, until I was utterly exhausted by the effort. In all this I had failed to see the grand end to be secured, which is nothing more or less than perfect submission to, and harmony with, the will of God. I had yet to learn that the great preparation to receive it was to get the consent and choice of my will that God's will should be done, and whatever else I might do a deficiency in this would defeat my effort.

"I had now fairly entered the gospel field. My long neglected and much dreaded duty I had now made my life work. I began with singleness of purpose to seek this precious pearl. Yet, fearful that one so utterly unworthy might be denied so great a boon, I longed to lay my heart open to some one who could instruct me; not knowing that this state can no more be comprehended before its attainment, than justification can be by an infidel. At last I heard that a good old gentleman who had enjoyed this blessing for more than forty years was coming to make his annual visit to his children with whom I was then boarding. In due time he came, and I took him to my room one day, closed the door, and with a sense of my own unworthiness, I asked him if God was will-. ing that such an unworthy person as myself should possess so great a blessing as perfect love. The enemy was all this time suggesting to me that he probably would say, No! You are too young and presumptuous to think of that great and exalted state yet. But no, with deep and tender emotions the good old father answered, 'Why, bless your dear heart; why, yes, the Lord wants you to be holy.' And I felt such gratitude towards the old man, because he thought God was willing to indulge me with the gift of so great a grace, as I never can describe. From this I took fresh courage. I now asked him, 'Can you tell me how I can get possession of it?' To this he replied, 'By faith.' But he might as well have answered in Hebrew, for I understood not his meaning. I dreaded deception, and I could not suppose it possible that a state of grace that I had set so high an estimate upon could be secured short of a correspondingly valuable price or gift, instead of a single cheap and worthless act of believing. [So faith appeared to him then.— EDITOR.] If he had told me to do some great thing, or to be very faithful, and expect to grow up into it by a long and tedious process, I could have thought his instruction more rational. I remembered the soul-tearing process which I witnessed in a brother who was seeking the blessing at the camp meeting where I was converted, and I thought that must be the true way. I had serious doubts, however, about my constitution being able to endure the agony necessary to obtain the blessing.

"While conversing with a person upon the subject one day, an elderly brother standing near, asked, 'Why don't you go across the town to R—— street, where they have meetings every week at Dr. Palmer's? They can tell you how to find the blessing.'

"Another elderly brother who stood by, and in whose piety I had great confidence, but who, though he believed in that state of grace and had been seeking it for about twenty-six years without success, now said to me aside, ' You must be very careful about having anything to do with Dr. Palmer's people, for they will tell you to believe that you already have the blessing, and besides many people do not think them so pious as they pretend to be, after all their sanctimonious airs, uniform dress and great pretensions.'

" From that moment I so greatly feared them that I would have received instruction from them no sooner than from a Mahometan. Indeed, I think I would have avoided them at all hazard if about to meet them on the street. I now remembered hearing Dr. Fisk answer the questions of my mother, as to what and how she should believe, 'Believe,' said he, 'that you have it, and you have it.' I did not then see the difference between 'believing that you are receiving it, and that will bring it,' and 'believe that you have received it, and that will make it a fact that you have received it!' Both, alike, were utterly opposed to my reason; and I could have as easily endorsed Mahometanism as holiness secured by these irrational means. I now began to think I could see through the vagaries of these people; that their holiness consisted in giving up all concern about the matter, and then by imagining that the end was gained, the cessation from the struggle would leave them quiet, and this quiet they called the witness of holiness.

"Of course I had abandoned all hope of attaining the blessing in the way I had pursued so long and so unsuccessfully. And now I went to work with all determination, hoping if my body could endure the agony through which I expected to pass, I might by this desperation gain the land of Beulah. Hearing there was to be a camp meeting within the bounds of an adjoining conference, I determined to go, as a stranger, and thus avoid being seen by any of the brethren of the society where I belonged. I knew they had confidence in my piety, but I was afraid should they see me in great agony seeking the blessing of holiness, they might not know what to think of it; and possibly they might conclude that I had been committing some grevious sin; and not being able to explain all to their satisfaction, they would feel grieved, and I thereby would be the occasion of great injury to the cause of Christ.

"When I reached the campground I found there a number of the brethren I desired to avoid. Well, thought I, it is my duty and privilege to be holy, to fit me for the great work I have to do; so I shall attend to that and leave God to take care of results. I was called upon to preach, but as I had come to seek the blessing of holiness, and to make that my business, I declined. When I began in earnest to rein myself up to the work, the devil became in earnest also, and induced me to begin to inspect the external evidences of other people's piety. It seemed to me that I never saw the corrupt state of the church as I saw it then. One person's mode of dress was trim, and that to me was evidence of pride; another's was careless, and that indicated pride of his fancied humility. I felt grieved at these evidences of spiritual decline, and my tears flowed in abundance.

"While walking in the grove alone, and grieving thus, I met the good old man who had given me such comfort in saying he thought God was willing that I should have the blessing of holiness; and I began telling him how I had come to the meeting to seek it, but that such evidences of decline in the church made me feel so badly that I could not attend to it with any hope of success. The old gentleman saw this to be a trick of the devil to divert my attention and efforts from the great work, and with a few words he set me right.

"'I,' said he, 'was once troubled as you are now, and I got out of it by resolving, if everybody else goes to' hell, by the grace of God I am going to heaven.'

"This broke the spell of what I then saw was one of the

devil's pious frauds, to hinder me from gaining the precious prize I was after.

"I now thought, if ever I gain the blessing, I must call my New York brethren into a tent to pray for me, and thus risk every evil coming through their possible misapprehensions of my moral state. This I did, and when I had stated my object and purpose, I asked them to pray for me. I had an idea that they would pray for me with all their might, and possibly create a wave, so to speak, on which my little bark could come to land. They began to pray at random, for everybody, and everything, without touching my case, just as people generally pray when they don't expect anything. I was now compelled to learn that no delegated power could reach my case, and I must go to God for myself. I then, while still on my knees, concluded to do my own praying and struggling; and supposing that the successful mode of prayer must be that which is characterized by great vehemence and will power, I watched my opportunity to break out in vociferous tones, and then I tried it; but I could not have uttered a loud word if it would have saved me, for my lips seemed to be sealed. This taught me the meaning of the words, 'Not by might nor by power, but by my Spirit, saith the Lord.'

"I then turned to look into my heart to see what progress I was making, and was overwhelmed to find nothing but what caused loathing and abhorrence. It seemed to me that I had lost all my religion in trying to get more. The enemy now suggested, 'You have lost all in trying to get holiness; you might better give up the struggle if such is to be the success of your effort,' and believing this to be a fact, I arose and left the tent to mourn over my last and greatest calamity. As I was passing along I met the good old man again, and while telling him what a disaster I had met with in trying to get holiness, I asked, 'Don't you think I have done wrong in aspiring after such an exalted state of grace? I know I have lost all I had, for I certainly had the witness of the Spirit when I left New York, but now it is gone.'

"'Why, bless your dear heart,' said this good man, 'don't you know the Lord is just emptying you?' Then, in a few words he set me right again. I had supposed holiness to be given in installments, and when a succession of blessings combined had filled my heart about so full, I might call it holiness; first, the pardon of sins, then the joys of salvation, and then a succession of indefinite blessings, which in the aggregate would make up the sum total of holiness. Now I learned that every blessing I ever had must be emptied out, for God would not fill a vessel with the wine of Canaan while it was half full of manna. I had now passed the days for relishing manna, and my Father had enough of the old corn and wine and this hereafter was to be my food. I had been seeking the last installment to complete the blessing.

"I now asked him, 'What shall I do?'

"Said he, 'You must believe for the blessing.'

"I went out into the grove alone, and while waiting upon the Lord and trying to believe, I thought I saw Jesus with my inner eye, just as I saw him at the time of my conversion. It was the appearance of Jesus as crucified. A voice seemed to say to me, 'All you can do now is to believe in this crucified man, Jesus' (for the time his divinity was hidden from me). But the idea of trusting my soul's salvation on a dead man, aroused all my old infidel notions, and I dared not risk it. That image appeared as distinctly as that of a person to my outward eye. He seemed to be in the twilight, and but a few rods distant from me. The camp meeting came to a close, and I went away without the great blessing.

"So away I went to another camp meeting which was to be held the next week. There again I stirred up myself to a desperate effort to seek for holiness, but with no appreciable advance! One day some one told me that the Palmers

from New York were on the ground, and had a tent for the
promotion of holiness. This family I feared more than the
enemy of all righteousness; but as my success in seeking
holiness was so poor, I finally thought I would find that tent,
and take a seat in some corner where if I saw they were
pressing error upon the people I could quietly leave them.
Strange as it may seem, an impression beset me that they
might, without, or against my reason, or consent, fasten error
upon me; so I resolved to be on the alert, and if I saw it coming to avoid it by flight. I reached the tent and took my
seat as I had determined. I saw here a large number of persons, and among them some Presbyterians, and some of other
denominations. They were all sitting very composedly while
one was reading from the Bible. I thought, 'Can this be
the way to seek holiness? I wonder that they don't get down
and pray with all their might!' Still I could not complain
of their reading the Bible, for that must be right. After the
reading a lady arose whom I guessed to be the one from
New York, whom I most feared, and I thought, I must now
be on my guard; but the first words she uttered were, 'I be-
seech you therefore, brethren, by the mercies of God, that ye
present your bodies a living sacrifice, holy and acceptable,
unto God, which is your reasonable service.' 'A living sacrifice,' she said, 'is a perpetual sacrifice.' Well, thought I,
that is Bible, and all right, so far. She then went on to
state the preliminary steps to be taken: 'First, a thorough
consecration of ourselves to God.' 'Very well,' said I to myself, 'all this I have done, over and over again.' She then
made this entire consecration to appear as a reasonable demand. She also showed the reasonableness of believing that
God meant what he said, and that he would do what he said
he would do, and that our faith must rest mainly on his
promise. 'He has said if I will do thus and so, he will meet
me there and then, and faith consists in taking him at his
word.'

"I then saw the way of faith as never before, and I said to myself, 'I have tried everything else but faith; I will now go out and make an experiment.' So I went out back of the encampment and stood reviewing my consecration to be certain that all was thoroughly devoted to God in an everlasting covenant. In a moment there appeared to me that image of Christ crucified; but I saw only his humanity. I seemed to be standing upon the edge of a fathomless gulf, and Christ stood upon the opposite side. The distance seemed too far for me to leap it, yet it was the thing for me to do. I must trust that crucified Christ to save me from ruin. It seemed to me that if I should make the effort and it prove a failure, I must from that moment bid adieu to all hopes of the world of blessedness, and abandon the profession of religion forever. I saw that everything I hoped, feared and desired was now, with all that I expected in the world to come, all, *all* to be staked on a single act, to be lost or won forever. I was intensely aroused by the thought of hazarding every hope of heaven like that, and I offered this prayer, 'O Lord, thou knowest all hearts, and that I want to do thy will. I have tried honestly to know all, and to do all I could to get right, and thou knowest that I stand ready to do or to suffer anything imposed upon me by which to secure the great blessing of perfect love. I have tried everything but this single and apparently inefficient and hopeless act of faith, which looks to my reason more like presumption than like an act that can do me good; and now, O God, seeing no other untried way, I will make the venture, and if it fails, on thee must rest the responsibility. If I am lost for believing in Christ, I cannot help it.'

"I seemed now to open converse with the Holy Ghost, and asked, 'How shall I believe? with my head or with my heart?'

"The answer came, 'With the heart man believeth unto

righteousness, and with the mouth confession is made unto salvation.'

"I now made the leap, as distinctly as if it had been in body, and in the same moment found myself in the arms of Jesus, who held me safely. I felt that I could risk a world in his hands; for I saw that 'in him dwelleth all the fullness of the Godhead bodily.'

"Oh, how changed did all things seem in that glorious moment! 'Surely,' said I, 'this must be heaven, or like it, for it comes up to my highest ideal of that place.'

"The next moment the enemy suggested, ' This is not the blessing of holiness, for you did not lose your strength, nor have you shouted, or made any great ado about it; but on the other hand you do not want to speak aloud.' And it did seem as though a single loud word would mar the rich spell which held me captive.

"I then took my eye of faith off from the Saviour, to examine this temptation, and in a moment I was back on the other side of the gulf again, and was as empty as ever. 'Well,' said I, to myself, 'I felt all right while believing.' That emboldened me to try again, and with greater daring than before, and with the same happy result.

"Now the temptation, 'You cannot keep it,' took my eye off again, and again I was back on the other side of the gulf. I then sprang off again, when the tempter said, 'No one will believe you,' and again succeeded in robbing me of my witness.

"And so did I alternate between faith and doubt, joy and sorrow, until I learned this fact, that it is not for believing, but *while* believing that the work is done. I hang upon the atonement, and realize the response of the Holy Spirit assuring me that the work is done. So I now determined to make the leap again, and to keep my eye on Christ. This I did; but the enemy asked, 'How will it be to-morrow?'

"I answered, 'I don't know, for to-morrow has not yet come.'

"'Well, how will it be in five minutes?'

"I answered, 'I don't know nor will I concern myself about it; I believe I am saved now.' I now saw the philosophy of faith. I breathe but one breath of air at a time; that is all I need; when I want another, it will be allowed. So I do not need a stock of the joys of salvation for future use, but take it, breathe it, by acts of faith just as I have need. Continuously acting faith brings a continuous supply. Faith to the soul is what breathing is to the body.

" 'Now, too, I learned the philosophy of consecration. It is to make room by emptying out the heart.

" Now,' said the Holy Spirit, 'go and tell brother M—— what the Lord has done for you.'

"I went onto the campground and when I found him, I began: 'Brother M——, I believe'——

" 'If you tell him,' said the tempter, 'he'll tell you to be very careful about making great professions, for sanctification is a very great blessing.'

"Brother M—— stood gazing at me without saying a word.

"Then I began again, 'Brother M——, I believe,'—— but fearing he would think I was boasting, I began to qualify my statement, but did not speak, and finally broke out, '*If I don't keep it five minutes, I believe that Jesus has sanctified my unworthy heart. Glory to God!*'

"Said Brother M——, 'Go and tell my wife.'

"I had now gathered strength by the testimony I had given, and the confidence Brother M—— seemed to express; and away I went to his wife, and said to her, ' Sister M——, Jesus has given me the great blessing.'

"She rejoiced, and said, 'Now go up on the stand and profess it to all the people.'

"I did so, and it seemed to settle and establish me.

"From this I learned to confess the exact thing done for me, and to guard against even hesitation in professing the thing as it is.

"Dr. Palmer found me, and said, 'Mr. Wesley says that one sanctification is equal to ten conversions, as it will result in that.'

"I took a cue for my future labors from this, and resolved to make a test of it now. I went into a tent and began at once to invite. my brethren to come *now* to the cleansing blood. We started a meeting, and God began at once to work in awful power. I have always found that making the experience of holiness the principal feature in revival meetings does not hinder the work of conversions. Here one or two penitents came in unasked, and one said, 'I was impressed to come to this very tent.' In a few minutes they were converted. The work in this manner increased until the end of the camp meeting.

"Now I began to learn a distinction between the joys of sanctification and those of justification. Formerly, if a camp meeting had been a good one, I would feel sad to leave the hallowed spot. The striking of the tents was to me like a funeral. Now I found it a matter of joy, for I carried a camp meeting with me. In holiness I found all the elements of a good meeting. When I reached my room in the city, the thought came, ' You will sleep off all this as you have other blessings.' I retired to rest, and the last words from my lips were, 'Glory to God!' When I awoke in the morning, it was 'Glory to God!' still. Thus I found the old corn and wine of the Canaan of perfect love was unlike the manna of justification, it was hearty, solid and abiding. Sabbath came, and I found no more shrinking from doing duty. I went over to the church, and in offering the closing prayer I had special liberty, and was sweetly blessed.

"On passing down the aisle a good brother met me and said, 'Do you know how you prayed? Why you prayed directly to Christ, and you did not even mention the name of God, but seemed to pray as if you could get anything you asked of Jesus.'

" 'Well, brother, it did seem to me that "in him dwelt all the fullness of the Godhead bodily." And don't you know that Jesus said once, "Hitherto ye have asked nothing in my name. Ask and receive that your joy may be full." '

"I now felt the power of the words, 'No man can call Jesus Lord, but by the Holy Ghost,' as never before. It seemed no risk to hang a world's salvation on the merits of Christ. In this light I saw the sin of unbelief to be the great soul-destroying sin of the world, and in comparison with it murder, robbery, and other sins were of small account."

9

CHAPTER XV.

Mr. Redfield's pastor was a good man, but he did not enjoy the experience of entire sanctification. Like a true man, he stood by this doctrine of the church. He said, that some years before, while he was earnestly seeking it, the blessing began to come upon him in great power, and he was tempted to believe that it would take his life, and he refused it. From that time he had thought that he must pass through life without it as a punishment. Strange as it may seem, many intelligent and sound theologians are troubled with just such difficulties. While this man could not enter into the work with the zest which otherwise might have characterized him, he encouraged others in the work.

With a full heart and strong purpose Mr. Redfield set about inviting his brethren and sisters to claim their privilege of enjoying this great blessing. He was a class-leader, and besides attending his own, he visited other classes; attended all the prayer meetings, and preached often. He appointed one meeting each week for the promotion of holiness and in it God wrought in great power. Holiness became the theme all through the society, and in the neighborhood; and in a very short time there were more than one hundred who could testify in love-feast that they were fully saved. These all became workers for God, in season and out of season, for the conversion of sinners. The latter now began to fill the meetings, and soon to seek the Lord, and sanctifications rapidly followed justifications, and the laborers increased in the same proportion, and so the work went on.

One sister who kept a school did her own housework, took care of her children, and prepared all the meals for her husband, yet found time to bring from six to twelve sinners to Jesus every week.

The work of conversions at last broke out with great

power, and extended rapidly, until the membership ran up
from five hundred to nine hundred, and the society had to be
divided, and then again the second time, and furnished a large
number for a third church. A heavy church debt was also
rapidly decreasing by the free-will offerings of the people.
Visitors from other churches, and from the country, some
from sixty miles away, came to gain a knowledge of full salvation, and then returned to spread the holy fire. Speaking
of these times, Mr. Redfield says:

"I wish the truth did not require the statement of some
facts that show that the work at that date met with hinderances.
Justice to the cause of holiness requires me to do it, that the
honest hearted may know that the slow progress, and almost
final extinction of this blessed doctrine, was by no means
due to any inherent weakness in itself.' It began to wane
under the combined hostility of a few who would not pay the
price of getting right with God. Some of them had dances
in their houses; some said, 'We want no more revivals in our
church, for it dirties up the house, and if sinners desire to get
religion let them go somewhere else, we have enough members now for one church.' Others cried out for order, and
neatness, and taste, lest their children go off to other and
more fashionable churches. So they had the church newly
and fancifully painted on the inside, introduced instrumental
music for the choir; then sold the seats. Then God quit
them, the congregations ran down, church debts ran up, and
the last end was worse than the first. And then the complaint was heard, that 'Redfield had done more hurt than
good.' Some who had professed to believe in holiness began
a determined warfare against it. They would go to some
who professed to have experienced the blessing, and begin
thus: 'You say you are sanctified, do you?'

"In great modesty they would reply, 'I do believe Jesus
has wrought that great work in my heart.'

"Then these opposers would say, 'You must be very careful how you profess anything like that, for some people simply get excited and call that sanctification. I have been praying for it a good many years, and I have not got it yet; nor do I know how long before I shall get it. Besides, we think you who have been converted only a short time, do not treat us old people with due consideration, even if you do enjoy the experience when you step in before us and profess it.',

"I asked one who made this complaint to me, 'How long have you been seeking the experience?'

"'Twenty-six years,' he answered.

"'How much nearer are you to it now than twenty-six years ago?'

"He hesitated, and finally answered, 'I cannot say that I am any nearer to it.'

"'Well, at this rate, how much longer will it take you to get it?'

"This stopped his caviling with me, but not his hostility to the work.

"Such arguments against the possibility of young converts entering into the experience so early, caused many of them to give up the doctrine and the testimony, and then they lost the witness of it. Then these opposers would approach them, and ask, 'Do you think you have sanctification now?' The answer would be honestly given, 'I am not clear, I may be mistaken.' Then the opposer, in triumph would say, 'If you had really received it you would not have lost it so easily.'

"I was, of course, deeply grieved and hardly knew what to do. I had felt so sure that I had found the secret of how to convert the world, and believed that Methodists and Methodist preachers needed only to see the practical workings of their own doctrine, and they would at once return to it in preaching and practice, and their methods and polity would enable them to take the world. I believed, though, that this manifestation of opposition was exceptional and that this doctrine of the Wesleys, Fletcher, Bramwell, Abbott, and Fisk would yet succeed. I determined not to abate one jot, but to keep on preaching and pressing the doctrine which I knew from the experiment so far, would work wonders in saving sinners. I felt to say, 'I know this to be right, and if everybody fights it, it is of God, and I'll stand by it, if I stand alone.'

"I now felt my commission to the world was renewed and extended, and I determined that, regardless of difficulties, 'I will go as far as I can and stop only when I must; if I never get through I will try, and if I die, I will die trying, and at my post; and like the old Syracusan, when he had discovered the power of the lever, I'll cry, "Eureka! Eureka!" I have found it, I have found it. For if some oppose, some will embrace the blessed doctrine, and the results will give them confidence, and Methodism will fulfill its mission in the world. Whether I am countenanced by men or not, I do know, bless the Lord, that Jesus approves of me, in my purposes and course; and whatever becomes of me, the world shall have it to say, that there is one man who will either prove true to God or die trying. If some will pull down the work of God, I must work the harder and faster to build it up.'

"I was soon to be put to the test. Not long after this a brother came to me one day and said, 'You must not go to your class to-night, you must attend the official meeting, for there is trouble about to come on you. You must not be surprised if your class-book is taken from you, and if your meetings for holiness are stopped.'

" 'What is the matter?' I asked.

" 'Some of the official board dislike your talking about holiness very much, and they say you have already done more harm than you can do good.'

"But, with this wonderful work of God before me, I failed to see the evil they claimed I was doing, and believing that God bade me go on, I said to him, 'I can't go to the official meeting, for God wants me to go to the class meeting.'

"Another and another came to me with the same message, and one of them said, 'If you don't go, I shall.' I told them all, 'God calls me to my class, and he will defend his own cause. If not, I don't want to contend for anything he will not stand by.'

"The preacher then came and advised me to go, but I answered, 'With all deference to you as my pastor, I must decline, for I feel I must go to my class and leave consequences with God.'

"When I went into the class-room I found it filled as full as it could be, while the passage way was full out to the street. In opening the meeting by prayer, I said, 'O Lord, if we are engaged in a work that pleases thee; if this is thy cause, give us a token in such a blessing as we have not known.' Instantly fifteen or twenty were struck down by the power of God, myself among the number.

"The commotion was as great outside the class-room as inside. As soon as I could speak, I said, 'Go on! for you have a greater leader than man to-night.' Immediately one sister who had recovered her strength arose and said, 'I have been powerfully tempted this day, from hearing that there was going to be an attempt made to stop these meetings, and to take Brother Redfield's class-book from him, and I have been praying about it all day, and just before night I got the witness that God would not allow it to be done.'

"Then arose another, and another, and still another, until some twelve or fourteen had testified in like manner as to their temptations, their prayers and the answer to their prayers, in regard to the matter. Of course they could not know beforehand what the action of the official board would be. The meeting closed and the next day I heard from the board as follows: 'A motion was made to arrest the holiness work and put a stop to the meetings; but the preacher in charge interposed by saying, " *While I am in the chair, I shall exercise my prerogatives, by not putting any such motion to vote. If you pass them without me, I shall act upon my authority, and tell you that you cannot interfere with those meetings, or abridge Brother Redfield's liberties.*"'

"All at once one or two of the strongest opposers to the work arose and confessed that they felt their opposition to be wrong, and that they were contending against God. For awhile the opposition ceased and the glorious work went on.

"One evening I shall never forget. We were in the main audience-room. I had been urging the membership to seek holiness, as the best means of promoting a revival, and that sinners would be convicted while the church was seeking holiness. They came around the altar, filled it, and then the large aisles nearly to the doors. I saw a door open and in came a man, who pushed his way through the mass kneeling in the passage, until he reached the altar, and then extending his hand to mine, said, 'As I was passing the church a moment ago, and knew not what was going on here, I was suddenly impressed to come in; for what I could not tell; but now I know; and I ask, "Is there salvation for me?"' He then knelt among the seekers."

Soon after a delegation from another church waited upon Mr. Redfield and invited him to come and labor with them, saying, "We believe if you will come we will have a revival." Said he, "Brethren, if you desire a revival, let your church seek holiness, and God will work among sinners at the same time." He finally went and preached as well as he could to the church and to sinners, but without any results. He then, one evening, appealed to the church again, and urged them to seek holiness; and after stating the cost and conditions connected with it, invited the membership to the altar; at the same time barely saying to the unconverted, "If you desire religion you may come too;" when eleven immediately came. He went home and in a week or ten days he was sent for again.   The committee said, "You must come again, for the revival has come to a stop."

He asked, "But were not the eleven converted?"

"Oh, yes," they answered "and then it all went down."

"But, have any of the church members experienced holiness?" he asked.

"Oh, no, we were so rejoiced to see sinners get religion, that we forgot all about that."

"I thought so," was his reply.

He was persuaded to go again, but he had no success. At last he said to the church, "You know, brethren, what God did when I was here before. Now try it over again, and hold on until God saves you." They came forward again, and nine sinners followed them to the altar; and the meeting went on for some time with great success.

CHAPTER XVI.

THE annual conference came on, and there was a change of pastors. The new pastor was a younger man than his predecessor. He was evidently ambitious, and tried hard to please the party opposed to holiness, as that was the predominant party in the church. When his first year was drawing to a close, and the time for the last quarterly conference was at hand, Mr. Redfield was laboring some eight miles up the river above the city. A revival of glorious power was in progress, and it seemed to be his duty to stay with it. He called on his pastor one day and asked him to look after the passing of his character, and the renewing of his license. His pastor assured him that this would be done. He went back to his work, and soon after learned that his pastor took advantage of his absence, to bring in a complaint of heresy against him, and the question of the renewal of his license was laid over. But the presiding elder sent word to him to go on, and he would sustain him. He labored on until the next quarterly conference, and when the time came was greatly tempted to let this obstruction settle the question as to his continuing in the work; and let those who opposed bear the responsibility. Then came again the message, "Live while you preach, but no longer." Both sides of the case were vividly presented to his mind, the fearful consequences of not going forward, and the blessedness of heaven's approval should he diligently pursue the path of duty. Yet he suffered much over the thought that those who should have made the way smooth for him, were hedging it up. He could but say, "If they knew how much of suffering it costs me to follow this path, and would ask themselves what motive must it be that governs him, they would not do so."

With great reluctance he attended the quarterly conference. There was a full attendance of its membership, numbering forty-five or fifty. At the appropriate time he was

called upon to answer to the charge of heresy. It consisted
of two points; *first*, his views of the nature of the millenium;
and *second*, his views of the doctrine of christian perfection.
He arose, and invited all to correct him, if he did not tell the
truth, and to prompt him, if he did not tell all the truth.
When he had finished his statement of his views, respecting
the first, the presiding elder said, "Brethren, we must accept of his views, for he is with Dr. Clarke. He now asked
for the same thoroughness on the second complaint. He told
them his experience, as much of it as had a bearing on the
doctrine of specific holiness, of his teaching, preaching and
belief. When he had finished, the elder again interposed,
and said, "Brethren, we must accept of that, for he is exactly
with Mr. Wesley."

The call was then made for a vote on the renewal of his
license, which was granted by a vote of forty to five.

He then told the conference he had a little business for
them to do. He said, "During the past three months, the
report has been kept in circulation that my own church
would not renew my license, and the public know not the
cause; and even some preachers to whose charges I have
been invited, have had to search for these facts to satisfy
their official boards, before they would consent to allow me
to labor among them. I now desire you to give me a certificate stating that I have been examined on the points of
doctrine for which my license was suspended, and that I have
been exonerated from the charge of heresy, and found to be
a sound Methodist."

At this his pastor arose and said, he could not vote Mr.
Redfield a sound Methodist, because, said he, "We as a
church do not believe with either Clarke or Wesley on
these points, but with Benson."

One of the official board who was grieved that Mr. Redfield was let off so easily, arose and said, "If any man says

there is anything in the doctrine of sanctification, he's a liar."

The presiding elder exclaimed, "Stop! stop! Brother Redfield is a Methodist and you are not. I did not know that this church would tolerate such anti-Methodistic doctrines as this."

The motion was finally modified to suit the preacher in charge, and read, "That the quarterly conference having examined Brother Redfield, found nothing against him."

Of these proceedings Mr. Redfield says, "Oh, how my heart was pained, not only to see this unsoundness as to the truth, but such quibbling and dodging when it came to the issue. I also saw that among the preachers there was an element that was not Methodistic. Still, my confidence in the ultimate success of the doctrine of holiness was unshaken."

He soon learned that this hostility was not against himself, but against the cause which he represented. He also learned, as many have since, that he who declares himself on the side of God, has virtually declared war against earth, hell, dead formality, and ambitious ministers of the gospel.

Mr. Redfield says: "A friend of mine, an uncompromising champion for God and the truth, was so much feared, that the preachers in his conference sought his ruin. Like the accusers of Daniel, they were compelled to find the occasion in his religion. They appointed a preacher's meeting where each was expected to give a specimen of his abilities by reading a sermon or essay, which should then be criticised by the rest. They assigned to this brother a sermon on holiness. Waiving his scruples against written sermons, he did as he was bidden. When the time came the sermon was read, and then the criticisms commenced. Said one of the preachers, 'I have often heard that this brother was anti-Wesleyan on the doctrine of holiness, and now we have heard it from his own lips.' He then followed this with a criticism so severe that some began to sympathize with the author of the sermon. And they said to him when the first critic was through, 'You have a right to defend, yourself.' 'Never mind,' said the brother, 'go on and say all you wish to.' Then another took the sermon to pieces and showed its heretical character. Then another, and still another. Finally the presiding elder was called upon to make some remarks, but he only said, ' The anti-Wesleyan character of the sermon is such that I shall have to reprove the brother first, privately, according to the Discipline;' intimating by this that he would bring charges against him at the conference.

"'Well, are you all through?' inquired the brother; and on being answered in the affirmative, he said, ' Now, all I have to say is, I have copied every word of that sermon from John Wesley's, and in my manuscript you will find I have given the volume and the page from which it is taken. And I ask, Who is Wesleyan, you or I?'

This was an unexpected turn, and some began to excuse themselves by saying they had not refreshed their memories of late by reading Mr. Wesley's writings on the subject. Another attempted to parry the stroke by complaining of unfairness in the preacher's taking out isolated portions of Mr. Wesley's writings and reading them as if they were his own productions.

This circumstance, when it came to Mr. Redfield's knowledge, convinced him more strongly that the opposition was not personal, but against the cause of holiness itself. At the same time he was impressed that he would be made to feel this hostility more keenly still, and perhaps would be forced to quit the field. But he resolved to go to the last link of the chain, for God and purity, and stop only when he could go no farther.

With a clearer understanding of what it meant, he now more fully than ever committed himself to the work of spreading scriptural holiness over the land. While aware of the deep-seated opposition to holiness now beginning to be manifest, he had the hope that great success, in the conver-- sion of sinners, would demonstrate to the preachers that God endorsed the doctrine, and at last their opposition would give way. He saw, too, that the literature of Methodism and the Discipline were in its favor, and he looked to see those who stood out against the doctrine brought to account for their criticisms and opposition.

About this time, also, Rev. L. L. Hamline was elevated to the episcopacy in the church, a man whose experience and preaching, and holy life, made him one of the brightest examples and witnesses of the doctrine in the annals of the church. For many years after this he was the confidential adviser of. Mr. Redfield, and, to a great extent, guided his labors, as to place and time.

CHAPTER XVII.

Mr. Redfield was now invited to join the traveling connection of the Methodist Episcopal Church. For a season he looked upon this with favor.

While considering this matter he became convinced that from some cause many of the conference preachers had lost their experiences, and most of them their freedom. He searched for the causes of this. He found that most of these desired to be and to do right, but that they were timid. Some of them acknowledged that they were afraid of proscription in case they should make a specialty of the doctrine and experience of holiness. In view of this, and of the fact that he felt more especially called to the work of an evangelist, he concluded that his place was in the local ranks. Here he would be more free to go where the way opened before him.

At this time there were but few evangelists in the field. It was the beginning of a new era of evangelistic effort. James Caughey had just commenced his great work, and was going like a flame of fire over England and Ireland.

John Newland Maffit, one of the most eloquent preachers of this century, had been laboring as an evangelist throughout the country with marked success; but the eclipse of his brilliant career, which by many was believed to be the result of his own indiscretion, now produced a public sentiment in regard to evangelistic work which was embarrassing and unfavorable to others who would enter upon it. Finney and Burchard of the Presbyterian Church, and Knapp among the Baptists, were the leading men, if not the only ones in this particular department of church work, except Mr. Redfield, who represented the Methodist Episcopal Church.

We have seen the terrific struggles through which he passed before he would consent to enter the sacred office. Now we see him about to enter its most untried and difficult phase of work. His first thought was to go where there were no organized churches, and so become a pioneer to other local preachers in such fields. But the truism, "Man proposes, but God disposes," has been made a truism by such experiences as we are now contemplating.

At this very time he had been invited to go up the river about twenty miles above New York city, and add his efforts to the labors of other local preachers who had broken the ground and, as he says, "begun to see some hopes of good." He found that formerly the people here had heard but two sermons a year, and those on week-day afternoons, and by a rank Predestinarian. Mr. Redfield's first visit was on a beautiful Sunday; and the first service was in a grove. The people came from miles away. The evening meetings were held in private houses, and God was present to save. He says the people were simple-hearted and natural. They used no fine phrases nor religious cant, for they were utterly unused to listening to the relation of Christian experience.

"At a meeting one day in a private house, a woman with a child in her arms sat swaying to and fro with suppressed emotion, when her face suddenly whitened out. Another woman seeing the state of things, took her child from her, when she arose and said, 'I don't know as I have got this good religion what I hear you talk about, but I do feel so good and warm all along up here,' at the same time putting both hands on her breast. It required no doctor of divinity to tell that she was happily converted to God. Soon forty or fifty were converted and formed into a class, and then the people set to work to build a church. In eleven months from the time of the first conversion, the house was finished, paid for, and I was invited to come and preach the dedicatory sermon. It was in the evening. Just before preaching I said to the first convert, 'Jacob, when I am done preaching, I want you to give an exhortation from the altar, and invite the people to come forward to seek religion.' When I was through he did as I told him, and such another exhortation I never heard. Its effects convinced me that God's tools are adapted to their work, and far more efficient when selected from among the people who are saved, than all the labored and scientific productions of those unexperienced in the things of God can be.

"The exhortation ran something like this: ' Now, sinners, I tell you, look a' here; I tell you, you don't know how good this good 'eligion is. Oh, I wish you would come up here and kneel down and get it! You know I used to drink rum like anything, and swear, and play cards. But, oh! how good this good 'eligion is! Oh, do come, and kneel down and get it.'

"To my astonishment stout-hearted men as well as others flocked to the altar of prayer. When the meeting closed, I said to Jacob, ' You and I must go all over this place and exhort the people to get religion; and we will begin to-morrow morning.'

"In the morning we started on our mission. In the first house we visited were two families. In the first room sat an elderly woman weeping, who was at the meeting the night before. Jacob left me to talk with her, and he went into the other part of the house to talk with those there. As soon as he was gone the old woman said to me with deep emotion, ' Oh, that sarment Jacob preached last night made me detarment to get this good 'eligion.' "

CHAPTER XVIII.

MR. REDFIELD was now invited to a church in one of the suburbs of New York city. This church was sustained mostly by the Home Missionary Society. He found a small class of humble people, who had been kept down by the proselyting efforts of a worldly church in the same community. One of the difficulties had been that the revivals, in the Methodist Episcopal Church had been of such a superficial character, that this proselyting was possible. Deep and thorough religious experiences would not be so easily overcome. As this church was fashionable and worldly, he was satisfied that it was from no abundance of piety that it so strongly persisted in its attempts to draw away the Methodist converts. He clearly saw that the only protection to those who would be converted in his meetings, as well as the prosperity of the church for which he labored, was to lay the foundations of the revival in holiness. This would be so out of harmony with the efforts of the other church, as to make it difficult for it to sustain a claim to being *Christian*. At the same time the revival would be seen to be so in harmony with the Bible and the will of God, and that would make young converts strong to resist proselyting influences. Again, it would require such a deepening of the experiences of those who were already members of the church that they would be prepared to lead young converts wisely and safely. This church struggle had been of practical benefit to the Methodist' class, in that it had kept the eyes of the membership open to the evils of worldliness in the church, and also the evil of mere church zeal. It also made them the more ready to receive and stand by the strong truths of the Bible. Here he had an opportunity to labor freely, without opposition from within the fold, although there was plenty of oppo-

. 10   (117)

sition without. He scarcely had commenced operations, before
two clergymen of the other church commenced to war against
him. At first they advised the people to stay away, because
the Methodists were simply going to have one of their usual
times of excitement. When the meetings began to get hold
of the people, and particularly of some of the more choice in
the community, one of these preachers began to visit them
and to coax them to join his church. It soon became necessary for Mr. Redfield to defeat these efforts, if possible, the
immediate occasion of which, Mr. Redfield says, was as follows:

"A man who had been converted and whose wife was a
seeker, had been strongly urged, and finally had consented,
to join this minister's church. One evening the man came
inside the altar to labor with some of the seekers, and I said
to him, 'I am told that you and your wife design to join the
other church as soon as she is converted.' 'Yes,' said he,
'that is our design.'

"I said to him, 'Don't you do it; for they will press your
religion out of you, and press final perseverence into you, and
you will lose your soul by it. You won't join them, will you?'

" 'No,' said he, 'I will not.'

" I went to his wife, who was kneeling at the altar, and
asked her, 'Why is it you do not find what you are after?
Do you give up your whole will to God?'

" 'Oh, yes; I think it is given up.'

" 'Well, if God wants you to join the Methodist Church,
will you do it?'

"She was startled with the question, and I saw her will
was against it; and fully believing that for her to join that
church would be to surround her with influences that would
make it almost an impossibility for her to be saved, I said to
her, 'You may rest assured, God will never touch your case
until you are willing to join the Methodist Church.'

" 'Do you think so?' she asked.

" 'Yes, I know it,' I replied.

" 'Then, I'll be willing,' she said.

" 'But, *will* you join the Methodists?' I asked.

"Again she seemed to draw back, and I saw that here the difficulty lay; and I said, 'I am satisfied you will never find the Lord until you make up·your mind to join the Methodists.'

" 'Well, I will,' said she; and instantly shouted, 'Glory to God! I have got it.'

" Various other plans were adopted to draw our people away from us, but without success. All the converts, without an exception, united with us, which so strengthened the society that it ceased to need missionary help, and began to help others.

"After the failure of . the two preachers either to stop the revival or proselyte from us, their own people dismissed them. One of them was so displeased at this that he exposed the fact that there was but one communicant in the society, the remainder simply sustaining the minister as an item of upper-tendom luxury. The other, for drunkenness, stealing church funds, horse-racing and night-reveling, was soon after silenced."   *   *   *   *   *   *   *

"I have also learned that the great opposition to the thorough work of God, is from · nominal professors of religion, who have never been converted, or who have backslidden from a good experience; but the severest of all is from professed ministers of the gospel. I also came to know that whatever others might say or do, I must maintain God's rights, and will, at all risk and expense. In doing this I found I must contend against any and everything that did not bear the mark of God's approval, and that nothing short of this will give that character to the church that will prevent it from downright formalism. The supposition that there are redeeming traits in human nature which only need disciplining, rather than a radical change; and the use of appliances to polish and adorn, instead of rooting them out, will, if allowed to prevail, banish heart-felt religion from the world.

"I have also learned another important lesson, namely, that God demands harmony and purity among his people. One night, at this place, when the altar was well filled with seekers, we came nearly to a stand-still. My soul for a moment seemed crushed within me. I cried to God to remove the hinderance; when I was instantly impressed that there were those among us of whom God would say, 'Remove from before me the vile, and then offer your sacrifice.' So strongly did this come, and so plainly did it appear to be in the way, that I arose from my knees, and getting the attention of the congregation, I stated my impressions, and asked that those present who were conscious of wickedness in their hearts, and of opposition to the work now going on, to have the goodness to leave the house. Three members of the class immediately left; but no sooner had they done so than the converting power of God fell upon the congregation, and souls that were seeking were soon set at liberty. What was more remarkable was the fact that for twelve or fourteen successive nights after, we had a like experience until we could succeed in getting those very persons to leave. One of those persons was afterward expelled for gross immoralities. Another was proverbially deficient in the Christian spirit, and the other was hypocritically acting the part of a friend to our faces, but behind our backs and with infidels talking against the work of God.

"While we were holding meetings at the church, the colored people held meetings in a private house, and the power of God was among them in a wonderful manner. One night a young woman who had been under deep awakening for some time, suddenly arose and ran toward the door, determined to get away from the leadings of the Holy Spirit. Before she reached the door she fell to the floor in great agony. She would rise on one elbow and cry, 'O Lord, have mercy! Lord, have mercy! Lord, have mercy!' and then sink back to the floor again, to all appearances, sense-less. In a few minutes this was repeated, and so continued for seven days and eight nights. Some thought she would die, and called me to go and see her, which I did. She had then been in this condition several days. I tried to offer Christ to her, and also to find out what her particular trouble was. Though I persisted in my efforts for some time, and called to her in a loud voice to tell me what the matter was, she paid no regard to me, and seemed neither to see nor hear anything. Still, at regular intervals she would rise as I have described, and utter that cry, and then sink back to the floor again. She obeyed no call of nature during this time, except once when she swallowed a few drops of milk which was put in her mouth. She lay on a bed prepared for her on the floor, and there continued during the period stated. Two Christian women slept in the room, nights, to watch her. The eighth night, when all had retired to rest, and the light put out, the poor girl continued to be exercised as before. At last she changed the wording of her prayer to, 'Here, Lord, I give myself away. 'Tis all that I can do,' and instantly began bounding, and jumping, and praising God. As soon as the first gust of glory passed, she sank to the floor from weakness caused by her long fasting and want of rest; and they fed her by the teaspoonful until she could bear a more hearty meal. When she came fully to herself, she said that she had seen the awful state of the damned, and it was that which had so distressed her and kept her in such agony for so long a time. She proved to be a remarkable specimen of the converting power of God."

CHAPTER XIX.

The success of the meeting described in the last chapter, deepened Mr. Redfield's convictions that the preaching of holiness would conquer the world for Jesus, and that it was his duty to follow the same course wherever he went, since it had proved successful in every instance heretofore. In conscience he could choose no other course.

In response to a call, he went to a neighboring city. Before he commenced work in the church to which he had been invited, he met the pastor of another society in the same city, who desired his services for a few days first. A meeting had been in progress here for six weeks, but not one conversion had occurred. He accepted the invitation, and went to work.

Speaking of his experience here he says, "I tried to preach the class of truths which the Holy Ghost led me to preach. I called upon the membership as Methodists to seek the blessing of holiness, as the sure course to have a revival among sinners. But they would not. move." The preacher then expressed to them his surprise at this, and urged them to come. But they did not respond to his invitation. After the meeting was dismissed some of them sharply reproved him for pressing them to take such a stand before the world. To save himself he threw the blame on Mr. Redfield, and the next day told him plainly that he did not like his preaching, and that he believed he was backslidden, and for that reason thought everybody else was. Mr. Redfield says, "A few years afterward the same minister astonished me with his attentions and endorsement, in a place of considerable importance, where the dignitaries of the church, because of my success in the place, were paying me unusual attentions. There he could not do enough in words and affability to show himself friendly. But his course deeply pained me. I thought, if I am not right I ask. no man to endorse me, and I value no man's friendship who cannot do it when I am an object of scorn for representing an unpopular truth."

He returned to the church which first called him. Here he found a people and pastor right in theory and effort, and the first night fifteen professed to have found the blessing of holiness. The work among sinners also broke out in great power; and in a short time about three hundred were converted.

He now felt sure that the church would see that success would follow the preaching of holiness, and the effort would become general. But he was doomed to disappointment. He says, "I learned little by little that there was a deep-seated hostility to holiness, especially among the preachers, who evidently leaned towards a worldly policy, and a desire to prune Methodism of all that was objectionable to pleasure-loving professors. I had heard that one of our preachers had said in urging worldly people to become religious, 'The time has come when a man without a profession of religion cannot find access to genteel society.' I also had another proof that a worldly policy was gaining ground in many places, and that a time-serving spirit swayed the councils of the church sometimes. One of the bishops, who has since learned that it is hazardous to stand with God against all sin, told me of some things that indicated the downward tendency of Methodism to an extent that I had not known. He was deeply grieved over it, and feared the final results. But he gave me some counsel, advice and encouragement, that led me anew to hope for success and to resolve undauntedly to pursue the thorough way. I could now say, 'I know of one bishop and one preacher who will try to stand for God and the right.' I believe that the most of them were as they thought in favor of a high degree of piety; but I was equally sure that they had more confidence in their own ideas of propriety and consistency than they had in the leadings of the Holy Ghost. But in charity to them I believed that, taking a rational standpoint, they did the best they could. I thought that with the accession of new preachers who were clear and straight (and I knew a goodly number of them that were about to enter the work), and with one bishop who could be relied upon, that the work of holiness would certainly be revived, and we should again see our Fletchers and Bra nwells and Abbotts, blessed men, whose influence would be like ointment poured forth. Again I was doomed to disappointment, for I found not only hostility to the doctrine, but successful efforts were put forth to put down these revivals, and when it was accomplished, the sneering remark would be made, 'It is another of Redfield's revivals, and you see what it has come to.' "

At times he would be greatly discouraged, and almost give up the struggle. Then the words would come, "Live while you preach, but no longer," and again he would arouse to greater diligence and faithfulness than before. At such times the manifestations of the divine favor that he received were beyond even his wonderful powers to describe. He would say at such times, "It is worth a life of toil and disgrace to feel that God approves, and none can know the sweetness of it who has not tasted it."

He found new fields of labor were opening before him, and calls came on every hand; but, usually, they came from mortgaged churches, and nearly extinct societies. Here there was but little to lose, and the authorities would give him freedom. This was good so far. To succeed in such places it was necessary for him to raise the standard of piety to where the Bible puts it, and this would greatly shock both pastor and people. The piety and even the morals of the membership were generally of so low a type, and the contrast between the standard he presented and the characters they manifested was so great that it was with difficulty sometimes that he could induce the pastor to suspend judgment until God could redeem his cause by giving unwonted success. In speaking of this he says, "The good results of course would follow, as God's Holy Spirit will always work with the truth." When the victory came, pastors would say, "I did not think your course would result so gloriously. I shall now know what to do at my next station."

One said to him about this time, "I once saw things in this light, and tried to pursue the course you do, and had the same results; but I found that influential ministers in the conference began to look upon me suspiciously, and to utter murmurings against me, such as 'unsafe,' 'injudicious,' 'behind the times,' 'an old fogy,' and 'not a good representative of our church.' Besides, I knew what they did to other men who took the same course you do; they were proscribed, sent to starvation appointments, or were located."

Mr. Redfield says the ministers would sometimes ask him, "What system do you use, that works so successfully? Do you preach a regular course of sermons?"

"My answer would be, sometimes, 'Oh, no! I take the rough, unpopular Methodist truths that preachers who hope to be bishops and presiding elders dare not use.' Though I would leave them at such times evidently in the best of feeling, thanking the Lord that one more preacher was won back to primitive piety, and could now be depended upon to do thorough work for Jesus; still, I have been shocked often to find that within one year the same preacher had fallen back to the same state of cowardice, inefficiency and indifference, and some of them would enter their protests against the Redfield revivals."

In one place to which he went, the preacher was sick and unable to attend the meetings. The work broke out in glorious power. Some of the members immediately began to seek and obtain the experience of perfect love, while others opposed it. "When the former would go to the pastor," says Mr. Redfield, "and speak favorably of the meetings, he would fall in with them and approve of all. When the latter would complain to him of my preaching on dress, etc., he would fall in with them and promise to stop me when he could get out. After a little he began to circulate slanderous stories about me. These came out after I left. I remarked to some one that I would not be surprised if he was out of the ministry in less than five years. In a very short time he was called to account for a scandalous crime, and deposed from the ministry."

He found in this place some who had once enjoyed perfect love, but who, from yielding to persuasion not to testify of it, had lost the experience. One of them was a class-leader. When Mr. Redfield began to preach holiness, he was the first to come out and seek it. The baptism came upon him in great power. He was employed in a large factory, and the next time he went to work he asked permission of the foreman to address the other employes on the subject of salvation. This was granted, and Catholics and infidels listened to him as, with streaming eyes, he told them of Jesus' power to save. Some cold members of the church heard of it, and were terribly shocked at his course. But God wonderfully blessed the man; so much so that when he got home from his work he sat down and shouted aloud the praises of God. One member of the church, greatly shocked, came in great haste for Mr. Redfield to go and see the brother. From the words and manner of the messenger he supposed the brother was in a fit of some kind, and he caught up his medicine case and hurried to the house; but on entering he found the brother clapping his hands and shouting, "Glory, glory to God!" while his face shone with a heavenly radiance. The excited messenger was now more shocked to hear Mr. Redfield join the brother in the praises of God. Excitedly he exclaimed:

"I don't like this, at all!"

"Well, it's none of your business," replied Mr. Redfield;

"this brother is not your property; he belongs to God, and
God has a perfect right to bless him all he pleases."

"But," said the other, "what if he never gets over this?
what will become of him?"

"He'll never be fit for another horse-race, as long as he
lives," was the reply.

"Well, I wouldn't have that spell on me for five hundred
dollars," said the frightened man.

"Make yourself perfectly easy about that matter," said
Mr. Redfield, "for I assure you, you are in no danger, for
God will keep clear of you while you are in this mood."

"About this time," says Mr. Redfield, "I was called to go
and visit a lady, dying with the consumption. She was reduced to a mere skeleton, and to all appearances, might die
that night. I tried to point her to Jesus as the great physician of souls, and besought her to cast herself upon him at
once. To encourage her, I told her of a man whom I had
lately visited, who was sick like her, and without hope, but
who was so desirous of salvation that he tried to get on his
knees, though he was so weak that as often as he made the
effort he would fall over. But he found the Lord, and died
in peace. I told her she need not try to get on her knees;
that the Lord could hear her just as well when she was lying
down. But as soon as I was gone she insisted upon getting
on her knees, and with the assistance of a woman who was
watching with her, she was enabled to do so, and while kneeling by her bedside the Lord saved her and healed her in the
same moment. One or two Sabbaths after that she was in
church, giving glory to God, who had healed her soul and
body

"Soon after this, I was called to see a brother who had
lately been converted, but was now dying with the consumption. I found him apparently breathing his last. His wife
and sister stood weeping by his bedside; and looking on was
his only child, just old enough to know that his father was

sick, and that his mother and aunty were feeling badly.   The sick man was suffering terribly from suffocation, but his face was filled with smiles.   I said to him, 'Dear brother, if you are able to speak again, tell me if you feel Jesus sustains you.'

"With a desperate effort, in monosyllables, he answered, 'Oh,—yes;— I —am—so—hap—py—I—don't—feel—it—and —if—this—is—to—be—my —heaven —for— ev—er, —its— e—nough.'

"I was also invited to go and see a good old sister who, for many years, had enjoyed a deep experience in the things of God, but who was now passing away to the spirit land. I went in company with her class-leader, and when we en- tered the stairway leading to her room, the counseling phy- sicians in the hall at the head of the stairs had just given the opinion that she was then dying.   We were invited into the room, and her daughter told her that we had come, and then with her ear close to the old lady's lips, she was able to get her request for us to pray.   This we did, and then withdrew; but scarcely had we got outside the door when her spiritual vision caught a full view of her coming Lord, and so great was the strength imparted by it that she raised to a sitting posture in the bed, and waving her hand in triumph, declared that she saw Jesus; and continued thus to triumph until she passed beyond the clouds."

CHAPTER XX.

WHEN the spring came Mr. Redfield went to Long Island to spend the summer and recruit. He preached in the villages on Sunday and attended prayer and class meetings during the week. Before preaching he would go into the woods and plead with God until he received assurances of divine help.

Referring to these times, he says: "While under the Spirit's influence and power in preaching, I would often see and proclaim truths that put my own experience and piety to the test. I have profited more by trying to practice the truths which I have seen at such times, than from the preaching of others."

At a camp meeting in the early fall, his presiding elder requested him to supply a vacant pulpit until the season for holding revival meetings. This charge had been abandoned by the preacher appointed by the conference. Mr. Redfield had no sooner consented to go than he was advised by an old preacher not to go, for, said he: "In all my labors for twenty six years I have never seen a place so hopeless." But Mr. Redfield resolved to make the trial. When he arrived at the place, he learned that the society was organized by Jesse Lee, of blessed memory, who at the time was sent of God in answer to prayer; that the church had once been in a flourishing condition; that four classes had been reduced to one; that many of the members had not been in class for three years; that one leader had not met his class for a year; that some of the members were Universalists; that some were habitual drinkers; and that there was an old, unsettled quarrel of twenty years' standing between some of the members. This made him very sad. He says: "My first visit was to an old man, the principal on one side in that quarrel. He asked me if I had come to be their preacher. I told him I had. 'Well,' said he, 'there is no use, unless you put the people through a course of discipline.' He then, in a rapid and zealous manner, began to bring their sins to light, and to tell me how much he had suffered by them. I said, 'Hold on a moment.'

" 'I tell you,' said he, 'they are not worthy of church fellowship.'

" 'Wait a moment,' I interposed.

" 'Oh, there's no use of your trying to do anything here, amid so much of wrong; and everybody knows it.'

" I had to let him go on. When at last he was almost out of breath, I managed to make him hear me and got him stopped. I then said: 'Now, brother, you are much older than I am, and I don't feel myself capable of attempting to settle the matter until I have asked God for wisdom.' At this I knelt, and he knelt with me. I then determined not to rise until God melted his heart. I struggled in prayer for some time, when at last he began to cry out, 'O my God, what have I been about! Lord, have mercy upon me! Oh, how wickedly have I sinned against thee!' Finally he said, 'I want a meeting called, so that I can confess my wrong and my sin, for I am the one to blame.' A meeting was called, and the offended members readily received the old man's confession and forgave him, and the breach was healed.

" One of my visits was to old Brother V——'s, who was one of the first members that joined the society. At his house, for many years, the few pious ones used to meet to ask God to send them a preacher 'after his own heart'. It was in answer to their prayers that Jesse Lee came and organized them into a class. The old brother had been a very efficient leader and exhorter, but now his understanding and memory were in ruins. His good wife said to him, 'Father, here is the preacher who has been sent to us.' The old man raised from his stooping position in the chimney corner, and, with a vacant, wavering stare, said, 'Why—how—is your

mother? Well? Why—you look good.' I had heard that
pious old people, however broken, would sometimes remember well matters of religion; and after satisfying myself that
he was only able to converse in a very incoherent manner, I
abruptly inquired, 'Father V——, do you know one Jesus of
Nazareth?' Instantly his whole demeanor changed, and, with
an intelligent air, he answered, 'Yes, I have known him a
great many years. He is my Saviour, and he'll not turn me
off;' and then repeated many passages of Scripture and several hymns, so appropriate to the thought he first expressed
that I was amazed and could hardly assure myself that he
had not been trying to play a deception upon me.

"The Sabbath came, and I went to church. A goodly
number had come, probably from curiosity, to see the new
preacher. I had resolved to deliver my own soul regardless
of persons or conditions, by declaring the whole counsel of
God. But I saw no favorable indications. After a few
efforts during the week following to bring about a change,
and finding it all in vain, I went to sinners and exhorted
them to flee from the wrath to come. The response from
them was, 'Go look after your ungodly members.' Sabbath
came again, and I delivered my message in view of the judgment. When I was leaving the church, I met the principal
member of the official board, who accosted me thus, 'We
don't like your preaching here at all, nor the chapters you
read from the pulpit. Hell is not very popular here.'

"I inquired, 'Will you tell me, brother, what I have
preached that is not Bible truth?'

"'Well,' said he, 'I believe it is true.'

"'Do you want me to preach lies?' I asked.

"I went home, weeping along the street. I now saw if
I was going to accomplish anything, I must do it with my
might. So Monday morning I went to the grove, and knelt
before the Lord in prayer. It seemed as though the powers
of darkness were all about me. The sensations I experienced

were as if by the hardest effort I was overcoming great obstacles and rising higher and higher until my head struck
against a rock, and L sank back overcome. I arose and sought
another place to plead with God, and there experienced the
same. Thus I continued day after day through the week. I
would go to the house once in a while and get something to
eat, and then return to the struggle. Sometimes my agony
was such that it seemed to me I could rend the heavens with
my cries for the salvation of sinners. It seemed to me that
if I could hold on until the victory came I should see them
saved. When Saturday night came my very brain seemed
sore, and the jar of my step gave me pain. I felt a kind of
bewilderment coming on, but I had received no answer.
I had resolved, in the name of God, to see a break and salvation come to the church on the next Sabbath, or an end
put to its standing as a stench in the nostrils of the Almighty and the world.

"Sunday morning came, and with eyes sore from weeping,
and my brain tender from the continual struggle of the week,
I walked softly and carefully to the church, and into the pulpit.
In opening the service, I said to the membership: 'This day
ends my labors in this place. You do not want me here, and
I do not want to stay, for I am heartily tired of pouring
water on to rocks. But if God will help me, I will either see
a break to-day, or see this ungodly apology for Methodism
annihilated. I have asked no man's money; I go at my own
expense; but I shall go straight for God.' Nothing seemed to
move in the morning. In the evening I went into the pulpit
again, and announced that I should redeem my pledge. Of
course this aroused their hate to a high pitch. As God
helped, I pointed out the track of an acceptable disciple, and
the only one that could possibly pass the gates of Paradise.
At the close of the sermon, I asked those, and only those
who meant it and would take this track, and where needed
go to their neighbors and confess to them, and pray with

them, and who would seek for the blessing of holiness until they knew they had it, to rise. I didn't believe I could get them to come forward. Two only arose, and they were of the most lowly. 'Well,' said I, 'there seem to be but three of us, counting myself as one, and God besides; but I think we will try. and have a prayer meeting.' Those two and myself were all that would kneel, I in the altar, and they at their seats, about half-way down the church. I opened with a short prayer, and began to rise in spirit until I struck that rock again. I then asked some one else to pray, but no one responded, and I tried again with the same experience and result, and the third time, and the fourth, and fifth, until the sixth time, in immediate succession. I now felt that this is the last time, and that if I did not get the victory, God would say to me, 'Let them alone.' The case was a desperate one, and I knew the world and the devil were against me, and the church members who would not kneel; but I said in my prayer, 'O God, I'll go as far as I can.' Again in spirit I began to rise, and soon I struck that rock again, and it seemed to shiver to atoms. Instantly the house was filled with the divine glory. The two who were kneeling with me fell, and their shouts and screams were so loud that they alarmed the village. The people came running in to see what was the matter, and as they crowded up the aisles and saw the two prostrate under the power of God, tears chased each other down their faces; and the poor tempted members began one after another to confess their hostility, and ask for pardon, and promised to take the track pointed out to them. I staid one more week, and forty-five sinners were converted. The preacher who had abandoned the work returned, and the revival went on in power for some time. Ten or fifteen years afterward, I heard from that society, and it still was doing well."

He was now waited upon by a preacher from a place about seven miles away, who said, "I want you to come to

11

our church. We have been holding meetings for three weeks, and not one soul is yet converted. And it is the request of the Baptist and Presbyterian ministers also, for you to come." He went, and without consulting the minister as to what course he should pursue, he followed what he be-. lieved to be the leadings of the Holy Spirit. The first night while he was preaching, some arose and went out of the house in great haste, slamming the doors as they went; but they soon returned, and did the same thing over again. He learned after the meeting was dismissed that they were members of the church who took this method to show their disapproval of his preaching. They went to the preacher and told him that he must send Mr. Redfield away, or he would ruin the church. The Baptist and Presbyterian ministers gave him similar advice. The next night the congregation was larger than before, though these opposers had prophesied to the contrary. He preached as he felt God desired him to. Now none even came to the altar, and it was said he had broken up the revival. Two or three who had been forward before he came now refused to come. He sent the next day to see what the difficulty was, and was informed that they had no design of changing their lives at all, but had thought if the Methodists praying for them would do them any good, they were willing to let them do it. Now they did not care to go any farther. From this Mr. Redfield was satisfied that he had not harmed the revival, and resolved to keep on in the track on which he had started. Now the opposers became very angry, and began to advise the people to stay away, for the preacher was not fit to be heard, and was no proper representative of Methodism. A prominent infidel met some of them face to face, and said, "Let that man alone; he is the only honest man among you, for he dares to tell the whole truth. He cuts me up ''fore and aft,' but I shall still go, for I like to see a man who is honest for his God." He did keep on, and was converted. Now the

war began in dead earnest. Ministers of other denominations continued to counsel and advise, and their conclusions
were that to allow him to stay any longer would be the ruin
of the Methodist Episcopal Church. This greatly emboldened the opposers in the church. The Baptists and Presbyterians left their churches and appointed meetings each side
of him to keep their members away.

Mr. Redfield went before the Lord with the matter.
He says, "I felt to say, 'O Lord, thou knowest I don't know
what to do. Give me thy help for this once. Tell me what
the message is.' A text and subject were presented to my
mind from which I shrank. I said, 'O Lord, that will never
do; for the people are so much offended now that this will
produce a perfect tempest and break up the meeting.' The
instant I shrank I was in the dark, and distressed beyond endurance; I now cried out, 'Lord, show me the way, and I'll
follow.' Then that text and subject came again. Finally I
asked the Lord to direct me to some appropriate text as cor-
roborative, if that was his will. I opened the Bible at random and put my finger down on the words, 'Be not afraid,
but speak, and hold not thy peace, but speak for I am with
thee,' etc.—Acts xviii. 9, 10. I said, 'Lord, I will venture it
at all hazards, although I am sure that I shall be stopped before I am through.' When I went to the church I found instead of a small congregation the house was so crowded that
it was necessary to throw open the unfurnished galleries,
which had never been used before. The two meetings on
either side of us, which had been appointed to draw off the
people, were deserted. But now was to come the tug of
war. One thing encouraged me: the preacher in charge was
a very devoted man. Though he said but little, I knew he
was ready to identify himself with the right and to rise or
fall with it. But I expected trouble with the people, and
especially with the official board. When I went into the
pulpit I thought, 'They will order me out before I can read

the first hymn; but I will proceed until they stop me.' I read for the first hymn the one commencing:

> " 'Shall I for fear of feeble man,
>   The Spirit's course in me restrain?
> Or undismayed in deed and word,
>   Be a true witness of my Lord?'

"Such an unction was given that every word fell upon the congregation with great power. When I had finished I thought, 'Well, I have read my hymn, and I have not been ordered out yet;' but the temptation came: 'If you pray as you feel you will be collared by some of the officials and taken out.' I resolved to go as far as I could, and just as the Holy Ghost should prompt me. When I finished the prayer I thought, 'I have prayed, and I am not ordered out yet.' I read another hymn, and after the singing, I announced for my text: 'I AM hath sent me unto you;' and as the Spirit gave me utterance, I tried to show them, first, that my authority was from God; second, that the message was from God; third, that the message was unbending in its requirements, and was not to be trifled with.

"I felt an unearthly thrill charging me from head to foot, while the place was filled with a sense of the awful presence of God. I soon saw that the minds of the congregation were in great commotion; and in a few minutes the power of God broke like a thunder clap upon the people, and such screaming, falling, shouting, and crying for mercy I had no thought of seeing in that place. All denominational lines were obliterated in an instant, and Baptists, Presbyterians, and Methodists took each other by the hand, and with deep emotion declared this God to be their ·God. After this the work went gloriously. One brother said to me that night: 'I now see what was the matter with our revival five years ago; we did not go deep enough. It was for the want of the strong doctrine of holiness that it all fell away, for out of five hundred converts we had hardly one left that has not backslidden.'"

Mr. Redfield was now invited by a good old brother to come to his help in a place about five or six miles away. He had been doing his best to start the work without presenting the heart-stirring doctrines of holiness. Mr. Redfield felt it his duty to tell the people how gloriously the work of holiness would move the work of conversions forward, and called upon the church to begin to seek the experience. He then asked those who desired to seek pardon to rise to their feet, when fifteen immediately responded. The next day the preacher and he visited from house to house. At the first house at which they called they found the woman rejoicing in the fullness of salvation, while busy at work over the wash-tub. She said: "I came from the church last night fully resolved to seek for perfect love, and immediately set about it, and before morning came God gave me the desire of my heart. It does seem as though I never found it so easy to get along before. I tried to sweep this morning, and the very broom seemed to move itself. My children never seemed so obliging and good as they do this morning. Oh, glory to God in the highest!"

His calls to help the preachers were now so numerous that he could spend but a short time in each place. He had met with a preacher at a camp meeting in the fall who now desired him to come to his assistance. It was about ten or fifteen miles distant, in a large and fashionable church. There had been a very extensive revival in the church the winter before. He went, but with great misgivings about coming under the minister's influence, for he seemed to be very superficial in his work. They had hardly commenced before he informed Mr. Redfield one day that they were invited out to tea. This Mr. Redfield feared was a trick of the devil to dissipate his communion with God, and he frankly told the minister he dared not go out to afternoon parties of any kind, for he had only time and strength to do God's work, and he felt the need of being closeted with God every moment when not at church, or traveling from place to place. The preacher told him he need not fear any irreligious tendencies. Mr. Redfield says: "I was overpersuaded, and for once I yielded. When we arrived, I found the parlors filled with gay, but intelligent women, some of whom were members of the church. My heart sank within me, and I desired to withdraw. But the preacher assisted in giving a religious tendency to the gathering; yet this forced apology for religion only pained me. Tea was soon passed around, and I had paid all the compliments I desired to. As soon as this was over I sang a spiritual hymn, and then knelt in prayer, and we continued until all the nice and shaped-up order was broken, and God came in slaying power. This good beginning was a sample after which we patterned, and held social meetings every afternoon in private houses. These fitted us for the public services at night in the church, where God saved a multitude of sinners. Yet I must say, I think it is hazardous to undertake a system of fashionable visiting in connection with a revival meeting.

CHAPTER XXI.

Mr. REDFIELD now received a letter from a preacher whom he had met at the camp meeting alluded to in a former chapter, and whom he had promised to assist during the winter, if possible. At their first meeting this preacher was a seeker for perfect love. He had inquired of another preacher how he should seek for it, and was referred to Mr. Redfield. At first his heart revolted at the idea of going to a local preacher for advice; but finally he concluded to do so. "When he came," says Mr. Redfield, "I felt the opposite from what he had felt, and shrank from attempting to give him advice. I said to him, 'I am but a poor unworthy local preacher, and it is asking a great deal of me to advise you; but with your leave, I will tell you some part of my experience, and then I will ask you a few questions.' When I had finished my experience, I asked, 'Brother, can you say to begin with, "The will of the Lord be done?' "

" 'I ought to,' he answered.

" 'But do you say, "O God, thy will be done"?' I asked.

" 'I do,' said he, very emphatically.

" 'But hold a moment, brother. Let us see what possibly, may be the will of God, and then when you comprehend it, see if you can still say, "Thy will be done." God's will is comprehended in two tables—what you must do, and what you must suffer. Now it may be the will of God that you should be put down as a very inferior preacher, and be sent out on to the frontier, as unfit to represent Methodism in any populous town. Now, do you say, "Thy will be done"?'

" 'I do,' he replied.

" 'But stop again. It may be God's will for you to go to Africa, and spend your life there; to leave home and society and let your bones sleep in the hot sands of that country; now can you say, "Thy will be done"?'

" 'I do,' he again answered promptly.

" 'But brother, that may not be your track; for God wants poor-house preachers, and I don't know but that you can in poverty and rags, in the poor-house, show the power of grace to triumph, and that your sufferings there will so preach the power of the gospel that some one by that means will be pressed to seek religion, who would not by any other. Can you now say, "Thy will be done"?'

" 'I do,' was his prompt reply again.

" 'But it may be, brother, that God wants you to testify by the triumphs of his grace over pain, and your calling may be to suffer distress of body, that the power of grace may so shine out in your case that some infidel may be won to Christ, and he become the honored instrument in the hands of God of bringing many to Christ, and thus you do more than in any other way; now can you say, "Thy will be done"?'

"And again he said, 'I do.'

" 'Well, brother, you have got just half-way through; and by this you know you have the consent of your will to suffer the will of God. Now about doing the will of God: you may have duties to do from which your heart up to this time has shrunk; the little duties which will put you at variance with every one who is not in harmony with God—"Who is deaf as my servant; and blind as he that is perfect," says God —to take sides with God, and never allow yourself to set up a defense of self, to be thorough, straight, and honest; to vindicate the rights of God, as you would within five minutes of the judgment. You can stand for God when protected by men of influence in your conference, but will you be as tenacious for all of God's will when all turn against you? Remember you will be considered an old fogy, unsafe, imprudent in want of charity. You need not abuse men to win a bad name; only be unflinching for God, and your name is worth more now than it ever will be again. If a man of wealth should pick you up out of the ditch in a starving condition, and take you under his care, provide for you, and make you one of his heirs, on condition that you keep watch of his interests, would you think it right to allow men to come and steal his property, for fear you might make some of them your enemies? God has called you to be a watchman, and you must on no condition allow, in silence, an infringement of his rights. You will meet with ministers who will regard it a small thing to be so particular; but no man is too particular in matters of sufficient importance for the Almighty to notice. The world, a dead church, and time-serving ministers will protest against you, and resort to all manner of means, more or less dishonorable, to humiliate you. Now can you, do you say, O Lord, I will do thy will, if I stand alone? Can God count on you as one who can be trusted to do the exact right, when his back is turned, and the church and the world conspire to outlaw you for your fidelity?'

"'I do say,' he replied, 'the whole will of God shall be done in me, and by me, at every cost.'

"'Well, now you are all the Lord's, are you not?'

"'Oh,' said he, 'it seems to me there is ' something ' that I have not yet comprehended in this surrender.'

"'Well, brother, tell the Lord, when that 'something' is made apparent, that you will then give that also.'

"'I do,' said he.

"'Well, then, you have given all to do and to suffer the will of God, have you not?'

"'Oh, yes.'

"'Well, then you are the Lord's. Now, brother, who has required all this surrender at your hands?'

"'Why, God; has he not?'

"'What, everything?'

"'Yes, has he not?

"'Oh, yes,' said I, 'now, if he has demanded all, and you have given all, do you think he will ever accept it.'

"'Oh, yes; if he has required all, and I have given all, he will accept it, for he is not trifling with me.'

"'Well, if he will accept, when will he do it?'

"'Oh,' said he, 'I don't feel,'——

"'Well, you are not ready to feel; you are just now ready to believe; not that you have the witness, for you have not; but believe on the bare promise of God, that having complied with the conditions in giving yourself to him, God now finishes the work by accepting you.'

"'What, must I believe before I feel?'

"'Brother, do you tell sinners when they are seeking to wait until they feel? or do you tell them to take the promise of God for the face of it?'

"'Why, I tell them God is to be trusted, and they must credit his word.'

"'Is not the promise of God to the sinner, just as good for the preacher? or do you want better security, than the sinner has, that God will keep his word?'

"'Why, I ought to ask no better security, and I'll try to believe. But,' said he, 'I don't feel yet!'

"'You have not done all yet. Now, finish the condition: "With the heart," not simply the assent or consent of the head, but "with the heart man believeth unto righteousness." You finish the work of doing right in your compliance with the condition. But, now, it is "with the mouth confession is [to be] made unto salvation."'

"'What, confess that I feel what I don't feel?'

"'Oh, no; that would be telling a lie; confess what you *believe;* viz., that God is true to his word, and that, on the bare say-so of God, you now believe that he accepts what you have given him.'

"He immediately went to a tent and confessed, not to what he felt, but to what he believed; and while in the act of doing so the witness came; and referring to this experience in a testimony given some six weeks afterwards, he said, 'It seemed to me that I was like a vessel lost in a sea, without bottom or shore; and I was so filled with the divine glory and power that I prayed for God to stay his hand.'

"This brother now desired to engage me to come to his charge and assist him in a protracted meeting during the coming winter. I told him I would, if the Lord permitted, but also told him to go home and persuade all the church, as far as possible, to seek the blessing of sanctification, and that I would guarantee that, in the meantime, God would work upon sinners. He said he would do it, and the following will show the results:

"About two months after this I received a letter from him saying, 'I wish you to be here next Tuesday to begin a protracted meeting.' I took a public conveyance, and reached his place on Monday evening. On arriving at his house I learned he was gone to a private house to hold a holiness meeting. I found the house, and on opening the door, I saw the place was filled with people whose faces fairly shone. The remainder of the evening was given to testimony, mostly of those who had entered into the experience of holiness. These were clear and strong. There were a number, also, who testified as seekers of the experience. The meeting was one of glorious power. After it closed, as the minister and myself were on our way to his home, I asked, 'How long have you been holding these holiness meetings?'

"'About two months,' he answered.

"'How many of the church now enjoy holiness as a distinct blessing?' I asked.

"'I think the largest proportion of them are now in the experience, and almost all the remainder are pressing after it,' was the reply.

"'Do you remember,' I asked, 'what I told you at the camp meeting? that if you and your people would keep at the work of holiness, God would work in the awakening of sinners?' I inquired.

" 'Yes, I do,' said he.

" 'Do you know of any cases of awakening?' I further asked.

" 'No; I don't—not one,' he replied, and then calling to one of the leaders who was walking near us, asked: 'Brother H——, do you know of any sinners who are serious?'

" 'No,' said the brother, 'I don't know of any.'

" 'Well,' said I, 'this beats me; for I never knew it to fail. I believe yet that you will find that God has been doing something.'

" Tuesday afternoon came, and we met at the church, but there was no sign of any stir among sinners. It was the same at the evening service; also Wednesday afternoon and evening. Thursday afternoon we seemed to have come to a halt, and could not stir. As a last resort we called upon the church members to come to the altar to renew our consecrations, and others to seek the blessing of holiness. In a few minutes it seemed as though the powers of darkness were let loose upon us. The preacher cried out: *Hold on! Steady faith! Steady faith!*' and all at once the power of God fell upon us, and there was a great crying out among sinners; and one or two came to the altar screaming for mercy, and soon were hopefully converted to God. From this moment the work went on in great power.

"The next morning one of the class-leaders came to the preacher and said: 'Brother O——, my cousin who is an infidel and never goes to church, does not seem to be as hard as usual. He goes with his head down; and I would not wonder if you might be able to talk to him about religion. Will you and Brother R—— go with me to his house and see him?'

" Down to his house we went and were introduced to his wife, and sat down to wait for the leader to go to the man's shop to call him. As soon as he came in at the kitchen door and saw us in the other room, he wailed out, 'O God! O God! what shall—what shall I do? Oh! oh! oh! God, what shall I do?' I felt like getting the Bible and directing him to a promise to the broken-hearted sinner to read for himself, and asked his wife, 'Have you a Bible in the house?' She arose and went to a cupboard over the fireplace and took one out; he caught sight of it as she handed it to me, and broke out, 'Oh, that poor neglected Bible!' I took it and turned to the words, 'Come unto me all ye that labor and are heavy laden, and I will give you rest. Take my yoke upon you and learn of me; for I am meek and lowly in heart; and ye shall find rest unto your souls. For my yoke is easy and my burden is light.' I held them before him, and said, 'Look at that and read it.' He brushed his long hair from his eyes with his hand, and gazed through his tears upon the precious words. 'Read them for yourself,' I said.

"With emphasis he replied, ' I am reading it.'

"'Well, I want you to believe it,' I continued.

"'I am believing it,' he answered, and burst into such a tempest of shouts as made the whole house ring.

"His wife now cried out, 'O God, have mercy on me,' and commenced to wring her hands, walking the floor back and forth, and crying, 'What shall I do? what shall I do?' The little children, who were too young to appreciate the feelings of the parents, began to cry aloud. In a few moments the mother was happy in the Lord.

"As soon as the first gust of glory had passed over, and the man had so far recovered from the overpowering effects of his joy that he could talk, he said: ' Now, I know what all this means; I know what all this means.' He then said he had not been to a church for two years; but, about two months before had felt sadly impressed that some great calamity was about to befall him. 'I thought,' he said, 'perhaps, I am going to die, or some member of my family is going to be taken away. But now I see, it was the Holy Spirit convicting me; and now I have got religion.'

"The preacher went down through the main street of the town, calling upon the people, and I returned to his house. After awhile he came back with the glad tidings that God had indeed broken up the entire place. Said he, 'As I was passing the first store one of the proprietors called me in, and there at one of the counters stood his partner weeping, and as I entered, he inquired if I could tell them how to be saved. I directed them as well as I could, and started on down the street. As I was passing the court-house the jailor asked me to come in and pray for him, for he wanted religion. When I left, and was passing a lawyer's office, he accosted me, and asked, 'Sir, can you tell me how to be saved?'

"I continued laboring with this brother a few weeks, but as the work was going well enough without me, I went where I was needed more. In one of the meetings, before I left, I counted about forty who testified about like this: 'Some two months ago, while I was at work in my store (or shop, or on the farm, as the case might be), I felt the awakening Spirit of God had got hold of me, and I sought and obtained mercy.' But not one was there of all who professed to be saved while I was there who referred to any preaching or any meeting whatever, as the means for awakening them."

He now went at the request of a minister to a small city where the Methodists for many years had been robbed by systematic proselyting of all who would be of financial benefit to a church; and this by open hostility.

Mr. Redfield resolved to break it up, by the help of God. He plainly saw that people of such a spirit would not properly care for converts, and that it would be positively dangerous, in a spiritual sense, for them to go into such associations. As soon as he commenced his labors they commenced their operations. He made a public statement of the case, and told them they must get religion enough to stop such wicked work, and go to work and quarry out their own converts, for their success in proselyting was coming to an end. He then warned the people against them; saying it would be at the peril of their souls to have anything to do with such folks. One minister began to preach against the Methodists, and soon after was dismissed by his church. Another attempted the same, but his church stopped him after his first effort. Some five or six different churches were engaged in the same work, but such was the thoroughness of the revival that the young converts could see the difference between the true and the false, and none of them were lost.

But a poor drunken Universalist preacher, who had once been a Methodist, but after being expelled, turned Episcopalian, and then became a Universalist, was not so easy to get along with. He went to New York city to find something with which to shake the confidence of the people in Mr. Redfield. He was stirred up to this by some of his members being converted and leaving his church; and because the new church he was building had come to a standstill from lack of interest in its completion as one result of the revival. When in New York he foolishly laid his plans before some who knew Mr. Redfield, and who kindly informed him of them.

When the Universalist minister returned he reported that Mr. Redfield came to the place on a stolen horse, and that he had run away from a city about two hundred miles distant in deep disgrace. Mr. Redfield concluded to say nothing about it, but leave the man in the hands of God, and soon after he died with the delirium tremens.

CHAPTER XXII.

Mr. Redfield's extreme and incessant labors now began to tell severely upon his naturally frail constitution. For some time each effort to preach had greatly exhausted him, and sometimes it had seemed as though he would never be able to preach again. Severe attacks of vomiting had now set in that indicated cancer of the stomach. He became so weak that he was obliged to lie down at the close of his sermons, and let others take charge of the altar work. All remedies failed, and, obliged to leave the field, he went home, as he supposed, to die. For a long time his sufferings were of the most excruciating character. It was six months before he entered a church again, and eight months before he preached another sermon. During this time his communion with God was uninterrupted, and, as the sequel shows, his affliction was to be a means of building him up more strongly in the faith. He says:

"In the midst of the severest pain my soul was so filled that sometimes I would cry out, 'O Lord, I would not have one pain less.' My happiness at the thought of having fallen with my armor on, and that I was suffering for my zeal for God, and not for wickedness, was indescribable.

"I had found a home with a very kind family who did all for my comfort that lay in their power. To all appearances I could live but a short time; yet I would not allow any one to sit up with me, and these dear friends, without my knowledge, would come into my room in the night to look after me. When I found this out, I desired them not to do so. One night I locked my door so that they would feel themselves excused from watching me. I had scarcely laid down before I felt a peculiar sensation like a wave pass over me, from my head to my feet; and with it an impression as of a clear voice saying: 'This is death.' I realized my condition, and thought, 'They will find my door locked in the morning, and after awhile will force it open and find me dead.' Then I thought, 'If this be death, I'll go singing;' so I began the song commencing:

"'I am on my way, passing over.'

I sung the first verse and began the second, when my voice failed, and I finished it in a whisper. I tried the third verse and my breath stopped. I then tried to move a hand, and then a foot, but could not. I felt a sensation all through me as though my spirit was about to leave the body. My eyes turned upward, and myriads of angelic spirits seemed to be hovering over me, as if waiting to bear me home. All my previous conceptions of the 'innumerable company' were eclipsed by this vision. I thought: 'How great must be the whole number if the escort for one poor man is so without number!'

"With the same suddenness with which it came on, that wave of death passed, and my heavenly visitors were gone.

"I had often prayed that I might have some testimony that was reliable, that the visions that dying Christians so often declare they have, are true, and this seemed to be in answer to my prayer.

"I had seen two sisters, both of them Christians, in quick succession, pass away with the consumption. Both of them professed to have found the experience of perfect love in one of my meetings. The first one gave me a kiss with her dying lips, and declared she saw angels, and heard them singing, and that children were mingled with them. She called upon her watchers to listen and to look. But one suggested to the other that she was out of her mind, to which she responded: 'Oh, no! now look there! now listen!' But the scene and sound were only for herself.

"Soon after I was called, in company with the attending physician, to make the last visit to the other sister. On approaching the sick room, she asked:

12

" 'Who has come?'

" 'Your physician,' was the answer.

" 'Well, let him come in. And who is the other?' she asked.

" They told her, and she said: 'Let him come in, too.'

" I approached the bed; around it stood her weeping husband and friends. Her eyes were already dimmed with the clouds of death. She asked her physician: 'Doctor, am 'I not dying? I think I have been all day.' But the doctor knew not the power of divine grace and dared not answer. The more he hesitated the more she urged an answer. 'Say, doctor, am I dying? You must tell me.' He touched her pulse and then her temple, and finally said: 'Yes, you are now dying.' An indescribable smile instantly spread over her face; and she said: 'Now let everybody come in that I may testify to them of the power of salvation in death.' She then sank into a gentle doze for a moment, and then again aroused herself, and with that heavenly smile upon her face she said: 'Oh, yes, bless the Lord, I am dying.' She then reached out her hand, with the chill of death upon it, and, taking mine, she asked: 'Oh, do you see those beautiful stars? I want to testify once more if I can to the power of this great salvation. O brother, do continue to preach holiness, for, oh, how it saves!'

"She had been quite offended at first, because I pressed her so strongly to give up conformity to the world, but now she seemed eager to encourage me to press it on others with all my might, for the glorious results were so rich."

These incidents had made a deep impression upon his mind, and the vision described at the opening of this chapter he always thought was the fruition of the desire that was created by them.

While recovering from his sickness, he was invited to preach in one of the New York churches. After service he went to Dr. Palmer's to dinner. When he had an opportunity

to do so, he related some of these incidents to Sister P——
and asked her views in regard to them. She replied, "I believe we should have more of them than we do, if we would
not make a bad use of them;" and then added, "I wish
Sister B—— was here to tell you some facts concerning her
mother." The door bell that moment rang, and in came Sister B——. Sister Palmer turned to her and said, "I wish
you would tell Brother Redfield about the remarkable scenes
at your mother's death-bed." When seated, Sister B——
related the following:

" My mother enjoyed the blessing of perfect love for
more than forty years. When she came down with the sickness that ended her life, my sister and I watched with her
by turns all through it, until the last night, when mother said,
'Now daughters, you must go to rest, for it will disturb me if
you do not, for you are so worn.' But I said to her, 'Mother,
you do not know how sick you are.' But she replied, 'I now
feel quite easy, but I cannot rest and know that you are not
resting, when you are so weary.' My sister left the room,
and I fixed me a place to lie down out of mother's sight, and
hid the light behind the fire-board. I had scarcely laid down
when the room become as light as day. I could see all the
furniture plainly, and the texture and stitches of the bedding
that was spread over me."

"But were you not dreaming?" asked Mr. Redfield.

"No," she replied, "that could not be, for I thought of
that, and I arose, and felt of myself, and tried various expedi-
ents to assure myself of the truth of the matter. I finally
turned and looked at the bed where mother was, when I saw
a crowd of angels hovering over her, with most heavenly
faces. They were looking most intently toward where I
knew mother's face was. I gazed, and wondered that I felt
no fear. Thus I continued, until I finally thought, 'I must
have some sleep, and will now lie down.' But the instant I
closed my eyes, my mother called me. I sprang up and ran

to her side. Daylight had come, and as I approached her, she raised her hands and said, 'Oh, what a night I have had!'

" 'Why, mother,' I asked, 'were you in pain? Why did you not call me? I did not leave the room.'

"'Oh, no! daughter,' she said, 'I was in no pain, but as soon as you left me, the angels came and staid with me all night.' The family were now called at her request; she gave them her last charge, and then passed away."

Sister Palmer then related a circumstance of interest concerning a young lady of deep piety; who, with those around her when she was dying, heard most delightful music over their heads; and what was more strange, when the funeral procession was on the way to the grave the same music attended them, and returned with the family to the house. For months afterwards, it was occasionally heard over the place where she died.

CHAPTER XXIII.

As Mr. Redfield's health began to improve, he entered the evangelistic field again. He was now more hopeful than ever before that the Methodist Episcopal Church, to which he belonged, would have her commission renewed "to spread scriptural holiness over these lands." His views of the doctrine and the experience, and his methods of advancing them, had undergone a new test to him—a thorough and solemn review on the brink of eternity. He now entered the field with stronger faith, and courage, and determinations than ever. Several ministers of prominence and promise had entered into the experience and were clearly and boldly teaching it to their people, and the blessed fruit of it, in the conversion of sinners and the sanctification of believers, was gloriously manifest. He was now invited by one of these ministers to come to his assistance. A protracted meeting had been in progress for some time, and a goodly number had been converted. All at once the work stopped. Mr. Redfield immediately was in an agony, not knowing the cause. He resorted to prayer as usual at such times, and one night in church, while thus engaged, his distress was almost unendurable. He afterwards thought he ought to have given vent to his feelings before the people, but instead of that, he deliberately cast it off. As he did so the impression came very strongly to him, "Let them alone;" and then he had such a view of their desolation, and being forsaken of God, and of their being visited by death, that he could but pray it out before the people. He left the place, but meeting with the pastor some time afterwards, he was informed that a peculiar disease broke out among the people after the meeting closed, and many were swept into eternity. The minister also informed him that one cause of the revival being checked had come out, and that was the banding together of a large number of young men to resist it.

Again he was invited to a place where he had been before, and was assured by the Lord that it was not his will for him to labor there. But the correspondence opened the way for him to go to another place where Methodism had never succeeded in gaining a footing. Here he experienced much opposition from other churches. It was about ten miles from G—— (probably Goshen). There was one church in the place occupied by a bigoted old minister who claimed the ground as a sort of a parish. He had another flock about three miles east, and still another about five miles in another direction, to whom he preached about twice a year, besides attending their weddings and funerals. A short time before Mr. Redfield's visit, a Methodist man attempted to hold a prayer meeting in the village school-house, but so great was the opposition that the doors were nailed up so he could not get in. When Mr. Redfield arrived he found an Episcopalian lady who knew something of the power of salvation, and she invited him to make her house his home. Her husband was an infidel, and apparently made so by the unholy type of religion he saw about him. The school-house was now open and Mr. Redfield gave out an appointment to preach in the evening, and though the weather was severe the people came in large numbers. The women kept closely veiled, or stood outside and looked in at the windows, and he had to do his own singing and praying. He commenced a regular visitation of the people from house to house. As an illustration of his reception he records the following as having occurred in the house of Deacon ——:

"'Good morning, Deacon. How are you prospering in the way to heaven?' I inquired.

"'We don't want any of your fanaticism here,' was the answer.

"'But I suppose you love God, and his ways?'

"'I tell you, we don't want any elements of discord introduced here.'

"'I suppose you have often prayed for the salvation of your children?'

" 'Yes, sir; I have.'

" 'Well, suppose we pray for them now.'

" 'You are not wanted here, sir; we want none of your disturbance, for we are all at peace now.'

" 'But, Deacon, I think we will pray for your children now.'

" 'I want you to leave my house.'

" 'Well, but I think I will pray first.'

"So down on my knees I went, and prayed for the old man and his family; and then went on to another deacon's house. I found him alone. His face was white with rage. I tried to draw him into religious conversation, but he would not answer me. After a long and fruitless effort to get him to say something, I at last asked to pray with him before I left. 'Pray if you have a mind to,' was his short and gruff reply. I needed no further invitation, and I knelt down and thanked God for the kind and Christian deportment of the deacon who was so willing to let me pray in his house. The next day the deacon was in the school-house, and as soon as there was an opportunity he arose and asked the privilege of speaking. I gave him permission, and he proceeded to tell the congregation that I was at his house the day before; how mad he was at the sight of me; how roughly he treated me; and how I prayed for him like a Christian. 'But,' said he, 'after Mr. Redfield was gone I began to reflect, and when night came, I went to bed, but not to sleep; for I could not. Finally my agony of mind was so great that I got up and knelt down before the Lord. It seemed to me I should die before morning, and I dared not sleep. I remained all night upon my knees praying for my soul, and about day-break God spoke peace to me, and now I have got religion.'

"This testimony took hold upon the congregation with great power."

Concerning his method of work in this place, Mr. Redfield continues: "I did not feel called upon to put any
great task or cross upon the people, such as coming to any
particular place or bench. I could discern by their manner
those who were sufficiently awakened to make the right
move. So I asked, simply, that all who desired to be saved
to stand up. The work soon broke out in great power.

"An old lady sent for me one day, whose two daughters
had been very clearly saved, and whose bright testimonies
had put the old lady's hope in the shade. When I reached
the house and was introduced to her, I saw her face was
the picture of despair. With great emotion she said, 'O sir,
my daughters tell me they know their sins are forgiven,
and that they know they are the children of God;
and I don't know what to think of myself.' Not to
shock her too badly, I thought best to accommodate my language to her by the use of the terms in which her church
was accustomed to speak of religious states of mind. So I
replied: 'I suppose, madam, that you already entertain a hope.'

"'Oh, no!' said she with evident horror; 'I would not
dare to be so presumptuous;' and then in a nervous, senten-
tious manner, she said, 'I—do—think—I—can—say—that—I
have—a—desire—that I—might have—a hope.'

"This is a type of most of what passed for religious experience in this place.

"I found one, however, who knew the power of salvation.
She was in the last stages of the asthma, and in great suffering from suffocation. Her minister had been sent for to visit
her, but he did not come. When I entered her room I was
greatly moved to see her gasping for breath. As she could
not lie down, she was bolstered up in the bed; her face was
swollen, her breathing very short and labored, and her voice
could be heard but a few feet from her. Her sister, with her
ear to the sick woman's lips, could catch the answers to my
questions and repeat them to me. I asked her if she found

religion a satisfying portion in the midst of such great distress.

"She answered: 'I am so filled with comfort and joy that if this agony of dying is to be forever I am perfectly content and happy.'

"I went to the afternoon meeting, and there saw the minister, who had been persuaded to come and give this poor flock an extra sermon. He was about opening the services, so I took my seat and listened. After a formal opening, he began his sermon by stating that he was set for the defense of the gospel, and while he was upon the walls of Zion he must protect his flock from ravening wolves. He then opened his batteries on John Wesley and the Methodist Church, and warned his people to keep clear of them, and not to forsake the religion of their fathers. He then, in substance, told them that he would relate to them what he had read in a New York paper. (I had read the same and knew what was coming.) 'But,' said he, 'I shall not call names.' He then proceeded to say: 'A man came from New York to a village about thirty miles from there, and told the people that they had the devil in them, and they must take an emetic which he had prepared for them, and vomit him up. But I am not going to speak his name now. Well, he got some to take it, and it was found that they would die, and the constable was after this man, but I shall call no names.'

"The meeting closed, and one of the principal men in the place said to the minister: 'You had better stay to the meeting to-night, Mr. E ———, and hear this man preach, and see if you have treated him just right.'

" 'No,' said the minister, 'I cannot stay with you.'

" 'But you have implied some very hard things against Mr. Redfield, and I think it no more than right that you should be at some pains to learn what you evidently know nothing about.'

"But away he went. One of his members approached

me and said: 'Mr. Redfield, I have hated the very sight of
you; and when I saw you passing along the street it has
been with difficulty that I could refrain from whipping you.
But I won't see you so abused.   And if you will build a
Methodist Church here I'll give you fifty dollars.'   Another
immediately said: 'I'll give you a lot.'   And still another:
'I'll give fifteen dollars.'   And so it went on, and in a
short time we had a church erected and dedicated, and the
last I heard from the place they had a flourishing Methodist
circuit there.   The minister's opposition laid the foundation
for three new churches and built one, and made a good appointment for a preacher, and has been regularly supplied
from conference ever since." (1863.)

Soon after the close of these labors Mr. Redfield attended
a camp meeting where he met many of the preachers who had
promised him to stand by the work of holiness; but he found
they had backed down and did not know it.   They took
him one side to counsel with him.   They said: "Brother Redfield, you know that everywhere you go revivals break out
in great power, and the people are converted by the hundred
and sometimes by the thousand."

"Yes," said he, "I know it, and I know too that it is but
the legitimate workings of holiness in the hearts of the
people."

"Well, well," said one, "that is all granted; but, Brother
Redfield, are you willing to take advice?"

"Most certainly, if it is good."

"Well, now if you could adopt any way by which thousands would be converted where now you see only hundreds,"—

"Most gladly do I desire to do all I can."

"Well," said he, and the rest all concurred in it, "if you
will not say so much about 'holiness,' 'perfect love,' and 'sanctification,' and not press any one up to these things, for that
makes many people mad, and many of our preachers afraid

of you; some say you can never do good enough to over-
balance the harm you have already done; and you get so
many prejudiced against yourself, and it must be very
uncomfortable for you to have to meet so many prejudices,"—
"Well, what would you have me do?" said Mr. Redfield.

"We would have you cease to use these terms which
arouse the prejudices of some, and, Brother Redfield, you can
preach up Bible religion as high as the Bible warrants, but
drop the objectionable terms."

One of the preachers then said: "I am pastor of the
church in ———, where the people were so offended at you
that they would not let you stay; but I have preached the
doctrine of holiness up very strong, and have done it so cautiously, that no one knew what I was preaching about.
And they have endorsed it; and now they are willing to have
you come back." (Mr. Redfield says: "I afterwards went
back, and found them worse than before.")

In speaking of this advice, he says: "It was just the
thing to take with me, I thought. What a Godsend that
these brethren have helped me out of all my difficulties! I
do find, certainly, all the opposition I can stand under. I am
willing to work without fee or charge, but my nature shrinks
when called unflinchingly to stand for God, and either in
word or tacitly tell the time-serving preacher that he is the
enemy of God. I don't ask any office in the church higher
than that of a local preacher, but I dare not do otherwise
than take that. But now I have found an easier way apparently, and a way to accomplish much more for God; a way
to be for once and forever free from slanders and misunder-
standings which follow me all over the land. So out I
went as soon as the season for protracted meetings began, and
attempted to preach the best I knew how, and yet avoid the
objectionable terms. But I found my power with God and
man was gone. Two or more weeks resulted in but one person being moved, and she so slightly that she did not stand

a week. Well, thought I, my mission is ended, and God has got through with me. So I can now go home and attend to business, and bid farewell to this rough, toilsome and heart-aching cause. How good it will be to feel once more that I am not an Ishmaelite, with my hand against every man, and every man's hand against me. But before I leave the field I'll take counsel of some good man. In casting about for some one to give me that counsel, I thought of a pious old colored man who, I thought, would be unprejudiced in every way. I went to his home and took him out into a grove, and told him all my experience in holiness; about my labors; how God had manifested himself in saving souls through me, when the doctrine of holiness was preached. I then told him that my mission with the great power God had given me was gone, and that I thought God was done with me.

"'My brother,' said the old man, 'haint you nebber com-permised?'

"'Compromised?' said I, 'why, no! I would as soon cut off my arm! I dare not do that.' But recollecting myself, I said: 'I have been counseled by some good preachers to avoid the use of the terms, perfect love, sanctification, holi-ness, etc., because the people's prejudices were so strong against it that they became angry at me and I could not do them the good I desired. But I try to preach the Bible truth as high as ever.'

"'Dat is it. Dare is just where de trubbol lie. Now what God call sanctification, you no bizness to call anysin else. It isn't you de people hates; 't is de Lor'.'

"God so let the light shine through this old black diamond that I saw there was the very place where I lost my mission and power; and I said: 'I'll go right back and preach these doctrines right in the notch where I used to, and in the mean-time seek my power over again.' But scarcely had I touched the old key before the power came. God had not condemned, but dropped me, that I might learn this lesson, that we must follow him in all things, great and small."

He now went to a place where the parish minister not only cautioned his people against him, but brought to light an old law which gave him authority over the people, even to the use of the rod on minors, and he threatened to use it if they did not stay away from the meetings. This moved the hearts of the people in the right direction, and a Methodist church was built and supplied with preaching as the result.

He then went to the place where the preacher had won the people over to love holiness by preaching it in such a guise that they did not know what he was at. But Mr. Redfield found the state of affairs bad enough. There again, he had one of his awful burdens. He thought he must be fainting away, and went to a window and raised it, and when he found the fresh air did not help him, he knew it was a burden. But so intense was his agony that he thought he could not endure it, when the suggestion came: "Cast thy burden on the Lord." He knelt down, and gave vent to his feelings in sobs and groans and tears. The burden passed away, and as it did so left him with the feeling that God had withdrawn from the place, and his labors there were at an end. This proved to be true, and he left.

CHAPTER XXIV.

Mr. Redfield was next called to visit Middletown, Conn., the seat of a Methodist university.

Referring to his call to this field of labor, he says: "My heart dreaded the conflict which I knew must follow if I did not lower the standard of gospel truth, unless there were those who would take a stand for God. But I had promised to go, and I made up my mind to meet the worst."

Rev. B. T. Roberts, now General Superintendent of the Free Methodist Church, but who, at the time of Mr. Redfield's labors in Middletown, was a student in the university, describes the state of the work there at that time as follows:

"The state of religion in the church was extremely low. Professing Christians were chiefly distinguished for their conformity to the world. The Methodists had ceased to be persecuted, and were fast becoming a proud and fashionable people. In the university, intellectual rivalry had well nigh supplanted zeal for the cause of God. But a small proportion of the students professed religion, and these exhibited but too little of the power of godliness. Dr. Redfield's preaching created a profound sensation. His deep-toned piety, his fervent, moving appeals to the throne of grace, and his unearthly, overpowering eloquence disarmed criticism, even in that congregation of critics, and prepared the way for the reception of the truths he uttered. Had he lowered the standard to suit the pride and prejudices of his hearers, his popularity would have been unbounded. He insisted upon the Bible standard of entire conformity to the will of God in all things. The church was crowded, and the people seemed amazed. Such exhibitions of truth they had never listened to before. It was for some time doubtful how the scale would turn. Dr. Olin heard of the commotion. He was unwilling to take the representations of any one, but arose from a sick-bed and went and heard for himself. His majestic intellect and deep experience in the things of God could not easily be imposed upon; and a candid hearing satisfied him both of the sincerity and soundness of the preacher. 'This, brethren,' said he, 'is Methodism, and you must stand by it.' His word was law. The faculty, the official members, and the church received and endorsed the truth. Such a work of God as followed we never witnessed. Professors in the college, men of outwardly blameless lives, saw they were not right with God, frankly confessed it, and, laying aside their official dignity, went forward for prayers. The city and adjoining country were moved as by the breath of the Lord. For some eight or ten weeks the altar was crowded with penitents, from fifty to a hundred coming forward at a time. The conversions were generally clear and powerful. Dr. Olin seconded the effort in the university, and went beyond his strength in exhorting the students and praying with them. This great man never seemed so great as in prayer. Then he seemed clothed with the

"'Awful majesty of man
Who talketh often with his God.'

"Nearly all the young men in the college were converted, and of the converts a large number became ministers of the gospel. The fruits of the revival remain, and have been multiplying ever since."

More than three hundred were converted at the church. At the same time the work was going gloriously forward in the college. The tutors who had experienced entire sanctification entered into it heart and soul. At first a band of them met together and united in praying for such students as they thought were leaders of influence and mischief. At these times they would hold on until they thought they had received an answer. The first time they met thus, the young man for whom they were praying went running and rollicking through the halls as though he was possessed by evil spirits. They took this as an indication that the Holy Spirit was striving with him and held on. The next night the young man was converted at the church. They then informed him of their especial season of prayer for him; and asked him to unite with them in the same work for others. They selected another, and he soon was converted. They then divided into two bands and held meetings in separate rooms. A remarkable feature of the work was that the conversions took place in the order in which they selected these subjects of prayer. Their method and success became known, and had such an influence that a student went to one of these praying bands one day and asked, "Have you got my name on your list?" On being told that they had, he said, "Well, I thought you must have, from my feelings; and I may as well give up now." In a few minutes he was converted, and that night in the church told what great things the Lord had done for him.

President Olin took a lively interest in the work, and though in ill-health, he undertook to give a ten-minutes talk to the students in a large recitation room one day, but the minutes swelled into hours; and the speech was afterward published as one of his great intellectual efforts. The result of the revival in the city and at the college, all together, was nearly four hundred conversions. Twenty-six of the college students became ministers of the gospel. Here the sainted William C. Kendall learned the art of soul saving, and went from here to preach the same gospel for a short season with great success. His was a short but a shining track. He too found himself much opposed, for daring to stand for the right.

Such was the success of this meeting, and the glorious stand taken by President Olin and his faculty, that Mr. Redfield began to hope again for the cause of holiness in the Methodist Church. He felt sure that such an endorsement would silence opposers and give that doctrine the right of way through the land.

Mr. Redfield was now invited to a church in New Jersey to spend a Sabbath. He arrived on Saturday night, but did not enter the church until Sunday morning. The pastor was to be in New York over Sunday, and requested Mr. Redfield to fill the pulpit for him both morning and evening. He was careful, also, to request that he would not present the subject of holiness that day. When Mr. Redfield entered the church he thought he understood the reason why the pastor had made such a request. The church was new, and had been ornamented in the highest and most costly manner.

"I felt," says Mr. Redfield, "I must do my duty, no matter what the results. But I felt sure the people would not endure it; and in all probability I would have to find shelter in a tavern over night. I took the money I had from my pocket to assure myself that I had enough to pay my fare. When I saw that I had enough, I was at rest, and resolved the people should hear holiness for once. I went through regardless of consequences, and when the service closed I met some in the aisles who grasped my hand and said: 'Brother, I believe in holiness, and mean to have it.' "

He went to a prominent city in the same state to hold meetings. He preached on his usual theme, and God responded in power. The people often fell from their seats to the floor while he was preaching. But he soon found the preacher very much afraid of holiness.

Here, he again was asked in regard to his family. He told the inquirer that it was a matter he disliked to talk about, but that only made the matter worse. At last he was obliged to ask that he might meet two of the presiding elders, to whom he could tell the whole story. His request was granted, and they coincided with his view of the matter, that silence in regard to it was his best course. But from this on the matter grew worse and worse, until after counsel and advice

13

he put the matter in the hands of a lawyer and obtained a
divorce.   Mr. Redfield had not seen nor heard directly from
her for over five years, but had heard rumors of her death
several times.

CHAPTER XXV.

Mr. Redfield, about this time, met with opposition from the preacher in charge of the society where he held his membership. The issue was made on his license, the preacher taking the position that he should belong to the society where he labored. This was done on the floor of the quarterly conference. Mr. Redfield replied to this that it would be very inconvenient for him to do so, as he staid but from four to five weeks in a place. The preacher was insisting upon it and crowding the quarterly conference to refuse the renewal of his license, when the presiding elder, Dr. Heman Bangs, came to Mr. Redfield's relief by saying: "Brother Redfield is a very useful man, and he must have his standing. somewhere, and if he wishes it he must have it here. Let his license be renewed." It was done, and Mr. Redfield went on his way, but with a sore heart. In speaking of it, he says: "If these men only knew what it costs me in my feelings to go without home, and face the constant apprehension that the misfortune of my family affairs may be taken advantage of by my enemies to destroy my influence, while my friends are more or less perplexed about it until they understand all, it seems to me they would not try to make my way harder than it is."

He could but observe that the men who were engaged in this opposition were not the spiritual men, nor the revivalists, but those who were laboring to make the church take rank in culture, splendor and influence with other churches. They could but see that the preaching and experience of holiness were attended with a renunciation of earthly pomp and glory that was fatal to what they were struggling for. They also saw that where the doctrine and experience of holiness obtained a footing there were marked indications of utter abandonment to what was supposed to be the divine will, and demonstrations of great joy at the consciousness of the divine approval. This was attended by more or less of reproach, and all was fatal to their worldly ambition. It was doubtless true that these men were blinded by their own desires and prejudices; but this was not strange. It has been the case in all ages of the church. Caiaphas was misled in like manner as to what should be done with Jesus.

One marked feature of the holiness revival was that the churches were filled with the poor, who gladly listened to truths from which the proud turned away. Again, the thorough renunciation of worldliness and sin that holiness requires brought such a cloud of reproach upon those who preached and professed it as none but the truly consecrated could endure. This has in all ages saved the church of God from sinking into utter worldliness and degeneracy. Once make Christianity acceptable to depraved human nature, and men will embrace and profess it without regeneration.

Mr. Redfield at this time busied himself during the summer in earning the means by which he could pay his expenses during the revival season. His laboring without fee made it possible for him to get into places where otherwise he could not have gained admission.

About this time he was invited to go to the assistance of Caleb Lippincott, a preacher of the primitive stamp, and one of the most successful in the church. Mr. Redfield now thought, as he had found a preacher who was not afraid of the power of God, they would see a glorious work. But he found that the enemy was still upon his track, and had more than one way to wage war upon him. The Universalists here became the agency to humiliate him. God soon began to pour out his Spirit in a remarkable manner, and many had been added to the church. Among these were some promising young people from among the Hicksite Friends. One night an old lady, whose daughter had just been converted, became so enraged that she broke out in the meeting in denunciations of all about her. In a loud voice and with violent gestures she said, "I don't like this at all. I am mad at you." In the night, at her home, she became so distressed in mind that she sent for some of the religious women to come and pray with her. She surrendered to the Lord and was gloriously saved. Her first utterance after the assurance of salvation came was, "Oh, how I love everybody!" The work went on in great power for some time. The house was crowded with people and the altar with seekers. All at once, Mr. Redfield noticed a falling off of the congregation, which continued until the attendance was so small and the interest so low that he concluded that his work in that place was done. His next appointment was but fourteen miles away, and he procured a conveyance and drove to the place. This was on Tuesday. When he arrived, the minister with whom he expected to labor told him that the meeting was advertised to commence the next Sunday. Mr. Redfield could not bear the thought of four days' idleness, so he returned to the place he had left. During his absence that day the secret of the decline of the meetings came out. A Universalist paper had been circulated in the community in which Mr. Redfield had been published as a notorious villain, connected with John Newell Maffit, the noted evangelist, who was at that time under a cloud of dishonor. Of the matter charged in this paper Mr. Redfield had never heard. It was also charged against him that he was making the revival meetings he held a matter of gain in money and fame. As soon as he had read the article he determined to meet it with a public statement. That evening in the pulpit, before preaching, he made a statement of what had been published, and said to those present, "When the congregation is large enough, I'll tell you something worth two of this." The next night the congregation was greatly increased, to which he made a similar statement; and again, in like manner, the third evening.

On the fourth evening the house was crowded, and a
great many stood outside around the open windows. When
he arose, he said, "I will now tell you my story." He pref-
aced it by reading the newspaper item; and then proceeded
to say, "Of this matter in regard to Mr. Maffit, I can say,
first, I am able to prove that I could by no possibility have
known anything of the matter at all; second, I was never
alone with Mr. Maffit five minutes in my life; and as to
being in league with him to break up the Methodist Episcopal
Church, I never knew until now that he was charged with
any such thing. As to going about in this manner for money
and fame, I can say, I have never in any way negotiated with
any church or persons for one penny for all or any of my
traveling expenses. I will allow, however, that when I left
here last Tuesday morning a brother of this church put in
my hand two dollars and compelled me to take them. Now,
it cost me twenty-one shillings to come here, and this
brother gave me sixteen. So you see I have not made anything here, nor did I ask or expect it. As to my laboring
for fame; these charges are the fame I get. I will sell any
man all of it for three cents. I am aware that the curious
desire to know why I am thus going about, and what is the
impelling motive for it. I will tell you. You yourselves
must know, that I am either a fool, or crazy, or honest. If a
fool, do not be too hard upon me. If crazy, I need your pity.
Now no man in his senses will follow the track I am on
without a motive; and I'll frankly own, though I do not
make a practice of dwelling on these matters, that I am
where I am and doing as I am, because I dare not do otherwise. For this I have been brought to the verge of
the grave, and then let off on the promise that I would go
and preach the gospel. And the last time, the word came to
me, 'You may live as long as you preach but no longer.' I
dare not disobey. Now, if the president of your Temperance society (he was the one who had circulated the paper

with the charges in against me) was to be thus treated, because he tried to win your drunken husbands and sons back to a virtuous life, do you think he would deserve it? While I have been here in your midst every day, when the weather was pleasant I have spent the most of my time out in yonder grove on my knees, and sometimes on my face, before God, pleading with him to spare you and save your husbands, and wives, and sons, and daughters. You yourselves will bear me witness that I have not tried to persuade any one here to lie, steal, swear, fight or get drunk, or to do anything that is wrong. On the contrary I have tried to make everybody better, kind, loving, happy and comfortable, and to help them to get ready for the world to come—and this at my own expense, and in the face of slander and persecution."

Here Mr. Redfield's feelings overcame him and through his tears he concluded by saying, "I do not think I should receive this kind of treatment." The tide of influence turned, and the meetings went on with greater power than ever.

Mr. Redfield says: "This was the only instance where I felt called upon to say a word in self-defense." •

Soon after he was invited to go back to the city of New York to hold meetings in one of the large churches. He says: "We began on Monday. The church immediately commenced to seek the experience of holiness. The first night fourteen were converted; the next night, eighteen; the next, twenty; and so the number increased through the week. Sunday the house was greatly crowded, and especially so in the evening. During the preaching in the evening God was present in great power. When through with my sermon, and I was about to invite seekers to the altar, the preacher stopped me, saying: 'Wait a while; I am going to marry a couple before the prayer meeting.' I said: 'O brother, don't! I am afraid you will divert the attention, and destroy the interest of the meeting.'

" 'I can make it very solemn, and besides I have promised to do it,' he replied.

" 'For the Lord's sake, and souls' sake,' I pleaded, 'don't do it. You will crush out this interest.'

· " 'Well,' said he, 'I shall do it.'

" 'Can't you take the couple into the basement?' I asked. 'Don't break us up here.'

"But in spite of my entreaties he arose and commenced the ceremony by a brief lecture on the nature and solemnity of marriage. In a few minutes I saw our opportunity for getting people saved that night was lost. He finished the ridiculous affair, and we tried to have a prayer meeting, but the Spirit had been grieved, and the effort was a failure. The revival came to an end right there."

Mr. Redfield went from this to another church where some three hundred had professed conversion. He expected to preach but one night. When he was through with his sermon the pastor followed with remarks, and asked if the meetings should close. The congregation voted, No. He then asked: "How many will seek religion if the meetings continue?" About five hundred arose. The meetings went on for some time, and the conference minutes showed afterwards that about five hundred additional ones were taken into the church.

These successes were very assuring to Mr. Redfield of the wisdom of preaching the doctrine of holiness. He was also much encouraged by the promptness and thoroughness with which a minister was dealt with in an eastern conference for publishing a pamphlet opposed to the Wesleyan view of the doctrine. He was required to renounce his pamphlet, and to promise not to preach his peculiar opinion. This minister then took a transfer to another conference.

About the same time Jesse T. Peck, afterwards bishop, published a work on the subject, entitled, "The Central Idea of Christianity." Quite a controversy on this subject had arisen in the church, and the new book was written in defense of the true doctrine. Much of it appeared in one of the church periodicals first. It was finally published in a permanent form, after being enlarged and adapted to popular use. This work discussed every feature of the doctrine that now attracted the public attention, but not in a controversial manner or spirit. To read it now, one would scarcely gather from its pages that the doctrine was ever disputed. The work soon became an authority on the subject, and has been used in the course of study for preachers in at least one of the Methodist bodies of America.

Some strong men were enlisted on both sides of this controversy. In favor of the doctrine as held by the early Methodists were found Nathan Bangs, the first historian of American Methodism; the author of "The Central Idea"; Joseph Hartwell; and, not the least in the tribes of Israel, Phœbe Palmer. On the other side were Hiram Mattison, C. P. Bragdon, and others.

Mr. Redfield now thought the doctrine was safe, and the return of the church to her ancient simplicity and power was assured; but he subsequently wrote, "I had yet to learn that hostility to right never ceases."

He went to spend the winter in Philadelphia. He labored for a while in St. George's Methodist Episcopal church, the oldest church of that denomination in the city. It had been the cradle of Methodism. The pastor had lately been brought into the experience of perfect love, and entered heartily into the methods and labors of Mr. Redfield. God greatly poured out his Spirit, and many were saved. In the midst of this success, the minister who had been required by his conference to renounce his pamphlet and promise not to preach his peculiar views, appeared upon the scene and commenced to oppose the work then in progress. But God had given the doctrine of holiness such favor in the eyes of the people that the work went on in triumph.

Mr. Redfield now visited another church by especial request, but was permitted to preach but once.

He then visited another church. Here he found a state of revival. Some three hundred had already been converted. The pastor said: "We have had a great work. I desire you to preach a few sermons on holiness to help us regain the spirituality we have lost in our efforts for others. I think it will do us good for you to do so."

Mr. Redfield had a favorable opinion of the moral state of the church, and thought it in a good condition to take hold of the doctrine of holiness. But he asked the pastor: "Do you know what you ask? Are you prepared to allow the doctrine of holiness to be pressed upon your people?"

"I don't know what I have to fear," he answered.

"Well, let me tell you," said Mr. Redfield, "my impression is that the introduction of that doctrine will be accompanied with results beyond your conception as to their magnitude. Why, sir, this work has but just begun."

"Well," said he, "I'll risk it."

The doctrine of holiness was made the theme of the meetings. In a few days it became necessary to close and even lock the doors after the church was comfortably filled, in order to work with success. The scenes of power were most remarkable. The saved would shout, jump, fall, so as to block the aisles. Sinners in the midst of this would crowd their way through and sometimes climb over the seats to get to the altar, and when that was filled, they would sometimes fill a row of seats clear across the church. So great became the press of seekers, and the violence of the commotion, that the preacher became alarmed and abruptly closed the meetings.

Mr. Redfield then went to two other churches, but was permitted to preach but once in each, and then took the meetings to private houses. The work of holiness went on in power. The last afternoon meeting, fourteen were sanctified.

He then visited many places in quick succession, stopping but one or two weeks in each. During this time he saw many souls saved, but afterwards thought he had made a mistake in leaving most places so soon.

CHAPTER XXVI.

Mr. Redfield went now to a place on Long Island where a Methodist church had been compelled to contend for a bare existence against the opposition of other churches. One minister was very violent in his opposition. He warned the people against attending the meetings, especially while Mr. Redfield was there. This only aroused their curiosity, and the house was full from the beginning. Among those who came the first night was an infidel school teacher. The next day he said to his scholars: "Tell your parents I have been to the meetings and have heard the new preacher. Tell them I say he is the only honest preacher in the place, and if what he preaches is religion, it is worthy of their fullest confidence. Tell them to come out and hear for themselves."

They did come; God owned the truth, and revivals broke out in different places in the vicinity besides, and many souls were saved. The minister here was a good man and had been very successful; but he was now nearly worn out from excessive labors.

From this place Mr. Redfield went to the former home of Freeborn Garrettson, one of the pioneers of Methodism. Here he found the widow of that soldier for Jesus still living, and in readiness waiting for her summons to the mansions of the blest. Among the tokens of friendship he received here was a set of Benson's Commentaries from Mrs. Garrettson. These had belonged to Mr. Garrettson, and had his autograph upon a blank leaf. Here some fifty or sixty were saved.

Mr. Redfield next went to C——, about fifty miles distant. Here there was a powerful work among sinners, resulting from the church entering into the experience of holiness.

On leaving C——, Mr. Redfield went to labor in the suburbs of New York city again. Here there was not much accomplished, as the church did not readily embrace the experience, nor welcome the doctrine of holiness. It was early

in the fall, and the people did not feel sufficiently released
from business to enter upon a revival campaign; so he abandoned the effort.

While here he was constantly waiting upon God to know
where he should spend the winter. One day there came
before him the peculiar sign that had indicated the will of the
Lord many times before. He got a map of the United States
and found the sign to point in the direction of Cincinnati.
He had before this been invited by Bishop Hamline to visit
that city, and he now resolved to enter every open door that
led in that direction. Soon a brother from Philadelphia
came and invited him to return to that city where he had
spent the previous winter. He resolved to go because it
seemed to lead toward Cincinnati. But that night his track
was laid out for him in a dream. He must begin at Goshen.
The next morning an invitation came from Goshen to help
in a protracted meeting there. He told the minister from
Philadelphia that he would go to Goshen and write to him
from there. His reasons for this decision he kept to himself.

Goshen was a county seat, and had a very bad name. A
Methodist bishop on passing through the place some years
before found that there was no Methodist preaching in the
place, and at the next meeting of the Home Missionary
Society presented the matter. A minister was sent, but
found no place in which to preach. The principal church
building in the place was an old affair, and the membership
of the church led such inconsistent lives that it had very
little influence for good. The place seemed almost given up
to skepticism and drunkenness. A new church was finally
built by the denomination that owned the old one, and the
latter passed into the possession of a gentleman who allowed
the Methodists to occupy it. But it was in such a bad condition that many considered it unsafe. The Methodist preacher
finally raised money to build a church, but when he came to
purchase a lot, the only one he could buy was a frog pond.

Undaunted by this, he had the pond drained, and built his church. The new church was to be the scene of Mr. Redfield's labors. The preacher was a gentleman and a Christian, and stood by the evangelist as he endeavored to preach the straight, plain truth. Some of the poor members were badly frightened, at the thought of losing caste with the established church of the place if they should obtain a higher type of piety than they now enjoyed. The editor of the local paper was a deacon in that church, and he used his paper to bring the meetings into disrepute. The rumsellers became violent in spirit, and accused the evangelist of proving himself a bad man by destroying their business. They complained that they had lost about sixty dollars during the first three weeks of the revival; and if the meetings went on, their families would soon suffer for the necessaries of life.

When the other churches found they could not drive the Methodists out of the town, they tried to build themselves up by proselyting. Some of their members began to come into the meetings and to sing with the young converts, and to make much of them, and at last to lead them before their church officers to be received into church fellowship. When about sixty had been received into the church to which the village editor belonged, his paper changed its tone, and instead of saying anything more about the unhealthy excitement of the Methodist meetings, it spoke of the gracious revival in the ———— church.

The infidels, to cast odium on the meetings, got up a mock prayer meeting. The wife of the ring-leader, at whose house this meeting was held, became frightened and left. Her husband went insane before their meeting closed. He declared he was lost forever, and in a few hours he was dead. The next Sunday this man's funeral sermon was preached in the Methodist church by the pastor. This interposition of Providence put a stop to all opposition to the revival, and the work of God went gloriously forward.

An attempt was made, soon after, to proselyte the more influential of the converts. Mr. Redfield finally announced from the pulpit that he was aware of what was going on, and threatened if he found them trying to proselyte the colored people or the ragged poor he would expose them. One of the converts was a rich old man, who some twenty years before was awakened, and went to a deacon, and asked how to find peace. The deacon asked him what was the prevailing sin of his life, and, on being informed, told the man that he was a reprobate, and there was no mercy for him. The man then concluded that he might as well enjoy himself as best he could. But eight years before the meeting now being described, this man had a dream, in which he was told that he would yet see a man who would tell him how to be saved. This made such an impression upon his mind that the next morning he told his wife and the deacon that he was sure he was not a reprobate. The night of his conversion was the first of his attending the meetings, and when he returned home he said to his wife: "I have seen the man of whom I dreamed eight years ago. He has told me how to be saved, and I have found it. Now I shall join the Methodists."

Another was a wealthy merchant, who had been president of the village corporation and was quite influential. The same old deacon who had told the other man that he was a reprobate could not bear the thought of losing this man; so he came early one morning to talk with him, but found Mr. Redfield present. At this he seemed disturbed, and said, "I hope I do not intrude." When assured by the man of the house that he might feel perfectly free, he inquired: "Well, Mr. B——, how do you feel?"

"I don't have any evidence of my acceptance yet," the reply.

"Evidence!" said the deacon. "You know Deacon R——? He never had any evidence; and everybody thought he was a good man. But all the evidence he ever had of his conversion was, his heart felt as hard as a stone."

"But," said Mr. B——, "if I only knew that God heard my prayers, I should take hope."

"Hear your prayers?" said the deacon. "Why, we have been praying for more than twenty years for a revival, and you see it has just come."

Said Mr. B——, "I am now anxious that Mr. S—— should go with me."

"Oh," said the deacon, "you need not trouble yourself about Mr. S——, for if the Spirit begins with him he will have to come."

Mr. Redfield had felt that the man to whom the deacon was talking needed, especially, to have a thorough experience. He had been seeking earnestly for a number of days, and that night he was at the altar again for prayers, when the following conversation took place:

"Brother," said Mr. Redfield, "what is the reason for your not being converted?"

"I don't know," he answered.

"Do you make a full surrender to God of all you are and have?"

"I do."

"Will you give to God every dollar you own, and let him make a draft upon you to any amount, at any time?"

"I will," was his prompt reply.

"Will you at once begin to pray in your family?"

"Why, would it be right before I am converted?" he asked.

"Certainly. God commands all men to pray."

"I will," said he.

"Further, my brother, will you go out and exhort sinners to come to Jesus?"

"Would that be right before I get religion?"

"Surely; for God says to every one that heareth not only to come, but 'let him say, come.'"

"I will," said he.

The meeting closed without his finding relief. He went alone to his store; the clerks were all gone, and going down upon his knees, he gave himself up to God—person, property, and all. He then went home, and set up his family altar. In the morning, early, he went to the home of the gentleman he had felt such an interest in, and said: "Mr. S——, I have come on a strange errand to you this morning. It is to ask you to go with me and seek religion."

In deep emotion, Mr. S—— replied, "I will. Mr. B——; pray for me."

"I have never tried that yet; but if you will kneel down, I will try."

They knelt, and while Mr. B—— was praying for his friend, God converted his own soul.

The deacon heard that Mr. B—— was converted, and went to see him again. He now insisted upon Mr. B——'s going before the session of his church. When he had him there, he pressed him hard to unite with that church. Said he:

"You will not think of joining the Methodist Church; it will surely injure your standing if you do."

"Oh," said Mr. B——, "I may be too zealous for your church. I must go where I can save my soul alive."

He finally united with the Methodist Church and became a useful class-leader.

The doctrine of holiness was made the prominent theme of this revival meeting, and the young converts were, many of them, a few days after their conversion, in the clear enjoyment of the experience.

One young lady who had been thus saved, was badly burned by the explosion of a fluid lamp she was filling. While her friends were endeavoring to extinguish the flames at the pump, she sang the hymn:

14

"Am I a soldier of the cross?
A follower of the Lamb?
And shall I fear to own his cause,
Or blush to speak his name?"

A physician was called, who pronounced her not in danger
of death. But she declared she was going to die; that her
soul was full of glory, and that she wanted to be with Christ.
On dressing her arms, the flesh fell from the bones. She
lingered for a few days in great pain, but glorious triumph,
and then passed away. Thus was demonstrated the genuineness of this work of grace, and the soundness of the teach-
·ing that was used by the Holy Spirit in bringing it about.

It was estimated that more than four hundred persons
were converted in this revival. This mission appointment
became self-supporting, and an aid in the support of other
missions.

Mr. Redfield next went to a place seven miles from
Goshen, where the Congregationalists had been holding a
meeting until it was broken up by the roughs. He found
the community greatly demoralized, and mostly through the
scheming of a professor of religion, a member of a church
which was jealous both of the Congregationalists and the
Methodists. He and an infidel commenced operations the
first night of Mr. Redfield's meeting. After the service had
closed, Mr. Redfield asked the membership:

"Why do you allow such conduct in your meetings when
the law protects you?"

"They always do so when we commence a protracted
meeting," was the answer. "They have just broken up the
Congregationalist meeting."

"But you must stop it."

"We dare not meddle with it."

"Well, I hope you will not put that burden upon me; but

one thing is certain, if you don't take the matter in hand I shall," said Mr. Redfield.

The next evening the house was greatly crowded, and in the gallery was that professor of religion, and his infidel accomplice. They began their disturbance by throwing missiles at the ladies who were coming in. The congregation was engaged in singing. Mr. Redfield called upon them to stop, and pointing to the infidel, said in a loud voice, "I hope that young man with the white cravat, will be civil enough to cease throwing things at the ladies." The infidel made an insulting reply, and Mr. Redfield said, "Sir, we know our rights. A Methodist church is not a tavern nor a grog-shop, and our rights are respected by the law, as well as those of any other church. Upon my honor as a man, I promise to see that the ladies who attend these meetings shall be protected by law. The legal penalty for disturbing a religious meeting, is a fine of twenty-five dollars, or imprisonment in jail until the fine is paid. I will meet every person who disturbs these meetings at the magistrate's office, and will see that the law is executed. And you may tell your friends that they can come to the Methodist church and be respected."

It was very quiet that night, but the next morning one of the rowdies with some companions was seen standing in front of the church. He began to curse the members and Mr. Redfield, in a loud and very blasphemous manner. Suddenly he fell to the ground. His comrades thought he was dead. They took him to the tavern, removed his clothing, and put him in bed. After a while he came to, and exclaimed, "O God; what have I been doing." He confessed his wrong: his companions were frightened, and all opposition to the meetings ceased. Within ten days from the time the meeting commenced, more than one hundred persons were converted. The church that had inspired such opposition now tried to gather the young converts into their communion, but they were too clear and strong to be easily taken in that manner. After Mr. Redfield was gone, the pastor of that church undertook to have a revival. The first night he announced that they wanted no shouting, nor singing of the songs used by the Methodists, nor any fainting away (as he called the losing of strength). But he invited all who desired to become Christians to rise to their feet. Only one arose, and that one had been seeking at the other meeting. In a few days the meeting came to a close with no further result.

A request now came to Mr. Redfield to return, and make an effort to save the respectable part of the community, as the uncouth rabble had all been converted, and the probability was that the others would now be willing to accept of salvation. He considered that there was but one gospel and one salvation, for the rabble and the genteel, and as they had refused that, he had no other to offer.

His next meeting was in P—— I——, on Long Island. Here he found a state of things similar to that at the last place. He told the preacher he must command order, as God had given them the benefit of the law. But he replied, "The great difficulty is, some of the disturbers are children of our own members." Mr. Redfield then determined to do his duty. The second evening came, and the rowdy element was very boisterous. He tried to quiet them by kind words for a season, but in vain. At last he got their attention, and told them to make one more demonstration if they dared, and he would see the law enforced the next morning. All were hushed immediately. The next night seventeen of the rowdies were at the altar, seeking for salvation.

In this meeting, the afternoons were devoted entirely to the experience of holiness. The second afternoon the wife of a sea captain was forward, seeking for perfect love. In her consecration she came up against the question of giving up her husband. The enemy tempted her to think that if she gave him up the Lord would take him away, and she would never see him alive again. At last she was enabled to make the consecration, and the power of God fell upon her. As soon as she could she arose and testified to being saved. The work now opened with great power, and many were saved.

CHAPTER XXVII.

MR. REDFIELD was next sent for to spend the winter in Boston. But before he started he received a letter from the preacher in Chelsea, near Boston, asking him to spend a few days there before commencing in Boston. He agreed to this, and went immediately to fill the engagement. He found the preacher a courageous, faithful man. His congregation was worshiping in a hall, as their church edifice was not yet completed.

As usual, Mr. Redfield commenced his work by showing the standard of religion to be what Wesley and Fletcher and the fathers of Methodism had declared it to be. God owned the truth. The hall was crowded nightly with a congregation made up from various orthodox churches. He had labored but a few days before he was waited upon by a committee consisting of several laymen and one Methodist preacher. They told him they had come to labor with him, and, if possible, to disabuse his mind of some misapprehensions that he evidently entertained.

He replied, "Brethren, do your whole duty."

Said the preacher, "By your strong and sweeping declarations against all who do not come up to your standard, you reflect upon the Unitarians and Universalists. You evidently don't know them. Besides you offend some of our members whose friends belong to these communions. I regard them as good people, especially the Unitarians; and if there is any choice between them and the Methodists, it is in their favor."

Mr. Redfield could hardly repress his astonishment at such a declaration from a Methodist preacher; and replied, "Your good Unitarians and Universalists have the devil in them."

He was interrupted by one saying, "You ought to know

that such rough deportment will not be accepted in a place as refined as the city of Chelsea."

"Well," said he, "if you know the doctrines of Methodism as you ought to know them, if you are members of the Methodist Church, as you claim to be, I will this night prove to you that what I say is true. As Methodists, you know that our doctrine of holiness is love, and nothing but love. I think matters are ripe for it, and to-night, I design to present the doctrine of perfect love; and if it don't smoke out devils I will give up that I am wrong."

Accordingly, the theme that night was holiness as a state to be attained now. While he was preaching, a young man, of a large and powerful frame, fell like a dead man to the floor. The people were alarmed, supposing he had fallen in a fit. Several went to him and carried him out of the hall. As soon as he could speak, he cried out, "Glory to God! You need not hold me. God has given me the great blessing." He came in again, and walking up the aisle, testified as follows: "While Mr. Redfield was preaching, I said, 'O Lord, I never heard about getting the second blessing. Now if the doctrine is true, let me know it by laying me out on the floor.' Instantly I fell as if I had been shot. Now I know I have got the blessing; and I love God with all my heart."

One of the class leaders immediately arose and said, "If that doctrine has got in here I am done with the Methodist Church. I am a Universalist."

Then another leader arose and said, "I will have no more to do with Methodists for I am a Unitarian."

But the work went on in great power, and when Mr. Redfield's time was out about one hundred had been converted.

He now went to Boston, and presented himself at the parsonage of the church in which he had engaged to labor. The minister was an old man, and had never met Mr. Redfield. When he found he had come he seemed frightened, for he had heard terrible stories of the measures used in Chelsea, reported by the preacher of the committee already alluded to and the infidel Methodists who had left the church.

The good old man, to make it as easy as he could, said, "We have had some meetings, and I don't think the brethren will be willing to open them again." Mr. Redfield saw his embarrassment and dilemma, and as quietly as possible withdrew and returned to Chelsea. But the good man went over and saw for himself, and, when he returned, persuaded his people to let Mr. Redfield come and preach once, that they might know him for themselves.

A goodly number of his congregation were superannuated Methodist preachers, engaged about the book-room in the city. Of course they had heard all the reports that were in circulation, and were afraid of Mr. Redfield. When the time came for the appointment, the meeting was held in what was called the small lecture-room of the church. Mr. Redfield perceived what this meant, but went straight forward about his work. At the close of the meeting several of these old preachers said, "You must stay to-morrow night, and we will open the large lecture-room." Mr. Redfield did so, and took the strongest stand he could for primitive Methodism. God blessed the truth, and in a few days the main audience-room was opened, and in a fortnight forty or fifty were converted.

He had now accepted an invitation to a place about two hundred miles distant. But the preachers of Boston, who saw how they had been deceived by false reports, urged him to remain. The old preachers of the congregation had told them that the objectionable things were the peculiarities of old Methodism, and that those who had left the church of Chelsea were Unitarians in sentiment. About the same time Prof. ——, of the Wesleyan University, came to Boston and bore testimony to Mr. Redfield's soundness as a Methodist. This so broke up the opposition that the ministers of the city endeavored to engage him for a year. Greatly encouraged by this, Mr. Redfield promised, if it was possible, he would return. But the opportunity to do so never came.

He now went to U——, as he had promised. Again the doctrine and experience of holiness was the theme and the apparent means of arousing a great religious interest, and many were converted.

One night he observed a youngerly man sitting in the front seat who appeared to be greatly interested in the work. Others sitting with him manifested the same kindness, though none of them took part in the altar work. After the meeting Mr. Redfield asked one of the brethren, " Who are these persons who seem so pleased when people come forward?"

" Why, don't you know them? They are ——ists, and ——ists, and ——ists."

" Well, what are they doing here?"

"Oh, they are watching those who come forward, to see if there are any that they want. If any of influence come forward, they will soon be after them. They never allow the Methodists to get any one here of importance if they can help it. They say they can do better by the upper class than we can; and that we are well adapted to help the lower classes. They help us financially, for they say we are doing a good work, both in filling up their church and ours. One of our preachers once asked one of theirs, ' If the Methodists should hold all their converts what would be the result?' The answer was, ' Our growth would be comparatively small.'"

Mr. Redfield saw one night that these watchers were greatly elated over something that had occurred. After the meeting closed he asked one of the brethren what it meant.

"Oh," said he, "the man who knelt at the corner of the altar was one of such as they are after."

The next evening Mr. Redfield heard the bell of one of

the churches ring, and he asked, "Are they going to commence revival services?"

"No," was the answer, "they are to have an experience meeting to-night."

"What is that for?"

"Don't you remember a man who knelt at one corner of the altar last night who attracted much attention?"

"Yes; I do."

"Well, they are to open the doors of the church for him to-night."

"But he was not converted last night!"

"That makes no difference in this case."

The man was received, settled down satisfied with what he had done, and having been addicted to strong drink, within a year was in the gutter.

While here Mr. Redfield met a local preacher who was also a school teacher, whose wife had opposed his preaching. But if he did not preach to a congregation at least twice a week, he would preach in his sleep. He would repeat the hymns, call on some one to pray, and then take a text and preach in a regular manner, but so loud that it drew the attention of the neighbors, who would gather about the house to listen. This so humiliated the wife that she gladly yielded to his preaching regularly.

CHAPTER XXVIII.

MR. REDFIELD visited Newburgh just before the camp meeting held near there that year. He endeavored, as usual, to present the truths of real Methodism. Some Episcopalians who had united with the church, entered into the experience of holiness, and shouted in their new-found liberty; while some Methodists who had never belonged to any other church, became angry and opposed the work. The pastor was displeased, but the old presiding elder stood by the doctrine, the experience, and the work.

In its early history Newburgh was completely under the control of infidels, who intimidated Christians and those who desired to be Christians. They were very violent and blasphemous, but nearly all of them died violent deaths, and their passing away left impressions that went far to contract the influence of their lives. Mr. Redfield spent but a few days here, as the camp meeting soon commenced.

At the camp meeting he did not feel much liberty for a day or two. There was evidently an effort on the part of the preachers to get along without him. On Thursday afternoon, one of the preachers, after exhausting his skill in trying to make things go, turned and said: "Brother Redfield, can't you do something?" He answered in a loud voice, "No! but I know of one that can. The Lord Jesus Christ will take the whole matter into his own hands, and no man can stay it, if you begin at the right end by getting holiness." He was permitted to take the meeting, and in his peculiar way he set forth the conditions of full salvation, and called upon all who would meet these conditions to kneel at the mourner's bench. They were in a large prayer-meeting tent. Many immediately knelt, evidently understanding what they were about. But scarcely had they engaged in prayer before the slaying power fell upon them, and sinners, without an invitation rushed forward to find a place to kneel as seekers. The tent was eighty feet long with a row of seats running the whole length through the center. During the remainder of the camp meeting, without cessation, that bench was filled with seekers, and sometimes two and three rows on each side, the men on one side, and the women on the other. As soon as any were converted, they would be taken away to make room for others, and there seemed to be some one waiting to take the vacant place at all times. No one had to exhort, or to persuade penitents to come. God was there in awful power. One remarkable thing was that many, in relating their experiences, testified that they were convicted at their homes two and three miles away, and on coming to the campground, were drawn to this tent. Nothing was said at any time on the subject of dress, yet fashionable ladies, with their bonnets filled with artificial flowers, would struggle and weep and cry, and when all else failed, would put up both hands and tear the flowers out, and in a few moments, smiling through their tears, they would make the woods ring with their shouts of joy.

Such was the crowd of penitents that it was necessary to open another, though a smaller tent, for those seeking holiness; and these two tents became great centres of spiritual power.

The first night after starting the meeting in the second tent, when ten o'clock came, the hour for closing all services according to the rules, the meeting in this tent was going on in greater power than at any time before. The Committee of Order sent one of their number to close the meeting. When he came several remonstrated with him against his action, but he persisted in it. While engaged in his effort, he was suddenly stricken to the ground; and the Spirit seemed to be poured out in greater power still. The increased noise showed the other members of the committee that their

man had not succeeded, and they despatched a more resolute
one to his assistance. He had not more than reached the
tent before he was also smitten to the ground. Again the
shouts of praise and the cries for help from the Lord rose
higher and stronger than before. A third man was then
sent with orders to bring the meeting to a close, at all hazards. When he arrived and saw the other two committee-
men prostrate, he beat a hasty retreat, and informed the re-
maining members of the condition of the first two, and that
if they desired the meeting closed they must do it, for he
would have nothing to do with it. The meeting was no
more interfered with, and ran on until after daylight the next
morning. It was estimated that more than one hundred
were converted in the other tent during the night. When
we consider that this wonderful work commenced immediately after Mr. Redfield took hold of the meeting in the circumstances of the afternoon previous, we cannot but conclude that it was a demonstration of the correctness of his
method.

This incident gives a clue to his wondrous power to break
through to victory on occasions like that; and also illustrates
the close alliance of the two phases of revival work,—sanctification and pardon.

The afternoon following, Mr. Redfield was leading a
meeting for holiness, and while pointing out the details of
perfect submission to the will of God, an old minister present, exclaimed, "You lay too many burdens on the people;"
but when Mr. Redfield came to speak of the final act of
faith, he cried out, "You make it too easy." When Mr.
Redfield finished speaking, the same old minister said to him,
"If I could see this course accompanied with demonstrations
of power, I would think more favorably of it." Just then a
call came for Mr. Redfield to go to another tent where several persons were anxiously seeking, and he invited the old
minister to go with him, saying, "Perhaps the Lord will give

you the demonstration you desire." When they arrived at the tent they found a large number of persons present, all seated, but some of them in deep struggles of soul.

In his own account of this matter, he says, "Among them was a large, strong woman, whom none would call nervous, but who was wringing her hands, swaying back and forth, and audibly praying, 'O Lord, I must have it; I shall die without it. I can't live any longer in this manner.' I perceived that her consecration was complete, but she was making the mistake of trying to obtain the experience by will power. All present seemed to expect me to get down and by vociferous praying to heighten her emotions, and by this tempest to help them all. But instead of that I sat down by her side and endeavored to get her attention. This was quite difficult to do, but I finally succeeded, and then I inquired:

" 'What do you want?'

" 'Oh,' said she, 'I want to be entirely sanctified.'

" 'How much do you want it?'

" 'Oh, I would give all I have.'

" 'Are you sure of that? Are you willing I should turn your heart inside out, and let all your desires be seen just as they are?'

" 'Yes, I am,' she replied.

" 'Well, I can't do that, but I asked it for your own benefit. You now know you are honest. This is the starting point, honesty. Don't let the devil drive you from that point. Now, with that honesty, can you, will you say, The will of the Lord be done?'

" 'I do,' was her prompt reply.

" 'Will you say this, and let God take you at your word in a moment?'

" 'I will,' she answered, very emphatically.

" I then described to her a possible example of suffering, and remarked: 'Remember, God may take you at your word.

Now, in view of anything he may ask, do you yet say, 'Thy will be done?'

"Again she answered, 'Yes.'

"I then described to her an example of duty, of going from house to house in the city of New York, where she lived, and asked: 'Will you do this if God wills it?'

"She answered: 'I will do that when I have the grace to do it with.'

" 'But, sister, is God at fault, that you have not the grace of perfect love up to this time?'

" 'Oh, no! God is not at fault.'

" 'Well, can you, will you, say, blessing or no blessing, if visiting and exhorting from house to house would be my duty if I had the blessing, I will not let my disobedience in the past be an excuse for disobedience in the future; I will go and do that duty?'

" 'Yes, I will,' she replied.

" 'Well, sister, who has required all this of you?'

" Enquiringly she looked up and said, 'Jesus; has he not?'

" 'Oh, yes!' I replied; 'and now I ask, sister, if Jesus has required all this and you have surrendered, do you believe he will *ever* accept of it?'

" 'Most certainly,' said she, 'for he is not trifling with me. He will, won't he?'

" 'Oh, I don't doubt it,' said I. 'But the only question now is, sister, *when* do you think he will accept of what you have just surrendered?'

"She stopped as if a new thought had struck her; her face changed, and the next moment she shrieked out, 'NOW!' and fell to the ground, where she lay and made the woods ring with her hallelujahs.

"But I do not think the old minister was satisfied with this exhibition, for he shortly after was making complaints of some who fell while they were repeating the doxology, though several were converted and a number sanctified.

"The sister who came out so brightly, went home from the camp meeting, lived a faithful life, and died triumphantly a few years after."

CHAPTER XXIX.

IMMEDIATELY after the camp meeting described in the last chapter, Mr. Redfield went to a small village a few miles away to spend the Sabbath. A number of retired business men, residing in the village, had built a commodious church and had presented it to the Methodists. The preacher appointed had staid away from the camp meeting to prepare a controversial sermon on baptism, which Mr. Redfield was destined to hear the following Sunday. Of course the appointment was out for this special sermon, and the door for the evangelist was closed for the morning. The minister was careful to keep it closed in the evening, also. An invitation to conclude the service gave an opportunity for a brief exhortation, in which Mr. Redfield set forth the type of religion that would save. The minister was very restless, but did not interfere. At the close of the service one of the men who had built the church came to the minister and asked who the stranger was who had spoken. The preacher thinking he was about to be reprimanded for allowing Mr. Redfield to speak, began to apologize, and said, "He is a local preacher from New York city."

"Well," said the inquirer, "if that is Methodist doctrine, why do you trifle with us as you have, by giving us bosh? Why not like an honest man tell us the truth?"

The poor preacher for the time was humbled.

Mr. Redfield began to observe many such instances of unfaithfulness, while men of less talent and learning but more zeal and faith, and consequently more efficient, were either kept out of the conferences, or crowded out on to the frontiers. He also found that some of these, both in the ministry and the laity, like the one just described, seemed to conspire against genuine Methodism. He saw that Asbury,

15   (197)

Bramwell, Abbott and Nelson would not be tolerated by such ministers. He saw the lives of these worthies on sale at the book rooms, and sometimes peddled among the membership of the church by these ministers who took pains to hold up to ridicule those who strove to walk the same way. This caused him seasons of great depression of spirits. At these times he would be greatly tempted to give up the battle. Sometimes he would conclude that he had looked on the dark side so much, that he might be deceived as to the real state of things.

Just at this time Sister Phœbe Palmer informed him of a brother in Western New York who felt the same as he did, and was engaged in the same kind of work. He determined to find this brother and by his aid settle the question that troubled him. It was also made known to him that this strange brother desired his attendance at a camp meeting about to be held, and he needed no urging to accept the invitation, and in due time was on his way to the place.

Speaking of his visit to the camp meeting and of his introduction to the man he wished to meet, Mr. Redfield says:

"I was full of conjectures as to the appearance and spirit of the man I was about to meet. I knew some Congregationalists and Presbyterians who were welcoming the doctrine and experience of holiness as it had been taught by the early Methodists; but to see a living Methodist who saw, felt, and labored, as I saw, felt and labored, was to be to me a treat indeed. On reaching the campground, Sister Palmer introduced him to me. He was very cautious, but courteous and hearty in his deportment. The next moment he was gone, I knew not where. I soon heard a voice leading a holiness meeting, to which I drew near and listened for some time, and finally said to myself, 'I am not alone in my peculiar views of holiness.' I drew nearer, where I could see as well as hear, and found the speaker to be the very man whom I had come so far to see.

Referring to this meeting, Mr. Redfield continues: "I went into the stand one day between services, and found my friend in conversation with a pale, sickly-appearing man, who was confessing to him, with deep emotion, that he had wronged him. The sick man said: 'I expect to die; I want to die in peace with all men. I have tried to injure your influence, and now I ask your pardon.' This was readily granted; and soon after I took my friend aside and said to him: 'My brother, that confession is worth something, but I think you should never let it be known; let it die with you.' But how greatly was I shocked to see in the public prints a short time after, a more severe criticism on my friend from this same man than he had ever given before.

"This man included Sister Palmer and myself in these criticisms. I made no attempt to reply to him, and he soon dropped me. But Sister Palmer, or some one for her, returned the fire, and a newspaper war upon the subject of holiness here began, which to my knowledge was a prime cause of awful backsliding. I found places in my labors where confessions were made of this stamp:

" 'So many years ago I enjoyed the blessing of holiness; but when I saw in one of our Methodist papers articles against the doctrine of holiness, I first was shocked, and then began to reason: if ministers, who ought to know more than I do, say the doctrine is untrue, it may be I am mistaken. And giving up the doctrine, I soon lost the experience.' One of these owned up that it brought him to the gutter.

"Some of the preachers who encouraged the sickly man I have described, a few years after were glad to get rid of him."

From this camp meeting Mr. Redfield went to another, and there found that the sickly minister, whose confession he had heard, had so cautioned the presiding elder, who was in charge, against him, that he was not allowed to labor much.

From here he went to Peekskill, where forty or fifty were converted in a few days.

CHAPTER XXX.

From Peekskill Mr. Redfield went, on invitation of the chaplain, to visit the Marine Hospital of New York city. Not knowing his congregation, he committed himself to the guidance of the Holy Spirit. He was led to treat them with all the kindness he could command. The main drift of his preaching was to offer hope, and they would break down and cry like whipped children. Many were clearly converted, and some of them died soon after in the triumphs of the Christian faith. He staid but a short time, and after he was gone, some of them entreated the matron to send for him, "for," they said, "nobody understands us as he does. The ministers who come here think we are a hard set and preach to us of hell; and that don't do us any good, for we are used to that; but when one preaches to us kindly, that breaks us all down."

When Mr. Redfield heard this he made inquiries in regard to these broken-hearted mariners who had come here to die, and found that many of them had served terms in the state's prison; and, when discharged had changed their names and enlisted in the United States service. This made a deep impression upon him, and taught him that these men were not hypocrites; that the terrors of the law do such no good for they are already in a hopeless state of mind. Hope only can reach them.

He went from here to the Sing Sing state's prison by invitation of the chaplain of that institution. Here he followed what he believed were the leadings of the Holy Spirit, and preached to the prisoners in the same manner that he did to the sailors in the hospital. He says: "I could not see that they were different from the mass of mankind. These had been caught, the others had not. I felt drawn to address their better nature; if possible to arouse it to respond to the truth and the call of God. I told them God condemned men when the decision is made to commit sin; while man condemned for the action only. I tried to show them that each had redeeming traits, and that they might, if they would, by the grace of God, rise to a life that would be acceptable in the world to come. That though men might look upon them as degraded and lost, yet they were capable of bearing the image of God. To men they might appear criminal, but with God all men are criminals. What if men do brand you with names of dishonor and disgrace, and chisel those names in the monuments of human remembrance; and what if you die unhonored and are buried in yonder prison graveyard, and no stone to mark the spot? if you will avail yourselves of the means God has provided, your names shall be written in the Lamb's book of life, and angels shall keep watch over your sleeping dust, and in the morning of the resurrection you shall come forth to be honored by the King of kings.

"I did not attempt to apologize for their sin, or to soften the color of their crimes, but tried to refer the question of the difference between them and the rest of mankind to the judgment day, the proper place for the settlement of the question. I told them that it was honoring themselves to say to the Almighty, 'Against thee and thee only have I sinned.'

"The magical effect of kind words addressed to their hopes was wonderful to behold : the dropping tear, the anxious look, with now and then a flash of gratitude, as they gazed upon a poor mortal like themselves, who instead of upbraiding them was endeavoring to induce them to try once more to rise to true manhood, and to aspire to the society of heaven.

"The next day as I passed through the prison, I thought I experienced some of the emotions of the Angel of Mercy. I was allowed to converse with some of the prisoners, and found some of them penitent, and quite a number of them genuinely converted to God. I was astonished to see the depravity and entire alienation from God of some. Some awakened ones desired me to step one side that they might talk freely to me. One among them, who had been sentenced for ten years, who had already served out five, and had given his heart to Christ, now with tears running down his cheeks, confessed that his sentence was just; and that God in mercy had allowed him to come to that place for his own good. He said he had not a relative or a friend to come to him in his disgrace, and yet he was so happy and so contented that he could not bear the thought of leaving the place lest the snares of the world should entrap him again. He said, 'When I go to my cell and sit down on my bunk, Jesus comes and sits with me, and we have such sweet communion that I would rather stay here than lose it.'

"The warden told me that there were some prisoners so violent that they had to be kept with a ball and chain fastened to their ankles. They had once taken a stand in one of the cells, in defiance of the authority of the prison, refusing to obey orders.

"I asked if I might see them. The warden answered, ' I don't know whether it is safe.' I pleaded, ' Just give me permission to go to them.' This was finally granted, and I went in and sat down among them without any manifestation of fear, and trusted myself to them. In the spirit of kindness I conversed with them. They claimed they had been greatly abused. But I appealed to their sense of right and wrong; that it was their duty to do right whether others did or not. My kindness of manner and speech, and my treating them as though they were reasonable beings touched them, and soon they consented to change their course and submit to the discipline of the prison.

"I found one man, a foreigner, who from not understanding our laws, had committed an offense in an effort to show kindness to one apparently in distress, and had received a sentence of five years at hard labor. The warden was greatly interested in his case, and was desirous that some one should make an effort to obtain a pardon for him. I undertook it with the assistance of another gentleman. It was necessary to get at all the facts in his case so as to lay them before the governor of the state. In order to have access to the man for this purpose, I was obliged to hire him of the state; and to meet the expenses, it was necessary to furnish him with employment. The only employment at hand that the man was fitted for required a second man, and one more skilled than he. The second man was a genius in his way. He was serving out his fifth sentence. He was very ambitious to excel, and loved to be appreciated, and withal very affable and agreeable. But he seemed to have a passion for stealing. The first man told me I must be on my guard or he would pick my pockets. He also told me that the man kept an old bag in a by-place in which he hid bits of coal and bits of cloth clipped from prison garments brought to him to be mended. In regard to the first of the two men, the effort to obtain a pardon succeeded, and he went forth a free man.

"While engaged in the effort to procure this pardon, I saw several instances of the fidelity of woman's love in the face of disgrace brought upon the family. Wives came to visit their husbands who were prisoners, but though there were several married women in the prison, there was not a single instance of a husband coming to visit his wife during all the time I was there."

During his stay at Sing Sing he held a series of meetings in the town. As usual, the doctrine and experience of holiness was made a prominent feature. There was much opposition, but victory was won for God and his truth, and many were saved.

CHAPTER XXXI.

ABOUT this time the preacher from Bridgeport, Connecticut, came to Mr. Redfield and invited him to assist him in revival services at that place. He said:

"We must have a revival or lose our church. Our people have been robbed for years of the fruit of their labors by the proselyting system of other churches; and they at last came to the conclusion to build a church which would overtop all others, and thus gain a position in the community which would command respect. But now we must lose it, for we are owing twelve thousand dollars, and we cannot raise that amount. "You must come and help us."

Mr. Redfield replied, "I am sorry your people have been trying to win a name by worldly policy. I dread to meet the spirit which such a state of things is sure to foster. My experience has taught me that such a state of things is against the faithful preaching of the doctrine and experience of holiness."

The preacher acknowledged the mistake of the people, but said, "We have it, and can't afford to throw it away. What can we do? Must we give it up and let Methodism be driven out of the place? Or shall we try to save it?"

Mr. Redfield finally said, "I will go;' but it was with a heavy heart. He knew God would hold him responsible for the faithful presentation of the truth and thorough dealing with men. He was almost certain that he would meet with great opposition. Referring to the state of things at this place, he says:

"When I arrived I saw a stately edifice, eclipsing all others in exterior splendor. Two great towers, one bearing a bell and the other a clock, reared their massive proportions in front; the whole of antique architecture and 'loud' appearance. My heart ached in view of the prospect. I thought, 'This course will destroy the last vestige of real

Methodism, unless God come to the rescue.' I could see none among the ministry who dared to risk their chances of preferment by attempting to stem the tide. But somebody must fearlessly take sides with God, and he will possibly be crushed for his pains. I thought I comprehended the situation; I realized my own weakness; but I resolved in the name of God and pure religion to do my duty. When I had done so, I felt a strengthening of my soul, and the sweet assurance that God approved of the vow."

In his preaching, from the commencement, he endeavored to arraign the conscience before God. At the close of the first service the pastor, on the way home, asked if a less objectionable class of truths could not be used. Mr. Redfield replied: "Do you think Jesus would mutilate the truth, and tacitly give men to think that he had preached the whole? and this when he had not touched the real evil of the case?"

"Well," said he, "I am afraid your course will ruin us."

"Brother," said Mr. Redfield, "what time does the next train leave here?"

"Why, you must not leave?"

"O my brother," said Mr. Redfield, "I certainly shall leave if I cannot go the Bible track. I will allow you to call me to account at any time when you find me outside the Bible and the Methodist discipline, but I must be free to preach the whole truth."

"Well," said he, "you must stay, and we must have a revival or lose our church."

"I feel no interest in your saving your church in the present condition of things. It would be no calamity to religion to lose it, unless it can better represent Methodism than it does at present."

Said the preacher, "You must stay; and do be as easy with us as you can."

Mr. Redfield replied, "I'll be as easy as God will let me,

but no more so; and I wonder that any one can ask me to lower the standard of the only religion that can save!"

Mr. Redfield went on with his work in the name of God and truth. In one of the afternoon meetings Fay H. Purdy, who was assisting him, fell to the floor while Mr. Redfield was praying. This was something new to the congregation, and unexpected to the minister.* The husband of one of the members, a man who paid well, but was without salvation, arose, apparently in great anger, and left the house. At this the preacher became alarmed. After a little, one sister arose and began to confess to dancing, playing cards, novel reading, and conformity to the world. The preacher became very uneasy, and finally arose and cautioned the people against looking on the dark side, and referred them to the old prophet who complained that he only was left to serve God; and how God corrected him with the assurance that there were seven thousand in the land who had not bowed the knee to Baal.

Mr. Redfield saw the tendency of this was bad, and arising, said: "That is all true in the case of the old prophet; but I insist that if these members have been dancing, card-playing, novel-reading, and behaving in general as the followers of the meek and lowly Jesus ought not, it is due to him and the truth and the world that they confess their sins as publicly as they have committed them. It is only thus they can restore themselves to the confidence of the world as the representatives of the religion of Jesus. The cause of Jesus has been slandered by their conduct; and is in disrepute because of it. Common honesty demands that the wrong should be charged where it belongs. If Jesus has not disgraced his own cause, do not compel him to bear the odium that now rests upon it. If they have done this thing, it is the honorable way for them to say to the world that neither Jesus nor his gospel is at fault."

The Lord soon began to manifest himself in great power

---

*Rev. Clement Combos, who was present.

in the conviction, conversion, and sanctification of souls. When victory began to seem certain, the other churches began to accuse Mr. Redfield of bigotry, because he had not invited them to participate in the meetings. His experience in other places enabled him to perceive the motive that underlay this, and that was their desire to gather the converts into their own churches. He also saw that it would not do arbitrarily to rule them out, and that it would be for the good of all concerned if they, like the Methodists, should become as thoroughly reformed. He then gave them an invitation to unite in the work, but at the same time insisted that they should humble themselves before the Lord, and that as many of them as had been addicted to dancing, and card playing, etc., should make the same confessions the Methodists had. He told them they would have to do this if they ever regained the confidence of the community, and were in a condition to assist in the work. This had a salutary effect. It removed the objection which had been made, and put the responsibility of their non-affiliation where it belonged.

One of the ministers still stood out upon the technical objection that he had not been invited in writing. But his motive was so apparent that his attitude was no hinderance to the work. He was the one above all others who had despised the Methodists, and yet had labored the hardest to gather their converts into his church.

The skeptical portion of the community now put forth an effort to check the work by disturbing the services, and the strong arm of the law had to be invoked to stop their proceedings. The same persons then attempted to accomplish their purpose by petty annoyances beneath the notice of the law. To meet this, one Sunday evening at the opening of the service, Mr. Redfield told the Christians present not to fear the opposition, for victory was as certain as that God was the author of the gospel. God might allow these annoyances and persecutions for a while, but if they were likely seriously to hinder the work, he would take life if necessary to stop them. He then related a number of instances of this character which had come under his own observation. The next day, at dinner, in a house opposite the church, a daughter of the family residing there, amused the company by relating what Mr. Redfield said, and characterized it as an attempt to frighten the people, and said, "I would like to know who will be the first to be knocked down in this place for ridiculing religion. Let us try it!" She then began clapping her hands, and shouting, "Glory, glory, glory," and instantly fell to the floor in great agony. Word went out that she was dead, and was smitten down while ridiculing religion. An eye-witness of the scene related it in a large boarding house, where were a number who had been engaged in a similar manner, and who were now greatly shocked at what they heard. All opposition of this kind now ceased and the revival went forward with increased power. In a few weeks over five hundred were converted.

The young girl who was so suddenly stricken down lay four or five days in that condition, and then was restored, but with a permanently impaired mind.

As Mr. Redfield was about to go to another place, the minister in B——— said, "Before you go you must take the converts into the church." It was arranged for this to be done the following Sunday. At the close of the sermon in the morning, Mr. Redfield requested all who desired to unite with the church, to come forward and be seated in the front pews. A large number came, when he addressed them as follows:

"It is your duty to unite with some church. You need to be under its watch-care. I do not ask you to join the Methodists, nor do we want you unless you are in every essential point a Methodist. I do not know as one here desires to join the Methodists, but if there should be, I will tell you what we shall expect of you. We desire no one to come among us who will engage in proselyting from other churches. We shall expect you to live up to our rules. (Here he read the General Rules of the Discipline, commenting on them as he passed along.) You perceive from these, there can be on your part no more dancing, nor card-playing, nor novel-reading, nor pleasure parties, nor wearing of jewelry, nor worldly conformity. This may seem hard to you, but there are other churches that are not so strict as this, where you will be welcome. You will only be a curse to us by your example and influence if you do not conform to our rules. Some of you know how faithfully we have had to deal with some here during these meetings, who have lived contrary to these rules. And I would say, if there are any still among us who are not in sympathy with our rules, and have not determined to obey them, you had better do so immediately, or take your letters and go where things are more to your mind." (Here the preacher became very uneasy, and Mr. Redfield expected to be called to order, but he was allowed to proceed.)

"I have now told you only what you cannot do and be a Methodist. I will now tell you what you must do to be a Methodist. We shall expect of you a faithful attendance upon all the means of grace; class and prayer meetings, the preaching services, and family religion. We shall expect you to be active in seeking the conversion of sinners, by personal labor for them and with them. You will be expected to make religion the first business of your lives. All worldly matters are to be considered but the small chores of life. If you cannot make this pledge to us, that you will conform to these rules, you had better go where it will not be required of you. If you go elsewhere to have the privilege of a life of inactivity in the cause of Christ, and of doing as you please in loving the world and conforming to it, you will come, by and by, to death, how soon none can tell; it may be a year; a month; a week; and you will open your eyes to see that .

you have exerted an influence, which is still in operation, that turns immortal souls out of the way to heaven, and into the way to ruin. Now pass on to the judgment and see how it will appear there. Behold the souls over which your influence preponderated, like the grain of sand which turns the scale, and fixed their destiny forever among the lost. On the other hand, if you choose to join where all these things are required of you, which you perceive are in harmony with the word of God, your influence will be felt, and will tell on the side of salvation. If your probation in this life should be long or short, in death you may pillow your head on the bosom of Jesus, and leave behind you an influence in the Christian activity of those whom you helped to decide aright, that shall work on through the ages while you are sleeping in the dust; and in the great day of God there shall stand among the redeemed the blessed fruit of your decision, to rejoice with you forever."

Both the church and the preacher, if Mr. Redfield rightly interpreted the indications, were in great fear as to the results of this address. But when he asked those who wished to do so, to give their names to the church, more than one hundred responded; and in a few days some four hundred more did the same. And what was peculiar, not a single one united with any other denomination. Soon after this, the debt that hung over their church property was paid, and a second church had to be built to accommodate the congregation. This demonstrated that faithful work makes good Methodists.

About this time Mr. Redfield met with the following anecdote which gave him much encouragement:

"When Elijah Hedding, who afterwards became bishop, was stationed in or near Boston, a servant girl of the celebrated Hancock family, was a member of his church. One Sunday she took home from the church library a volume of Wesley's sermons. Soon after the lady of the house picked it up and after reading in it for some time, called the girl and asked where the book came from. The girl informed her, and added, 'Our minister preaches just like that every Sunday.' The lady inquired his name, his street and number, and then ordered her carriage and drove to his house. Mr. Hedding himself answered the bell, and she asked, 'Is this the house of Rev. Mr. Hedding?'

" 'That is my name,' he replied, and invited her in. When they were seated, she said,

" 'I have come to talk with you about joining your church.'

"Mr. Hedding looked at her in surprise,—at her attire, at her carriage before the door, and concluded there must be some mistake in the matter. He asked: 'To what circumstance am I indebted for this call?'

"She then related to him the incident of the volume of sermons, and the remark of the servant girl, and then added: 'Those so fully accord with my views of what a Christian life should be that I hasten to identify myself with the people who hold to those views.'

" 'But, madam,' said Mr. Hedding, 'do you know our discipline, and can you conform to our rules?'

"He then opened the book and read them to her, and repeated the question.

"She replied promptly: 'I can, and will.'

"Still desirous of dealing faithfully with her, and to get rid of her if she was not willing to be a Methodist indeed, he said: 'Madam, you are a stranger to me, but as we are to have a love-feast next Sunday morning, you had better come to that; and in the meantime I will consult with my official brethren, and, if there is no objection, I will receive you on probation.'

"She came to the love-feast, was received into the church, and became a worthy Methodist."

CHAPTER XXXII.

Towards the close of the meetings at Bridgeport, several Methodists from New Haven visited the services, and were desirous that Mr. Redfield should come to their place. But little did they know of the conflict which preceded the victory they had witnessed. Soon an invitation came for him to spend a season there. As usual with Mr. Redfield, he underwent a season of great spiritual suffering before he gave his answer. The first question for him to settle was, always: "Is it God's will?" Then came his natural shrinking from the conflict that awaited him. He had heard enough of the state of the church in that place to know that the struggle would be a hard one. Past experience had taught him that his spiritual conflicts would be great, and attended with great suffering. He knew, too, if the opposition prevailed, the attempt would work against him in the future. The tide of worldliness had now set in so strongly, and had become so general, that wherever he went the battle must first be fought out in the church. And it was no light matter to attempt to bring a dead church into that spiritual state where it would be a successful working power for God and souls. He had learned that the tendency of worldly policy in the church was to benumb the conscience and blind the perceptions of the membership and ministry to the spiritual truths touching consecration and holy living, and that it would take a greater degree of divine power to awaken them than to awaken the ungodly. He had also learned that the carnal reasonings and fears of a worldly church and ministry were more serious obstacles to scriptural awakening than the combined opposition of all forces outside the church. It was because of this that he suffered so in spirit. Yet he reasoned: "Somebody must do the work. Whoever enters upon it, must lay every interest upon the altar of God—reputation, the good opinions of friends, all outlook for the future; and with a single eye to the truth and the glory of God, stand for the exact right, and take whatever comes as best he can. It may as well be me as any one. If I go down in the conflict, my calamity may draw the attention of some honest and daring one who, following God fully, may finally triumph."

Reader, would you call this cowardice? True bravery does not shut its eyes to the dangers that surround it, and then go forward blindly. He is the bravest man who is most conscious of the danger and still goes forward. Some natures less finely strung than Mr. Redfield's would have gone forward easily and readily, but their work would have been more crudely and less thoroughly done.

After a full consideration of the matter, Mr. Redfield consented to go, and informed the messenger who had come for his final answer, that he would be in New Haven the next Thursday night.

New Haven was the seat of Yale College. The influence of this institution was hostile to Methodism, and had been from the beginning. It was a city of many churches, and these likewise all hostile to Methodism. At this particular time there was no manifestation of opposition, for Methodism had ceased to be a power in the city. The membership had cowered before the lofty claims to superiority of these churches, and had contentedly settled down in a subordinate position and almost ceased to have an independent life.

The time came for Mr. Redfield to take the cars, but it was with the feeling of a soldier going into battle, and not that of one who has gained the victory. He went with the determination to do his full duty if he was not allowed to hold more than one service. When he arrived he found a number of brethren waiting at the depot for him with a carriage to take him to his boarding place. He felt grateful for this, yet he saw that it would make the cross heavier to do his duty to them when the time came for it. He found that a great effort had been made to advertise the meetings, and

16

by the manner in which this had been done, much curiosity had been excited to see and hear him.

When he entered the church he found a large congregation present. At the proper time the pastor arose and said: "Brother Redfield has finally come, and will preach to-night, to-morrow and next-day night," and then sat down. Mr. Redfield arose, and addressed them somewhat as follows:

"It may be so, and it may not. You may not desire me to stay after to-night. But, by the help of God, I mean so to preach that if I am called to the judgment within five minutes after I am through, I shall be ready. And it makes no difference to me whether I stay one day or six weeks, I shall certainly preach the straight judgment truth of God,— the same truth we must die by, and be judged by,—if it takes the last brick from the foundations of this church."

With his usual unction and power, he endeavored to define the type of religion which was necessary to enable a soul to enter the kingdom of God.

The mass of the membership was frightened, and with it the pastor. But one good old man, who knew what primitive Methodism was, came and took him by the hand, and bade him Godspeed.

One of the leaders came and said: "You have altogether mistaken this people. That kind of preaching will not take in this place. You have tacitly reflected upon the other denominations in this city, and we believe they are pious people."

An ex-mayor of the city somewhat relieved the feelings of the pastor by saying to him: "That is the kind of preaching we need in this city. We have not a minister here who dares to risk his reputation to preach like that. That is the reason why the churches have been so inefficient for the last twenty-five years. Here, give him that, as a token of my approval," and handed him a twenty-dollar gold piece.

Before the pastor got away from the church a lawyer met him, and said: "That is the kind of truth we want here."

Soon after, several more of the influential men gave their sanction to the truths Mr. Redfield presented, which greatly allayed the minister's fears.

In a few days the rabble began to serenade Mr. Redfield with doggerel songs, to send him ball tickets through the post-office, to hoot and shout after him in the street, to hold mock prayer-meetings and to mimic his voice and manner. The careful were greatly distressed at this, and came to him with the matter, but he rejoiced, as he saw in it the evidence that Satan was being disturbed. He told them, "The devil will soon exhaust his resources, and we'll see many of these made happy in God."

For seven or eight weeks he preached wholly to the church. At last he was waited upon by several members of the official board, who told him that his course would ruin the church, if not soon changed. They also informed him that they knew of more than fifty persons who were waiting for an opportunity to present themselves as seekers, and they were afraid this perpetual labor for the church would soon become stale and offensive to them. One of them said, "There are many of us, and I am one of them, who will never get out clear until we get to laboring for sinners."

Mr. Redfield replied: "I know of many who desire to become Christians, but I tell them we are not ready for them yet. Now, brother, the trouble with you is, you desire to get on the wrong side of the altar. You can't warm up by the exercise and call that a revival."

"But what will become of sinners if we spend all our time praying for ourselves?" he asked.

Mr. Redfield replied by asking, "What will your prayers be worth for them if they do yourself no good? It would be better to ask the penitents to pray for the church."

He saw, however, that nothing but a failure would convince them, and the next evening he gave an invitation for penitents to come to the altar. Before they were through singing the first verse of an invitation hymn, the altar was filled. He then invited the brethren forward to pray for them. A large number of them came. The first brother who prayed asked for the blessing of God on the missionary and the Bible cause, and almost everything else but the seekers at the altar. Others followed in like manner.

Mr. Redfield then arose, and said: "It is time to close, but if any of these penitents have been blessed, let them confess it to the people." He tried to encourage them to do so, but it was in vain. He then said to the congregation: "I will never again while I am here ask penitents to come to the altar for the benefit of such dead, meaningless and formal prayers. We will keep to work at ourselves until we get so we can pray."

The next night the very ones who had been so anxious to warm up by praying for others, began in good earnest to pray for themselves. One or two received such a view of their own hearts and lives that they appeared to be in despair. He now appointed two meetings to be held about an hour before preaching, in two of the class-rooms, for the benefit of those who desired to seek perfect love.

In a few days God gave a few witnesses to the experience. The number of witnesses then began to increase faster and faster, until soon their aggregate power moved the entire city. Frequently there were more than one hundred at the altar at one time seeking for pardon. Other churches now availed themselves of the opportunity, and reaped great benefit from the general awakening. In one of these churches it was reported there were received above four hundred persons. The revival got into Yale College, and many of the students were converted. All hostility in other denominations, for the time being ceased, except the proselyting to gain members.

A good deacon came to Mr. Redfield, and told him that one minister was preaching to his congregation that it made no difference how people lived, or conformed to the world in dress and manners, if only the heart was kept right. Mr. Redfield felt it his duty to say publicly in regard to this, that God's requirements were unbending; that his word commanded them to "love not the world," and to "be not conformed to the world." He warned the congregation against ministers who taught the contrary. He urged that all men must settle these questions with God alone, and the Bible was to be their guide. As a result of his faithful dealing, one woman laid aside several hundred dollars worth of jewelry, and went from house to house confessing the wrong of her fashionable life. She then tried to undo the bad influence of her worldly life upon her own family, and in two weeks had the pleasure of seeing each member of it converted to God.

Another woman saw her husband, who was considered a model Christian, in such agony over his own state, that his cries aroused the whole block in which he lived. She then cried out, "If my husband sees himself in such a light, O Lord, where am I?" She sought the Lord now in the most earnest manner, and when she found him, so great was the blessing of God that she could not rise from her bed, and remained thus for more than one week. When Christian people came to see her, with her face all radiant with the glory of God, and with great power she declared, that she saw the church did not believe the Bible.

Such experiences had a powerful influence in the community, and in a few weeks from the time that the work broke out more than fifteen hundred had been gathered into the kingdom of God. The Methodist church in which this meeting was held, was so filled with members that more than thirty families were unable to find seats, and another church had to be built in another part of the city. Yet strange to say, the pastor afterward became an opposer of Mr. Redfield and spoke disparagingly of this revival.

CHAPTER XXXIII

WHILE the work was moving in great power in New Haven, a deputation from Stamford waited upon Mr. Redfield and invited him to that city. He accepted the invitation, and, immediately after closing his work at New Haven, repaired to that place. On being introduced to the pastor, the following conversation took place:

"How many inhabitants have you here?"

"About eighteen thousand."

"How many churches?"

"Eight or ten. Our own people have three, but one is closed."

"What is the prevailing tone of religion?"

"Unitarianism."

"How long since the Methodists had anything like a revival?"

"About thirty years. But we have become quite respectable. The time was when we could not get a spot in the place on which to build a church, and we had to build some miles outside the town. A great change has come over Doctor O———, who so bitterly opposed us then, and now he says we ought to have the same privileges the other churches have. Now we have this fine edifice in an eligible part of the city."

Mr. Redfield said nothing, but he feared that this respectability had been gained by abandoning real Methodism.

In due time he proceeded to the church for the first service. The message was to the church; the theme—the New Testament standard of religion, and the unlawfulness of all others. The meeting closed, and he returned with the pastor to the parsonage. As soon as they were seated, Mr. Redfield was asked:

"Is that the course you design to pursue?"

"Yes, sir."

"I do not think it will do here. I think I can give you some valuable advice if you are willing to receive it."

"Very good; good advice is always acceptable. Tell me just what you think."

"Well, I think our conference preachers have done admirably here for many years. Brother ———, who was here years ago was a perfect gentleman, and the people all loved him. Brother ———, who followed him, took the same course; and so all of them down to the present time. These men won their way into the affections of the people, and have gained for us the position we occupy now."

"Then you think that is the course for me to pursue?"

"I do."

"Will you tell me what time the next train leaves?"

"You do not think of leaving, do you? We have sent for you to hold these meetings, and we want a revival."

"Brother," said Mr. Redfield, "God has made me a rough man, and given me a rough gospel for rough hearts. I shall leave; for if you think a little more of the same stuff which you have had is necessary, and which you acknowledge has been a failure for thirty years, you have all the tools necessary, and have no need of me. I will go where the people will allow me to use God's only tools for saving men."

After some moments of silence, he replied: "Well, my time is nearly out, as this is near the close of my last year; and I will allow you to go on."

Two days after, in an afternoon meeting, an old man, a member of the church, arose and said: "I went home from meeting last night, and went to bed, but I could not sleep. I thought I was sick, and would die before morning, and I dared not sleep. I arose and knelt down and tried to pray. I struggled the remainder of the night, but about the break of day God spoke peace to my soul." And then raising his voice very loud he cried: "My brethren, this is the same kind we used to have thirty years ago." Then arose a sister, who said: "Brethren, when I heard what a great revival was in progress in New Haven, where Brother Redfield was laboring, I thought, 'If he will only come here, what a good time we would have.' But when he came, and began to preach, I said: 'O Lord, I can't have it come this way.' I thought he would put it on to the sinners, but when he preached so sharp to us, I thought 'I never can endure it.' But last night, when I went home I could not go to bed, so I sat up all night and prayed God to have mercy on my soul. And early this morning he came in power to me. Oh, this is the same kind we used to have years ago!" and she fell, as though dead, to the floor.

Another and another arose, and gave in substantially the same testimony. Dr. O——, who had come to the meeting, evidently out of curiosity, by this time had become quite angry, and now arose and left the house. As he passed out he said to one: "Such things ought not to be tolerated; and Mr. Redfield ought to be shut up at once."

The meetings went on in great power for several weeks, and many were saved.

CHAPTER XXXIV.

AFTER his labors in Stamford, Mr. Redfield visited the camp meeting at ———, and there saw such an illustration of the power of divine grace to save as he had never witnessed before. It was the case of a man who had become so abandoned that several times he had been a candidate for the penitentiary. To all appearance, his mind was but a wreck. He was a fish peddler, but when he could find any one who would gamble with him, he would leave his fish to decay in his cart. So wretched and vile had he become that some thought it was useless to pray for him. Some months after this, Mr. Redfield saw him again, and the change in him seemed like that in the demoniac of Gadara, when Jesus had cast out the evil spirit. His body was still a ruin; his mind, stupid; his person, filthy; and his whole external appearance, very repulsive; yet when he spoke of his experience there was such a charm in his artless testimony as gave a most vivid illustration of the power of grace to overcome the devil.

At this same camp meeting he met with an Indian preacher whose religious experience was very marked. In relating it he said:

"I was powerfully awakened. I sought to get help from the white man. I heard of a camp meeting and thought, 'I'll get help there;' I went to the place, but seemed to get no help. I was uneasy and wandered from place to place about the grounds. I went from tent to tent, looked into them, and seeing nothing to help me, turned away. I was most wretched. Finally the meeting closed; the last tent was struck; the last wagon driven from the ground, and I was yet unsaved. Night came on. I walked into a little ravine, the bed of which was dry, and laid down on the grass, determined never to rise until I found peace. During the night it began to rain, and after awhile the water began to run down the ravine. It came up around my sides, and then ran over me. I raised my head so I would not drown. At last, when it seemed as though I would drown if I staid there longer, God blessed me, and I crawled out of the water and went on my way."

While at this meeting he also became acquainted with another Indian, the son of a chief, who told of the great concern he felt for his people, and how God had used him in bringing his relatives to God. He related the following story:

" I procured a Testament printed in the Chippewa language. Having found Jesus myself, I wanted to see my red brother enjoying the same. I asked him to go out into the woods with me. We took our seats on a log. I then read to him about the death of Jesus. I read on and on, when at last he laid his hand on me and said, 'Just stop there.' I stopped, and he started to leave me. I knew from his looks what he meant, and neither spoke nor followed him, but remained sitting on the log. He went over a little knoll and began to pray in good earnest. He continued to cry for mercy until the sun was going down, when suddenly he bounded to his feet like a deer. God had saved him. He now started for his father's wigwam, and going in, knelt down and began to pray. Soon his mother came and knelt by his side, and then a sister, and then another; and finally his father came and knelt down. By the morning all were converted. His father was so happy over his new religion, and so anxious to spread it, that he started for the store of the white man who sold fire-water (whisky) to the tribe. When he got there, he said to the white man:

" 'We have lived together here for a long time. We have been good friends, and never had a quarrel.'

" 'That is true,' said the white man.

" 'Now, I want you to do me one good thing as a friend. You know I never asked you for anything before.'

" ' Well, I'll grant you the favor if I can; what is it?' asked the white man.

" Then said the Indian, ' Don't sell any more fire-water to the Indians. You know many of them have come here and bought the fire-water, and some of them when drunk have tried to cross the river and have been drowned; and some of them have fallen in the snow and have frozen to death. And our people have been made wretched by drinking the fire-water.'

"The white man made the promise, and the old Indian returned home to pray for him. The next morning he went near enough to see that the store was closed, and then went back to pray for the white man more; and to let him have time to think it over. The next morning he went again to see, and found the store still closed. The third morning he found the store was still closed; but he went now to see how the white man got along. He found him in despair. He tried to comfort him, but he said: 'No! no! it is true; I've been the means of the deaths of those who were drowned, and of those who were frozen, and there can be no mercy for me.'

"The old Indian tried to think of something that would give the poor man hope, and finally said: 'There must be hope for you, for the Lord had mercy on me. If he can save an Indian, he can save a white man.'

"The poor man laid hold on this, and was saved. He then went among the Indians and became a successful missionary among them."

At another camp meeting during this season, Mr. Redfield met a converted Jew in whom he became greatly interested. He was a son of a rabbi. He told Mr. Redfield the following story of his father's death, as an illustration of how Christ comes to some of his people in the dying hour. When his father was drawing near to death, and while uttering the usual cry of his people at such times, "he called for me," said the son, "and said to me, 'O my son, I have tried to live in good conscience all my life. I have tried honestly to serve the God of my fathers; but now in my great extremity I do not feel prepared to die. I have done everything I can think of to prepare me to meet God, except to have a sacrifice offered for me. But that is impossible; we have no temple and no high priest.' Some of our Jewish friends came as usual at such times, and exhorted him, as a last act of fidelity to God, to curse Christ, and thus deny all fellowship with idolatry. But he broke out saying: 'God forbid that I should deny my only hope of salvation.'

"This," said the young man, "is of frequent occurrence among the more devoted Jews."

This incident afforded Mr. Redfield much comfort, for the thought of missionary work among the Jews, and how to do it, had been much upon his mind.

During the summer, while visiting in Stamford, as he passed a house one day a lady called him in to see her husband who was in despair over the doctrine of election. He had, in childhood, been taught the Calvanistic faith, and although he had been a Methodist for years, he could not shake off entirely that teaching.

Mr. Redfield asked him, "How long have you been in this state of mind?"

"For twenty years," he replied. His wife said he would sometimes shut himself up in a room and pray and groan for hours together without any relief.

Mr. Redfield said to him, "Tell me as near as you can all about it."

"Oh," said he, "I am afraid that I am a reprobate; that Christ never died for me. Sometimes I feel my heart a little softened, so I can weep a little; and then I take comfort and hope that I am not lost. But the hardness returns, and then I am in distress again."

"Well," said Mr. Redfield, "I am not going to use any

arguments against that false doctrine; but I want you in your heart to say, *I believe Jesus died for me.*"

"Oh," said he, "I would not dare to do so wicked a thing, for if he did not die for me, I should then be believing a lie."

"Never mind that," said Mr. Redfield, "for if Christ did not die for you, according to this miserable doctrine, you are lost any way, and to believe one more lie cannot make your case a great deal worse; you had better risk it."

The old man repeated aloud, in measured tones, "I believe—that Jesus—died for ME. Oh, glory to God! I've got it! I've got it! I've got it."

Here Mr. Redfield saw demonstrated that one act of faith would do what twenty years of praying had failed to do.

In another place, that season, he attended a holiness meeting held in a private house, where a room overhead was occupied by a gentleman boarder, whose strange conduct is recorded below. God graciously manifested himself in the meeting and several were sanctified, and a number more converted. In the midst of it, the man overhead began to rave like a madman. He came down into the hall, and began to howl and bark and growl like a dog, and that so rapidly and violently that it sounded as though a number of dogs were fighting there. He then burst in the door, and when he saw Mr. Redfield, his eyes flashed, and he moved towards him as if to do him harm, and yet harmed him not. At last he left the room. The next day the man of the house asked him why he could disturb a religious meeting like that.

"Sir," said he, "I do not with to do such things, but I cannot help it. I know that I am forever lost; I have known this for years. Ever since the time when I was forsaken of God, I cannot endure the sound of prayer or of religious song. It completely unmans me."

CHAPTER XXXV.

As winter approached Mr. Redfield was invited to return to Stamford to one of the forsaken churches in that place. The condition of Methodism in the vicinity may be seen from the following facts. Three miles away was a church which had not been occupied for three years; one and a-half miles away was one to be closed the following spring; two miles in another direction was one that had been unoccupied for many years.

The pastor who had invited Mr. Redfield was a devoted man, but poorly adapted to resurrect a dead church. Under the strong truths preached by Mr. Redfield a general awakening was coming on, when other Methodist societies in the vicinity opposed to the resuscitation of this one, forced the meetings to close. The African Methodists then opened their doors, and the revival went to them. Here God wrought mightily, and some of the most wealthy and influential people of the city came to the altar and were saved ; some of them that the deadness which had reigned in the churches had well nigh made infidels. Among themselves they started a subscription to build a new church, and desired Mr. Redfield to become their pastor. He consulted his presiding elder, who advised against it, and the matter was dropped.

He was now having all the calls he could fill; and to have accepted that proposition would have turned him aside from his peculiar mission. He had many friends among the more spiritual of the ministry, who would have called in question the propriety of such a step; and the step once taken, might have involved him in circumstances such as would have rendered it impossible to retrace it.

Before leaving Stamford, he went with the pastor to hold one more service in the old church that had been closed so long. During the service he observed a young man in the congregation who seemed deeply interested and who closely watched everything that was said and done. When the invitation was given for seekers of sanctification, he came forward boldly. He was a Methodist preacher, and after the service closed he invited Mr. Redfield to go to his charge five miles away to labor with him for a season. He said the church was not inclined to receive him when he was appointed the spring previous; but after pleading with them for some time, they yielded, and let him stay. He now desired Mr. Redfield to go with him to assist in a revival meeting.

The following conversation then passed between them:

" Now will you go?" said the young preacher.

" Do you believe in the doctrine of sanctification as held by the Methodists?" inquired Mr. Redfield.

" I do," was the ready answer.

" Do you enjoy it ?" asked Mr. Redfield.

" I do not, ' the preacher answered.

" Will you seek it with all your heart until you find it?" further inquired Mr. Redfield.

" I will," was the immediate reply.

" But let me tell you what may be the consequences of your taking this stand," said Mr. Redfield. " If you obtain this experience and preach it, you will have a living, active church, and sinners will be converted in great numbers. They will be converted so they will know it in power. Then perhaps when conference comes, some one else will be appointed to the charge. And the membership and converts may injudiciously speak in great love of yourself as their former pastor; and if the new preacher has not the grace to endure it, he may become jealous, and will speak lightly of you to the other preachers; and by impressing the conference that you are an unsafe man, and poorly calculated to keep up the dignity of Methodism, as a result you may find yourself crowded out of the best paying appointments, and on to frontier work. Now, if you thus lose caste and standing among the preachers, and have to go on alone, unappreciated, will you seek for this experience, and preach it to your people? Can you afford to wait for the great day of judgment to adjust all these matters?"

With great emphasis, the young preacher replied, "I will accept the conditions."

"Very good," said Mr. Redfield, "I will go to your place: and further, if ever you get into a hard spot, because you take the honorable course for God, just let me know, and I will come to your help."

Mr. Redfield went to the aid of this young preacher, and found the utmost freedom "to go the straight way for God and the exact right." At the close of the first sermon, the young minister took his stand as he had promised. He said:

"It may seem strange to my congregation that I have never preached this doctrine to you. But as an honest man I could not preach to you what I did not enjoy as an experience. When I joined the conference, I told the bishop and the preachers that I believed in this doctrine, and would seek it. And now I ask you to forgive me for not having done it before; and I also ask you to come forward and pray for me."

He then knelt at the altar, and the members of his church around him. The power of God fell upon them in a wonderful manner. The work of God began with unusual power, and soon the entire community was deeply moved. Skeptics, who had not entered a church for twenty years, were convicted, until unable to leave their homes.

The place of worship stood on a corner where five streets came together, and was the scene of glorious things. Sometimes the saved, as they returned to their homes, made the night air ring with their shouts.

This young minister, soon after, thought it best to take a transfer to a Western conference. We will not consider his case further at present, but shall hear from him again.

Mr. Redfield was now called to go to the aid of a con-ference preacher who had made himself offensive by his plainness. He had been appointed to a village that could boast of a tavern, two churches, one blacksmith shop, and four or five painted houses. But the people rebelled at the "imposition," as they called it, of having a preacher appointed to them, who was so far behind the times as to be opposed to worldly amusements. Mr. Redfield staid but a few days, as he could not discern that he would have any especial help from God in the work.

A short time after he went to a camp meeting in Central New York. There he found strong opposition to the doc-trine of holiness among the preachers. This was very pain-ful to him, and aroused his fears for the future of the doctrine and the church. One preacher, in a sermon, opposed the doctrine as taught by the early Methodists. In the midst of his argument against it, one of the preachers in the stand quoted two or three passages from the Bible that upheld the doctrine, but was told by the presiding elder to "stop"; yet, this elder had no rebuke for the man who was antagonizing Wesley, Clarke, Watson, and other standard authors in the church. This sermon threw the people into great confusion, and many of them left the congregation, thinking to strike their tents and go home. Mr. Redfield and others went to them and endeavored to dissuade them from this, while the elder, seeing the disaster the sermon was bringing upon the meeting, required the minister to stop. Rev. Hiram Mattison, who at this time was the leader of this opposition to the doc-trine of holiness, was present, and attempted to allay the excitement by speaking somewhat as follows:

"The doctrine of sanctification is true and good. There are various opinions in regard to some of the details of it. I can best express mine by using an illustration: On an orange tree you will find blossoms and green fruit and ripe fruit. My experience is similar to that. When I was converted I was

17

partially sanctified. When I joined the church I was a little more sanctified. When I took a license to preach I was still a little more sanctified. And so you see we are more and more sanctified as we pass along; and the way to become sanctified is to progress in the divine life."

He said much more, but this was the substance of it all. This made the matter no better with the dissatisfied brethren. Brother Purdy was present, and in his inimitable manner tried his hand upon the storm. He prepared a place for a prayer meeting in an unoccupied part of the ground and called the people together. He then said: "I think it will be well to take the testimony of the people upon this question. Now, how many of this company know, by a heart-felt experience, that entire sanctification is distinct from justification and regeneration, and that it is received instantaneously by faith? Arise and stand upon your feet." About three hundred arose. "Now," said he, "let all those who know they have experienced it, but received it gradually, and not instantaneously, arise." Not one arose.

This was thought by the opposition to be a very unfair proceeding; and yet they saw nothing wrong in staying in the church and openly opposing one of its fundamental doctrines.

The following are some of Mr. Redfield's reflections in regard to the matter:

" I could but think, when a preacher, in a place like this, will be allowed to attack one of the fundamental doctrines of the church, and receive encouragement from the presiding elder, we are in a very bad state. Methodism must come to an end, or another people be raised up to carry on the work. But I shall probably be numbered with the dead when that day arrives. God helping, I will do all I can to save what spirituality remains, to check the waning of its power, and to keep it as efficient as possible while I live."

These circumstances led him to see the necessity of a greater degree of spiritual power than he had ever known, that he might be more efficient in the Master's service.

CHAPTER XXXVI.

At the close of the camp meeting mentioned in the last chapter, Mr. Redfield went to Syracuse, N. Y., in company with a Brother Hicks and wife. While tarrying there for a few days, he attended a prayer meeting with them at the church where they belonged. On leaving the church there came to him his old sign which had always tokened to him a great outpouring of the Spirit. He said to Brother Hicks, "I tell you God is going to visit this city in awful and glorious power."

"Yes," said Brother Hicks, "I believe it. A goodly number of us have been praying for it, and we feel that he has answered our prayers; and now we are looking for it."

These friends were desirous that Mr. Redfield should come and lead a revival meeting, but were fearful that their pastor would be unwilling, as he had not manifested any sympathy with the doctrine of holiness. Mr. Redfield had never before received this peculiar token of a revival except when he was to be an active laborer in it; and as yet there was no indication that he would be connected with this. So without waiting further he started for his home in New York city. But before a great while he received a letter from a preacher stationed at Salina, now a suburb of Syracuse, requesting his services. He accepted the call as a possible step towards Syracuse.

On his way while traveling up the Hudson river on a night boat, he began to have a wonderful manifestation. The especial impression was of the presence of the heavenly host; and its effect was to comfort, cheer and strengthen him. This lasted all through the journey. He seemed rapt in a contemplation of God, and the work of God, such as no words could express.

As he approached Syracuse, there came to him again the

same token of the coming revival. He reached the city, and went to the house of Brother Hicks. Here he took courage again, for this man could appreciate the strongest type of salvation. His house was like the temple of God, where the altar fires were constantly burning. It was a sanctuary for the oppressed and the persecuted. For years one could not enter it often without finding there some one who had made it a refuge. Seasons of prayer there often lasted all night, and sometimes complaints of this were made to the magistrates.

Brother Hicks took Mr. Redfield to the home of the minister he was to assist; and on crossing the bridge that lies between the two towns, the old token appeared again, but this time, it stood over the place to which he was going. When he reached the minister's house, he found him in very poor health. The state of religion was such, that because of a small amount of indebtedness on the church property it was about to be sold. The society had about concluded to dismiss their preacher, because of the lack of funds to pay him. There could be no possible objections to Mr. Redfield's labors in such a place. For some time he had found that ministers were perfectly willing that he should work in such places, and that with the greatest freedom, for he could not possibly make things any worse.

He also found that this place had been overrun with mesmerism, spiritism, and finally unionism; that is, the discarding of all denominational distinctions. The next step was to Unitarianism.

. There was a fear upon the part of good people that if a revival should take on the old-fashioned type that characterized early Methodism, it would be called spiritism, or mesmerism, or something else besides real religion. His reply to them was, "I believe that the old gospel has as much power to day as it ever had, and that God will come to our rescue; and if men try to imitate the work, as in the days of

Moses, the rod of Jehovah will swallow up their rods, and they will be obliged to confess the true God."

The revival-had not been in progress long before a good woman from another town felt constrained to come to see Mr. Redfield. She came to the house where he was stopping, was introduced, and when about to shake hands, she gave two piercing screams, so sudden as to startle him. He had never heard anything like them before, and knew not what to make of them. He thought it best to wait until he had an opportunity to investigate them before he allowed himself to be disturbed with them. When meeting time came he started for the church, and this woman with some friends followed. Occasionally he would hear her give the same two peculiar screams as they came along the walk. When he had reached the pulpit and turned about, he saw her coming in at the door, holding her hands over her mouth. She came up near the pulpit, and as she turned to enter a pew she gave the same two screams again, so loud as to shock all in the house, and then clapped her hands over her face and appeared greatly mortified; but, evidently, could not control her voice.

In a subsequent conversation with her upon the subject, she told him the history of this strange phenomenon. She said, " Once while conversing with an honorable gentleman, a member of the Methodist Church, he complimented me upon the quiet and unostentatious character of my piety. I replied, 'It is a source of gratification to me that I am not as demonstrative as some.' Instantly a power seized me that I could not resist, and I uttered those two screams. Since then I have found it in vain to resist when that power is upon me."

As soon as Mr. Redfield could get the attention of the congregation, he began the service. But often during the evening she gave those two peculiar screams. The curiosity of the people was aroused to know what it could mean; yet when the invitation was given for seekers of holiness, the altar was crowded with them. The prayer meeting began, and in a few minutes a seeker at the altar screamed in like manner; and then another, and another. Finally, one woman's scream was entirely different from the rest. It sounded as you would imagine a woman would scream if a knife was suddenly and unexpectedly thrust through her heart. A sister of hers came, took hold of her, and shook her, commanding her to stop; but it was all in vain. Some six or eight were exercised in that manner during the altar service.

In the midst of this, Mr. Purdy, who was assisting in the meeting, asked,

"Don't you think you had better check it?"

"I do not yet. If God makes the duty plain, I will; but not till then."

"Well, what do you make of it?"

"I don't know. But I shall not wonder if God is preparing to meet and overcome the magicians in this town. You perceive no one can possibly make such a sound of themselves. Besides, there is no fear of hypocrites attempting it, for it is too humiliating."

The service closed, and Mr. Redfield returned to his boarding place.

The sister of the lady of the house was stopping there also, and she was one of those who had been so strangely exercised. Mr. Redfield now thought he would have a good opportunity to study the phenomena. This woman was about thirty years of age, and married. She, as well as all the rest of those so exercised, was of good repute and good standing in society. Before retiring for the night the entire company knelt in prayer. She commenced those screams again, and continued them for about five minutes with a rapidity that he believed no one could imitate. After rising from prayer, all retired for the night. In the morning Mr. Redfield had an opportunity to talk with her in regard to the exercises of the evening before. She appeared very solemn when she came into the room, and immediately, in a subdued tone of voice, and in humbleness of manner, asked him:

"Can you tell me what this means? When I went to bed last night it all stopped, but commenced again when I arose this morning. You know what a spell I had at family prayer last night. Well, I thought I saw my dead sister who passed away triumphantly a few years ago. I also seemed to see my father's house, and my mother very sick; and that they want me to come home."

Her sister, the lady of the house, then came into the room, and asked, "What do you make of this?"

He replied: "I cannot tell; and yet my opinion is, that it is something God has sent, or permitted, to put cavilers to silence."

"Do you think it would be right for me to pray the Lord to stop it?" she asked.

"I do not, sister. My impression is, that you should not court it, nor fight it. Let it alone; seek only to be right with God, and if it is allowed to come, then there is an object it will serve. Let it come, or go, upon you."

"Oh, I would not have it come upon me for ten thousand worlds."

With a scream, her sister replied, "It will come upon you."

At that she began to tremble, and sat down. She was holding a wash bowl and pitcher in her hands, and so violently was she shaken that Mr. Redfield feared they would be broken, and he took them from her. At this, with a shriek louder than any he had yet heard, she was thrown upon the floor, and then, as if seized by a giant power, she was lifted up and taken into another room. This was attended with those screams, or rather those movements attended the screams, for the screams came first. After a little she was able to converse.

"Well, what do you think now?" asked Mr. Redfield.

"Oh," said she, "I would not have them taken from me for ten thousand worlds."

"Are you in pain when you scream?"

"I was at first, but soon it was the joy that filled me. It was beyond anything I ever dreamed could be this side of heaven."

"Is it because you feel such joy that you put forth an effort to scream; that is, is the scream the result of your effort?"

"Oh, no! I put forth no effort at all. But a power seems to take hold of me, and I am compelled to scream. I cannot resist it."

Of all the other cases which he examined, and there were a large number of them, some of screaming, some of jumping, and others of a kind of dancing, in every case they testified the same; that is, it was produced by an unseen power, unexplainable by them, that took hold of them, and over which they had no control. In one case, the woman prayed that it might leave, and it did leave; but she was instantly in an agony of despair, and found no rest until she prayed for its return. Another had a similar experience.

In the case of the first one he examined, who seemed to have the vision of her father's house and the sickness of her mother, in a few hours after her statement to Mr. Redfield, she received a letter by mail, in which the foregoing was corroborated.

Whatever the reader may think of these incidents, if candid, he must admit the wisdom of Mr. Redfield's advice: "They are not to be courted, or fought." Since that day there has been much of such demonstrations. Some of the best of Christians, persons of clear understanding, and of pure lives, have had them. It is also true, that many of inconsistent, and in some cases of impure lives, have had them.

Usually where there has been, extreme encouragement of them, it has resulted in mischief. The same may be said where there has been determined opposition to them. Those who have neither courted nor fought them have got along with them the best. It has been demonstrated,—beyond all doubt, in the minds of the observing,—that they are not infallible marks of piety. Another thing is also true,—as yet mankind knows but little of mental science, and probably many of the strange phenomena of mental operation are yet to be explained.

CHAPTER XXXVII.

WHEN Mr. Redfield began his work at Salina, as usual he tried the best he was able to set forth the standard of holiness in view of having "something to work up to," as he expressed it. He pressed the people to seek this experience. Many came forward for that purpose, but were unsuccessful in seeking it. He then made the discovery, after careful examination, that the mass of them were backslidden from God. So he publicly confessed his mistake in preaching holiness to them, when they needed justification. He then attempted to impress the truths related to that phase of religious experience. But again they were brought to a stand. More thorough searching, and humbling themselves before God, and it was discovered that the mass of the people in the religious confusion that had reigned, had fallen below even morality. So he confessed his mistake again, and began preaching to them the first principles of the kingdom of God.

He now began to have some of his own peculiar experiences again, that had often attended his most successful efforts. He began to be "burdened" for the work. He had often had these struggles, and sometimes with a severity that threw him upon his bed as if with a fit of sickness, and held him there until victory came. One night in the church he was filled with unspeakable agony for souls. If he could have howled like the old prophets, it would have relieved him; but this he could not do. He thought he could not endure it. He attempted to go out of the church, but was checked by the Holy Spirit. He then said, "Lord, I'll try to hold on." He then began to cry out, "O my God, this people must be saved." At this he was instantly relieved. The whole church was now in commotion. Screams for mercy mingled with shouts of rejoicing were heard on every side. At this time commenced the strange demonstrations described in the preceding chapter.

When the revival was fully under motion, and these demonstrations were becoming common, then the curious began to come to witness the strange sights. One night several came near the altar and asked permission to observe them closely. It was given them, and soon they began to make remarks as follows:

"It is nothing but hysterics."

"Do you understand physiology?" asked Mr. Redfield.

"Yes, well enough to know this is nothing but hysterics."

"Are people usually happy when they have hysterics?" They did not answer.

Another said: "It's nothing but psychology."

Another said: "It's spiritualism."

Another said: "It is easy enough to produce it all."

Mr. Redfield was afterwards told that some of these men held meetings in which they tried to imitate these phenomena, but failed. They then declared it to be supernatural. Many of these men were soon after converted to God.

The experience of a Unitarian woman well illustrates the thoroughness of Mr. Redfield's methods. She was of high standing in the community because of her wealth and benevolence. In years past she had been an active member of an orthodox church, and none had been more deeply engaged in revival work than she. Of late she had pretended not to believe in anything of that kind. God now got hold of her by his truth. When she came forward some of the more worldly of the Methodists seemed much elated. The expression on their faces seemed to say, "Now, she will give our church character, and we'll be thought something of." Mr. Redfield thought he detected this, and resolved that she should go through it if it was possible. He knelt near her and asked her loud enough for all to hear it, "Madam, what is your wish in coming to the altar?"

"I want religion."

"Then pray right out loud for salvation."

"Oh," said she, "I cannot pray for myself."

"Well, then, I cannot pray for you."

"Why, I have said I would go to hell before I'd ever pray in such a place as this."

Raising his voice, he repeated her words, and then said, "Madam, you will either take that back, or you *will* go to hell. You need not think of succeeding in your rebellion against God."

"Do you think there is any mercy for me?" she inquired.

"I don't know," he replied, "your case is a hard one, and it may be you have already passed beyond the limits of mercy; but I would try to pray."

"Well, I'll try."

"But will you pray in your family?"

"Oh," said she, "I have said I'd sooner be damned than pray before my husband."

"Well," said he, "you'll take that back, or be lost forever."

"Well, I will," she replied.

"But you have exerted an influence against God and Christ among the Unitarians; now will you go to them and confess this, and cut your acquaintance with them, and tell them why you do it?"

This was a hard task, but after being shown that her course had been one of hostility to God and the right, and if she desired to make clean work, she must now do this, at last, she said,

"I will do it."

"One thing more. Will you exhort them to seek Jesus, and then pray with them before you leave them?"

Some may think this was carrying the matter too far, and

she felt it was a hard thing for her to do.   But Mr. Redfield thought it a wicked thing for a woman in high position to use her influence against Jesus of Nazareth, so he insisted upon her making the thing right with God and man.

"Well, I will," said she, at last.

She then turned and asked one to pray for her, of whom she had said, "I never want him to pray for me." The moment she made this request she fell helpless to the floor. She was truly saved, and did her duty faithfully, and God was with her in power.

One of the Unitarian ministers came to him one day for a talk.   After a formal introduction, he said:

"I am happy to make your acquaintance. I have attended some of your meetings, and I desire to say to you, that I extend to you the right hand of fellowship.   But I think you might adopt one suggestion I will make, and that to your advantage."

"What is that, sir?" inquired Mr. Redfield.

"Let us win our way to the hearts of sinners by showing Christian love among ourselves.   Just let them see how our religion unites us all together, and this will recommend the benign religion of our Saviour."

"But how far would you have me go with this?" asked Mr. Redfield.

"All who even take the name of Christian, are entitled to our charity and brotherly love."

"But suppose a man tells me there is no more virtue in the blood of Jesus than in the blood of a hog?" (This had been preached in this man's pulpit, unrebuked.)

"Well, it will do no good to hold a man off and deny him your charity for opinion's sake."

"Further," said Mr. Redfield, "suppose he tells me he does not believe in God, nor heaven, nor hell, nor Christ, nor a future state?"

"Well, it is a free country, and any one has a right to

believe what he pleases; and we can do no good to a man by prescribing what he shall believe as a condition to his receiving our charity."

At this Mr. Redfield said: "Let us pray," and kneeling down, prayed for his visitor as a poor, deluded man.

At the afternoon service this man was present. After a time he arose and said:

"I desire to say here, to this church, that I feel a great interest in these meetings. They meet with my hearty approval."

When he sat down, Mr. Redfield arose, and said: "I want this congregation to understand that, as a church, we have no fellowship with infidels or atheists. And I know this man to be such from conversation with him to-day. God calls upon us and angels, to worship Christ,— to worship Jesus."

Instantly the power of God seemed to fill the whole house.

These services continued a short time longer. The church edifice was saved, the debt paid off, the minister received back for another year, and well provided for; there was a large addition to the membership, a good parsonage built, a second church built near by to accommodate the congregation, and that all paid for, and the whole within a few months, as the fruit of this revival meeting.

CHAPTER XXXVIII.

MR. REDFIELD now went back to the city of Syracuse to see if he could find an opportunity to labor there. He. went to the house of Brother Hicks, and sent for the preacher in charge. When he arrived, Mr. Redfield immediately stated his reasons for sending for him.

He said: "For the first time in my experience, I ask for an opportunity to come here and hold a revival meeting. I am a Methodist; and I have had a wonderful experience with regard to this matter; and I am sure God has designs of great mercy for this city; and from my feelings, I think he designs that I shall be identified with it. Now, I desire to know if you will allow me to hold a meeting in your church?"

"Oh," said he, "if God designs you to hold a meeting in this place he will open the way for you."

"But will you allow me to hold a meeting in your church?"

"It will cost too much for expenses."

"I have anticipated that objection, and I have brought money enough with me to pay expenses for a few months; and I will labor free of charge if you will allow me to come into your church and hold a meeting."

"Well, you cannot be allowed to come into my church."

"Then, brother, you will not feel afflicted if a way should open in some other denomination for me to labor here."

"Of course not," he replied, with an expression on his face that indicated his doubts of that ever coming to pass.

The next mail brought to Mr. Redfield a request to come to Palmyra, the home of his friend, Fay H. Purdy, to hold a meeting. In response to this, he took the cars for that place. As he drew near, his old sign of coming victory made its appearance again. He had no knowledge of the place, not even its exact location. When he arrived at the station where he was to leave the cars, he found himself about nine miles away, and that the public conveyance was a stage. While waiting, a gentleman approached him with the question: "Will a ride in a private conveyance, at the same price, be agreeable?"

"Yes, sir; and much preferable," Mr. Redfield replied.

As soon as he was seated, and on the way, the following conversation took place:

"Do you live in Palmyra?" asked Mr. Redfield.

"Yes, sir."

"Do you know a man by the name of Purdy?"

"Yes, sir."

"What of him? I hear a great many things about him. What is he?"

"Oh, the man is in bad repute among the people where he is best known."

"He is a Methodist, and labors in revival meetings, I believe?" remarked Mr. Redfield.

"Yes; but the people here have no confidence in him."

"He is, probably, a man who swears?" said Mr. Redfield, enquiringly.

"Oh, no; I don't think anybody would accuse him of that."

"Well, he probably lies?" Mr. Redfield continued.

"Oh, no; not that either."

"Well, he must be a great cheat,—a dishonest man?" said Mr. Redfield, in the same inquiring tone.

"Oh, no."

"Well, what is it?" he then asked.

"I will tell you," said the man. "I am a Methodist, but it is the world's people who find fault with him."

"Well, what is it they have against him?"

"The world says, 'If he is so zealous for religion, why doesn't he stay at home where his work is needed?"

"You have a new preacher since conference, I believe?"

"Yes, sir."

"Well, how do you like him?"

"Oh, not at all."

"What is the matter with him?"

"Why, he is too old, and he does not keep himself tidy. He is no honor to Methodism."

Said Mr. Redfield, sternly, "I know what the trouble is with you; you are all backslidden from God. I am going to the house of Brother Purdy."

When he arrived and had a proper opportunity, he asked Brother Purdy, "What is the matter with your new preacher?"

"Well, I will tell you. He is a good man, but our church is backslidden and formal, and they think he is not up with the times. We have not had a revival in sixteen years. In spirituality the Congregationalists have far outstripped us. They have revivals, but we do not. Our church has been mortgaged, and the mortgage foreclosed, and it is to be sold in a short time. Spiritual worship has been turned out of doors, and an organ has been put into the gallery to make up the deficiency, and to pander to the tastes of the world. The preacher was not received, and the elder has been denounced as a 'pope,' because he will not remove him. The dandy preacher who was here before him, wore his gold spectacles, and carried a gold-headed cane, and acted the fop, and now the contrast is too great for them to abide. They have not paid the new preacher a cent, and say they will not. So I have given him a shelter, and am supplying his wants."

Mr. Redfield now understood the state of affairs, and looked to God for direction and help.

He was now taken to the house that was to be his home during his stay. He had scarcely got to the room assigned him, when a Brother B——was brought in and introduced to him. Mr. Redfield found him to be a good man, who lived some seven miles away, and had come to spend the Sabbath in the meetings.

18

The next morning Mr. Redfield arose early, and went down the stairs. Soon he heard Brother B—— groaning loudly in the room adjoining, and a glance through the window revealed a large number of people standing on the walk who had been attracted by the noise. Mr. Redfield asked the family, "What does this all mean?"

"Oh," said one, "it is Brother B—— at his devotions."

"What kind of a man and Christian is he?"

"Oh, he is one of the very best of men. Everybody knows Brother B—— to be an excellent Christian."

The preacher in charge was to preach that morning, and Mr. Redfield did not go to the church until time for the sermon. As he entered the church he heard quite a commotion in the basement; and on reaching the pulpit, the old minister said: "We have been having awful times down stairs this morning!"

"What is the matter?" asked Mr. Redfield.

"Oh, Brother B—— fell to the floor, and made so much fuss that he scared the people till they ran out of the house. My wife is very angry about it. Hark! hear Brother B——!"

And there came up from the basement a cry of anguish, and the words: "O God! I shall die if this church is not saved!"

Said the preacher: "I think I had better go and lock him in a class-room."

"Brother," said Mr. Redfield, "let him alone. The spirit that would interfere with him, would drag Christ from the Garden of Gethsemane."

"But I am afraid he will come up stairs!"

"Well, let him come."

"But he makes such an awful noise!"

"Well, you need an awful noise. If you get salvation enough, you'll get where you will be able to hear a hallelujah without fainting away."

"There he comes," said the preacher.

"Well, let him come."

And sure enough he did come, and crying out in great agony as he came. As he reached the altar he fell to the floor, and Mr. Purdy cried out, "Amen!" at the top of his voice. One of the old members who sat near by asked in an angry voice, "What did you say amen for?"

"Because I'm glad to see God get one more chance to breathe in this church."

"Well," said the preacher, "I will go and put him into a pew."

He did so, but soon Brother B—— rolled off onto the floor, and made more noise than ever.

The old minister tried to preach, but the struggles and cries of Brother B—— made it almost impossible for him to do so. When the sermon was ended, Mr. Redfield took occasion to endorse Brother B——; and seeing the preacher was in great distress of mind over it, he thought it best to go home with him. When they arrived at the house they found one of the lady members almost in hysterics over the matter. The preacher tried to soothe her, but Mr. Redfield said to him, "Don't smooth over the matter; she is fighting against God." After a little she began to confess that she was not right. The preacher now declared his intention to send Brother B—— home the next day.

"Well, said Mr. Redfield, "then I'll go, too."

"Oh, you must not go. We must have a revival or lose our church."

"I don't care about your church. It would be no calamity to lose it," replied Mr. Redfield. "They have managed to keep God out for sixteen years, and it is now ruled by the spirit of the world. The members are on the road to hell, and will get there if they don't repent."

"But they will not pay me a cent of my claim, and want to drive me off; and I am dependent on Brother Purdy for shelter and for the necessaries of life; and the church is to be sold in a few weeks."

"Let it go; it's a curse in its present condition."

"Well, don't leave us, and I'll let him stay."

"But, brother, there is another item I want in the conditions, and that is, if you believe that brother to be a good man, you must give him the right hand of fellowship. If you do not, you'll have two parties in your church over this very matter. The people saw this morning that you were greatly tried with the good brother, and unless you settle the matter at once you will have sympathizers with you. Now, by prompt action on your part you can stop all that."

"Well," said he, "don't leave, and I'll do it."

"Very well; do it to-night when I am through preaching."

When the time came he stood up in the altar and confessed to the congregation, and to Brother B——, how he had been tried, and turning to Brother B——, said, "Brother B——, I give you the right hand of fellowship, come into the altar;" and instantly he dropped to the floor. As soon as he could command himself, he said, "If I had given way to my feelings I should have made a great deal more noise than Brother B—— did this morning. I have not had such a blessing in twenty-three years."

Now began the war. One infidel, a merchant, who paid ten dollars a year for a seat in the church, and did the same thing for a seat in another church, in great wrath arose and left the church. His wife pulled out the cushion and started after him; both declaring they would never have anything more to do with the Methodist Church. But this only created the more stir, and curiosity brought the people out from near and from far. The house became so crowded that it was necessary to have services both in the basement and in the upper room at the same time. One night there were thirty conversions, and more than five hundred were converted in a few weeks. The preacher was taken into favor and provided for, the liabilities against the property paid; and Methodism took hold anew in that community.

CHAPTER XXXIX.

Mr. Redfield now received a letter from the Congregational society of Syracuse, inviting him to hold a revival meeting in their church. He obeyed the call at once. When he arrived at Syracuse he went immediately to one of the deacons of the society to talk over the matter. He asked:

"Is it true that your church wishes me, a Methodist, to hold a protracted meeting?"

"Yes, sir," said the deacon, "we passed such a resolution."

He then took Mr. Redfield to see one of the other deacons, who corroborated the statement of the first.

"Well, deacon, how long since you had a revival in this city?"

"Oh, we had a kind of a stir about fifteen years ago, but nothing to amount to much in twenty-five years."

"Have you put forth any effort?"

"Oh, yes; we have had Finney, and Lovering and Knapp, but nothing scarcely was accomplished. There are now five churches in the city without pastors, and the place is given over to the Unitarians."

"Well, deacon, had you not better put that question to vote over again, that you may do this thing with your eyes open? I am sure the old gospel is as potent as ever. I can do nothing, but that can. You must prepare yourselves for a great conflict, and many things that will shock all your ideas of order and propriety. I will tell you what I'll do: if any fighting or setting the church on fire takes place, I will do all I can to regulate that; but if God comes,—and that he will in awful power,—and the people shout or lose their strength, or anything else that God owns by working in the midst of it, you must not interfere."

One deacon said, "I have taken my stand, and I have no back tracks to make."

The other said, "The devil has had full swing for fifteen years, without let or hinderance, and I think it no more than right that God should be allowed to have one chance more." "Very good," said Mr. Redfield, "I will go forward."

He then went to see a Methodist preacher who lived not far away, and asked him to assist in the work, but he declined on account of poor health; but he felt there was no use of asking the one who had refused to allow him to work in his church, and who had so sneeringly said he had no objections to Mr. Redfield laboring in the city with other denominations. Yet this minister was soon active in circulating the report that Mr. Redfield was making war on Methodism.

Mr. Redfield had preached but a few times, when in one of the afternoon meetings, one deacon arose and vehemently protested against the Congregational church being used to make the people confess.

Mr. Redfield replied, that he had been invited with the understanding that he should not be trammeled in his measures; that he labored for nothing, and other churches were calling for him, and that he had no time to spend in contention. He then said, "I want to know if I am to be allowed to go forward or not." A vote was taken which resulted in his favor, and the deacon was quieted. The meetings went on a few days more, and the deacon could endure it no longer; and he became very bitter and violent in his remarks. Again the vote was taken and again the deacon was voted down. In a few days more he arose in a meeting all broken in spirit, and made a most startling confession to the church and congregation.

The Spirit was now being poured out in great power. Two Presbyterian elders fell under the power one night. While they lay there a deacon approached Mr. Redfield and said, "You Methodists get greatly excited."

Mr. Redfield replied, "Do you know that man lying over there?" "No!" "Well, that is a Presbyterian elder."

"What! can that be possible?" he asked.

"Yes, sir;" said Mr. Redfield, "and you all have Methodist hearts, and if you would give God a chance at you, he would do the same things with you."

Among the confessions made was one by a young lady, who said, "I have been a member of the Methodist Church for ten years, but have been deceived all this time. I never knew until now what religion was. But I know it now."

A Unitarian lady, who came to the meetings, she said, to prevent a friend of hers from going forward, when returning home the same night, fell while passing the Unitarian church, and cried out in great agony for mercy. Several persons who heard her, guided to her through the darkness by her voice, went to her assistance. The first words she spoke to them were, "Can any of you pray?" They took her to her own home, and one of them who had a religious friend, went for that friend to come and pray, but the friend was backslidden from God, and was obliged to become a seeker first, before he could aid her; and both were saved that night.

So great was the religious interest, and the danger to the Unitarians, that they sent to Boston for Theodore Parker to preach in their church for a season. He came, and flaming handbills were posted through the city announcing his arrival, and the themes of his discourses. But a violent storm which swept over the city a few days after he came so damaged their church that he returned to Boston.

Some of the fruit of this revival still remains. In after years, in the West, Mr. Redfield was welcomed and cheered by the faithful ones who in this revival were brought into the light. Rev. M. V. Clute, of the Illinois Conference of the Free Methodist Church, has given me the following incident: "I was a lay member of the Congregationalist Church in a neighboring town. During the time of Mr. Redfield's labors in Syracuse I visited my brother in that city. While at supper the first evening, I was asked to go and hear him. When we arrived at the church we found the seats near the door occupied, and were obliged to take one near the pulpit. In a very short time the house was crowded; those who filled the aisles stood, while those between the seats and the pulpit sat on the floor. He had been preaching but a few minutes when the heavy breathing of a person attracted my attention. For some time I could not make out who it was, when at last a man sitting on the floor threw up his hands, and exclaimed in a loud voice, 'O God!' The next moment he sprang to his feet, and with arms extended, started down one of the aisles toward the door, groaning as he went. The people made way for him, and he crossed behind the body seats and returned up the other aisle. As he reached the pulpit, he screamed and fell to the floor. During the time Mr. Redfield, in perfect silence, stood leaning on the pulpit watching him with great interest. For a few moments after he fell there was perfect quiet throughout the room, when suddenly from eighteen to twenty persons sprang to their feet and ran, praying, to the altar."

CHAPTER XL.

Mr. Redfield was now invited to Albion, N. Y., by Rev. W. C. Kendall, of blessed memory. Mr. Kendall was a minister of more than ordinary ability, and of deepest piety. He was noted for his faithfulness as a pastor and preacher. He had been well received in Albion at first, but when it was found impossible to get him to moderate his zeal, to lower the standard of piety, or to cease insisting upon the membership living up to the rules of the church, some of the most influential members turned against him. He commenced revival meetings amid great opposition, and finally sent for Mr. Redfield.

Mr. Redfield was well received at first, and soon conviction became general. At last the power of God began to come, and one night two or three fell. One was a Baptist. This frightened the people, and many hurried out of the house. Some ran for water to resuscitate the prostrate ones, while others broke window-lights to let in fresh air. Now some cried out that Mr. Redfield had mesmerized these people, until many in the church became alarmed and others angry. Then persons began to lose their strength at home, and some even miles away. It was well for the revival that Mr. Kendall was preacher in charge, for he was in full sympathy with Rr. Redfield, and gave him complete control of the services. In meeting and breaking through opposition, he was one of the most successful of evangelists. If permitted to act freely he scarcely ever failed to succeed. He now had the utmost freedom, and soon the tide of conviction rose above all opposition. The scenes of power in the services and in the homes of the people were marvelous. In the midst of this the following incident took place.

Rev. J. M. F ——, a former pastor of the church, was overheard to make the remark, in the Methodist Book Room, in Buffalo, that " Kendall has got Redfield to help him in a

revival at Albion, and I must go down and attend to matters
there." The word was brought to Albion by Rev. Brother
T ——, who heard J, M. F —— say it. This brother related the matter at Mr. Kendall's tea-table. With a look of
serious alarm, not easily forgotten, Mr. Redfield turned to
Mr. Kendall, and said: " It is my request that you do not
ask Mr. F —— into the pulpit, if he attends the services. It
is obvious that his errand here is to guard his friends against
my peculiar teachings, and for him to sit with me in the
pulpit is to pretend to be my friend. God cannot endorse
such a two-faced act; and my soul abhors such hypocrisy.
If you want God to help me to preach to-night, see that you
do not ask that man to take any part in the service."

Mr. Kendall, after a few moments thought, replied, "I
do not think I could ask him, no matter what the consequences may be."*

Mr. Redfield's description of his feelings and motives
will give a view of his character, and a clue to his wondrous
power.

"This man (J. M. F.) came into one of the afternoon
meetings, and knowing what his object was in coming to
Albion, I was overcome with grief. I went up into the pulpit, and got down out of sight and prayed, 'O my God, why
hast thou sent me out at the loss and cost of all things, and
then allowed such men to make my way so hard? He lives
on the fat of the land; is pampered with a large salary,
while I go unpaid, meet the brunt of battle, and have
to fight the devil, the world, and a dead church, and preachers besides.' I felt as though my case was too hard. My
bursting heart was so full that I put both hands upon my
mouth to keep from bellowing aloud. And I said, 'O,
Lord, I can go no further!' Then the old voice rang
again in my ears, 'You may live while you preach and
no longer.' Oh, how I wished these ambitious, wicked
men could have seen how God had to push and crowd me

* Mrs. M. F. LaDue, formerly Mrs. Kendall.

out against their opposition. But as usual, I had at last to come to the point where I could say, 'I have not yet resisted unto blood striving against sin. It will not be long before I will be called away, and I'll let God settle all this.' I saw somebody must stand up for God and the right, and it may as well be me as any one."

In the evening, as the congregation were seated after singing the second hymn, the house being very crowded, this man entered and made his way down to the altar. He looked up into the pulpit, and, as he was not invited to enter that, he seemed embarrassed, his face reddened, a pew door opened, and he was provided with a seat. That night Mr. Redfield preached one of his most awful sermons, from the text: "And for this cause shall God send them strong delusions, that they should believe a lie that they all might be damned, who believe not the truth, but have pleasure in unrighteousness."—2 Thess. 2: 11, 12. Those only who have heard him can imagine the pictures he drew of those who had lived in the church for years without saving grace; who had sat under the most searching gospel ministry; had seen the truth exemplified in the lives of some around them; and yet closed their eyes and ears to it all, rather than pay the price and humble themselves by repentance and confession, and take the way of self-denial and the cross of Christ. He then outlined the track of those ministers who have managed for years to preach without the Spirit, and have learned to lie to the people by telling them the way was not so narrow after all. They had become such adepts in lying that they preached and seemed to believe that we have "peace in Christ, and joy in the world," in common with all men (a doctrine this very man had preached). They lived for money, and had found that some churches would pay the best to the man who would preach to them such stuff. And no wonder they were in trouble, when a man came along who would preach the whole truth, and plainly point out that the wrath of Almighty God was upon sin and sinners in the church.

The effect of this sermon was electric. The Holy Ghost so attended it, that members of other churches were shaken as by a whirlwind. Some cried out, some fell prostrate before they could get to the altar, and others fell at the altar. That night and the night following, the prostrated ones lay in some places upon one another, until the aisles were closed for hours and the congregation literally hemmed in.

The minister referred to, fled as if in consternation, as soon as he could make his escape. Before he left the place, by the circulation of slanders against Mr. Redfield, he alienated many of the members of the church, who finally withdrew from the meetings, and at last became bitter opposers of the work. Among those whom he attempted to influence was an ex-senator. This brother came to Mr. Kendall to labor with him, when the following conversation took place:

" I feel very much grieved and tried with you. You preach to us that we should treat each other with Christian courtesy, yet you have not invited Brother F —— to preach since he has been here, and he feels very much hurt over it."

" Well, Brother H ——," replied Mr. Kendall, " I can now say to you what I could not have said before in regard to that: and I'll ask you, How could I invite him to preach or take part in the meetings when I knew he had come here to put a stop to them?"

" What do you mean?" asked Brother H ——.

" I mean just what I say."

" How do you know that he came here for that purpose?"

" Brother T —— came to me and informed me that he heard Mr. F —— say, before he came here, 'Kendall is holding revival meetings at Albion, and has Redfield to assist him, and I must go down and stop him.'"

" Is that so?" asked Mr. H ——.

"It is even so," replied Mr. Kendall.

Mr. H—— went home and found Mr. F—— there; and said to him, "I am greatly astonished to learn that your business here at this time was to stop this revival; and more, that you should claim to feel grieved because you were not invited to preach!"

"It is all a lie," said Mr. F——, "let who will say so. I never intimated any purpose of that kind."

"It is true, sir," said the minister who brought the report, and who happened to be present. "I heard you say it before you left Buffalo."

In this instance this opposer's efforts were a failure. If the same could be said of all his efforts to oppose the work of holiness, different results would have occurred in many instances. Mr. Redfield told the congregation, that observation for some years, had taught him that any person who passed through a genuine revival without yielding to the truth of God, became from that time a standing committee to fight God and holiness. This proved true of many in the place. They became the persecutors of those who undertook to follow God fully. The minister who came to Albion to oppose the meetings became a bitter persecutor of holiness teachers in the ministry, and has claimed the doubtful honor of producing the state of things which caused the rise of the Free Methodist Church, an organization which resulted from this same persecution.* This man entered the army after the breaking out of the rebellion of 1861, was subsequently accused of defrauding the government, was indicted for the offense, but for some reason was never tried. At the time of this writing, December, 1887, an effort is being made in Albion, where he attempted to stop the revival described in this chapter, to raise money to relieve him from severe destitution.

An incident occurred during this meeting worthy of note,

---

* General Superintendent Hart.

and which illustrates the thoroughness of Mr. Redfield's
work.

He labored to bring all to the gospel level by noticing the
poor, and especially the colored poor. We have already
seen him identified with the anti-slavery struggle. In the
Albion church there were some who set themselves against
the colored people strongly. Mr. Redfield told them several
times that he never saw a revival that was complete until all
such feelings gave way.

One night a colored woman, who was a model of neatness
and unobtrusiveness, arose and testified to having found salvation. Mr. Redfield, noticing that some received her testimony with disdain, made his way through the crowd until he
reached her, and taking her by the hand, began to sing an
inspiring salvation song. The colored sister became very
happy, and jumped and shouted aloud. The Spirit of God
very evidently endorsed the action of Mr. Redfield, for the
power of God came upon the people in a remarkable manner. One family refused afterward to kneel at the altar with
such trash, but a score of families from among the poor came
and found salvation.

The following letter, from the pen of Mr. Kendall,
written at this time, will give something of an idea of the
work and the circumstances:

"ALBION, February 3, 1855.

"Dear Brother P——:—I was glad to hear from you and
of your prosperity in the narrow way. I rejoice with Brother
Tinkham and the pilgrims in Taylorville, that salvation de-
scends there.

"That man of God, Dr. Redfield, is with us. We have
hard battles. The Doctor came a little more than a week
since. His shots are finding a lodgment in the hearts of the
King's enemies. He says that 'many here are stuck down in
the slough of *I won't.*' Our official members are great
hinderances. Entire holiness is gloriously prevailing; young

converts and little ones are pressing into the possession of it, and their influence is being felt.

"We have good congregations—very attentive. Brother Redfield is much thought of, and I have no doubt will be the means of great good. * * *

"The pilgrims are having a fight of afflictions in this region, such as they never saw. You may know something of it when I say that I have received five letters of remonstrance lately; *i. e.*, before Brother Redfield came. They have called us 'stumbling blocks,' and frequently 'fanatics.' They have said: 'the devil was speaking, through me; that my course was 'unhallowed,' 'unchristian,' 'self-sufficient,' 'impudent,' etc. One local preacher has said about town, of Dr. Redfield, 'That old *fanatic!* he don't know anything about preaching!' But glory to God! he 'rules the whirlwind and directs the storm.' It is breaking; and at the same time we hear talk that the trustees are going to close the house against us. We have no fears. It is one of the devil's scarecrows. Such times were never before in Albion. I wish you were here. * * *

"Our house was crammed Sunday night from top to bottom; but salvation came. Last night, also. Two lost their strength—a thing never known in Albion until this winter. The people are filled with wonder and dismay. Officials, thus far for the devil, begin to cower. There is great danger that Jesus will become popular. Dr. Redfield says it will take the devil six months to repair the damage done to his kingdom already. 'My voice is still for war,' is his watchword. We look for a mighty shaking. Glory to God for salvation!

"Your pilgrim brother,

"W. C. KENDALL."

From the following letter it would seem that Mr. Redfield was having more calls than he could fill. The letter gives us a glimpse of his inner life, of his deep concern for the Kingdom of God.

"ALBION, January 31, 1855.

"Dear Brother Hicks:—Your letter was received yesterday and my heart was deeply pained for the pilgrims at Syracuse. If I could cut off and send my feet one way, and my arms another, and then the stumps of this old body another, I would do it. I want to go twenty ways at once, and would, if possible. My spirit feels oppressed and bowed down by one little body, and it seems sometimes more than I have patience to bear. I see so much to be done, so little to do it, and so few that dare do the right thing for God, I feel distressed and ask, O God, must all this work be left undone? I cannot bear the thought, and yet what can I do? My spirit struggles and gasps to be free, and go free all over the world, like the lightning on telegraph wires. But I cannot. What shall I do? Only snail it through the world? But I must have grace to bear it.

"I cannot leave here for a few days yet. God is coming, and promises to come in more awful power.

"My love to all the pilgrims.

"Yours forever,

"J. W. REDFIELD."

19

CHAPTER XLI.

At the close of his labors in Albion, Mr. Redfield went directly to Bridgeport, Conn., for the last protracted meeting of the season. Here he found a pastor with a clear head, a pious heart, and unflinching integrity. But the meeting had scarcely commenced before he felt one of his old burdens coming on. At first, as usual, he misread the feeling, and concluded it was preparatory to an attack of apoplexy. He attempted to leave the meeting, but failed. He then turned to his medicine case, and took a remedy he thought would relieve him; but with no good effect. He then began to see that it was a "burden,"—the spirit of prayer. His agony for souls became very great. The sensation was as if a mighty hand took hold upon his brain, drew it up, and then thrust it back with a painful shock. This occurred several times. Every time he would cry out, "I will hold on until salvation comes." When suddenly he was relieved, and the power of God fell upon the people in a wonderful manner.

A Baptist deacon arose from the altar, and went reeling and tottering about, his face all radiant with the joy that filled his soul, and professed to have experienced the great blessing of perfect love. This was a surprise to his people, for they thought him eminent for piety, and in their opposition to the doctrine of holiness, they had been known to say: "But there is Deacon O——, and he never says anything about holiness." But, now, after the deacon had professed to have experienced it, they said: "Well, we have always been a little suspicious of him."

So great was the ingathering of souls during this meeting that it was necessary to build a new church to accommodate them.

The following are some of the incidents of the work:

A lady member of one of the city churches came and was convinced that she was without the saving grace of God.

This brought her into great distress of mind. Her mother came to Mr. Redfield and made a statement of the case. She said: "My daughter is in despair. She has been a member of the —— church for ten years. Her minister has been to see her, and has tried to persuade her not to give up her hope. But she told him that she had been deceived for ten years, and had just found it out. She then requested him to let her alone, and not to deceive her again. The deacons of the church came to see her, also, but she tells them the same story, and refuses to be comforted. Now, what shall I do? Shall I try to comfort her?"

"No, madam," said Mr. Redfield, "by no means; unless you desire to deceive her again. When she yields up her will to God she probably will find relief."

"But I fear she'll become deranged," replied the mother.

"Better be deranged and die so, in trying to be honest and to get right, than to go on as a deceived person, and die in that condition." -

"But she has eaten nothing for three days."

"Well, some spirits have to be starved out."

"Well, what shall I do?"

"You can pray for her; deal faithfully with her in pressing her to yield to God. But for her soul's sake, don't speak peace; let God do that."

About 12 o'clock the next night God spoke peace to her soul. Mr. Redfield was greatly encouraged when she related her experience the next afternoon. She told the congregation, that at first she was very angry at Mr. Redfield for disturbing her peace of mind, and then with a radiant face, she exclaimed, "But, oh, how glad I am that he dealt faithfully with me"; and turning toward him, said, "Do let me exhort you to be faithful wherever you go."

For a day or two during the meeting, Mr. Redfield had missed a brother who had taken a very strong stand for holiness, when one day he and his wife called. He seemed in

great distress of mind.   He said: "When I went from meeting a few days ago, I was fully determined to follow the
leadings of the Holy Spirit.   When I got home the Spirit
said, "Lie down on the floor and prophesy that you will now
die."

"But you did not die?" interrupted Mr. Redfield.

"Oh, no!" said he; "then the Spirit told me to prophesy
that the man in the house opposite would die before morning,"—

"Did he die?"

"No!   Then the Spirit told me to go into the streets and
sing, 'Pink and senna'; and to go singing it into the drug
store, and call for a large amount of it.   Then I was to make
a decoction of it, and give it to my children, to guard them
against sickness.   I did so, all but giving it to the children.
Next the Spirit told me that as I had once loved a lady before I married my present wife, that, therefore, I was guilty
of adultery with her; and I must go and confess it to her.
But I knew I was innocent of such a crime.   The Spirit
then told me I must now part with my wife.   Now what
shall I do?"

"Were you all this time led by this spirit?"

"Oh, no!"

"Let me ask you further, when this spirit was upon you,
did you not feel wretched?"

"I did! and it seemed I would die, my agony of mind
was so great."

"Well, brother, when any such influence comes upon you,
no matter how like conviction of duty it may appear, if it
brings distress of mind instead of filling you with love and
peace, resist it as you would the devil, for it is the devil.
God's Spirit never distresses one except those burdened with
guilt.   He leads by light, and love, and peace."

In connection with this incident Mr. Redfield penned
these thoughts upon the subject:

"I have occasionally met with similar cases. To my sorrow I have known some of the best of people to get frightened, and thinking insanity was being caused by the meetings, have insisted upon their being closed. I saw, I thought, that in following the track of Jesus, we must pass these temptations also; and if the church did not have the discernment to distinguish between temptation and insanity, we would be liable to do irreparable injury to the work of Christ."

From Bridgeport Mr. Redfield went to the scenes of his childhood. There he attempted to do his duty in the fear of God. He preached the same gospel that he had heard in the same pulpit from the lips of Wilbur Fisk, A. D. Merrill and John Lindsay, all of precious memory. God responded to his truth with power, but in the midst of it, the unspiritual pastor arrested the work by bringing the meetings to a close. Full of sadness, Mr. Redfield visited the graves of his mother and other saints who, in former days, had worshiped God in the church near by. Here he wept over the desolations of Zion, and consecrated himself anew to the work of spreading holiness over the land.

CHAPTER XLII.

In November, 1852, Mr. Redfield was invited to Henrietta, Monroe county, N. Y. The preacher was J. K. Tinkham, known for many years through Western New York for his powerful singing, and who passed to his reward in 1885. On his way to Henrietta, Mr. Redfield called on the presiding elder, who asked him where he was going.

"To Henrietta, to assist Brother Tinkham," Mr. Redfield replied.

"Well, I am glad you are going there, for there you can do no hurt," was the elder's reply.

But Mr. Redfield was becoming somewhat accustomed to such thrusts. On his arrival at Henrietta he found, truly, there was no danger of making matters worse. A once flourishing society was now reduced to eighteen members, and these were cold and formal.

Mr. Tinkham proved to be a pleasant pastor to labor with. He feared not the truth nor its effects. In a few days came the tug of war. Men saw they must resist strongly or yield; indifferent they could not be. The Holy Spirit pressed home the truth until men began to confess their delinquencies. One night, an official member of the church confessed that although he had tried to keep up the forms of religion, yet he had been unsaved. His two boys who had grown up infidels were present in the congregation. He went to one of them and asked his forgiveness for living before him as he had. The young man was much mortified, and tried to quiet him. The father then went to the other, and confessed and asked his forgiveness; and with the same result. He then returned to the altar, and falling on his knees, cried out in agony for their salvation. There was no appearance of the answer before the meeting closed. But during the night the oldest son arose from his bed, came down the stairs into his parents' room, and begged of them to rise and pray for him. They did so, and soon he began to pray for his brother. The father went to look for him, and found him on his knees crying for mercy. He was brought down stairs, and their prayers continued until nearly morning, and both were gloriously converted. They came to the afternoon meeting the next day, with shining faces, ready to work for God. Such was the earnestness with which they went at it, that in some instances sinners left the house to get away from them. One of these fell outside the door, and another sprang over the fence near by, and fell there. They cried for mercy, were converted, and returned to the house before the close of the service to testify of what Jesus had done for them.

The work now went on in great power, and awoke the opposition of the minister in another church. He tried first to proselyte the converts, but this failed, because of the thoroughness of their conversion. He then began to cry out against the work. Mr. Redfield now felt it his duty to speak plainly against a type of religion that would allow its possessors so to do. The opposition of the minister ceased and soon he was also saved, so that he would get happy in his pulpit, and shout, declaring he now knew what made the Methodists happy.

The man who had the charge of the church in which this revival was held, has told the writer within a few years, that such was his own indifference to religious things, under the wretched influence of the church, that for some time after this revival commenced, he would light the house and return to his home and wait for the congregation to disperse, and then go and close the house for the night. But he heard so much about the manner of Mr. Redfield and the truths he preached, and his unsparing denunciations of sin, that he ventured to hear him one night, for himself.

He says, "I thought I never heard it on this wise before.

At first I rather enjoyed seeing others get it, but at last the
lash came to my own back. Conviction set in, and soon I
was at the altar fairly howling for mercy."

Some of those who were saved in this revival are still living, and are illustrations of the thoroughness of the work
that was there done.

Mr. Purdy was present part of the time, and assisted in
this meeting, with his usual liberty and power.

While laboring at this place, Mr. Redfield wrote the
following interesting letter to Brother Hicks, of Syracuse,
N. Y.:

"Henrietta, N. Y., Nov. 11, 1852.

"Dear Brother Hicks & Co.

> "'Some time has passed away
> Since I began to pray,
> I love the Lord to-day;
> Bless his name; bless his name.'

"Brother P—— as usual ran away soon after my arrival.
Oh, what a pity that such talents cannot be controlled and kept
at work. But it cannot be helped. I suppose we ought to
be more thankful for as much as we can get out of him,
rather than to mourn because we can have no more. I will
not yet abandon all hope that he will see his error.

"Brother Woodruff is here. He is a man of God, and full
of the Holy Ghost. Brother Tinkham and he are shoulder
to shoulder pressing the battle, and resolved to have the
victory. You may well judge that it will take a large degree
of redemption power to raise from the dead the church in
this place. But it begins to move some. About twenty
have been converted, which in my judgment is equal to one
hundred in Syracuse.

"Brother W—— and myself go next Saturday, or the
following Tuesday, to Painted Post, where we hope Zenas,
the lawyer, will meet or follow us, and not run again, leaving

us right in the cramps.   From that place we expect to go to
Buffalo.

"Brother P—— has not yet decided about getting the
tent and going to Syracuse.· Yet he seems full of faith that
that is a move, which if carried out, promises much good to
the old line.   I think if such an arrangement could be
entered into, and sanctioned and sustained by men of the
right stamp, that there are many ministers who would will-
ingly join the flying artillery, and that great and glorious
results would follow.   I wish that Dr. Bowen, or some one
of his standing, would form a plan and lay it before one of
our bishops for approval, and then I think that H—— Mattison would find his guns spiked before he could do much
damage.   If the plan works, as I have no doubt it will, I
think that at the next conference there will go out such a
voice from that body as will make our way easy, and plain,
and successful.

" Could you not draft a plan and send it to Dr. Bowen,
and get him to enlist others whose influence will at once
protect and give character to the movement?   It seems to
me that such is the condition of the churches, that some
unusual effort must be made to check the progress of approaching ruin, and extend the borders of Zion to fields as
yet unoccupied.

"How are you all getting along? Are you at anchor?
or drifting down stream? or rowing up? Don't get discouraged; God will yet give you victory; for if you cannot
carry the opposition and turn them to the Lord, you can use
them as polishing brushes to make you shine the brighter. I
tell you heaven is in view.

"I desire you would remember me to Sisters A—— and
A——, Brothers B—— and G——, and all the disciples of
Jesus.   O Brother Hicks, encourage them to hold on and to
fight manfully. I much desire to see you all, but at present
I cannot see it possible.

"Brother Hicks, would you like to take a little stock in heaven's savings bank? I will tell you how. You pilgrims just spend a little time every day in secret prayer that God may be with us who are laboring for souls at Henrietta, Painted Post, and Buffalo.

"I would like to select my homestead near yours on heaven's public lands. If you assist me by your prayers we shall doubtless settle in the same neighborhood on the prairies of the New Jerusalem. Hallelujah! Amen!

"J. W. REDFIELD."

From Henrietta, at the request of a presiding elder, Mr. Redfield went to another place, where matters were in an equally bad state, though there were more members in the church. On his arrival, he found he must commence in the presiding elder's family, and he sternly rebuked the wife and some others for their bad example in wearing jewelry. They were much offended, of course. He found that the preacher in charge had no religious influence, because of his trifling manner among the people. But there was an old minister, who was without an appointment, but who had been on the straight track for thirty years, and who saw matters in the same light in which Mr. Redfield saw them. This was to him a source of great comfort and encouragement. He had often known ministers, in the heat of successful revivals, to take a stand for the right, but when they arrived at conference, and saw it did not meet with the approval of those in power, to look at their families, and almost empty pocket-books, and then draw back. But here was a man who had stood; who had dared to do his duty, to follow the truth, and risk the consequences.

The work had scarce begun before it became apparent that there were serious things in the way. Mr. Redfield consecrated himself anew to do faithful work. He said to himself, "I will only stop when I must. By the grace of

God I will not swerve from the right. If I go down with the truth, I know Jesus will go down with me; and he will have a resurrection. I will be as honest with the people as though I was going immediately to the judgment. I know I am already in bad odor with the worldly and pleasure-seeking, in the church, and, probably, faithful work here will not improve my reputation: but I will leave all that to be adjusted at the judgment."

He saw that representatives of Jesus must do something to restore themselves to the confidence of those outside the church. He urged the membership to make clean and thorough work in confessing their true moral state, so that the world would have the true standard of religion.

When he had finished a sermon on this subject, an old local preacher arose and said, "This Redfield has insulted us. This church will never disgrace itself by making any such confessions as he urges. He need not come here to accuse us of having no religion. I know I've got religion; and, Oh! brethren, what a glorious time it will be when we all get up there."

"If you ever get there," suggested Mr. Redfield.

Next a son of this old man arose, who was also a local preacher, and with great vehemence denounced Mr. Redfield. The meeting closed, and one of the equally dead members of the church approached the old local preacher, and said, "I know the reason why you are so bitter upon the preacher because of this confessing business. You know you are guilty of crimes that would make a decent man blush." Not knowing that his life was so well known, the old man tried to deny it, and asked for the proof. The other called up a man who was present, and asked him, 'Don't you know that this man is guilty of ——?" naming the crime.

"Yes, sir, I do," said the witness. And then another, and another, was called on to testify, who witnessed to the same. The old man left the house not to return again.

Mr. Redfield then took an expression of the congregation, sinners and all, whether the truth that will do to die by was what they wanted. A large number, by the uplifted hand, declared in the affirmative.

The next night Mr. Redfield plainly saw that they had come to a point where somebody must act; and said: "I have gone to my utmost extent in preaching the word of God to you, and it all fails. I will now try one more thing; not to appeal to your conscience, for you have none. Bible truth seems to have nothing sacred in your esteem. You may possibly have some sense of honor; I will appeal to that. Now, when you joined the church you either did, or did not, know its rules. If you did not, here they are [holding out a copy of the Discipline]. They forbid doing harm, and command to do good. They forbid conformity to the world. Yet, in all that you are deficient. Now, make up your mind; can you, will you, conform to these rules? If not, then do have the honor to go to your preacher and tell that you can't live up to the rules and ask him to drop your name."

Afterward Mr. Redfield learned that one of the principal members did so, and then said, "There, I have withdrawn from the church, for I am resolved to live and die an honest man." He also said to Mr. Redfield: "I have been kept in the church because I was reputed to be wealthy, and that, too, when it was known that I would swear."

But to return; this looked severe to many, but the sequel showed that God was in it. This course raised a tempest. Immediately one of the leading members arose and said, "We have borne this abuse long enough."

Mr. Redfield asked, "Will you show me what I have preached that is not truth?"

"We believe it is truth," he answered, "but we won't stand it."

The service broke up in a tumult. A large number came

around Mr. Redfield and vehemently accused him of causing the disorder,—five to ten speaking at once until he could not be heard. He went to his stopping place, at the presiding elder's, and fell upon his face before the Lord. He cried out, " O Lord, thou knowest I have not swerved from the right. I have gone as far as I can. I must now stop. I give the matter into thy hands." He then retired to rest with the rich consciousness of the divine approval. Soon the word came that two of the most faithful men in the society had fallen to the floor in the church, both burdened for the membership, and especially for the man who had talked so to Mr. Redfield. About two o'clock in the morning, he was awakened by a rap at his door, and was informed that the wife of the pastor was almost in despair, and desired him to pray for her. She had also requested them to bring Brother F——, one of the brethren who was prostrate in the church, and he had been brought to her house, but he was perfectly stiff, and had to be carried. When Mr. Redfield arrived, the pastor's wife confessed that she had slyly counseled the sisters of the church to keep on their jewelry. She was now in great distress. They had not prayed long, when a messenger came and said, "Several members of the church are in a house near here, and they desire, all who can, to come and pray with them. And they especially desire Brother F—— shall come." Several men picked him up and carried him there. After a little, a messenger came there with the word that a number of sinners were congregated in a house near by, and desired Christians to come and pray with them. Before daylight it became evident that the whole place was under awakening; and the result was a glorious ingathering of souls.

CHAPTER XLIII

From the scene of the labors described in the last chapter, Mr. Redfield went to a place only a few miles distant. The preacher in charge was present the first Sunday morning. He said to Mr. Redfield, "We are expecting you to begin to-day. Now, do you object to a melodeon in the gallery? If you do, we won't have it used."

"Don't let it sound a note," replied Mr. Redfield.

"What about the choir?" asked the pastor.

"Bring it down to the front seats, and let the whole congregation sing, in Methodist style," was the reply.

Again, he began at the foundation. Holiness, inward and outward, was urged upon the people. When the truth was beginning to take a deep hold upon the congregation, he was waited on by a committee one day, who announced their business as follows:

"Brother, are you willing to be faithfully dealt with, and, if possible, to remove all hinderances that are in the way of a revival?"

"Most certainly I am," he replied.

"Well, we have heard some reports in regard to you which are greatly in the way of the cause of God."

"What are they?" he inquired.

"We have heard that you are worth three hundred thousand dollars; that you own a most splendid mansion in New York; that it is furnished and decorated from top to bottom in the most costly manner; that your servants dress in livery; that you carry a costly gold watch, and that you come out here and pounce upon us for our paltry two and six-penny gold rings; and we think this ought to be corrected."

Said he, "I don't hold myself responsible for all the lies told about me, nor feel that I am required to correct everything that is circulated about me. If I did, I would have my hands full, and no time to work for God." Pulling out his plain silver watch, he continued, "That is all the watch I have. About the mansion: the report is true, except they have located it in the wrong place. As to the three hundred thousand dollars, I would not sell it for that sum. Indeed, I do not think I should be blamed for its possession, for it was willed to me by my elder brother, when he died. As to my describing it to please the fastidious, I shall not do it. This much I will say, it is fenced round with walls made of diamonds, amethysts, and other precious stones, and the walks are paved with gold. You may judge what the mansion must be."

The committee bowed themselves out, and he heard no more of the matter.

The revival was deep and extensive. It was estimated that nearly five hundred were converted. Some of the converts became remarkable for their piety, their activity, and their success as workers for Jesus.

One young girl, about sixteen years of age, came to the altar one evening, and, turning to the congregation, said: "Farewell to you all; I am going to seek religion; and I will have it." Dropping upon her knees, she prayed most determinedly for salvation. She soon arose, and clapping her hands, gave glory to God. Then, turning to a faithful old preacher, and calling him by name, she said: "O brother, this is good. Oh, how I wish Jane had it"; and running to her sister Jane, she brought her to the altar. "Now," said she, "I want Mary"; and she went and brought her. "Now I must have Susan," but Susan ran out of the house. She then went for another, but that one refused; and the young convert fell upon her knees for a moment, and then led this one to the altar also. This girl had not been converted more then ten minutes, before she began to work for others, and in less than an hour she had led eleven persons to the altar; a work far beyond that of many in the church in a life-time.

God seemed to have, on this night, complete possession of the place. One sister arose and said, "Oh, what shall we do for some one to lead us on when Brother Redfield is gone?" And turning to the preacher in charge said: "O brother, you must get the blessing of holiness, so you can lead us on."

The preacher arose, and instead of being offended, said, "I will have it; and I desire you all to pray for me." He did get it, and afterwards said to Mr. Redfield, "I had it once before, and I preached it; and I had just such revivals as this. But I saw how some in the conference ·treated Brother Purdy, who is with you, and I was afraid I should get into bad repute among my brethren, as he has,—so I lowered the standard, and lost the power out of my soul; and I have been thinking about locating. But now I shall take my old track, and risk the consequences."

But, like many others, he afterwards failed to keep his promise. The next year the conference sent a minister to the place who was opposed to preaching and teaching holiness. This caused Mr. Redfield much pain, but he was comforted by hearing that one of the members had died in glorious triumph, having kept her experience until the end.

Having closed his labors in this place, Mr. Redfield next went to labor in Bath, Steuben county, N. Y. Here he again raised the standard of holiness. Soon the work broke out in power. Here again the devil undertook to hinder the work by subjecting a woman, who experienced the blessing of holiness, to severe temptation. In her earnestness she promised the Lord she would follow the Spirit wherever it might lead. One afternoon, the impression came to her to go to the church to the meeting, and she arose and started. When about half-way there, the impression came to return home. She did this; and then it came to return again to the church, and when there to kneel in the end of the seat, so that the people who passed would have to step over her, and thus illustrate to them what stumbiing blocks they were; and she obeyed it. Then the impression came, "This church is very proud, leap through the aisles like a frog to humble them"; and she did so. Then the impression came to call an old lady who sat near her, a hypocrite; and this she did. Then, following the same leading, she went after her daughter, who was in the house, and the daughter fled to avoid her. By this time the confusion became so great that the service was brought to an end. She went home, and the impression came to test her faith by sitting between a very hot stove and a wall near by. While at this, her husband, who was a physician, came home, and was informed of all that had occurred. Very much frightened, he hastened to the parsonage to see Mr. Redfield and the pastor. He declared his wife to be raving crazy, and that the meetings must stop, both for her good and the credit of Methodism. But Mr. Redfield thought he saw that it was another effort to dishonor the work; that these temptations sooner or later came to every one who was fully determined to follow Jesus. He then said to the doctor, " Don't you know that the determining symptoms are not insanity? This is only temptation. She will come out of it all right."

"Well, what shall I do?" said the doctor.

"Be quiet, and pray for her. Let her entirely alone, and she will come out of it, and tell you it is all of the devil."

The doctor was finally persuaded to drop the matter, and not interfere with the meetings. The next morning she came out of it all right, and the glory and power of God wonderfully rested upon her. She afterwards said she saw clearly that the strange influences she experienced were all of the devil.

But the report went far and near that the woman went crazy. Those who circulated it were careful not to say she was all over it the next day. This was also charged to Mr.

20

Redfield's labors, and the people were cautioned not to employ him.

The work in Bath went on in great power, and soon a jeweler was saved, and his conscience refused to let him buy or sell or mend jewelry, and it was reported that he had gone crazy.

CHAPTER XLIV

AFTER closing his labors in Bath, Mr. Redfield went to the city of Buffalo, where he held a series of meetings in the Niagara Street Methodist Episcopal church. Rev. Benjamin T. Roberts, now senior General Superintendent of the Free Methodist Church, was the pastor of the Niagara Street society.

On inquiry of an old minister, Mr. Redfield was informed that he had nothing to fear from the pastor, and that the truth would be given the utmost freedom. When he arrived, he was informed by Mr. Roberts, and also by a leading man in the church, that Methodism was in a very low state in the city, and that it had been quite difficult to sustain prayer meetings in this church for a year or two.

In due time the work began to move. Soon, among others, came to the altar, a poor drunken local preacher, whom Mr. Roberts had found in the delirium tremens but a short time before, and God saved him. Then another one came, who had been attending horse races in Canada, and he was saved. One woman of high standing made the confession that she had been wronging her own sister out of her portion of their father's estate, and had to restore it to find peace. This created great excitement and opposition. But the work went forward with power in the reforming, converting and sanctifying of souls. Many of the people began to take a strong stand for Bible holiness and Methodism. A sister B——, one of the most fashionable members of that church, and who wore a very large amount of jewelry, laid it all aside, and went from house to house among her fashionable friends in the church, and upon her knees confessed to them the wrong she had done them in setting such an example, and came out into the light as a true and steadfast disciple of Jesus.

In the midst of this revival the meetings of the General

Missionary Society came on, and one service was appointed to be held in the Niagara Street church. Mr. Redfield called on the bishop and had a talk with him in respect to the decay of primitive Methodism, and asked him to say something during this gathering that would encourage the effort to build up the work. He related to him the cases of the two local preachers, among others, as illustrations and proofs of the genuineness of the work in progress. But the bishop turned upon him, and said, very abruptly: "I don't believe a word of it."

Mr. Redfield saw he must now prepare himself for trouble. When the bishop preached he seemed to take especial pains to impress the congregation that he did not approve of Mr. Redfield's work. Dr. A. S——, editor of the *Christian Advocate*, in an address went out of his way to declare that Christianity was not opposed to the luxuries and elegances of life, and indulgence in them was not inconsistent for Christians.

At this time there was a sharp conflict in the Genesee Conference in Western New York, over the question whether the modern innovations upon Methodism should prevail. Mr. Roberts, Mr. Kendall, Eleazar Thomas, who years afterwards was massacred by the Modocs, and quite a number of others, were standing for the Wesleyan doctrine and experience of holiness, and the simplicity of Methodism. Now there crowded into the Niagara Street church the leading opposers of all this, and mingling among the membership, who were being graciously moved by the revival in progress, they circulated scandalous reports that had a tendency to stop the work. After they were gone, a lawyer V—— came into one of the afternoon meetings to carry out the wishes of the opposition. He arose, and said, in substance, "We have been annoyed and disgusted long enough with this man Redfield, and now it shall come to an end. These meetings shall no longer be endured."

Mr. Redfield was kept perfectly calm and sweet amid it all. When the lawyer was through speaking, Mr. Redfield asked him to state what had been preached that was contrary to the Bible and the Discipline. He sharply retorted: "It's all true enough, but we won't stand it here anyway." Mr. Redfield was obliged to cease his labors there and go elsewhere.

The Niagara Street Methodist church was then heavily in debt. Mr. Roberts offered to become responsible for lifting the indebtedness, if the trustees would make the seats free. His proposal was not accepted. The church was afterward sold for its indebtedness. It has since been used as a Jewish synagogue, until, within the last year, when it was purchased by the Free Masons for the purpose of erecting a Masonic temple on its site.

During this time Mr. Redfield wrote the following letter:

"BUFFALO, N. Y., January 4,1853.

"Dear Bro. Hicks and Company:—I received your letter before I left Bath, which was last Friday. Since I last wrote you we have had hard battles, and some triumphant victories. Oh! how my heart ached when I learned how God's house of prayer has been turned into a den of thieves. But what can be done? I don't know! I don't know! May God help you to hold on a little while longer. There's a crown for you; hold on! *hold on!!*HOLD ON!!! Oh, how I want to see you! All your struggles and contests and toils make you all dear to me; and I know you are dear to him, 'who endured such contradiction of sinners against himself.' Think, dearly beloved, when you are writhing under persecution, God's word hath said, 'He that toucheth you, toucheth the apple of his eye.' Jesus has also said, 'If they have persecuted me they will also persecute you." And, again, 'It were better that a millstone were hanged about his [your enemy's] neck, and he cast into the depths of the sea,

than that he should offend one of these little ones which believe in me.' Fight on, fight ever! Live on, and live forever. Amen! Hallelujah! Glory to God!

"I want to hear from Mother A——, particularly. I
meant to have written her before this time, but do not remember her given name. Give my love to Sister A——, and
Brother and Sister B——, and especially Brother S——; in
fact, all who love the Lord Jesus.

"Brother W—— is here, running the old line straight for
God. I wish he could be preacher of the Brick church for
two years. But it is useless to hope; the powers and members
are all on the side of the opposition. It will not always be
so. Jesus will by-and-by come and straighten all these matters. O my God, my heart feels almost ready to burst
with anguish when I look at the desolations! What can I do?
I don't know. What I mean to do, I know. I mean, unless I
backslide, to throw myself into the hottest battles. They
may ride over me, fight me, spit on me; but in the name of
God, when I see them stabbing at Jesus, they shall sheathe
their swords in me first, if I can get between them and him.
If I cannot conquer for Jesus, I can die for him. I have
tried to make a bulwark of my reputation, and of all I hold
dear on earth. Let them batter me, I'll go singing, 'I'll stand
the storm, it won't be long.' But how much I need of salvation's power, of humility, meekness, gentleness, goodness.

"It encourages me as I go from place to place to think
of the precious few who are holding on. Yet when I see
some coming out into the light and shining with the blessing
of perfect love, I ask: Who knows what their next preacher
will do? Likely enough he will try to undo the whole
work. But I think of the little band at Syracuse and other
places, and I am again encouraged to hold on, and I sing
again, 'I'll stand the storm.'

"God bless you all.

"J. W. REDFIELD."

From Buffalo Mr. Redfield went to Townsendville to the help of his especial friend, Rev. J. K. Tinkham. A glorious revival occurred, and many were converted.

From Townsendville Mr. Redfield went to P—— B—— (probably Port Byron), to assist Brother P—— (probably Purdy), in a church which once belonged to the Presbyterians, but had been sold to pay the preacher's salary. What were the results of this meeting cannot now be told, but the need of a revival is seen from the circumstance just related.

He now went again to Syracuse to visit the brethren. After a few services had been held, it was determined to build a church. A cheap building of rough hemlock boards, and plastered with one coat, was erected and dedicated to God. An engraving of it, that heads a letter written from this place to Rev. W. C. Kendall, shows it to have been the extreme of plainness and simplicity. From the beginning of the effort their meetings were attended with great manifestations of power and success. The opposition manifested by Methodist preachers during the great revival in the Congregational church, a short time before, broke out anew. But the presiding elder favored the new movement, and those engaged in the work were organized into the Third church. The course of the elder changed the controversy to the question of the wisdom and legality of his administration. But the conference was willing to accept of the new society, without regard to the question of legality, and sent them a preacher. The society soon found, however, that the preachers appointed by the conference were opposed to the spiritual freedom enjoyed by the membership.

After some years an effort was made by the preachers to disband the society; but God had raised up a layman of deep experience and determined spirit, who could not be coaxed or driven from what he thought was right. This was Clark T. Hicks, to whom the letter in this chapter is addressed. He was a man of fine business abilities, which kept him in the recorder's office of the county, either as head officer or deputy, for more than forty years. It is said that in his work of recording, during all this time, there is not a mistake or an erasure to be found. In his religious life he seemed to follow the Lord in like manner. Radical upon every question in which morals, or the rights of God or man were at issue, pronounced in the expression of his opinions, and filled with the loving tenderness of the Christian, he was well fitted to stand in the front and take the blows and rebuffs that came in the path of duty. It was often his duty to pronounce the oath for witnesses in the court-room, and it is said of him, that men who were expected by their employers to swear falsely, were sometimes frightened into testifying to the truth by his manner.

The new society lived and flourished, more or less, at times; had its revivals and declensions, became at one time an independent church, and, finally, when the Free Methodist Church was organized, became attached to that body.

How long Mr. Redfield remained at Syracuse after the organization of the Third church, or where and how he spent his time after leaving there cannot now be told, but the next trace of him is found in 1855, where, in Burlington, Vermont, he was engaged in one of his most successful meetings.

CHAPTER XLV.

In February, 1855, Mr. Redfield was invited to visit Burlington, Vermont, and assist in a protracted meeting. Mr. Purdy had preceded him two weeks, and in his characteristically thorough manner had prepared the way for Mr. Redfield's coming. There had not been a revival in the place for twenty-one years. The pastor was favorable to old-fashioned Methodism, and stood by the work like a man of God. Opposition from other churches set in, as was often the case in those days, but God gave the victory. Many remarkable conversions took place, and the revival spread through the town and the community round about, until more than one thousand persons had been converted to God. So many were the accessions to the Methodist Episcopal Church that there was strong talk of organizing a second church, and erecting another place of worship. This met with great opposition from some of the conference ministers who thought that Methodism had become numerically so strong that one society and a stately edifice which would vie with those of the other denominations, was the better policy. Mr. Redfield advised against this, as those who were in favor of it among the membership were such as were of no assistance in revival work, and such a policy would bring them to the front and endanger the spirituality of the whole. Besides this, he feared the bringing in of a spirit to outdo other churches, which would undoubtedly grieve the Holy Spirit.

The next pastor, who came soon after the revival, endeavored to carry out the policy advocated by the preachers at conference, but failed, and the new organization was effected. An effort was now made to counteract Mr. Redfield's influence and build a fashionable church. To do this, slanderous stories were circulated about him, in regard to his wife, who had deserted him nineteen years before. But the

second church was built, much according to his advice, and
the society became a power for good.

In *The Congregationalist*, of Boston, Mass., for
February 11, 1886, I find the following with respect to this
revival. The writer, Rev. R. B. Howard, of the Methodist
Episcopal Church, in a sketch of Rev. C. L. Goodell, D.D.,
of St. Louis, who had lately died, says:

"Toward the close of young Goodell's last college year,
1855, a remarkable work of grace, beginning in the Methodist church, in the village below, under the labors of a
Doctor Redfield, a popular, eloquent, and successful revivalist,
gradually spread up to the college. Goodell, meantime,
with several other college students, had become greatly
interested in Doctor Redfield and his meetings, not so much
on religious grounds as on the score of his eloquence, and the
marvelous sweetness of his singing. The writer will never
forget seeing Goodell and another gifted classmate, by the
name of Robinson, night after night elbowing their way to
the front, and sitting flat on the carpet before the pulpit—
the house being too full for them to obtain seats—for the
sake of listening to the wonderful oratorical flights of that
now long since departed, but gifted evangelist; little dreaming, meanwhile, that he was himself so soon successfully to
engage in the same glorious work of calling sinners to
repentance."

In a letter to the *California Christian Advocate*, by the
same writer, about the same time, I find the following:

"It so happened that Dr. Goodell and the writer were
converted in the same revival at the University of Vermont,
in connection with the labors of an eloquent and successful
revivalist named Redfield. The revival proper was conducted at the Methodist church, but the good work extended
to the University, where, in a few weeks, twenty-five or
thirty young men were converted, many, if not most of
whom, became ministers."

A letter written to Rev. W. C. Kendall, at this time, reveals the spirit that actuated the man:

"BURLINGTON, VT., February 24, 1855.

"Dear Brother and Sister Kendall, and the church of pilgrims who visit your house: — " Your very welcome letter, postmarked the 21st, has this day arrived, and, oh! how my heart sunk within me, as I read that your church is wading through seas of conflict, and especially that your principal foes are among those from whom you have a right to expect better things. Your duty is plainly laid out before you. You must not, cannot, and I know you will not, sell out the interests of Jesus though all men forsake and persecute him in the persons of his disciples. Thank the Lord, there are some who will drink his cup and be baptized with his baptism. They can well afford to give all for God, for their record is on high. It does seem worth infinitely more than the cost to feel the blessed assurance that they are trying to be faithful representatives of Christ, and that he will say of them, as he did of Job, 'They can be trusted.' Yes, they will pass through the crucible and triumphantly shout, 'Though he slay me, yet will I trust in him.' Oh, how I want to bless you all! My heart, reputation, and life, are at the service of Jesus and the pilgrims. How it does encourage me to labor on, when I think there are a few faithful ones who dare to die for the blessed cause of the great salvation. I want you to greet all the blessed ones in my behalf. Tell Brother Seth [Woodruff, a layman of great religious activity and power in prayer], I will let him know when I go back to Syracuse, and I shall expect him to go with me. Remember me especially to Brother Roberts—God bless him—and your father, and Sister S——. I hope when I return to Syracuse that she and yourself will come down and visit the Syracusans.

"Brother Purdy left here on Monday last. As usual, he

left his mark here. Many of the church have been quick-
ened, and a goodly number of sinners converted. He received
forty on probation the Saturday night before he left. He is
now at Palmyra, but is to begin a meeting in Troy next
week. He says he has no more work in Western New
York, and of course I cannot expect him to go with me to
Syracuse. If I go there I shall depend on Brothers Woodruff, Tinkham, Kendall, Wallace, and Roberts, and others to
come to our help. I shall probably stay here two weeks
longer.

"Yours, etc.,

"J. W. REDFIELD."

He now, as the following letter will show, was connected
with another physician in starting a medical infirmary at
Syracuse, with a branch at Burlington, Vt.:

"April 25, 1855.

"Dear Brother and Sister Kendall: — "Ye troublers
of Israel; the Lord bless you forever and ever. I returned
to this place yesterday afternoon, and sat down to answer
yours of the 16th, but I was so exhausted that I was
compelled to defer it until this morning. It is refresh-
ing, my dear troublers, to know that there are those who
dare 'hazard all for God at a clap,' and then take the
consequences. Let history, common sense, and religion
answer the question of what would become of vital godliness in the churches in ten years if there were none to stand
up for the truth. The ashes of the martyrs have been, and
must be, the seed of the church. I think that neither you
nor Sister K—— are too good for such a fate. Jesus made
himself of no reputation, and got killed for it. It is enough
for the servant to be as his master. I thank God that some
of us are counted worthy of shame for the name of Jesus.
Oh, how it nerves me for the conflict when I remember that
others with me are enduring cruel mockings. Amen! Halle-

lujah!! Go on, *on, on, on.* I want to see you very much, and I greet you in the name of the Lord. If Sister K——— and others can come to Syracuse we can accommodate them now. I am boarding with Doctor Wager, who is making arrangements to accommodate a number of invalids. I inclose a card which will direct to the house and office. The house is pleasantly situated, and abundantly large to accommodate a goodly number of pilgrims. The Lord willing, we mean to make it a pilgrims' rest.

"I would like to go to your camp meeting, and will if I can make it convenient to do so. Give my love to everybody that loves Jesus. Business pressure compels me to be short this time.

"Yours forever and ever,

"J. W. REDFIELD."

"P. S.—We design to keep an infirmary.

"R."

On May 7, he wrote from the same place as follows:

"Dear Brother Kendall:—Your favor of the 3rd has just come to hand, and glad indeed am I to hear from you, and most of all, from the tone of your letter, that you have not been bought, coaxed, nor frightened from your stand for God and the truth. Oh, how my heart takes courage at the sound of the war-whoop from the few daring servants of God, who are big enough to be little, who know enough to be simple, and who have courage enough to dare to stand up and out, straight for the right! Our cause is right; it will triumph. We shall conquer. Go ahead, dear brother, and when your reputation is all exhausted in the war, you are at liberty to draw upon me for what fragments of a broken-down reputation I may have left.

"We had great times at Burlington. Brother Purdy as usual, under God, put things in their right places, and laid a foundation to build upon. How many were converted, as a result of his labors, I cannot tell, and probably it cannot be known this side of eternity. But if we may reckon on the reflex influence, as manifest in the many extensive revivals round about, that grew out of his labors here, I shall not go wide of the mark when I say that the number is about 2,000. Revivals sprang up in almost every quarter, from ten to one hundred miles away, as the result of Brother Purdy's labors. God bless him. You can form something of an opinion of it, when I tell you that at Burlington we had from sixty to eighty at the altar, and anxious seats each night in the main audience-room, besides a large number at the same time in the lecture-room; and that a new second church is now being erected, and the work is still going on; that in one place, fifty miles away, about fifty are at the altar each night, at another place twenty-five, and still another twenty, and in many other places from ten to twenty. One preacher, who came more than fifty miles to the meeting in B——, said that our meeting was shaking almost the entire state of Vermont.

"Well, dear brother, let them kill you if they can, and knock you all to pieces; Jesus will gather up every fragment at the last.

"I feel a great desire to be at one of your preachers' meetings, and especially at the camp meeting. But I must go back to Burlington for a season to take charge of a department in a large infirmary. I spend only part of my time here, and I may be compelled to be there at the time of your camp meeting. I wish I was able to devote all my time to the work, but I am compelled to use part of it for the meat that perisheth.

"Our terms, for board, washing and treatment, are $10.50 per week. This includes nursing, hydropathic and homeopathic treatment, and everything else pertaining to the good and comfort of the patient. But until we can get ready the great establishment we have in contemplation, we shall charge but $7.50.   Our large establishment will cost from fifteen to twenty thousand dollars.

"Yours as ever,

"J. W. REDFIELD."

Several important things may be learned from these letters:

1.   The absence in him of anything like rivalry, or vain-glory.   The letters of Rev. Mr. Howard show that Mr. Redfield was the principal figure in that great revival, but he gives the honor to his friend, Purdy.

2.   The fact that he did not make a gain of his work as an evangelist.   The fifty or one hundred dollars per week charged by some modern evangelists would have enabled him to devote all his time to God's work, as he desired.

3.   The peculiar work in which he engaged now and then to replenish his purse.

4.   His hearty sympathy for all who were suffering for Jesus' sake.   And there were many of these at that time.

CHAPTER XLVI.

While Mr. Redfield was engaged in the work of a physician at this time, he began seriously to consider the question of marriage. Nineteen years had gone by since his wife deserted him, and fourteen since the courts had given him a legal separation from her. Several years had also gone by since he, by two ministers of the church, heard that she was dead; and nothing to the contrary had ever come to his knowledge. A careful consideration of all the facts and of the law in the case, convinced him that there were no legal nor moral barriers in the way; and he determined to marry, if a suitable opportunity presented itself.

One of the causes that led him to this decision was, that his enemies were continually taking advantage of his single condition to fabricate and circulate slanderous stories about him. He thought the presence of a wife with him wherever he went would put a stop to this; but, to his sorrow, he found this was not so.

Among the many who came to the infirmary for treatment was a lady of more than ordinary intelligence, and who had had some experience in city mission work. She, like himself, had been unfortunate in her married life, and was now separated from her husband. Mr. Redfield finally proposed marriage to her, and his offer was accepted. Immediately after closing a revival effort at Keesville, N. Y., he was quietly married to this lady by a Methodist minister in the presence of a few witnesses.

Instead of this hushing the tongues of his detractors, it only gave them a double opportunity to harass him. Because of this occasion for offense, as some judged it to be, some of his warmest friends were greatly afflicted. This hedged up his way in many places, and destroyed his influence. His was doubtless one of those peculiar instances spoken of by

St. Paul, in which the lawful is not expedient. Since his death it has been remarked, and supposed to be true, that he regretted this step; but in a review of his life, written by himself, he has recorded this:

"I went to Keesville, to hold a meeting, and about the close I saw fit to be married to one whom I then believed, and now know, to be in every respect a helpmeet to me in the gospel field."

Mrs. Redfield, after a few days, went on a visit to her father's, while he went to fill an engagement to hold a meeting. The name of the place of this meeting he does not give, and the writer has no means of learning it. Of the effort put forth at this place he makes this brief record: "I again saw the power of God displayed."

A few days' visit among his own people with his wife, and then they were away to Lima, N. Y., where he had been expected for some time.

In a letter to Samuel Huntington, dated April 9th, 1856, two weeks after he left Lima, he wrote:

"I found that two years before the church door was locked against the preacher (probably Purdy) and the people by one of the college professors. The principal teacher in the seminary was dismissed, and a woman, who made no profession of religion, elected in her place. Subordinate teachers were employed, who taught the Methodist girls of the seminary to dance.

"Well, enough of this. We began the fight in the name of the Lord, and the opposition started. Then came out a large number of students—some of them confessed their opposition to the work when Brother Purdy was here—and soon came into the enjoyment of justification, and then of sanctification; and then they confessed that the college influence had killed them. Soon the Lord had the quorum, and the opposition was compelled to stack arms. This continued until one or two fell in the street, and lay in an agony

21

of prayer for the cause and the church.   A goodly number
of the young men are going out to preach full salvation, and
some of them, if faithful, will make workers like Brother
Purdy in zeal and firmness."

Mr. Redfield's criticisms on the doings of the church,
and the influence of the college and seminary on the young
Christians sent there, finally occasioned his leaving before
his work was done.

A card from Rev. Woodruff Post, of the Genesee Conference, Methodist Episcopal Church, contributes the
following:

"A Mrs. Wilbur Hoag, though a professed Christian and
a member of the church, had for a long time mourned,
unreconciled, the death of her husband,—to use her own
words, 'even to worshiping a spire of grass that grew upon
his grave,'—was gloriously saved, so that she was enabled
to triumph in the Lord, and with joy to say, ' I give up all
for Jesus.' The rest of soul which she then experienced
enabled her afterwards to triumph under the loss of her only
child Julia, whom she had educated for a useful life."

At this time a severe conflict was raging in the Methodist Episcopal Church, in the Genesee Conference, between
those who were preaching and professing perfect love, and
those who were opposed to the same.   Charges were being
brought against Mr. Kendall, Mr. Roberts, Mr. M'Creery,
and others among the ministry, while many among the laity
were also passing through severe persecution from the
worldly element in the church.

For several years a laymen's camp meeting had been
held annually near Bergen, Genesee, Co. New York, for the
promotion of holiness.   This had been under the charge of
laymen, to keep it from being controlled by church officials,
who were opposed to its object.   This meeting was attended
by such men as Seymour Coleman, B. W. Gorham, then
editor of the *Guide to Holiness*, George Wells, Benjamin

Pomeroy, Henry Belden, Fay H. Purdy, and many others, all mighty men of God, and noted for being advocates of the doctrine and experience of perfect love. This camp meeting was largely attended, and extensive in its influence. Wonderful were the manifestations of divine power that here took place. Multitudes were converted and sanctified, and many ministers received the baptism of the Holy Ghost, and went to their homes in distant parts of the country to kindle similar fires for God and souls. The grove in which these camp meetings were held was a magnificent one, held by a corporation, in trust, for religious purposes. When at last the administration of the church began to expel both ministers and laymen who were identified with this work, an attempt was made, and finally succeeded, to get control of this camp ground, to put an end to the meeting. Advantage was taken of a technicality in the articles of incorporation, in which the name of the Methodist Episcopal Church was used, and those who had contributed towards the purchase of the property, had it wrested from them under the forms of law. While the question of title was in litigation, those who were trying to get control of the same went, one winter, and cut down the entire grove and destroyed it for camp meeting purposes.

It was at such a time as this, and in such circumstances, Mr. Redfield was now laboring. Every mistake of his was magnified into a crime, and many of his former friends, through fear and misapprehension, turned away from him. Those who knew him best, who had been brought into the closest fellowship with him, now drew closer to him than ever. Their private fellowship became intensely spiritual, and many were the special manifestations of the divine presence and favor they received, as they communed together, of their trials and conflicts, and prospects.

CHAPTER XLVII.

From Lima Mr. Redfield went to Rochester, N. Y. For several years he had felt that he had a work to do in that city, and now for the first time the way had opened for him to go there. The meeting was held in the First Methodist Episcopal church. The pastor was one who dared to stand alone where principle was involved. Mr. Redfield thought he had reason to believe him prejudiced against him, personally, yet he acted like a nobleman. The presiding elder seemed to have been of another type, for knowing the revival meeting to be in progress, he appointed a special meeting to be held in the same house and at the same hour it was being occupied. The pastor, knowing his own rights, refused him the church. But when the power of God began to come, and some fell, and other demonstrations of primitive Methodism began to appear, he became frightened, and declared the meetings must stop. The other city preachers began to utter their protests against the work. One of them said to his flock, "If you don't keep away from the First church, I will vacate this pulpit." Some answered, "Then give us something to eat." When such efforts failed, the preachers collected together and discussed the propriety of allowing Mr. Redfield to stay any longer. In the midst of this, when the pressure was so great that he could hardly endure it, a man came to him one day and said, "We have $3,000 pledged towards building a church if you will stay and be the pastor." But he saw the result of this would be such a storm about him as he had never experienced before; and he replied that he could not accept of the offer.

Just at this time he received a letter from Rev. David Sherman, of St. Charles, Illinois, inviting him to come there and hold a meeting. In the next chapter we shall see the beginning of his work in the West.

During the time of his labors in Rochester, Rev. Charles G. Finney, the evangelist, was also holding meetings in the city, and occasionally came to the afternoon meetings conducted by Mr. Redfield. He, a Congregationalist, could endure and endorse what the Methodist preachers of the city could not. The two men seemed to enjoy each others' society, and to bid each other Godspeed in their mission of calling souls to Christ.

Among the results of this meeting, quite a number of persons entered into the enjoyment of perfect love. Some of these have gone to their eternal reward, while others still hold on their way. Among those who experienced this great blessing was the wife of the world-renowned florist, James Vick, who has now, for more than thirty years, held up the light of a full salvation.

Mr. Redfield was reluctant to leave the field and the little band who had been led into the light and who were beginning to walk with God. But the thought that perhaps he might find a field in the West, where the truth would be given free course, where the regular ministry were more humble and had more of the self-sacrificing spirit of the Master, helped him to a willingness to go.

Before leaving here he wrote to Samuel Huntington, a full outline of his life, giving all the details of his family troubles, and the circumstances that led to his last marriage. It is not necessary to go over these again, as there is so much of it in these pages now. Suffice it to say, this was Mr. Redfield's first attempt at anything like a vindication of himself. The letter now before me is in his own handwriting, and corroborates the narrative of his sorrowful life contained in former chapters of this book. In this letter he authorizes Mr. Huntington to use the facts put in his hands in any way he sees fit. He also authorizes him to say, to those who are maliciously following him, that the matter has reached a point where he feels that the cause of Christ demands that he shall hold them accountable to a bar of justice if they do not cease. The date of the letter discloses the fact that this correspondence was going on during a revival meeting of extraordinary power, in which were some marvelous manifestations of the divine presence. The whole gives us a view of a wonderful man, in many phases of his character; for no ordinary man could have done such work in such circumstances.

April 9, 1856, he wrote to the same brother as follows:

"Dear Blessed Brother Sammy:— "Your last came to hand, and no one can know but those who have been compelled to endure a living cancer, and smother it, and yet have the very misfortune made the occasion of persecution; I say none else can know how heart cheering it is to feel that there is here and there one to whom these troubles can be unbosomed, and who can appreciate them and offer consolation. But after writing you what I did, I felt some misgivings for troubling you; and on maturely weighing the whole matter, I thought I would trouble you no more with my woes. A main reason for telling you what I have, was to furnish you with reliable facts, to meet the preachers and people who defame me, and defend, not me, but the straight salvation; for I know that that is the true cause of all this opposition. I can give, if called upon, a justifiable reason for every act of my life, and good names and testimony of all matters connected with my whole misfortune. I have been so rasped and harrowed that I have thought I must give up and retire to private life. Finally, while conversing with Brother Burdick (a conference preacher), I made up my mind to make one more move, and take upon myself the responsibility to be myself, and cut off any further occasion for such slanders as were afloat in Burlington. And as there was no moral or legal impediment in the way, I have taken to myself a wife, one that is pious and well fitted to co-operate with me in labor. I meant to have seen you and laid the whole matter before you, but could not get the opportunity. And I further thought I was under no obligation to ask or inform the gossipers about the matter. You can find out all you wish to know of Brother Burdick.

"I mean, if I can, to be at your dedication; but of that I must determine when I get West. , When I see you, if you can bear with me, I will tell you frankly all the rest of my sorrows, if any good end can be secured by it.

"I go from here to St. Charles, Kane county, Illinois, next Monday, for my last protracted effort. Brother Purdy left here this morning, I think rather discouraged as to any great results. If I can open his way satisfactorily, I think he will go West this summer. I shall try hard for it.

"I have been in Rochester two weeks last Monday. The church will not get right, but the pilgrims from all churches come in. The altar is frequently filled, and we have some strong conversions. The house is very large, but will not hold the people. I never saw a greater chance for a great work in any place. But as soon as we get to a boiling point, the moderators put the fires out, and we have to start anew. My only hope is to strengthen the pilgrims, and get them to work for a salvation church. Many begin to see no other way than to go at it as you did in Burlington, and have a church where they can practice religion. But my ever blessed brother, happy day! God helping me, I will go the strong salvation to the last link of my chain.

"Yours as ever, and forever,

"J. W. REDFIELD."

The sainted William C. Kendall was still laboring at Albion, only thirty-five miles away, and Mr. Redfield could not think of leaving the East without a brief visit with that blessed man. The visit was made, and again blessed in prayer, with and for each other, they parted in the early morning the next day, never to meet again on earth.

At this time persecution was raging fiercely against many of Mr. Redfield's friends in Western New York. The *Christian Advocate*, a semi-official paper, published in Buffalo, was made the organ of those opposed to the doctrine and experience of holiness and the revival of the usages of Methodism. The columns of this paper were open to rumors, slanders, and ridicule of these devoted men. And even ex-Bishop Hamline was not spared, evidently, because of his identification with that doctrine.

The only opportunity there was for defense was through the *Northern Independent*, a Methodist paper, published at Auburn, N. Y., edited by Rev. William Hosmer, a man noted for his piety and integrity. He had been editor of the *Northern Christian Advocate*, the official organ of several conferences in central, northern and western New York, but because of his radical and out-spoken views on the question of slavery, which was then agitating both church and state, the preceding General Conference had elected a conservative man in his stead, against the wishes of the patronizing conferences. This led to the founding of the *Northern Independent*, with Mr. Hosmer as editor. Several prominent ministers were appointed corresponding editors, among whom was Mr. Redfield's friend, Rev. B. T. Roberts. Over his own signature about this time, he attempted to show the character of this opposition to holiness, in two papers, entitled, "Old School Methodism" and "New School Methodism." For writing those articles, he was arraigned before his conference at its next session, on the charge of unchristian conduct. There was no attempt to deny the truthfulness of those articles, neither was Mr. Roberts allowed to prove his statements. Yet he was declared guilty, and sentenced to be reprimanded by the bishop. From this, he appealed to the General Conference. The following year Mr. Roberts was expelled on a charge of contumacy, for publishing an account . of his trial the year before, and republishing in tract form, the articles on "Old School" and "New School Methodism"; though he proved by the real publisher that he had nothing to do with it, and the only evidence against him was that of one minister, who testified that Mr. Roberts handed him a package of the tracts for distribution; and the character of that minister, as a witness, was impeached.

Mr. Roberts joined the church again on probation, immediately after his expulsion, and the following year, the minister who received him into the church, and several more who allowed Mr. Roberts to speak in their churches, were expelled for so doing.

These historical matters will help to explain some things in Mr. Redfield's letters that otherwise would not be understood.

CHAPTER XLVIII

WHEN Mr. Redfield received the letter from Mr. Sherman requesting him to come to St. Charles, according to his custom, he refused to go, unless he was also invited by the official board of the charge. Accordingly a meeting of the board was called, and a resolution inviting him to come was unanimously adopted, and immediately forwarded to him. As we have already seen, he accepted of the invitation, and soon was on his way to the place.

On his arrival he found Mr. Sherman to be the young minister to whom he made the promise, when laboring with him in New England, that if he ever got into a place where he needed help, to send for him, and he would come to his assistance. He had been transferred to the West a few years before, and in the fall of 1855 was appointed to St. Charles and Geneva, in Kane county, Illinois. Mr. Sherman was one of that class of ministers who, in the absence of pulpit talent and commanding personality, was endowed with a copious fountain of tears; where he could not command, nor persuade, by forceful thought or well-put words, he could succeed by his tears. But for some reason he had failed to make much of an impression upon either the church or the world at St. Charles, and in his extremity he sent for Mr. Redfield. Mr. Redfield had preached but a short time before the various elements in the society were thoroughly aroused. The few who were endeavoring to serve the Lord drank in his teachings of the doctrine and experience of perfect love with avidity and delight. Some of these readily understood him and appreciated his efforts. A brother and sister Osborne who had known something of his work in Western New York., promptly responded in approbation. Then there was Sister Snow, afterwards known as "Mother Foot," a Methodist of many years, well read in the theology, history and biography of the church, and who, because of her intelligence and force of character, had been a class-leader for a number of years. Her watchful eye ever on the alert for any departure from "sound words," perceived that the doctrine, the experience, and the methods of Mr. Redfield were Methodistic, and she gave her hearty approval of them. Father and Mother Garton, who had listened to the preaching of Finley, and Strange, and Christie, and Bascom, and many others of like character, were now made to think of olden times, and the old man would sing his old-time songs and hymns with new unction and relish. And with these was Sister Emily Laughlin, daughter of Father and Mother Garton, a woman endowed with remarkable good sense, deep insight into character, and an excellent faculty of saying the right thing in the right time and the right place. And there were others who had not forgotten God, who listened and took fresh courage, buckled the harness a little closer, and went into the conflict again.

Some forty of the membership entered into the experience of perfect love. Some held back and refused to walk in the light. Several old church quarrels were stirred up, and the dirty sediment that by its settling to the bottom had deceived many with the idea that all was well, now rose to the surface in all its loathsomeness. Some became angry, some were frightened, and some "cared for none of these things," and the meetings were forced to a close.

But there were some glorious cases of conversion and sanctification. Among these was that of Charles Elliott Harroun, now and from that time a preacher of the gospel. At this time he was a member of the church and choir. One night he arose and spoke as follows: "Brethren—I—think —if this—is religion—I never—knew anything about it. And—yet—I've been—a member—of this church—for more than three years." He soon afterwards was gloriously saved.

He had been forward for several nights, and seemed to be struggling hard to find peace. At last, one night, he arose, and after a perfect silence for a few moments, and the congregation waiting breathlessly to hear what he had to say, he suddenly screamed at the top of his voice, "I'VE GOT IT!"

Enough entered into the experience of perfect love, in addition to those who already enjoyed it, to make "the St. Charles Pilgrims," as they began to be called, noted through all that region for their power in prayer, the clearness of their testimonies, and the joyfulness of their lives. Their prayer meetings became seasons of glorious power, and the church was often made to ring with the praises of God.

April 30, 1856, Mr. Redfield wrote to Samuel Huntington again as follows:

"ST. CHARLES, Kane Co., ILL.

"My dear blessed Brother Sammy:—I did not leave Rochester at the time I expected to, for the people would not let me off, and of course I did not receive your letters directed to this place, until I arrived here last Thursday.

"I had felt for years a strong drawing to Rochester, but the way did not open until this spring. But such a clinch and contest I never had before. Brother Purdy came and staid a few days, but the opposition was so strong that he left, and I fear that he blamed me for not leaving also. But I did not feel at liberty to do so while so many of the pilgrim stamp were urging me to stay.

"We opened meetings in the First church, and soon we were so crowded that large numbers could not find a place to stand in the church or its vestibule. In our congregation were the workers of all the Methodist churches and Presbyterians and Baptists, numbers of whom procured letters from their own churches and came and joined ours. Then the war began in earnest. Some of the Methodist preachers threatened to leave their charges if the members did not stay

at home; and the answer they received was, 'Give us something to eat, or we will continue to go.' This brought the
ecclesiastical batteries to bear on me. The presiding elder
came down upon us, and appointed a business meeting in our
audience-room, but the preacher-in-charge would not let him
have it, and the elder behaved so badly that he brought himself under great odium. Then the preachers began to
preach against us as croakers; but that did not take; and
then they held an indignation meeting, and threatened the
pastor with a conference castigation, and to publish me as an
irresponsible ranter, a heretic, a divider of churches, a maker
of the people crazy, etc.

"Then the men of the world took it up, and I was informed that about five hundred in number proposed to build
me a church where the great salvation could be preached
without hinderance. You may rely upon it that we began
to have pretty hot work by that time; and wonderful to tell,
amid all this, God came in 'power and some of the most hopeless cases in the city were saved.

"But I thought it best amid such a clatter, to break away
and come West. It was hard parting with the multitude who
followed us to the train; numbers of whom followed us for
twenty miles on the cars, and who gave us their blessing
and one hundred dollars in cash to help us on our way.
They also insisted that we should come back next winter,
and if the fight against us is too hot, to take the city hall until
a salvation church can be built.

"But I don't know about the propriety of such a move.
My heart sank within me, and I asked, 'Who and what am I,
and what have I done, to merit such opposition?' I must
say, I could but appreciate the great kindness of the true
pilgrims who came long distances to meet us at Albion, our
first stopping place, on our way to the West. Notwithstanding all we passed through in Rochester, I feel confident, dear

Brother Sammy, that the good Lord has made a mark in that place that will not soon be wiped out.

"We arrived here on Thursday last. We found the people in waiting, and a goodly number of whom had been praying for our coming. This is very hard soil, but I do not expect much opposition, yet for a while, from the preachers; for they are, in many instances, too much engaged in speculation, some of whom make their thousands yearly. One presiding elder keeps a real estate office, and does business up to the last moment on Saturday, before going to his quarterly meetings, and then returns immediately Monday morning. This is a great field, and must be cultivated for Immanuel. Night before last we had a powerful demonstration in this place. I believe, if we can get down under the crust, we shall see salvation power of the right stamp.

"This is a great place for backsliders who have come here from the East.

"I have done as you requested, and have written a note to the paper where my wife used to live, and from where our certificate dates her residence. I told you one of my reasons for not publishing the fact of our marriage at Burlington. I knew I was doing nothing morally or legally wrong. I knew I would be a subject of suspicion; and I did design to make it known, believing that good people would appreciate it, and others would be quiet after the first blast was blown. But my wife had suffered so much from surmises and stories, that she was unwilling to have anything more said for the gossipers and scandal mongers to use. Her cancerous affection is such that any great disturbance of the mind aggravates her most agonizing symptoms. In one instance, after one of these disturbances, I had to watch over her night and day for ten days, before I could subdue her agony. Even your kind letter, which we found in waiting here, so overcame her, that I was fearful of the results for three days and two nights. There was evidently a transfer to the brain. She became almost wild. I feared, that in spite of all I could do, she would lose her mind. Her great trouble was the fear that our marriage would injure my influence. Under this, her distress became so great that I feared her cancer would break out, and then there would be no hope; and she must endure the most painful of deaths.

"But, thank God, your last letter set all things right. O Sammy, how I did love you when I got that last letter! We both knelt down, and gave thanks to God for that blessed letter. I did think that my kind heavenly Father put it into your mind to write us that letter. May he bless you a thousand times.

"But your first letter led me to a deep heart-searching of the whole transaction, and I fail yet to see but that I have done just right. I did believe that God led me to make the selection I did. I had learned about the gossip concerning her, and I went to the proper source and found that it was all false. I have since seen a number of the most precious saints I ever knew, who had been acquainted with her for years, and they, with one voice, pronounced her one of the most blessed Christians of their acquaintance. And I believe her to be one of the best Christians I ever knew. In each place where we have been, God has given her seals of her mission. Her very large correspondence, reaching all over the country, even to England, with those who have been helped in their religious experiences by her personal efforts, is to me a consoling proof that God owns her, and that she is the very one to go with me and labor as she does from house to house, as well as at church. She is a praying, devoted woman. How I have wished that her enemies could happen in upon her devotions and listen to the ardent prayers she offers for them.

"I regretted that it was against her wishes for me to be open and to state what I had done, and what I meant to do; but when I saw how it affected her, I knew it was best to do as I did. In this I deceived nobody, for I was under no obligations to publish my moves and doings, as long as I did no wrong. I thought then, and I still think, that I was led by my heavenly Father to make the choice I did, and especially so after I found that she had been led to devote her life to religious work, visiting poor-houses and prisons, the sick and the suffering, distributing tracts and praying with the people.

"If I had time to tell you the many strange providences which conspired to bring us together, and to show you the fruit of her labors, and how happy we are amid all our conflicts, and the protection she is to me many times when opposers who neither fear God, nor man, nor the devil, but who show a little deference to a woman, I think you would come to the conclusion that our union is of the Lord.

"Yours in great affection,

"J. W. REDFIELD."

CHAPTER XLIX.

WHILE at St. Charles, Mr. Redfield wrote the following interesting letter to Mr. and Mrs. Kendall, which was evidently designed to minister encouragement in the midst of those degenerate times:

"June 2, 1856.

"Our very dear Brother and Sister Kendall:—How greatly did we rejoice this day in getting a few lines from you; and though we sympathize with you, yet with you we rejoice that your ties are accumulating in heaven. This may startle you, but I think I have good reason to believe that it is not essential to breathe the outer air to secure a sentient immortality. We often look at your very life like pictures, and I never see them without a spring of joy, and a kind of sweet assurance that the originals have written on their every motive, *Fidelity to God.* God bless you. We do love you; we can't help it; and we don't want to.

"St. Charles has never been truly broken up; and the standard of a genuine, living, active, aggressive Christianity has never been preached here until Brother Sherman came. Much yet remains to be done, but I do think it looks somewhat hopeful, when pilgrims dare to pass through the streets, giving glory to God with a loud voice.

"We would rejoice to be with you at your camp meeting, but we must be in Green Bay city, Wisconsin, and at a camp meeting near there about the 15th of June.

"I thank the Lord that you still hold on, and press towards the narrowest of the narrow way. You will see great good, but it will be limited. You will be able to gather but little wheat among the many tares. Be content to be in the minority, for you will never triumph; but if unflinchingly faithful, the wheat you gather will be pure wheat. The wrong always has been, and always will be, in

22

the ascendency. "Many will say Lord, Lord." Christ
alone will end the contest, gather the little wheat, and burn
the many tares. But, oh, my heart says, Go on; go straight:
the salt of the earth, the seed of the church, are the martyrs.
God will—he does—bless you; I know it, I feel it when I
pray for you. * * * * *

"I think the pilgrims will yet have to organize a new
church, and yet that will fail, if they do not guard every
part of the Discipline against hard feelings against their op-
pressors. * * * * The opponents of holiness will conquer the pilgrims as long as they remain in the church, as
slavery will certainly conquer in the legislation of the
church. There is no hope but in getting away from so great
a mass of corruption.

"We must maintain the right though in the minority. It
is better that few be really saved than that many be only half
saved, and be lost at last. Your opponents may be silent,
but not dead. They will bide their time, mature their plans,
and make you at last feel their power.

"Your presiding elder, —— ——, is fairly in for it, and
must now stand fire. I pray God that he may stand firm for
the right. If he keeps to the right, God will see him out in
the end, but not now. Now he must suffer, but the next
generation will see him righted. Above all, God will approve
him at the last.

"Yours as ever,
"J. W. REDFIELD."

After this meeting closed, Mr. Redfield spent a few days
in Aurora, a young and flourishing city twelve miles south.
Some of the St. Charles pilgrims went with him, and were
a great help in the services. Here quite a number, also,
entered into the experience of perfect love.

The next trace we have of Mr. and Mrs. Redfield is at

Mackinaw Island, recruiting their strength for the next season's campaign.

While at Mackinaw, Mr. Redfield writes the subjoined letter to Mr. and Mrs. Kendall, which, to many, will be of special interest because of the views it expresses concerning the division of the church which he believed would result from the opposition the revival of primitive Methodism was destined to bring with it:

"MACKINAW, Mich., July 27, 1856.

"Dear Brother and Sister Kendall:—Your letter of June 23 reached us day before yesterday. While we most deeply sympathize with you in your affliction, we thank God and take courage for the assurance we have that your faces are still toward Mt. Zion. The pamphlet you sent us is a rich and rare omen for good. It was read by the preacher at St. Charles before he forwarded it to us, and from his report I believe it has greatly strengthened him to hold on unflinchingly to the right.

"Now I am no prophet, but I think we will never succeed in cleansing the church. God and truth have always been in the minority. Men act out the impulses of their moral state,—they always have, and always will. You may, if you can, overwhelm and check their schemes, by gaining numbers to the cause of truth, but the devil never was known to surrender the wrong and to contend for the right. This will always be so as long as a single person is left unsaved.

"Some ministers have never been converted; and others have backslidden. None of them can be brought to appreciate what we know to be right, until they are saved. God himself cannot make them love and sustain a cause at which their nature revolts. There are two distinct and totally opposite elements in the church, which can never harmonize until one gives way to the other. There seems no possibility of this. As God lives there is no rational hope but in separation; and yet I would by no means hoist the banner of separation, for you cannot then keep out the spirit of carnal warfare, and that will be death to spirituality. If our daring brethren will persistently hold on to their plan of resuscitating Methodist usages, and keep the central idea of Jesus and a full salvation before the people, they will yet see the day when the masses will be saved and go with them, and formalists will compel the separation. You have the right men for your leaders, and you have more sympathizers than many of you are aware of. Some of these have not the daring to stand alone, or even with a few in a cause which though right is unpopular. May the Lord bless the faithful ones.

"We are getting recruited for the fall campaign. We have invitations to go into Illinois and Wisconsin, which, the Lord willing, we will respond to about the first or the middle of September.

"Remember us to Sister S——. If it is the Lord's will we would be glad to welcome Sister Kendall and her to this place. I don't know what success she will meet with in her application to Dr. Durbin [missionary secretary at that time] for a field of labor on missionary ground. I have my fears that she will not succeed, but hope for the best. However, the will of God be done. If I had a bank, and knew it was the will of God, I would open up a field in the West where she might begin to work for God at once.

"My dear wife says, 'Send her my love, with all my heart'; so you see you'll have to come here to bring it back.

"Yours as ever,

"J. W. Redfield."

Early in September they left Mackinaw, for Wisconsin. After a short visit with an old friend, they went to Fond du Lac, where a glorious work began. Here he was greatly annoyed by the jealousy of the pastor. After vainly attempting to array the members of the church against Mr. Redfield, he wrote to the East to find what he could to injure his influence. One of the parties to whom he wrote informed Mr. Redfield of this. Some one communicated to this pastor some rumors of Mr. Redfield's old family trouble, of which the most was made. Mr. Redfield went to him about it, but found him in a warlike mood, and concluded to let it go.

Under great temptation to give up the struggle, Mr. Redfield left this place with the thought of looking up a home, and engaging again in his profession. But his way in that direction was providentially closed up, and he turned again to the work of the Lord. He was engaged for a short time in A—— (probably Auroraville), where he found kind friends, and where God came to his help in old-time power, and many were saved.

From here he went to New London, where he found a good, kind preacher, but a small society, and only one, a Quakeress, to pray at the altar. Because of this, Mr. Redfield was led to invite forward only those who would do their own praying. They did come, and God blessed them in great power.

From New London Mr. Redfield went to Jefferson, Wisconsin, at the invitation of a preacher whom he had known in the East, Rev. G. H. Fox. Here the Spirit of God had free course, and blessed were the results.

While here he received the news of the grievous fall of one who had been a strong advocate of holiness. Several allusions in some of his letters which follow are explained by this.

In a letter to the Kendall family, dated at this place, he writes:

"JEFFERSON, Wisconsin, December 20, 1856.

"My very dear Brother and Sister Kendall:—Your letter came to hand yesterday, confirming what I would not entertain for a moment before. Well, God would not let the Israelites have the body of Moses to worship, and, as you say, we must learn that we cannot trust in any one but

Jesus. But oh, how I feel for ———. I cannot but believe if all the circumstances of the case were known, sympathy and sorrow would be our prevailing feelings towards him. I wrote part of a letter to him this morning, but after reading it over, I burned it. I will try again. But enough of this.

"I am glad to hear such good news of Johnny, as to both physical and spiritual things. My thoughts often turn to the poor pilgrims. My heart almost sinks when I hear that the tried and true are being driven from the field, and weakening the little band who stand for the right. Shall the enemy yet triumph? I am more and more confirmed in the opinion I expressed long ago that amputation alone will save vital piety. It has come to this, a candidate for the presidency of the United States, in order to election, must guarantee the people that he will do his best to crush out the humanitarian spirit that inspires the abolitionists, and offer premiums to its opposite; and in some of our conferences candidates to be received into the ministry, instead of being required to pledge themselves to uphold the doctrines and spirit of Methodism, are required, virtually, to oppose them.

"Just take a common-sense view of the facts. In contending for the right, some will weary of the conflict, and for the sake of peace will leave the field. Every instance of this will give fresh courage to the opponents of spiritual religion. Others will become dispirited and call for a cessation of the struggle, and when the little band is reduced small enough, they will be surrounded, and made an easy prey. To be in a minority is to be rebellious, while to be in the majority is to be loyal. You think that some already fear that you are too fond of war. But I ask: Have you any selfish motive in this matter? Is it to have your own way? Is it not because you see the cause of Christ suffering, and men perishing? You answer: 'Yes.' Well, should you not contend against everything that wars against Christ? Whenever the church ceases to be aggressive,—ceases to be a

conquering power,—she loses in spiritual life.   No! no! dear
brother and sister, 'contend earnestly for the faith once delivered to the saints.' Contend, at least, until you are equal in
zeal, faith, fidelity, and purity with the early saints; then if
the Lord intimates that you may slack your pace, or ease up
in your thoroughness, you will be at liberty to do so.   But
if you contend, not for an improvement, but for the right,
you will have battles, and all manner of evil will be spoken
against you.   Remember, it is of small concern what men
may think of you. The judgment day will adjust all wrongs.
How cheering the anticipations of the words from our
Father, 'My child, you have done right.' Oh, that is enough!
Let us fight on.

"This great West is famishing for the bread of life.   It
is all hurry and bustle, hastening to be rich.   You can
scarcely turn without running against a backslider.   I went
out early to build a fire in the church last evening, and in
came an old backslidden class-leader from Scottsville, N. Y.,
all broken down, and said, 'Sir, this is the first time I have
been in a church in seven years.   Myself and wife, and
children, are all backslidden.   But if there is any hope for
me, I want to get back to the Lord.'

"There is an awful spell on the whole place.   Brother
Fox went into a store the other day, and as soon as he spoke
to the first man, he broke down and wept, and soon all in
the store were affected in like manner.

"We expect to go to Appleton about the first or the
fifteenth of January.

"You don't know how I want to see your faces in the
flesh once more, and with you have another season of salvation and power.   My wife is being greatly blessed.   She
is trying to do her duty.   She spoke to a man the other day,
—one who is very prominent in the church, and had more
piety than all the rest,—but he became offended because of
her close questions, and went to Brother Fox, and requested

him to send us away. But a few nights after he was gloriously blest, and confessed clear down to the bottom, and now is being used mightily to break down others. He has forgiven Mattie.

"The Lord knows I love you. Remember us to all the pilgrims.   "J. W. REDFIELD."

On leaving Jeffersonville, Mr. Redfield went to Waukesha, where he found another old friend in charge of the work, and who was willing to let the truth and the Holy Spirit have free course. God came in glorious power, and many were saved.

"Mr. Redfield now made his contemplated visit to Appleton, Wis., the seat of Lawrence University. This was a Methodist institution, and with the church, made the place a strong Methodist community. Rev. William McDonald, now editor of the *Christian Witness* of Boston, and also president of the National Holiness Association, was pastor of the church. Then, as now, he was an earnest advocate of the experience of entire sanctification, and boldly stood by Mr. Redfield's work. Among the professors in the university, was Rev. N. E. Cobleigh, who afterwards was known as a strong man in the Methodist Episcopal Church, and Professor F. O. Blair, who was a student in Middletown, Connecticut, at the time of Mr. Redfield's great meeting there. Mrs. Blair was preceptress in the university, and with her husband entered heartily into the work of saving souls. For a long time, there had been a strong infidel influence in the community, and in the university an infidel club had been organized by some of the students. Regular meetings were held, and the members of the club were active in propagating their opinions. Christianity was unmercifully ridiculed, and professors of religion were subject to sneers and scoffs. Just before the revival opened, the faculty had forbidden the meetings of the club; and about the same time, Dr. Cobleigh preached a sermon in which he declared that personal experience was the true test, to each individual, of the truth and reality of the Christian religion, and proposed to these skeptics to make an honest test of the matter by believing on the Lord Jesus Christ. An invitation was then given them, to come forward to the altar, and several of the most prominent came. Of course they experienced no benefit, and they went away boasting that they had tested the matter, and found there was nothing to it.

The most aggressive of these skeptics was a young South Carolinian. He was very intelligent and an excellent scholar. Aside from his infidel sentiments, he was a model young man.

A daily prayer meeting was started in the college at the commencement of the revival meetings, for the benefit of the students. In one of these this young man arose and declared that there was not, nor could be such a thing as experimental religion, and that the idea was a delusion and a snare. Before he was fairly seated, Professor Blair arose and related the story of Gallileo and the priests who condemned him for teaching that the world moved. He described the scene: Gallileo recanting on his knees, but as he rises, whispering aside to a friend: "*But it does move.*" He then remarked, that the truth of the gospel did not depend on the belief of any man or of the world of mankind. The meeting then went on without any further interruption.

The revival had such an effect upon the students that from that time Christianity was so in the ascendency that the skeptical felt the atmosphere too uncongenial, and one after another dropped out from the college ranks and went away. Not one of that infidel club ever graduated from that institution.

The young Carolinian already described was the last to go. He was a member of a class in mental philosophy with Professor Blair as instructor. One day he was called upon to recite a lesson wherein the author makes the statement, and lays it down as a principle, that no one can have any knowledge of a sensation, emotion, or feeling which he has never experienced. He presented the author's views clearly and distinctly. The professor then asked him: "Do you think that principle correct?"

He answered promptly, "I do."

"Then you think that a person who has never enjoyed religion can have no knowledge of that experience?"

The infidel paused; for he saw the dilemma this placed him in, and remembered his words spoken in the prayer meeting. A deep crimson blush rushed upward from his collar over his neck and face till lost in his abundant hair; and then he gasped out, "I suppose not." He never recovered his assurance, and at the close of the term departed never to return.

In this meeting many were converted, and also many were sanctified.

When the summer came (1857), Mr. Redfield made his way to St. Charles, Illinois, again. He came in time to attend a camp meeting, held in June, near that place. The presiding elder, Rev. E. H. Gaunnon, was a good man, and stood nobly by the work. He gave Mr. Redfield the utmost liberty. On Friday evening he preached. A storm had driven the people into the tents. This was before the day of large tabernacles and rented tents. Each family had their own tent of their own construction; except when several families, or a whole society, united and occupied a very large one. In such a society tent, Mr. Redfield preached on perfect love.

Toward the close of the sermon he used the following illustration of the reason so many fail to obtain it. He said: "An old lady once, on reading the eleventh of St. Mark before retiring for the night, said: 'There, that is just what I want to have done. Here is this great hill between me and my neighbor's house. I'll just ask the Lord to take it away.' So down upon her knees she went, and prayed accordingly. In the morning, as soon as it was light, she hurried to the window, and there stood the hill where it did before she prayed. 'Well,' said she, 'I thought it would be just so.'" "So," said Mr. Redfield, "many pray, and when the answer does not come, they feel, 'I thought it would be just so.'"

The meeting closed, and most of the preachers retired to the tent provided for them, and went to bed. Soon one of them asked the question: "What do you think of the doctor's sermon?"

"It was all right," answered another.

"If he is right, we are all wrong," said still another.

"If we are wrong, we had better get right," said still another.

"I'll go at it now, if you will," said still another.

In a few minutes they were up and dressed and on their knees in prayer. Soon the people from the tents were kneeling round the preachers' tent, on the outside, engaged in prayer; some of them for their pastors, and some for themselves. On past midnight this impromptu service ran. One after another of the preachers entered into the experience, until fifteen were rejoicing in its possession.

This was the beginning of better days for the people of God in this section of the country. In the following winter —1857–1858—memorable as that of the great revival, these preachers, all aflame, entered into the work with a zeal born of the Holy Ghost, and many were the victories for Christ, strong and permanent. The work in what was called the "Fox River region" took on a type of thoroughness and clearness that made the converts marked and distinct wherever they went. Some were called Redfieldites who had never seen or heard of Mr. Redfield.

CHAPTER L.

On July 4, 1857, Mr. Redfield wrote the following letter, which indicates that hostility to vital godliness was becoming more intense and general throughout the church, and that his own long-deferred hope of reformation without separation was rapidly giving way:

"My very dear Brother and Sister Kendall:—God and my own soul only know what drawings I feel towards you, and how it rejoices my heart to hear from you once more. How gladly would I go almost any distance to see you! Your fame has spread even to Wisconsin, and among the preachers you are regarded as the offscouring of the earth. Praise the Lord! The *Buffalo* and *Western Advocates* have put their mark upon you. Bless the Lord! I have shown the Medina paper, you sent me, to some of the preachers, and I think some of them are getting their eyes open. It is with much tribulation we must enter the kingdom. With my whole heart I can say, I believe you and those who stand with you are the representatives of primitive Christianity and early Methodism. My soul says, The Lord bless and keep you to the end. Bonds and afflictions await you, and every one who dares to merge every interest in God's will. I often inquire, Will the pilgrims hold out? or will they be disheartened, and finally give up the contest, and be content with saving themselves, and let others go to perdition? I am sure that they who have arrayed themselves against you will never cease their hostility till they put you down. If they succeed, where is the hope of the church? God only knows how sorrow fills my soul when I look at the gloomy prospect. 'By whom shall Jacob arise? for he is small.' Will Brothers M'Creery, and Roberts, and Kendall, and others grow weary, and say, What is the use of the unequal contest? I am more than ever convinced that it is duty to prepare for a separate organization, which, if judiciously pursued, will build up a church, in the midst of severe persecutions, perhaps, yet a church that will bless the world, and compel the opponents of vital godliness to feel their deficiencies as now they cannot.   But, of course, you know your own duty.   My prayer is, that God may direct you.

"It sometimes seems strange that God does not come to your rescue, if you are in the right; and in some unmistakable manner demonstrate that.   But I remember that God must protect the free agency of man, and then hold him responsible for results.   He permitted his ancient prophets to be slain.   He permitted the papacy to clothe the church in sackcloth for 1200 years.   So it has been from the beginning, and probably will be until the end of time.

"But may not great good come to them who endure, though painful it may be?   It hurts the penitent sinner to humble down and confess his sins, and then accept the humble Nazarene.   It hurts the convert to sacrifice all, and become a whole burnt offering on the altar of God, before he can be sanctified.   It hurts to have those, who have been your friends, drop off one by one, because they cannot risk their reputations to defend you.   Here we must often stand alone, with none but Jesus who dares to own us: We may have to stand with the Marys, and see Jesus wounded in the house of his friends, and be unable to help him.   A word, or a tear, or a groan in his favor, may cause them to strike him the harder and deeper.   They may strike you down until you seek a place of solitude where you may weep out your sorrow alone; but to see them strike your Lord, who can endure it?

"May I say, I see all this in the distance as your cup? What if M'Creery, and Roberts, and Hard should shrink from the bootless task, and strong hands should be laid on you to put you out of the conference?   Will you and your dear wife stand for God, and trust Elijah's ravens for your supplies? Oh, my heart is full! May the suffering Jesus be with you.

"Yours,

"J. W. REDFIELD."

The following letter, written by a personal friend, will further show what influences were at work in opposition to a revival of primitive Christianity, and will also be of interest as showing the personal character of the man himself.

Mr. Kendall was serving the Chili, N. Y., circuit at this time, a strong country charge, and one where he had brave friends to stand by him.

"CHILI, Aug. 21, 1857.

"Dear Brother Phelps:—Since I saw you I have been at two camp meetings—on Niagara District and at Wyoming. At the former, the doctrine that we are entirely sanctified at conversion was boldly proclaimed. Brother Wm. Cooley requested me to exhort in his place, and set the matter right. I occupied forty-five minutes in trying to do so, while the Regency preachers prayed God to have mercy upon me. I felt a good conscience all through.

"At Wyoming camp meeting I preached on the same subject. Brother Abell arose, as soon as I was through, and backed what I said. The presiding elder and two preachers then exhorted against me, after which Brother B. W. Gorham, of the *Guide to Holiness*, stood by me and the truth nobly, for which the presiding elder, as soon as the service closed, took him off into the woods. Some of the preachers roar against me "like the bulls of Bashan." I know not but they will gore me, tear the ground, or something, at the conference. I do not expect to remain at Chili. I go to conference, not knowing what will befall me there; nor do I trouble myself at all. Naught can harm me while I abide in Christ.

"Your militant brother,

"W. C. KENDALL."

But the conspirators were already at work, plotting and planning against these men. When conference came, Kendall, talented, successful, and beloved by the humble and spiritual, was confronted by a bill of charges, and only escaped trial for lack of time; then was sent to West Falls circuit, "the whipping post" of the conference.

B. T. Roberts was tried on a charge of unchristian conduct, and, not being allowed to defend himself with testimony, was declared guilty, sentenced to be reprimanded by the bishop, and then sent from Albion, a strong station, to a country village,

Joseph McCreery was treated in like manner.

When the bishop concluded the reading of the appointments, for a moment the pilgrims hung their heads in sorrow at this manifestation of the bitter spirit of their persecutors. The bishop called for a verse of song, and Kendall, with a full and steady voice led off with:—

"Come, on my partners in distress,
My comrades through this wilderness,
Who still your bodies feel;
Awhile forget your griefs and fears,
And look beyond this vale of tears,
To that celestial hill."

The bishop was about to pray, but Kendall sang on,

"Beyond the bounds of time and space,
Look forward to that heavenly place,
The saints' secure abode.
On faith's strong eagle pinions rise,
And force your passage to the skies,
And scale the mount of God."

Again the bishop was about to kneel for prayer, but Brother Kendall continued to sing:—

"Who suffer with our Master here,
We shall before his face appear,
And by his side sit down.

To patient faith the prize is sure;
And all that to the end endure
The cross, shall wear the crown."

By this time every head of the persecuted band was up,
and as they sang they believed, and hope grew strong. Some
fell to the floor; some shouted aloud, while Brother Kendall's
voice continued still to make the auditorium ring with
heavenly melody, as he sang:—

"Thrice blessed bliss-inspiring hope,
It lifts the fainting spirits up,
It brings to life the dead.
Our conflicts here shall soon be past,
And you and I ascend at last,
Triumphant with our Head.

"That great mysterious deity,
We soon with open face shall see;
The beatific sight,
Shall fill the heavenly courts with praise,
And wide diffuse the golden blaze,
Of everlasting light."

The bishop then prayed, the doxology was sung, the
benediction pronounced, and the pilgrim preachers went to
their appointments without a sigh.

In the following letter, Mr. Kendall describes his new
circuit.

"WEST FALLS, Erie Co., N. Y.
"Sept. 16, 1857.

"Dear Brother Roberts:—I find myself on my new field.
Four or five appointments—no parsonage—one prayer meeting—some fifty or sixty members; and they have been giving their preacher two hundred and fifty dollars to live upon.
The starvation system is in full blast in my case. I shall
have a good year, however, if I have any year. One appointment is within ten miles of Buffalo; and I have serious
thoughts of establishing one within the heart of the city its-

self. God may have designed, by my appointment, to pour out a vial of wrath or mercy on the *seat of the beast.* I intend to watch the openings of providence, and to enter them in the name of the Lord.

"I think of you often, and fear lest you will be discouraged in view of the state of things. The Regency pressed you hard in LeRoy; but it was not you they were after, but the blessed Jesus. I never realized the corrupt state of our conference as when we were voting on your case. Such combination to crush a brother I did not suppose could be with us. As you said on the conference floor, 'Some of us will die hard.' Don't be discouraged, brother; we have not suffered much yet. As you said to me on the night of your sentence and execution, 'It is an honor to be denounced by those men.' Such bribery as they practiced is a disgrace to any set of men who make no pretense to religion. But I must stop, or my head will be off next.

"I spent the Sabbath after conference in LeRoy. Brother —— asked me to preach, after consultation with A. P. R., and to preach the first sermon. I had a very good time. The Lord blessed me. I have no doubt that he willed that I should spend that day in LeRoy. McE. invited Mrs. K. and myself home to dinner with him, and treated me as respectfully as he knew how. Brother Shepard, a class-leader, said in class that he did not know the brother who preached; but if that was Nazaritism, he was a Nazarite. R. cautioned the people to 'beware of troublers.' Brother Colton was very friendly. Brother Anderson, just as McE. was about to pronounce the benediction, cried out, 'Brother Kendall will preach in the Congregational church at five o'clock, the Lord willing.' The house was well filled, and we had another good time, and followed the sermon with a sort of love-feast. The N——s are becoming popular in LeRoy.

"I expect you, Brother McC. and Brother Cooley will see to the pilgrims in that northern region. Brother Colton

23

said, on Monday morning, as I was about to leave, that he thought Brother Roberts and myself ought to go through the conference holding meetings. Indeed, I was almost persuaded, as they did not locate me, to locate myself, and be free to go everywhere, preaching Jesus. We must circulate, as much as possible, among the people. God will give us this land yet. I give the Regency fair warning, the Lord helping, I will do my duty to them this year. My address is as above. Write if you have a mind.

"Yours, through the war,

"W. C. KENDALL."

On Nov. 5, Mr. Kendall also wrote in another letter as follows:

"Dear Brother Phelps:— * * * * You speak of our being scattered, and exhort me to keep up courage. I have no doubt that it is as I told some of my people; I was sent here to be whipped and starved, but I don't expect to receive either. I have five appointments, and preach three times each Sabbath. There is no pastor of any denomination living within the bounds of my parish. I preach in four comfortable meeting-houses—two of them Methodist, one Union; the fourth is owned by twelve sinners. Abundance of work—scarcely any religion, only one *choir* to bother. No revival has been here for years. My health is good— my courage, also.

"We have just had our first quarterly meeting—a very good season. One soul soundly converted—a little of the first fruits. A few were a little displeased on finding the door closed, they being late to love-feast. The love-feast was a blessed season. Many saw the benefit of the Methodist rule. * * * *

"Your brother to the end of the war,

"W. C. KENDALL."

This was Mr. Kendall's last appointment. In the midst of a glorious revival, he sickened and died. His death was one of the most triumphant. A short time before his departure, he said: "I've been swimming for two days in the waters of death, and they are like sweet incense all over me." Waving his hands in holy triumph, he repeated the lines:—

"Bright angels are from glory come;
They're round my bed, they're in my room;
They wait to waft my spirit home—
All is well,"

and passed away to that better land, where "the wicked cease from troubling and the weary are at rest."

The day of his funeral the pilgrim preachers gathered around his remains, and clasping hands above them, vowed fidelity to God.

It is said of this blessed man, that he was one of nature's noblemen in every way. A large, strong body, a frank and noble face — the radiance of which has smitten sinners with conviction — broad and well-cultivated mind, and a large heart. To know him was to love him; to be with him, was to be rebuked for sin, and to be moved towards Christ. Joyous, buoyant, faithful, untiring in zeal, he wrought amid fierce persecutions which followed him to the grave. His friends were of the choicest, purest, the most devoted. His enemies were the worldly, the carnal, the time-serving, and the untrue. His bitterest enemies fought him while he lived, and eulogized him after he was dead.

The venerable Father Coleman once said to the writer: "I knew him; and such a face as his I never saw before. I think he was the sweetest, faithful man I ever knew."

CHAPTER LI.

In December, 1857, we find Mr. Redfield in St. Charles, Illinois, again, endeavoring to break through the crust of which he spoke in a former letter; but for some reason, never explained, he was unable to reach the signal victory here, which he experienced in other places. A few were saved, the pilgrims strengthened, while those in the church who resisted the light, settled into a deeper hostility to the doctrine and experience of holiness.

On the 21st of December, he wrote a letter to Brother and Sister Kendall, of which the following is a copy:

"St. Charles, Ill.

"My dear Brother and Sister Kendall:—We received your very welcome letter before we started for this place. How glad we were once more to hear from you! We had heard from you and many of the pilgrims through Brother J. D. R——, a few weeks ago; and now and then we get a little information through Eastern papers, which give us a little clue of what is going on. But we want to see you, if the Lord permit.

"We are now on our way to a southern clime—Texas, probably—where we wish if possible to find a place for a colony, where we can establish a type of salvation which will live. We think that not less than one hundred and fifty to two hundred will go between this spring and next fall. Among them will be a number of preachers, and most of the remainder will be Methodists. We shall only invite those who have a living religion. I go to select, if I can, from ten to fifty thousand acres of land, in a body in some eligible location, this to be distributed among the colonists. A prominent object is to get a location where invalids like Mattie will be likely to gain health, more surely than in northern latitudes. What information I have with respect to Texas is, the climate is most delightful, fully equal to the best portions of California.

"We have been holding meetings here, and have seen some as powerful conversions as I ever knew. But our plow has run into some old roots, of from five to twenty years old. We tugged, and ground, put on more team, and cut our way through, until some thought we had got through all. But I think there is more yet, and may be worse than any we have yet seen. Whether we can force our way clear through is more than I can tell. Mattie is afraid to have me press it through, but I have no fears for myself, and would sooner run under than leave the work half done. How we shall succeed remains to be seen.

"We expect to leave here by the middle of January, and I wish to hear from you once more before then.

"Yours in love,

"J. W. REDFIELD."

An appendix to this letter, written by Mrs. Redfield, says they had been in St. Charles three weeks. God had been with them in power. Quite a number had been converted. She refers to the troubles, and thinks the preacher in charge ought to take hold of them, and not leave so much for Mr. Redfield.

This preacher in charge was Rev. Charles French, a good man, who loved God and the truth, and was in hearty sympathy with an earnest salvation. He remained a firm friend to Mr. Redfield for years.

How soon the visionary scheme, described by him in the last letter was given up, there is nothing to show; but this is the first and the last trace of it to be found.

About the first of January he went to Elgin, Illinois. The pastor was Rev. C. M. Woodward, who knew many of the ministers in the Genesee Conference, of which he had been a member. He knew much of Mr. Redfield's work in

the East, and was prepared to receive him here. The notion
that it was best to keep the control of the services in his own
hands, as preacher in charge, was somewhat in Mr. Redfield's
way, as the latter's experience in revival work enabled him
to surmount difficulties, where others knew not what to do.
In this meeting Mr. Redfield did the preaching and invited
seekers to the altar, but Mr. Woodward managed the prayer
service. Mr. Redfield's success was due largely to his skill-
ful management of seekers at the altar.

The work moved slowly at first, but after a little, it began to take hold of the membership. Quite a number of
them entered into the experience of perfect love. But there
was no general break among sinners.

While engaged at Elgin, Mr. Redfield was visited by
Mr. M. L. Hart, of Marengo, a village twenty-five miles
away, at the instance of the official board of the Methodist
Church, to request him to assist in a revival at that place.
Mr. and Mrs. Hart had been somewhat acquainted with Mr.
Redfield's labors in the East, and when they heard of his being in Elgin, they recommended him to the Marengo
church. He consented to go, on condition that the official
board would allow him the liberty to preach according to the
Bible and the Methodist Discipline. On Mr. Hart's return,
a meeting of the board was called, and a motion to invite Mr.
Redfield on his own conditions was unanimously adopted.
Mr. Redfield on learning of this determined to go as soon
as he could leave Elgin. In the midst of this he received a
telegram as he entered the church one Saturday evening, that
his friend, William C. Kendall, was lying at the point of
death. After the service Sunday night he wrote the following letter:

"ELGIN, Ill., 12:30, Sunday Night.

"My dear Brother and Sister Kendall:—I received your
dispatch while going into church last night. And as there

was no mail or train until Monday afternoon, it afforded me
time to think and pray over the matter. Brother Woodward had already left for Marengo, to fill my appointment
there until I came, that I might stay here over the Sabbath.
I laid the matter before the Lord last night, and in great
distress of mind, I asked: 'What shall I do?' When I thought
of the work of God, and of your sickness, I said: 'We
cannot spare Brother Kendall.' Then I said: 'Lord, tell
me which way I shall go'; and a sweet, blessed influence
came over me, which seemed to say: 'You attend to God's
business, and he will attend to Brother Kendall better than
you can.' And I feel at perfect rest when I trust Brother
Kendall in his hands.

"Elgin has about 3,000 people, and it is said they have
never known such power as we have in our meetings. And
there is a fear that if I leave it will go down. This night
we have had one of the most awful and glorious times. The
straight way of holiness has most signally triumphed. To-
morrow I must go to Marengo, about twenty-five miles from
here. The preacher there is used up, can preach no more,
and must have help. Here they are pressing me to stay.
There they say I may go the straight way. There are also
two other places awaiting me; one twenty miles south, and
the other at Galena, a city of 10,000 or 12,000 people. Amid
these calls and promises to let God have a fair chance, together with what we now have, you may well judge of the
rack on which my mind was cast by your dispatch.

"All I can get from the Lord is: 'Keep at work, and I'll
take care of Brother Kendall.' I fear to get out of God's
order, and it seems to me to be his order that I confine my
labors at present to Marengo and Elgin. I feel at rest about
you, some way. You know I had got started for the South,
but as this door opened, I felt I must risk Mattie's
health, and she is now better. This, to me, is another evidence that I am in the right field for the present.

"You did not state what is the matter with Brother Kendall. Write to me at Marengo.

"I feel wonderfully at rest in regard to Brother Kendall. It doesn't seem as though the Lord would take him to glory yet. I could die for him, and nothing but the strong impression of duty keeps me here. If it were not for that, I would take the first train to come to you.

"Glory to God, all is well. Hallelujah!

"J. W. REDFIELD."

When Mr. Redfield arrived at Marengo, he had an opportunity to listen to the religious testimonies of some of the membership, and saw that it would take very thorough work to give the stamp of piety that was needed in that place. It was also evident that a large portion of those who had professed to be converted knew but little about religious experience. In his first sermon he endeavored to show that it was the privilege of Christians to live in the land of Beulah constantly. This so shocked some of the membership that they could scarcely endure him from that time. One member of the official board has informed the writer, that if it had not been for the pledge that they would let Mr. Redfield go straight on the Bible and Discipline, it would have been difficult to have gained their consent to let him continue. They never had heard the truth presented in that way before.

General Superintendent E. P. Hart, of the Free Methodist Church, son of the M. L. Hart who bore the request to Mr. Redfield to come to Marengo, says:

"I had professed religion during the meetings that had been held previous to the Doctor's coming, but I knew scarcely anything of real religion. I had heard father and mother speak of the Doctor in such strong terms, and such wonderful reports had come to us of the meetings at Elgin, that I was full of expectation of listening to marvelous eloquence. I went to a friend and relative of mine, a lawyer by the name of Rogers, and invited him to go with me and listen to the wonderful man. I became very anxious that Rogers should be favorably impressed, and remarked as we approached the church, 'He may be a little embarrassed to-night, as he is a total stranger, and may not do as well as when he becomes better acquainted.' When we got inside the church, I found it very difficult to get Rogers a seat, and was obliged to take one of the pulpit steps for myself. As soon as the Doctor commenced, I forgot all about Rogers. My hopes of heaven were all swept away by the truth, and from that time I could not conscientiously profess religion. The Doctor had taken tea at our house, and now went home with us to tarry for the night. As soon as we had got seated around the stove, after our return, he asked me how I enjoyed the meeting. I replied, 'Oh, very well; I am not used to quite so much noise.'

"'My brother,' said he, 'has the Lord made you ear inspector of this community?'

"This settled me, as far as that was concerned, but I did not get out into a good experience until long after the protracted meeting closed."

This revival swept the town and the surrounding country. People came from five to twenty miles in their own conveyances, and often the house would be well filled an hour and a half before the time for service. Many were converted in their wagons on their way home. The number converted has been estimated at from four to five hundred. Every whisky-shop in the place was closed, and many of the worst of people were converted. Large numbers were entirely sanctified, and a light was kindled that has never gone out. Many have died, who were saved in that meeting, who honored God while they lived, and who triumphed gloriously in their last moments.

Among the many trophies of divine grace was that of the

village drayman, a man by the name of Boyington. He was very wicked and blasphemous. When he was saved he became more remarkable for his piety. Endowed with remarkable good sense, and with a quaintness of expression peculiarly his own, he was always interesting, whether in private conversation, or in public testimony. He lived for about twenty-five years, a monument of mercy, and then fell asleep in Jesus.

A physician by the name of Richardson entered into the experience of perfect love, and though rejected by the conference, when he applied for work, was taken to Minnesota, by a visiting presiding elder,* and given employment. He became very successful, and was made a great blessing to the church and the world.

As at St. Charles, so here, there were a number of deeply experienced Christians, who quickly recognized the work of God, and who rallied around Mr. Redfield, and gave great aid to the work. One of these was "Mother Cobb," who for many years was the only living witness to the experience of perfect love in all those parts. She had then walked in the steady light of it for more than forty years. She lived for nearly twenty more in the light of that experience, when God took her home. Another was, "Mother Combs," a woman of deep piety, clear understanding, and consistent life. Another was, the mother of Superintendent Hart. She had been led into the experience by Rev. James Caughey.

The pastor of the church was no help to the work, and providentially kept away. Soon after the close of the meeting he was arraigned before the presiding elder on a charge of drunkenness. He soon after went to one of the frontier states and engaged in the practice of law.

One of the results of this meeting was the starting of a Monday evening holiness meeting at the home of a brother Bishop, several miles out in the country, that was sustained

_____
*Rev. D. D. Cobb.

through summer and winter for several years. It was nothing unusual for people to come from six to nine miles to that meeting, and return the same night. Many were converted and many were sanctified in those meetings.

During this revival meeting, the news came of the death of Mr. Kendall. The following is Mr. R——'s letter of condolence to Mrs. Kendall:

"MARENGO, Ill., Feb. 22, 1858.

"My dear Sister Kendall:—I cannot realize that our dear fellow laborer is really reaping his reward in heaven. I could not make it seem possible, that one so faithful, and so honored of God, could be spared. I did not feel that God would take him so soon. But there must have been the best of reasons why our heavenly Father took him up to the society of the glorified. He is now associated with the sainted Fletcher, whom he much resembled. Brother Kendall's face came up before me in a remarkable manner two or three hours before I received your dispatch, and during the evening after. I deeply mourn with you over your loss. I am persuaded that angels are rejoicing over his arrival among them. I pray that his mantle may fall on me. From Sister S——'s letter, I judge that he was past help when I received your first dispatch; or, at least, would have been before I could have reached him.

"Like Mrs. Fletcher, you may tarry behind to do much for God. You now realize, as never before, the power of religion. Yours is a hot furnace, but remember the white-robed throng came up out of great tribulation. I try to make your case my own, and often fear, should I be called to see my best earthly friend laid in the cold grave, that I could never smile again. God and my own heart only know what a jewel I have, and I fear I have not religion enough to sustain me in such a calamity. But I may go first. I do not allow myself to think of it, but keep to work, and trust that

he who has called me, if I am faithful, will sustain me in
that awful hour, whether she or I go first. If you could
only be with us here, God would make you a great blessing,
and I am sure that he and your sainted husband would be
pleased with your labors. Be as cheerful as you can; you
will have friends below as well as above.

"Yours affectionately,

"J. W. Redfield."

In another letter to Sister Kendall, written about the
same time, after discussing the idea of the departed being
ministering spirits to their friends here, the idea of which he
somewhat favored, he wrote thus of Brother Kendall:

"I always felt, and do now, a kind of inspiration to say:
'Blessed, persecuted, faithful man!' While he lived, God
had one man that would not swerve a hair's breadth from
the exact right. Yes, God had one man in the old Genesee
Conference that could be trusted in any place; who in the
darkest night of discouragement was at his post. Yes, blessed saint! Glory be to God, that I ever saw him! I feel ·
the inspiration of his faithful spirit. I never felt so strong
in God, and so firm to stand up for the exact right as I have
since he, like an Elijah, has gone on before. It seems to me
he is commissioned to infuse his own daring, faithful spirit
into those who are ready to halt, I praise God that he ever
lived. I sometimes relate his experiences, persecutions, and
triumphs, to my congregations, and always with good effect.
He is now above the reach of flattery, and I can say what is
in my heart, 'Well done, good and faithful servant.' I may
yet drink of his bitter cup, but shall I ever be with him and
see his glory? In imagination I can see him, on the occasion
of which you wrote, when he was so grieved to think he
stood so alone for God; and in my inner heart I say: 'Well
done, blessed man.'

"J. W. Redfield."

Mr. Redfield was pained at one thing in connection with his work in Marengo—the want of care with respect to the results of the meeting. He says: "Could the Methodist Church have been persuaded to take care of the work, rather than to contend against it, it might have spread farther, and a more glorious harvest have been reaped." The presiding elder could but endorse the character of the work, but thought in the end it would work harm, as it would be impossible to supply it with preachers who would be acceptable to the people—that is, it was unfortunate to have such a revival, because there were so few preachers in the conference who were in sympathy with it.

CHAPTER LII

FROM Marengo, Mr. Redfield went to Woodstock, the county seat, twelve miles distant. Here he found the Methodist society weak, and worshiping in a hired hall. Quite a number of the newly saved, from various places, gathered here to assist in the meetings.

Among them was C. E. Harroun, spoken of in the account of the St. Charles meeting. Mr. Redfield's manner and matter in preaching were new to the people, and as usual drew large crowds to hear him. The curiosity of the masses, the cold indifference of the church, and the hesitating, doubtful policy of the pastor, for a time made the effort for a revival very hard. One brother, from Marengo, who had experienced the holy baptism, while engaged in prayer at the altar, suddenly was without voice or thoughts. Having never had such an experience before, he was filled with surprise, and looked about him in amazement. With Mr. Redfield this was no new thing, and fully aware of the feelings of the brother, he shouted a word of encouragement, and soon all was right. Inquiry showed that all the rest of the praying ones had a similar experience at the same time. It was but one of those onsets of the powers of darkness often met by those engaged in evangelistic work. The writer remembers an instance of the kind, during Mr. Redfield's labors in Elgin. A sudden hush came upon the meeting. Every voice at the altar was silenced, and soon the congregation was boisterous with merriment. Mr. Redfield, standing in front of the pulpit, suddenly stamped his right foot, and at the top of his voice cried out, "Lord, smite the devil." In an instant, the merriment in the congregation ceased, and every praying one broke out in loud supplication, which lasted for some moments, when the praying was turned to praising, and the noise of the latter equaled that of the former. For such emergencies Mr. Redfield seemed especially endowed.

At Woodstock, determined opposition set in against the work. At first the Baptist and the Presbyterian ministers appointed a union prayer meeting and invited both the Universalist preacher and Mr. Redfield to attend it. Mr. Redfield saw that it was an attempt to crowd him into a position where he would be misunderstood by the people; that is, where he would be obliged to refuse to attend the meeting because of the liberty given the Universalist minister. They well knew this from what they had heard and observed of his preaching. But if he refused to accept of their invitation, they would charge him with uncharitableness, and that with apparent grounds for it. But he met it squarely, by answering, "No! I have no fellowship with infidels." He then spoke plainly of what he considered the design of the thing.

Then an eminent minister, living at a distance, was sent for, to preach in one of the churches, and that failed. Then a prominent member was found standing at the entrance of the hall one night, asking persons if they were not ashamed to be seen at a Methodist meeting; and that failed. Then threatening letters were sent to Mr. Redfield, and that failed. Then a band of roughs congregated together, and pledged themselves to each other to mob Mr. Redfield, and he was guarded to and from the hall a number of nights. A dentist, an old Methodist backslider, by the name of Murphy, a man of great physical strength and daring, was his principal escort. But one night nearly every one of this gang was at the altar crying for mercy; and so that scheme failed. Then reports began to be circulated that Mr. Redfield was a gambler, and a drinking man. Some men went so far as to say that they had seen him engaged in both; but that failed. The Universalist preacher was annoyed by so many of his flock attending the meetings at the hall, and asked them: "Why do you go there?"

"To hear Redfield preach holiness," was their answer.

"Well, if that is your reason, I can preach holiness," he replied; and he attempted to do so.

But all this failed to stop the work.

One night, after an ineffectual effort to preach, Mr. Redfield said to the congregation: "I have been trying for two weeks to preach to you the truth. For some reason it does not do its work as it should." He then turned to the pastor, who sat in the pulpit with him, and asked:

"How long is it since you joined the conference in full connection?"

"Fourteen years," was the answer.

"Did you not say then you were earnestly groaning for full redemption?"

"I did."

"Are you any nearer to it to-night than you were then?"

"No, sir."

"Don't you see that something is wrong?"

"I do."

"Will you get right?"

"I will."

"Will you go forward right here, and now, and on the seekers' side of the altar, and seek it?"

"I will," said the now deeply-moved pastor, and immediately left the pulpit and knelt on the outside of the altar.

With a scream, a woman, a member of the church, some distance back from the altar, sprang to her feet, and came running, and knelt by her pastor's side, and in a loud voice said, "O Brother B——, you said I need not take off this jewelry; that it was no matter if my heart was only right. O Brother B——, you have stood right in my way.' At this, a number more ran to the altar.

That night the work broke. The revival swept the town and the surrounding country. Every county officer, including the sheriff and the judge, nearly every lawyer, and many other prominent men, were converted. One lawyer became a traveling preacher in the Methodist Episcopal Church, and the sheriff became a useful local preacher. The next fall, the conference sent Rev. Joseph Hartwell, a sound Methodist, and one who enjoyed and preached holiness, to supply the pulpit, and the weak society became strong and vigorous.

Before leaving Woodstock, Mr. Redfield had one of his old signs again; and he said to his wife one day, "Mattie, we'll have to spend the winter in St. Louis." For more than twenty years he had felt he had a work to do in that region, although the precise place was not made known to him until now. The more he considered the matter, the more he became satisfied that duty led him there, and he planned his work accordingly. He did not go to St. Louis immediately, but made his visit there at a later date, as we shall hereafter see.

His successes at Marengo and Woodstock, and encouraging reports from Western New York, cheered his heart, and gave him courage to drive the battle on.

From Woodstock, Mr. Redfield went to a country church, on Queen Anne prairie, a few miles away. Here God poured out his Spirit also, and many were raised up to testify to the power of the cleansing blood. Some of these have gone to their reward, while others are still contending for the faith.

When in June, the St. Charles camp meeting came on, there was a host of witnesses to perfect love, from Aurora, St. Charles, Elgin, Marengo, Woodstock, Queen Anne, and other places, reached indirectly by Mr. Redfield's labors. What power there was in the services! with what unction the witnesses spoke and prayed! It was the writer's first camp meeting, and all its scenes and events are still vivid to his memory.

Again, Elder Gammon gave Mr. Redfield great liberty, and entire sanctification was the theme of the meeting. But the last day the Rev. C. P. Bragdon, the minister alluded to

24

in another chapter, who preached the sermon, when Purdy saved the day so gloriously; this man preached the same sermon here. His text was:

"Gather up the fragments, that nothing be lost."

The first part of the sermon was anti-rum; the second part was anti-tobacco; and the third part was anti-holiness. In the last he set forth the idea that all the experience a believer had after his conversion, is growth in grace. The experience of entire sanctification as a second experience, was ridiculed and denied. This was the first manifestation of hostility to the doctrine and experience among the Methodists of Fox River valley; but it was only the beginning of what proved afterward the occasion of division in the church.

Elder Gammon desired Mr. Redfield to preach in the afternoon after Mr. B——'s strange discourse. But he replied: "I shall have to meet the false doctrine of this forenoon, if I do."

"But," said the elder, "it would hardly do to have any controversy on the campground."

So Mr. Redfield did not preach.

CHAPTER LIII.

Soon after the St. Charles camp meeting, Mr. Redfield made a visit to Western New York. At Pekin, in Niagara county, he found a general quarterly meeting, the first of the kind he had ever attended. Here he met with preachers and laymen from afar, who had gathered to wait upon God for baptisms of power for the Lord's work. His heart was cheered with their boldness and freedom, and unction. He remembered his hours of sadness and lamentation over the thought that so much of his work had been destroyed, by the opposition to primitive Methodism in the church. But here he looked upon and heard many who had been brought into the light through his labors in various parts of the country. He found that the work had been kept alive in some places, by the organization of bands, made up of those who enjoyed perfect love and were contending earnestly for real Methodism. He told them of his labors in the West, where, and when, and with what results; of the oppositions and the encouragements he had met. He thought he saw that these brethren were sure of one of two things: either they would win the people to Methodism in such numbers that those in power in the church would not dare to molest them; or they would be finally excluded from the church. That very fall, but a few months after this, the work of expulsion commenced. Mr. Roberts and Mr. M'Creery were expelled from the conference and the church.

Soon after this meeting, Mr. Redfield returned to Illinois, and, August 25, he wrote to Mrs. Kendall as follows:

"My dear Sister Kendall:—I have much to say and little time in which to say it. Salvation is our only theme. The strife against it has begun, but the pilgrims in these parts hold on as yet, and seem resolved to maintain their stand.

B—— has made himself very busy in opposing it, but has lost caste with many for his trouble. I hear that the people where he was last year refuse to have him returned. I keep scattering the tracts and pamphlets. The more the pilgrims here learn of the pilgrims there, the more they love them. I am accused of 'splitting churches.' I confess that is my object—to split them off from the world. But many good people, and some of the preachers here, are very much prejudiced against you. Brother Woodward (formerly of the Genesee Conference) says he cannot believe all is right among the pilgrims when such men as Fillmore, and Church, and De Puy, and Bowman, represent them as they do. I learn that De Puy and Bowman* are to emigrate to this country this year. May the Lord have mercy on us if they do.

"Mattie's health has been very poor of late, and we think of going to Missouri and Kansas about the 20th of September. I wish you could go with us.

"How goes the great work at West Falls? and how among the pilgrims? I shall look with great interest to the coming session of the Genesee Conference. Don't fail to inform me of all that occurs. Mattie reads your letters to the pilgrims here, wherever we go, and they set them all on fire for the work.

"That was a remarkable scene you described, when those two preachers thought they saw the sainted Kendall. Oh, how my heart leaps when I think of his fidelity, purity, and zeal! I know he was right. How the breaking of the last seal will let a flood of light upon his adversaries! Then will they confess: 'O William, you were right, and we were wrong.' My heart continually asks: Who will take up his burden and testimony, where he laid them down?

---

* Mr. Bowman, at a national camp meeting held subsequent to this, as the writer was informed by a minister who was present, confessed that his course in the Genesee Conference difficulties was wrong.

Blessed man! Redeemed saint! I am sure he now dwells forever above the strife of tongues.

"Remember me to Brother and Sister Roberts, and all the pilgrims.

"J. W. REDFIELD."

About this time was held the last quarterly meeting for the Elgin charge, and in the quarterly conference, of which the writer was a member and present at the time, the license of Mr. Redfield as a local preacher was renewed without any opposition. He was also given a written recommendation as a revivalist. Mr. Redfield was not present when this was done.

About the same time he attended a camp meeting at Coral, near Marengo, where he labored with great power. This meeting was under the management of Rev. Hooper Crews, presiding elder of Rockford district. Mr. Crews was an excellent preacher, of sweet spirit, and manifestly very sincere; but, at the same time, little calculated for leadership against tumultuous opposition. He had already expressed his fears as to being able to furnish preachers who would be acceptable to societies where Mr. Redfield had successfully labored. On Sunday morning of this camp meeting, in his sermon, he made this allusion to his experience:

"If I ever experienced entire sanctification, it was when I was converted, for I have been happy ever since."

So strong was the influence of the doctrine and experience of holiness at this camp-meeting, that every minister was compelled to recognize it in his sermons and testimonies. Here were the fruits of Mr. Redfield's labors in the great meetings he had held at the places heretofore described; and any minister not in sympathy with the doctrine of holiness was in a very embarrassing position.

Mr. Redfield preached in the afternoon of Sunday with great power, and multitudes were at the altar seeking. So great was the interest that he held a second altar service about five o'clock, when perhaps one hundred were forward seeking. This meeting was led in his characteristic way. After opening with singing and prayer, he gave a half-hour's talk on the way of salvation. In this he pointed out clearly and distinctly the successive steps each seeker must take to find salvation. While dwelling upon this, he explained the seeming confusion of many in regard to the experience of entire sanctification being a second work, and then remarked, "That is what ails your presiding elder."

Brother Crews sat immediately behind him, and was deeply moved by the remark.

When the invitation was given for seekers, there was a rush. They commenced praying aloud, and all at once, and in about fifteen minutes the prayer meeting was ended. Nearly all had entered into the experience. This service was a revelation to a large number of ministers present, as they never had seen anything on that wise before. Immediately after the service the presiding elder took Mr. Redfield aside for a plain, close conversation on the subject of sanctification. That conversation resulted in the presiding elder's entering into the experience, a few weeks afterward in a prayer meeting in Rockford. But, from not confessing it fully, he soon after lost it. He found and lost it three times during the following year; and finally at a camp meeting held in the northern part of his district the following year, he went to the altar like a little boy, was labored with by the laymen and the sisters of his district, and while looking at one of the promises of God, in an open Bible, held before him by an eccentric minister by the name of Irving, and asked if he believed it, with a scream of joy he sprang to his feet, and seeing his wife at a distance, he ran speedily to her, caught her in his arms, and ran about the camp ground like a deer, shouting, "Hallelujah!" at every bound. From that time Hooper Crews preached, and enjoyed and lived the blessed experience.

Soon after this camp meeting Mr. Redfield began to get ready to go to St. Louis. At the same time he became greatly tempted about going. For several days this lasted, during which Mrs. Redfield advised against going, and finally determined she would not go. But during a season of prayer at the house of a friend, they both obtained the victory, and went forward cheerfully to their work.

On their way to St. Louis they stopped for a few days at St. Charles. While here, an effort was made by his friends to have him hold a few meetings. The official board of the church was called together, and a petition, signed by a large number of the membership, asking that Mr. Redfield be invited to hold revival services, was laid before it. The preacher was a new man, and for some reason was unwilling to work with Mr. Redfield. When the vote was taken on granting the petition, nine were in favor of it, and five opposed. But such was the opposition of the five that the majority offered to leave the matter to the pastor, and he decided against it.

While waiting here, he wrote the following letter:

"ST. CHARLES, Ill., October 7, 1858.

"Dear Sister Kendall:—We cannot tell you in words how highly we prize your very welcome letters, giving the details of the events taking place in Western N. Y. We are with you heart and soul, and the evidence you give us of your resolve to keep the narrow, steep, thorny, and disgraced way, fires us with new resolves to urge, press, and fight for the same. Mattie reads and re-reads your letters to the weeping pilgrims who sympathize with the pilgrims of the East, and who vow anew to go on in the narrowest of the narrow way. How it moved our hearts when she read of that camp meeting, where your husband's brother accepted his mantle and his cross. How the scenes of the past, when that sainted man, the personification of fidelity,

walked forth to lead the battle on, regardless of foes, or the
odds against him.   One motive, one thought, alone con-
sumed him, and that was to battle for the right.   When I
think of him, my heart vows anew to go the same despised
way.   How like vapor appear the opinions of all men! What
a death was his!   Shall I die like him?   Will Jesus say to
me 'Well done?'   Oh, this salvation that saves is the only
thing that will bear the test at last!

"Mattie has written to you of the camp meeting. Oh, how
soul cheering it was to see the multitudes who were saved
last winter still battling manfully for God!

"We expect by week after next to be on our way to St.
Louis, where if the Lord permits, we mean to press the
gospel which divides households, and splits dead churches off
from the world.   We need the baptism of fire for our work,
and expect it, too.   Bless the Lord!

"The fire is spreading in this region rapidly, but the
fight will yet come, and the pilgrims here, who read with
avidity the history and doings of the pilgrims there, and who
deeply sympathize with you, will have need that others sympathize with them.   Many pretty good Christians who have
not been through the hottest furnaces must remain too gross
to appreciate that blessed freedom and faith which dare to let
God's Spirit impel them to act out heaven's simplicity.   We
will bear with them, but let no one beguile us of the precious
freedom to act out, as well as shout out, glory.   I know it
shocks their sense of propriety.   But, thank God, I feel that
heaven's propriety is full as rational as ours.   Could men
see that the unknown glory which cannot find outlet in
words must have other avenues of egress to reach the gross
heart of the dumb world; could they but realize that heaven's
blessedness is designed for man's every pleasurable emotion,
and that the manifestations of these emotions are the only
means by which it can be understood, they would see the
profoundest philosophy in tears, smiles, shouting, screaming,
and jumping.

"My dear sister, Jesus has made you free. You may be a gazing stock to men, but remember you are also to the innumerable company. Your name may be cast out as evil, but they cannot reach high enough to tarnish it on the pillars of heaven. Of course you will be called foolish, crazy, nervous; but I am persuaded that you long ago passed those chained lions. Some people will not believe, some will feel a pious concern for the cause of religion; but if God desires to make you one end of salvation's telegraph line, to make known what is going on in the London of Paradise, let him have his way. From the depths of my soul I say go on in the name of the Lord.   J. W. REDFIELD."

October 31, he wrote again as follows:

"ST. CHARLES, Ill.

"My dear Sister Kendall:—We have been watching the mails daily hoping to hear from you again. We last night received information of the doings of the Genesee Conference—at least enough—for us to see what disposition was made of Brothers Roberts and M'Creery. I must confess I did not expect all that. I knew well enough what some of the preachers desired, but I thought they feared the people too much to go to such an extreme. It looks now as though Brother Kendall had been taken from the evil that was to come. I have been sorely tempted and tried over such conduct in the conference preachers.

"We had a little gathering at the house where we are now stopping, and Mattie read to us your letter describing the Bergen camp meeting, and we all had a weeping and rejoicing time, and renewed our vows to keep the narrow way.

"The people here have been negotiating for us to stay and hold another meeting before we go south, but I have no hope that it will be permitted. There are four fighters in this church of one hundred and sixty members, and I will not make another attempt, unless they will stop the 'fiddle', and pledge themselves to go the straight religion necessary to meet the judgment. Some are discouraged, and say 'Let us start a salvation church.' But that will not work, for all opposers will then feel themselves at liberty to manufacture what testimony they please to put us down.

"What will the people do in your region about the expulsion of Brothers Roberts and M'Creery. I expect under the excitement of the hour some strong resolutions will be passed, and many sharp things will be said; but will the pilgrims move forward in the good work, in a proper spirit? or will they be frightened at the usage of these two men? Like your sainted husband, I sing,

'I belong to this band, Hallelujah!'

"I only wish I was worthy to suffer with them.

"The friends of the Eastern pilgrims are increasing here in the West. We must make the most of our opportunities now to spread Methodism over the vast fields about us.

"If the church here does not take the stand for the straight way, we shall leave soon for our southern tour. We expected to have been off before this time, but Mattie's health and some unfinished business have hitherto prevented. But we hope by the 10th or 15th of next month, at most, to be on our way.

"I suppose there are many items of interest in the proceedings of the Genesee Conference, that we shall not receive unless you or some one shall give them to us. I did not get a copy of the charges against them, but I suppose they refer to the quarterly and camp meetings. But God still lives; salvation is free; and heaven is our home. The great reckoning day will set all things right.

"May God still keep you.

"J. W. AND MATTIE REDFIELD."

CHAPTER LIV.

JUST before the time came to start for St. Louis, a few of Mr. Redfield's friends came together for a season of prayer. And those St. Charles pilgrims were mighty in prayer in those days. During this prayer meeting Mr. Redfield was greatly impressed with the saying of St. Paul, "I go bound in the Spirit * * * not knowing what may befall me, save that the Holy Ghost witnesseth, that in every city bonds and afflictions await me." He was afflicted to think he could not adopt the remainder of the passage, and say, "but none of these things move me." Referring to this experience he says, "If I had dared to turn back, I would have done so. I was confident that God had called me to St. Louis, but I knew no one there, and besides I had not money enough to run any hazard."

They stopped at Princeton, in Bureau Co., Illinois, about one hundred miles on the way, to visit Rev. Charles French, with whom he had labored in St. Charles, the winter before. While here, a friend said to him, unasked, "I have some money for you," and handed him enough to take him to his destination and a little more. While waiting at Princeton, he penned another letter to Mrs. Kendall, of which the following is a copy:

"PRINCETON, Bureau Co., Ill., Nov. 18, 1858.
"My dear Sister Kendall:—We received your letter dated the 11th instant, and with deep emotion, read the filling out of what was lacking in the reports we had received of the doings of the Genesee Conference. This gave us a clear view of the spirit as well as the doings of the Regency.* I confess that my anxieties for the future are most intense. I am continually asking myself, 'Will the pilgrims hold on

---

* A name given to the opposition in that conference.

amid this furnace of affliction? or will they tire out from the
discouragements of this evil time, and abandon the work
God has given them to do?' You have nothing more to
lose. You will never regain the forfeited favor of those deluded men if you forsake the work, and if you fail, who
will dare to repeat the experiment? And yet your work
must be done, if vital godliness is ever reinstated in the
church. Remember the years of toil, and, apparently almost profitless, which it cost to lay the corner-stone of Christianity in Burmah! Think of the many martyrs who fell
before Africa received the gospel! And think of the self-
sacrifice, toil, weeping, and groaning before God, amid
slander and reproach, of a Luther and a Wesley! What
if they had fainted? What would have become of the re-
formations which they led? Great moral reforms have
always had their victims. Reformers must be content to let
their reputations lie over, at least, for one generation.

"But I'll stop this strain. I hardly know why I should
be led out like this. But let me say, there are many hearts
in these regions who pray for you, and who are with you
heart and hand, and stand ready to enlist in any feasible proj-
ect that bids fair to re-establish the primitive life, power, and
simplicity of Methodism. And their number is increasing.
I am glad the scribes, Pharisees, and Odd-fellows were
led to overt acts which have done more to open the eyes of
the honest to see the necessity of some decisive plan of
operations in returning to the 'old paths.'

"You speak of severe mental conflicts, in which your
reason seems to suffer. May I ask, is it like unto a bit of
my own experience? While struggling to fulfill my obligations to God, enduring to my utmost power of endurance,
groaning and weeping before God, my labors were questioned, my motives impugned, my character slandered,—and
that by a Methodist preacher, who all the time flattered me
to my face. I cared not for myself, but when I found that

the cause of Christ was suffering because of this, I was almost wild with grief, and was on the point of abandoning the field. Oh, what agony I experienced! The world never looked so desolate to me before. My bleeding heart would ask, why does the Lord suffer this? Why don't he remove the woe, and let me spend my days in quiet? I knew not what the Lord was doing with me. But I learned a lesson that I could have learned in no other way. I found two things in me that needed correction: One was, that I had taken more care upon me for God's cause than I could well endure, and had come to think that I was somewhat essential to its welfare. I forgot that God had to carry me and the cause also. The second thing was, that God held me responsible for fidelity, and not for success. How I then saw I was groaning over a few wrongs, while Jesus carried, endured, and wept over the wickedness and backslidings of the whole world. By this light I saw that God holds me responsible for duty, whether men hear or forbear. I now saw that my bewilderment arose from an attempt to settle these matters by my own reason. Then this simple track was presented to me: Look only to Jesus when he commands; stop when he bids you; do the exact right; leave no duty undone, and let God manage the results. This saves from all policy working even to outwit the devil. It saves from all planning, and all fear for results. It is resting wholly in Christ, and in the use of God's word and plan for the redemption of the world.

"Down deep in my soul I feel God is with you and will lead you, if you give him a fair chance. You will be led to duties that will test your views of propriety. Our views of propriety are usually from our reasoning, which needs this discipline. This disturbance of our reasoning is due to the conflict between our sense of propriety and that unadorned simplicity which the Spirit of God would institute. Let God move you in harmony with his word and the history of the past, and all will be well.   J. W. REDFIELD."

The next day after receiving the money from his friend, they took the train for Burlington, Iowa, where they expected to take a steamer for St. Louis. Here they had to wait a week, as it was late in the season, and many of the boats had stopped running. Mr. Redfield's state of mind was anything but pleasant. It seemed to him that he was going to meet with trouble.

On reaching St. Louis they put up at a hotel, at great expense. In a few days he began to look for cheaper quarters. For awhile matters looked as though they would have to leave the city, but at last he found a place where they could board at $12.50 per week, and this to be paid in advance. As soon as they could get settled he went in search of a Methodist church. There were plenty of southern Methodist churches, but he desired a northern church, as he did not feel free to become identified with a slave-holding people. It was difficult to find any who knew of such a church as he desired. He had letters of introduction to Rev. Dr. Williams, but no one seemed to know his residence. Sunday morning came, and he found the Ebenezer church and Dr. Williams its pastor. At the close of the morning sermon, he handed the pastor his letters of introduction, also their church letters. The 5th of December, he preached for the first time, at the invitation of the pastor. After this, in one of the official meetings a motion was made to invite him to assist the pastor in revival meetings. But the pastor refused to put the question, saying, "I propose to hold the reins of this pulpit in my own hands, and only invite to assist me whom I please. If you are dissatisfied with me, and desire this man, I can pack my carpet-bag and leave." Mr. Redfield was not present, and knew nothing of the proposition to invite him until some time after.

During this time he had been in search of a still cheaper boarding house, and finding one that was more reasonable, he was about to remove, when his landlady refused to let him take his trunks unless he would pay another week's board. He went to a bank to get a draft cashed, and found it imperfect, and that it must be sent back to northern Illinois to be corrected before he could draw the money on it. To get out of his difficulty he had to pawn his watch. Before the draft returned, a Jew, learning of the circumstances, unsolicited, went and redeemed his watch and returned it to him.

But now the news came to him of what took place in the official board. He said nothing to any one but his wife, but he felt that jealousy was at the bottom of the trouble, and that he had better leave. But his wife said, "No. God has sent us here, and we must stay." They then concluded that if there was to be trouble in the church, their mission would be to the people in house to house visitation. They made some visits, and God began a glorious work, in which quite a number were blessedly saved. But this was called sowing dissension.

About this time he was invited to preach in a colored people's church, and when he consented to do so, advised that the white people be not informed of it, lest they come to the meeting, and he be accused of drawing off the congregation from Ebenezer church. The first night God blessed the truth, and nearly every sinner in the house was at the altar for prayer. This could not be kept secret, and soon white people from Ebenezer church began to come. Occasionally he was allowed to preach in Ebenezer, and his congregations, when it was known beforehand, were large. The doctrine of holiness, as he presented it, attracted much attention, and the membership, not only of this church, but of other churches, became much interested in 'it; and a general revival was manifestly coming on.

He says, "I was in the company of the pastor one day, and was desirous of convincing him of my honesty and sincerity; and this especially as I had heard that he and other preachers had branded me as a fanatic, and an impostor, and that instead of being a Methodist, I was a Campbellite, etc. Without adverting to this, I said, 'Doctor, I am so burdened for St. Louis, it seems as though I must see salvation come, or I cannot endure it.'

" 'Oh,' said he, 'I never allow myself to get such burdens. If they do come, I go to bed and sleep them off.'

"I saw I could awaken no chord of sympathy in him on that line, and I said:

" 'I am a Methodist, and you, yourself, cannot find anything in my preaching at variance with John Wesley.'

" 'But,' said he, 'there are many of us Methodist preach-ers who do not believe with John Wesley.'

"And so every effort to bring myself into communion with him failed.

"Soon after this, the quarterly conference met, and a vote was taken on inviting me to hold meetings in the church, from one to three weeks; and only one man voted against it. When the pastor saw the unanimity of the vote, he remarked, 'Well, give us a good collection next Sunday, and after next Tuesday he can preach.'

"I was not present, but this was reported to me by one who was. When the time came for me to begin, I felt a presentiment that I would meet with trouble of some kind, and so I went in good season. But when I arrived at the church, a presiding elder, who was known to be an opposer of the doctrine of holiness, was in the pulpit, and had com-menced the service. After the singing and prayer, Doctor W—— said to me, 'Come forward and preach.' I went into the pulpit and commenced. I had felt impressed to take a copy of the Discipline, and also a copy of Rev. Joseph Hart-well's tract, giving quotations from Wesley's views on sanctification, with me. In the midst of my discourse, I thought it best to say to the congregation that the official board had invited me to stay and preach from one to three

weeks; but if I do, it is due to you to know what I am.   I
then said, 'I am a Methodist,' and drawing the Discipline
from my pocket, I repeated the rules to which I had sub-
scribed, and which I tried to live to.   'You may want to
know also what are my views on the doctrine of holiness';
and then drawing from my pocket the extracts from Wesley,
I said, 'Here are my views, straight out of Wesley's works.'
These I read, giving page and section.   I then said, 'If I
stay, I must preach the same class of truths to which you
have listened from me since I have been here.   And I think
it is due that I make this frank statement, that if I stay, I
must so preach the whole law that I can meet it again.   And
I think it is due to me to know whether you want It, and
will abide by it.   So I will ask all, saints and sinners, to say,
by vote, whether you——

"I was going to say, 'will do so or not.'   But I was
interrupted by Dr. W——, who caught me by the arm and
said, 'Stop, sir; I am responsible for this pulpit.'

"I felt perfectly calm, and turning to him, said, 'Doctor, I
was not going to transcend the proprieties of the pulpit, but'—

" 'Stop, sir'; said he.   'I am responsible for this pulpit.'

"I tried again and again to make an explanation, but he
forbade it, and then commanded me to go on with my
sermon.

"Afterwards, this was reported to have been an effort on
my part to take a vote of the congregation whether I or he
should occupy the pulpit.

"While this was taking place in the pulpit, my soul was
talking with God.   An unearthly power rested upon me.
God seemed to be all around me.   He seemed to say, 'I want
you to preach the straight truth for once; will you?'

"My heart said, 'I will.'

" 'But if you do, you may be stopped.'

" 'Well,' said I, 'I will go on till I am stopped.'

" 'You, probably, never will be permitted to preach again.'
25

"'I will go the straight way for this once, if it is the end of my preaching.'"

C. H. Underwood, at that time a business man in St. Louis, but who was afterward converted and became a minister of the gospel, once told the writer, that Mr. Redfield's sermon that night was awful, in its arraignment of the unsaved and particularly the unsaved of the church, before the bar of God.

In the pulpit and around it, were seated, two presiding elders, one church editor, and several city pastors. While the sermon was in progress, these men seemed to listen in breathless amazement. Many were smitten by conviction that night, among whom was Mr. Underwood.

The next night, as Mr. Redfield was walking down the aisle to the pulpit, Doctor Williams met him, and said:

"I have received a strange letter from the official board. Let us go into the parsonage and read it."

When Mr. Redfield opened it he found it to read as follows:

"ST. LOUIS, Jan. 20, 1859.

"To Rev. Dr. Williams:

"Dear Brother:—The undersigned members of the official board of Ebenezer charge have witnessed with regret the unprecedented conduct of Dr. Redfield since the commencement of his labors, and more especially on last night. Shocked at his proceedings, and believing that his labors are calculated to do more harm than good, by creating schism and dissension in the church, and feeling an abiding interest in the welfare of the church, and prosperity of the cause, earnestly request that you quietly tell Dr. Redfield that he cannot occupy the pulpit any more.

"Yours respectfully,

"J. W. HEATH,

"D. CAUGHLIN,

"J. W. HATHAWAY,

"WM. SCHUREMAN."

Mr. Redfield was greatly shocked, to see that so few could reverse the action of the quarterly conference; that this could take place in so short a time; and that part of the complaints were of matters that occurred before the action of the quarterly conference that invited him to hold the meetings; and he said to Dr. Williams:

'Can you tell me why there are so few names to this letter?"

"This is from the board of trustees, and the trustees can control me and the pulpit. I am sorry", said he, "but I cannot help it; you and I are good friends."

"Well," said Mr. Redfield, "what shall I do? Should I go into the church to-night?"

"I think," said he, "you had better not."

Mr. Redfield sent some one in to call out his wife, and while waiting for her to come out, he was approached by one who said, "Is anything amiss?"

"No," answered he, only the board of trustees have requested the doctor to shut me out of the pulpit."

Another said, "That is one of Williams' tricks."

"No," said Mr. Redfield, "that cannot be, for I read the letter and saw the names of those who signed it."

It was soon whispered through the church, that Mr. Redfield was shut out of the pulpit, and a large proportion of the congregation arose and left the house.

CHAPTER LV.

THE next morning Mr. Redfield called on Dr. Williams, and secured a copy of the letter from the official board, and asked for his own and his wife's church letters. Referring to this, he says:

"I incidentally remarked that I should either go into a free state or join one of the other Northern Methodist churches in the city. And I took a copy of the letter from the trustees in order to refute the charge that Dr. Williams was its author. On my way home I met one who thus charged him, and I said, 'Here is a copy of that letter, and it shows that you are mistaken.' He read it, and then replied, 'Only one of those men is a trustee; and now I know that Williams is at the bottom of this affair.'

"Here, then, were the names of four persons who attempted to rule the whole congregation, and one trustee to rule a whole quarterly conference.

"From this brother I now learned that seventy-two members of the church had held a meeting the night before and sent the following declaration to the official board:

" 'To the members of the Official Board of the Ebenezer charge of the Methodist Episcopal Church:

" 'Brethren:—Whereas, by the uncalled-for exercise of official power of a few individuals of Ebenezer charge in the city of St. Louis, which has lately taken place, whereby a large proportion of the members of said church have been deprived of their rights and privileges guaranteed to them, as we believe by the word of God, and the Discipline of the church; and, whereas we deem it our duty to state the causes which have induced us to separate ourselves from said church, as well as to assure our brethren from whom we have thus separated, that in so doing we have no other motive than the promotion of the cause of the Lord Jesus Christ, and the

exercise of those privileges which we have lately been deprived of by the unlawful exercise of a power never intended
to be invested in these four men holding official position in
said church; and, whereas, we do not believe in the 'one-man
power,' nor the unlawful exercise of an authority of four
men, never conferred upon them, and that for the accom-
plishment of an unholy purpose, such as has lately occurred,
which we deem oppressive and unjust, before God and man;
therefore,

"Resolved, that we ask the privilege, as we claim the
right, of adhering to, and continuing in, the Methodist Episcopal Church, both from principle, and from a firm belief in
the doctrines of said church.

"Resolved, 2. That we have the utmost confidence in'
the Christian character and the holiness of purpose of Rev.
Dr. Redfield, a minister of the Methodist Episcopal Church,
and that his close-pointed preaching of the gospel is in accordance with the usage of the primitive church'in bringing
sinners to a saving knowledge of the truth as it is in Jesus
Christ.

"Resolved, 3. That we hold the mandate issued by the
four officials in Ebenezer charge, excluding Dr. Redfield
from the pulpit, thereby denying him the privilege of preaching to a congregation assembled for that purpose, as unjustifiable, unauthorized by the Discipline, and ruinous to the
church.

"Resolved, 4. That this unjustifiable and high-handed
breach of trust, by the said four officials, deprives us of the
social and religious privileges we have heretofore enjoyed in
said church; and being thus deprived by the arbitrary act of
said officials from the privileges aforesaid, we feel we have
no other alternative than to separate ourselves from said
Ebenezer charge, which we have now done in the fear of
God, who will judge our action in the great day of account.

"Resolved, 5. That we do hereby solemnly protest in

the name of the great I Am, against the course pursued by
these officials in Ebenezer charge toward Rev. Dr. Redfield,
and also against the known wishes of a large majority of
the said church and congregation.

"Resolved, 6. That a committee of three of our number be appointed to attend the next official meeting of Ebenezer charge, to lay before it this preamble and these resolutions, and ask that they be spread upon the records of the
board."

When this paper was presented there were attached to it
the signatures of ninety members of the church.

These members began now to call for their church letters.
At first, Dr. Williams endeavored to dissuade them from
their purpose, and after granting the request of twenty, he
then refused to give any more. When at last he saw the
blame thrown upon those four men, he acknowledged himself to be the author of that letter. Thus the whole thing
proved to be a fraud perpetrated by himself.

There is in this document, addressed to the official board,
an evidence of haste. Probably a delay of a few days would
have made a great difference in the character of that paper.
But there was strife in the air that affected this movement,
which was not clearly apprehended by some of the actors.
The following letter to the *Northern Independent*, written
about this time, will make this plain:

"GREAT SECESSION IN ST. LOUIS.

"Mr. Editor:—I see from the *Central Advocate*, published in the city of St. Louis, that there has been a terrible
thunderstorm, a great moral earthquake—a large secession
from one of the Methodist Episcopal churches in that city.
But let it not be forgotten that this secession has taken place
in slaveholding territory—in one of the 'border conferences.'
It has taken place, too, in a city where there are but two
copies of the *Northern Independent* taken, and they are sent
to editors in exchange. Yet, strange as it may appear,

Brother Brooks charges that secession on the *Northern Independent*. What a powerful influence the *Independent* exerts! From the predictions of our church papers, I had supposed that secessions were to take place in Central New York. But lo and behold, it commences in 'border territory.'

"From the braggadocio and insulting style of the editor, I should think him a relative of 'Bully Brooks,' of Washington notoriety. His editorial is unworthy of a Christian minister. But something must be done to put down Hosmer, Mattison, and company. Just hear him: 'It is high time that decisive steps were taken for the protection of the church. We seriously question the temporizing policy which has been adopted by our eastern brethren.'

"Why, bless your dear soul, Brother Brooks, the power of episcopacy and of the conservative press, has been in full operation for the last two years to put down our beloved *Independent* and its friends, but without success. This 'crushing out policy' don't and will not succeed.

"But Mr. Brooks is frank enough to acknowledge that J. W. Redfield, an itinerant local preacher, has been the main instrument in bringing about the above-named secession. Now we desire to state distinctly for the benefit of Brother Brooks, that Mr. Redfield is in no wise connected with the *Northern Independent*, nor, so far as I know, in sympathy with it, for he does not take it. Moreover, Mr. Brooks must know that the *Independent* is not in sympathy with that peculiar doctrine advocated by Mr. Redfield. But the editor must have something to rant about. I hope, after this awful vomiting of bile, Brother Brooks'will himself be greatly relieved. Missouri is said to be very bilious to old conservatives. If the editor would take a good dose of common sense, he would be greatly relieved; otherwise, I fear his disease will prove fatal.

"But after all the rant and cant about secession, Brother

Brooks says: 'We have not directed attention to this subject, because we have any apprehension that the Methodist Episcopal Church is in any danger.' Good. You think just as many do in this region, Brother Brooks. No, my good brother, the *Independent* will not injure the church, so shed no more crocodile tears.

"Allow me, Brother Hosmer, to thank Mr. Brooks for bringing the *Independent* to the notice of his readers in slave territory.

"April 20, 1859.   "THE SPY."

This letter indicates that an effort was made by Mr. Brooks, editor of the *Central Christian Advocate*, to connect the disturbance in Ebenezer church with the *Independent*. We have already noticed the origin and character of that paper. William Hosmer, its editor, was a strong believer in the doctrine of holiness, and much in sympathy with the pilgrims in Western New York, and the columns of his paper often rang with warnings to the officials of the church against the high-handed usurpations of power on the part of subordinates in the church, aimed at the crushing out of the holiness revival.

For years a hot discussion had been going on in the church papers over the doctrine of holiness itself. Nathan Bangs, Jesse T. Peck, Joseph Hartwell, and others, had written in defense of it. They held to the doctrine as taught by the Wesleys. Hiram Mattison, C. P. Bragdon, and many others, had written against it. The writings of Mattison had slowly, but surely, poisoned the theology of many of the ministry, who stood ready, by one means and another, to hinder and crush out the teaching of Wesleyan views.

The cringing attitude of the church on the slavery question had developed a policy of administration, and even of preaching along the border of Mason and Dixon's line, that was destructive to independence of character except in opposition to every form of radicalism. This policy-spirit had undermined the spiritual life, and the conscience of the church, until such things as have been recorded in this chapter were possible with both the ministry and the laity.

When men got their eyes open to the real character of this spirit, they were filled with horror and distrust of those who still were actuated by it. Mr. Redfield's preaching left no middle ground. He poured such floods of light upon the motives of men that they could but see themselves in their true character. Some repented, and, full of gratitude for being saved from such an abyss of moral corruption, perhaps unwisely, would speak in strong approval of the faithfulness of Mr. Redfield's labors. This roused the jealousy of time-serving ministers, and the hatred of men who would not walk in the light. His friends were of the most spiritual in the church, his enemies of the worldly. The friendship of his friends was strong as death, while the enmity of his enemies was bitter to the extreme. Thus the gulf of separation was deeper than the width of this church action would indicate. Spiritual men, on the ground, would be convinced of its impassableness, when those at a distance would see but little worthy of notice. Of the actors in this conflict we shall see more by-and-by.

CHAPTER LVI

A COMMITTEE now waited on Mr. Redfield, and asked him to become the pastor of the new organization. But he answered, "I cannot do that unless you are regularly organized and recognized by the presiding elder."

They went to see him, and he told them he was glad to know of their taking this course, and he would recognize them. They returned and drew up a formal petition to that effect, which was signed by the members interested, and then presented to the elder again. He now had changed his mind, and declined doing it.

In the meantime, many of those who had withdrawn from Ebenezer were demanding an organization; and if that was not done, they declared their intention to join some other of the city churches; but were unanimous in a determination not to return to the Ebenezer church.

Dr. Williams came to Mr. Redfield soon after, and commanded him to bring back the people he had taken away, or he would expel him, and then publish him to the world.

Mr. Redfield replied, "I cannot do that. I never took them away, and I can never bring them back."

"You have split my church all to pieces," said he.

"You know better than that," was Mr. Redfield's reply.

Soon after this, Mr. Redfield received the following letter:

"St. Louis, January 26, 1859.

"To Rev. Dr. Redfield:

"Dear Sir and Brother:—We are pained with the disruption of our church, which has occurred recently in this city. With the present light upon the subject, we are persuaded that the responsibility rests chiefly with you. That a more perfect understanding may be reached, and the schism, if possible, be healed, we respectfully ask an interview with you this afternoon at three o'clock, at the office of the *Central Christian Advocate*, 97 N. Fourth street. "We trust you may not fail to meet us.

"Signed,
"THOMAS WILLIAMS,
Pastor of the Ebenezer Church.
"WINTER R. DAVIS,
Pastor of Hedding Church.
"JOSEPH BROOKS,
Editor of the *C. C. Advocate*."

In a note at tne foot of this letter, the time was changed to 10 a.m. of the next day.

Mr. Redfield says: "I did not feel willing to meet these men, especially Dr. Williams, who was capable of that fraudulent letter; and Mr. Brooks, whom I too well knew, from report and otherwise, and trust myself with them. So instead of going to meet them I thought it best to answer the call by the following letter:

"ST. LOUIS, January 26, 1859. 11:30 p. m.
"To Rev. Dr. Williams, Rev. J. Brooks, and Professor Davis:
"Dear Brethren:—Your note of to-day, received after church, greatly surprises and grieves me. I know Brother Brooks intimated to me last night that I was the principal cause of the disaffection complained of, but I could not make myself believe that the sober second thought, after a fair investigation, would at all warrant such a conclusion. I claim to be a North Methodist, and have tried to build up the cause of Wesleyan Methodism, and am confident that all my teachings in this city will bear a comparison in their orthodoxy with our standard authors. I have acted conscientiously and trust your charity will award to me an approval consistent with this statement. I cannot see that I am blameworthy if others show an attachment, as Methodists, for Methodist doctrines. It is thought I can heal, by correcting all the

causes of the state of affairs complained of. I honestly believe I am not the cause, and I feel just as sure that I cannot heal what I have not wounded. I am willing to do, and will do, anything consistent with right, which you may prescribe, to reach such an end. When I took my letter I did design, quietly, to change my relation, either to another Northern Methodist church, or to go to a free state, hoping to get away from so troublesome a state of things. I knew not that another person besides myself and wife had any design to take letters; neither did I state to any one that I had done so, till I learned that others had done the same, fearing that it would be construed into hostility to Ebenezer church. I designedly refrained from expressing opinions, and likewise from attending preliminary meetings, having in view steps of separation. But when it was announced that a new organization was a fact, and the papers were duly made out to petition the elder to perfect the organization, and there was a unanimous desire that I should preach for them until the proper officers should make provisions to supply them, I accepted their invitation, believing I was violating no obligations in so doing, as a loyal member of the Methodist Episcopal Church. If others think I have, and will convince me of the same, I will correct my mistake if it is in my power to do so.

"Now if you can find one person who has taken a letter, and who will state that I, by word or act, directly or indirectly, have incited them to do so, I will quietly retire out of your midst, into a free state. Or if you can find a majority of two-thirds, or one-quarter, even, who will state that if I were gone out of the city they would go back and return their letters to Ebenezer, I will then leave.

"But will you permit me to ask you, brethren, if your united wisdom cannot devise some plan by which the cause of Methodism may be so extended that we all can work without this, to me, very unpleasant state of things? I am ready to serve the church free of charge, and I ask, will you not try some plan to meet the increasing demands of this great city? Will you not try in your wisdom to husband the present tide of religious influence? Are we not brethren? and shall we not harmonize in the great battle for the right? I will do anything that is right at your suggestion to reach so happy an end. God knows I desire to see St. Louis saved, and a fair proportion of the people gathered into our beloved North church. I trust you will weigh my motives in an even balance, when I state to you that I have no personal interest to serve in the part I act in trying to promote this end.

"I have chosen to write what I have to say to you, that I might say it more deliberately, and that you might review at any time what I have said, in making up your minds.

"Yours, most respectfully,

"J. W. REDFIELD."

The next day he received the following reply:

"ST. LOUIS, January 27, 1859.

"To Dr. Redfield:

'Dear Brother:—As you have declined to meet with the pastors of the Methodist Episcopal Church of this city, this morning, according to our request, to endeavor to heal the unfortunate disruption that has taken place since you came to this city, we feel compelled by a stern sense of duty, in the fear of God, as pastors of the Methodist Episcopal Church, to seek an adjustment of this painful affair in another form, so far as your responsibilities are involved in the matter. Therefore, at the request of these pastors, it becomes my painful duty to request, in accordance with the Discipline of the Methodist Episcopal Church, that you deposit your letter without delay in one of the charges of this city, and have your name enrolled in a class-book.

"Yours respectfully,

"THOMAS WILLIAMS."

Mr. Redfield says:

"I had a warning not three hours before, and I believe from the Spirit of God, that trouble was ahead, and said to my wife, 'Something is coming, and I feel impressed to send our church letters away at once.'   So I had a letter written, and our church letters inclosed in it, and sent to the post office, and then went to church.   At the close of the service I received Dr. Williams' reply.   He came to me soon after, and said, he should now go 'war to the knife.'*   Others said, a plan was being laid to compel me to leave the city; and that a course was to be pursued that would shut me out from all Methodist churches of the land.   Another friend came to me with the word that he had reason to believe that the preachers would raise a mob against me, by the cry that I was an Abolitionist.   Then Dr. Williams came to me one Saturday, and said, 'If you will go to our church once to-morrow, I will let you off'; and I promised him I would. When my friends found this out, they stoutly resisted it, as they felt sure there was a plot of some kind in it.   But I thought I would risk it and keep my word; but I was taken suddenly sick, and was unable to get out for three weeks. I suffered much from fear and grief.   Every noise at night seemed to me like the noise of a mob, and I expected to see the windows burst in at any moment.   I was grieved to think that ministers in my beloved church would resort to such means to accomplish wicked ends.   I became so sick that I despaired of life, and said to my wife, 'You'll have to leave my bones in St. Louis.'   At the end of this time I was taken to the church one Sunday morning, in a close carriage, and as I entered, the singers sang, as a voluntary,

'Jesus look with pitying eye,
Saviour help me or I die.'

Oh, how I felt the meaning of every word!   On attempting

---

*The writer, when a pastor in St. Louis in 1866, was told by a lady that she heard Dr. Williams make that declaration in front of the church where Mr. R—— was then laboring.

to read a hymn, I found that my eyesight had failed, and from that time I had to wear glasses.

"I was soon able to resume the charge of the society, and we thought it best that we should form ourselves into a Methodist church on the Congregational plan, but adding a rule against slavery. In the meantime I thought best to prepare to let the annual conference adjust our difficulties. Some said there was no use, but I thought there was.   But sure enough, when the time came, the conference refused to look into the matter.   At last we settled down to look after our work.   New appointments sprang up, and calls began to come for me to labor.   Visitors came from Richmond, Virginia, New Orleans, Natchez, Baltimore, Chicago, and other places; who had heard so much about us, They came to see for themselves, and said, 'This is what we need at our place.' So the good work went on."

The conflict continued to rage hotly in St. Louis for considerable time, as the sequel shows. During this time Mr. Redfield wrote the following letters, which are of interest by way of throwing light upon the character of events then occurring, and also by way of revealing the true character of the man himself:

"St. Louis, Mo., Dec. 25, 1858.

"My dear Sister Kendall:—We received a letter from Brother Hicks last evening, from which we learned the results of the Laymen's Convention at Albion, but not all the particulars.

"We are now settled for the present in this wicked city, and are trying to clear away the rubbish so as to get down to the foundation rock.   The novelty of the doctrine of holiness, and the measures we use, as well as the little power sometimes manifested, is startling to them here.   One man lost his strength night before last, and fell back on the floor. Some say such a thing never took place in Ebenezer church before.   Some few profess to have received the blessing of

perfect love, but the stamp does not come quite up to my
wishes. Most of the people seem sincere, but timid and
halting. Among the reclaimed backsliders is the son of
Father Wait, of Albion. He has been backslidden for fifteen years. He is one of the city justices, has a great deal
of energy, and uses it among his associates, lawyers and
others, and deals as plainly with the church as Brother Purdy
used to, is just about as impulsive, and feels he has a duty to
do, and I am of the same impression. We have a few here
who know what salvation is, and they stand up in defense of
the definite work. How it will finally turn I cannot say, but
hope and pray that before the fight comes on, which surely
will come, that God may have one victory which will establish a gospel standard.

"Our church is quite central, but small and old, while the
South church has its full supply of large commanding
churches, proud, fashionable, and world-loving. They
frown upon the North church, call us intruders, and set us
down with negroes (bless the Lord!). But the strong gospel doctrines are taking hold of the honest-hearted sinners,
and I hope they will have one chance to show what they can
do.

"I can see that Brother Kendall's triumphant translation
has done for the pilgrims what nothing else could have
done. That solemn vow of the preachers over his coffin has
told upon that little band, and nerved them to acts which are
felt for God. He died well. The pilgrims saw the divine
approval of his course. Those who waited to see how he
would fare have been thrown upon their own resources.
The gospel did not succeed so well until after our Lord's
ascension.

"I am strongly impressed that God designs in this movement, to fit the pilgrim preachers for their work. How
could they better learn to guard the entrance to the Christian
ministry than by their sufferings from bad men in the ranks?

The experience they are obtaining will help them, when the time comes, to frame a discipline that will put the devil to many years of hard toil to get it tangled up again. I am sure the movement must end in division and a new church at last; and yet I hope they will hold on until pushed from the last plank.

"Firm in the Lord and in the power of his might,

"J. W. REDFIELD."

"ST. LOUIS, Mo., Jan. 13, 1859.

"Dear Brother and Sister Foot:—We have long contemplated writing to you, but the great number of our correspondents, and the fact that we had written to some in St. Charles, has caused this delay. We greatly desire to hear from you, and are particularly desirous to know how matters have turned in that region.

"We have reason to believe God sent us to this city. The contest is very severe. Presiding elders and other preachers, who have advised the members to conform to the world, are greatly stirred. But God is raising up witnesses to testify to the fullness of salvation. Members of other churches are taking a bold stand for the truth. Some have expressed a great interest in the doctrine of holiness. One Congregationalist has experienced it, and now blazes with the fullness. A goodly number of Methodists now rejoice in a complete salvation. But the jeweled saints fight with a zeal worthy of a better cause.

"Some ask me to go into other churches and preach this blessed fullness there. Some ask me to set up a new church, and many outsiders and Presbyterians and Congregationalists are ready to sustain it.

"The powers of our church permitted me to preach a few times, and as the people received it the slaying power came, and then they stopped me. They tried to get along alone a few nights, but they could not make it move; and

26

then they called for me again, and again the work moved
with power. Then there was shouting, and that was stopped,
and I was stopped again. Again they tried to make the
work go their way, but it would not move. I am now holding
off, and shall continue to do so until they pledge themselves
that Bible religion shall be sustained. The outside pressure
upon them, to have me preach, is getting very strong, and
the contest waxes hotter and hotter. I am calmly waiting,
standing still to see the salvation of God.

"You would not wonder at this, if you could see the jew-
els, flummeries, feathers, and the whole wardrobe of perdition,
passing on the backs of Methodists, like loaded camels. And
further to hear some backsliders confess their wrong, and
then declare that preachers had told them to 'Dress up;—put
on all you can get on; and shine in the world.' And further,
that they need not attend class, etc. You cannot wonder
that such kind of stuff and Bible religion will strike fire
when they come together. How matters will turn I don't
know. One thing I do know. God helping me I will stand
for truth or die trying. I know you pray for us. I do not
ask you to pray that we may be released from the burden,
the labor or the reproach, but that our faith and fidelity fail
not.

"Yours affectionately,

"J. W. REDFIELD."

"ST. LOUIS, Jan. 30, 1859.

"Dear Brother and Sister Foot:—Your letter was duly
received. Glad we were, indeed, to hear from you. Yet
we are sorry that salvation cannot have a fair chance in St.
Charles, to save and bless the people with a full salvation.

"We are now convinced that God sent us to St. Louis.
But such a battle we never had before. Our pastor blew up
the official board for introducing a resolution to invite me to
conduct the meetings. I was called upon, however, to

preach, and the Bible salvation took most wonderfully. The people came out in great numbers, and then the preacher stopped me. The people urged, and now and then he would permit me to preach, and when the house would fill up he would stop me again. The church murmured, and he threatened to leave. On the 20th, I went into the church to preach, when he took me into the parsonage, and showed me a letter from the official board forbidding me to preach again. The people found it out, and seventy-two members demanded their letters. I asked how it happened that the leaders' names were not on the letters; and he said it came from the trustees. Then it came out that only one of the four names was that of a trustee. When the people repudiated the dictatorship of the four men, the preacher owned up that he was the author of the letter. The people then formed a new church at once, with the promise of 150 members. The preacher lays the separation to me, and has demanded my letter, and threatens to expel me, and cut off all that left. He has got the presiding elder, the editor, and all the conference preachers on his side against us, but the outsiders, and the members of other churches, sympathized with us, and opened a fine church for our use. This made our enemies more angry than before. God came in power, and sinners have been saved. The people and the Lord seemed to leave them, and then they threatened us with war to the knife. It so happened that I expressed no opinion about dividing, nor counseled it directly or indirectly, but I have to bear the blame. Our friends have drawn up a writing, stating positively that I did nothing in any way to promote the separation, which they have all signed. This has been published. Then came a charge that I split the St. Charles' church; but a man from there happened along here, who gave the facts, and that story was spoiled.

"I am waiting now to have the organization perfected, when, I expect again to enter the field. We need your prayers, that God may defend the cause of righteousness. Holiness is our theme. God comes in power. Mattie says, such a class meeting as she attended to-day she never attended before. There were ten seekers of religion.

"Many honest-hearted sinners desire that we build a new church of our own, and are ready to help.

"Yours in love,

"J. W. REDFIELD."

In a letter to Mrs. Kendall dated February 17, after recounting the history of the work in St. Louis down to that date, almost exactly as in the foregoing letter, he says:

"Now the question comes up: Where shall we attach ourselves? We have offered ourselves to the Methodist Episcopal Church, and they spurn us. We cannot go to the Methodist Church South on account of slavery. We are Methodists, and cannot be anything else. I said to them, 'Perhaps the pilgrims of Western New York will receive you, and look after you.'

"So they have organized congregationally until they can open up negotiations with the East. We have written to Brother Roberts to come on and take charge. There are a number of other places where matters are somewhat as they are here.

"I must go up to Quincy, Illinois, next week, if it is at all possible, to hold another meeting this season. That is about 130 miles north, on the river.

"The opposition have sent for Bishop Janes to come and help them out of their difficulty. He is expected to-day. But it is too late. The new church voted night before last, to make no further attempt at reconciliation.

"I have for years seen that we must come to this; but never once supposed that it would be done in my day. But we are forced into it.

"I think I never suffered more in so short a time in my

life, than while I have been here. The trouble laid me up, sick-a-bed for a fortnight, but I dared not run. It cheers my heart to think that the pilgrims are praying for me.

"Yours,

"J. W. REDFIELD."

On March 2, 1859, he wrote again to Brother and Sister Foot of St. Charles, Illinois, as follows:

"My dear Brother and Sister Foot:—Your welcome and cheering letter of February 27, was received last night. I answer thus early, and your questions in particular, that you may be able to form a just opinion of all matters pertaining to the division here.

"The Ebenezer charge, when the division of the church on the question of slavery occurred, eleven years ago, had more members and better prospects than at the time of our arrival here last fall. At the last conference there were reported 140 members. Those who have left to form the new church are all the spiritual members of the flock, with a few exceptions. Over one hundred of them left. Seven of them are local preachers. There are a few spiritual ones left, but their hearts are with us. Before deciding to form a new church, several joined the South church, and a large portion of the remainder were determined to go to some other church if we did not organize. To save them to the church North, it was necessary to form a new society. Just at the time when we were discussing the question, Where can we hold meetings? and a committee was seeking a place, a gentleman, the owner of a large church, offered it to us, on such terms that we accepted it: It is in the heart of the city, large and commodious. It was formerly occupied by the Baptists, but about this time the society broke up.

"If the new society was to dissolve to-day, it is not likely that ten of the members would return to the Ebenezer church. They have organized under a congregational form of government, and will wait until conference to see what is

best to be done. If at conference they cannot get a pledge
to be supplied with Methodist preachers, at least religiously
inclined, they will then unite with the pilgrims of Western
New York. The pilgrims here have not as much of the
laboring power as they need, but they are seeking it. And
yet they are comparatively free to what they were before
they left. There, if any got to shouting or exhorting, the
preacher would stop them, and in private call them 'gran-
nies.'

"Already we have a large, growing Sunday-school, and
are looking for one or two more places in which to hold
meetings, with the hope of establishing new societies.

"The people say we must not leave St. Louis, but I see
they are leaning upon us. I dare not tell them, but I always
feel like running away when I see symptoms of that nature. The most of those left in the old church, you may set
down as like Brothers ——, ——, and Sister ——, except
the few I spoke of, who, like Nicodemus, are disciples, but
secretly for fear of the Jews. The piety, the talent, and
the working force, are in the new organization.

"God is with us, and the number is daily increasing. Our
church on Sundays is crowded to its utmost capacity, and
many are obliged to go away for lack of accommodations.

"Dr. Williams and the few who stand by him, have been
trying every possible way to upset and destroy us, but so far
have signally failed. They sent for Bishop Janes, but since
he has gone, they have lowered the tone of their opposition,
and their threatenings have ceased. It is surmised that the
bishop has advised this.

"Wife and I expect to go to Quincy for a short time.
The people here say we must return, and stay; but I very
much need rest, and I feel I must have it. I would gladly
go to St. Charles and spend a short time.

"Our fight here has been the most severe I have ever
known. I don't wonder that Satan contends sharply to hold

his own in this Vanity Fair. Theaters, masquerade balls, rum holes, with Sabbath breaking, abound. The churches have so far kept in the good graces of his Satanic Majesty, that but little damage has been done to his kingdom since the city has had a being. Somebody has got to get a broken back for disturbing this state of things, and it may as well be I as anybody. The thing must be done, or St. Louis is lost. I have suffered so much that it seems as though I could never go into another such conflict. It laid me on my back for two weeks. I am hardly able to do anything of moment now. Yet God keeps my head above water, and the people are very kind and sympathizing. My whole heart goes out in prayer that God may remember them, for they have not been ashamed of my chain. I tell you this strong salvation makes strong friends and hot enemies.

"I don't feel equal in giving you advice in relation to your meetings. Yet I must say, dear sister, I cannot see how you can be true to God and truth, without throwing your whole weight into the scale of right. Will not some of the Marys, 'last at the cross, and earliest at the grave,' stand in the way and lift up the voice like a trumpet? God's cause must not go down! But who will hazard all, and die a moral martyr for Christ?

"The Lord bless you all.

"J. W. REDFIELD."

Mr. Redfield, during the time of these troubles and afterward, passed through severe mental conflicts in regard to the course he had taken. His naturally sensitive and shrinking nature drew back from everything like severity and cruelty. Anything like mental or physical pain in others would cause him the most intense anguish. The accidental injury of a bird, or beast, or even a fly, would cause him to weep. Such a nature felt intensely all the attacks made upon his character, the questioning of his motives, the withdrawal of friendship, and the open hostility of his enemies. Naturally

he was a coward; religiously, the bravest and most faithful
of men.   In the pulpit or in the social circle, when he felt
he stood forth in the name of Jehovah, his hearers would be
impressed with his bravery and fidelity; but when merely
himself, they would think him a marvel of human weakness.
He relates this incident in his experience at the time of the
troubles in St. Louis.

"I was now beset by enemies who tried to annoy me in
every possible way; and I felt heart-broken to think that
after being so pressed in spirit and crowded by the
Lord to go this thorough way, I must meet with such opposition from ministers of the gospel.   It seemed more than I
could endure.   And I could but examine my whole course
and motives, and then ask the Lord, 'If I am right, why
are these things permitted?'   I was talking like this to Sister M—— one day, when she related to me the following:

"'When we moved here from Cincinnati three years
ago, I told my husband I could not join the Southern church
for I was an Abolitionist.   I went to the Ebenezer church,
but it was so dead that I could not think of joining that.   I
saw so little of spiritual life in the city, that it seemed as
though I could not stay here. So I went to the Lord about it
in prayer, and he told me to hold on, and he would send a man
to preach the true gospel.   About the time you came, I began
to feel that the man had come, but I had heard nothing
about you.   I said to my husband one Sunday morning, "I
must go to Ebenezer church, for I feel the man has come the
Lord promised me he would send."   But he said, "Your health
is so poor, it will not do for you to go; and your doctor will
be displeased."   But I felt I must go, though the church
was two miles away from us.   I finally persuaded husband
to go along, and when we entered the door and saw you in
the pulpit; I said, "That is the man the Lord promised
me."   The Lord had let me see you, and I knew you.'

"This was of great encouragement to me, and allayed all
my fears for the time being."

CHAPTER LVII.

INFORMATION now came to Mr. Redfield that Mr. Roberts, who had been expelled from the Genesee Conference, was laboring under the auspices of a Laymen's Convention held in Albion, N. Y., during the first part of the winter. This convention after remonstrating against the course of the conference, in expelling Mr. Roberts and Mr. M'Creery, passed a resolution, asking Mr. Roberts to go through the country and discuss the action of the conference, guaranteeing him his support while so engaged. When Mr. Roberts was called in, and the resolution read to him, he declined the request, but offered to spend his time for a year in evangelistic work if they desired it. The resolution was then reconsidered and changed to harmonize with that proposition. Mr. Roberts and Mr. M'Creery had appealed to the General Conference which would be held in May, 1860, and both had united with the church again, on probation, according to Discipline. They did this that they might legally labor in spreading the gospel, while their appeals were pending. As Mr. Roberts' relation to the Methodist Episcopal Church, at this time was similar to that of their own, the new society in St. Louis now sent for him to come and take Mr. Redfield's place for a season. This would leave Mr. Redfield free to go to Quincy, Illinois, where a field had awaited him for some time.

Mr. Roberts went, helped to perfect the organization, and to make a rule against slavery that could not be evaded. One of the members, Joseph Wickersham, who for conscience' sake, when seeking perfect love, a few years before, had set at liberty $30,000 worth of slaves, was one of the most eager for such a rule. Thus on slave territory, these men and women who had gone into this new society, dared squarely to meet the question of slavery, when the Methodist Episcopal Church, as a body, through its conferences, annual and general, were cringing and dodging in regard to it. This circumstance shows that the difficulty was not with the laity, but with the ministry; and that all their pleas of toleration for slavery were baseless. Many of these persons were practical business men, and who knew the power of prejudice, and social ostracism, yet fearlessly they adopted this rule on slavery in a slave-holding city. Their action shows a conscientious boldness that will honor their names in time and in eternity.

The Laymen's Convention under whose auspices Mr. Roberts was now laboring, had passed a resolution, based upon Dr. Abel Stevens' declaration of the reserved power of the laity to correct the mal-administration of the ministry, viz.: the right to withhold supplies. This resolution read as follows:

"Resolved, That we will not aid in the support of any member of the Genesee Conference who assisted, either by his vote, or his influence, in the expulsion of Brothers Roberts and M'Creery from the conference and the church, until they are re-instated to their former position; and that we do recommend all those who believe that these brethren have been unjustly expelled from the conference and the church, to take the same course."

The resolution to employ Mr. Roberts and Mr. M'Creery reads:

"Resolved, That we recommend Rev. B. T. Roberts and Rev. J. M'Creery to travel at large, and to labor, as opportunity presents, for the promoting of the work of God and the salvation of souls."

The salary of each was fixed, and a committee of fifteen was appointed to collect the same.

The policy was soon adopted by their enemies, of reading out of the church as withdrawn, all who acted upon these resolutions. In some places the numbers so cut off were so large that temporary organizations had to be effected to provide places of worship and to appoint officers to take the oversight of the work. This made work for the two men, and Mr. Roberts' visit to St. Louis was for the same object.

The convention had also adopted the following resolution, that expressed its attitude toward the church:

"Resolved, That the farcical cry of disunion and secession is the artful production of designing men to frighten the feeble and timid into their plans of operation and proscription. We wish it distinctly understood that we have not, and never had, the slightest intention of leaving the church of our choice, and that we heartily approve of the course of Brothers Roberts and M'Creery in rejoining the church at their first opportunity; and we hope that the oppressive and un-Methodistic administration indicated in the pastoral address (adopted by the Genesee Conference) as the current policy of the majority of the conference, will not drive any of our brethren from the church. Methodists have a better right in the Methodist Episcopal Church than anybody else, and by God's grace, in it we intend to remain."

Mr. Redfield says of the state of affairs at this time in St. Louis: "We now expected our conference to set our matters right, and then to take us into conference; but if that failed, we had one hope left, and that was that the General Conference, to sit in about one year, would begin a system of correction which would eventually reach us. If that failed, we would be compelled to set up permanently for ourselves."

This expresses the state of things in February, 1859. But little did these laymen or ministers know what awaited them in the future. There was a deceptive quiet, politically throughout the nation, that proved to be the precursor of a terrible storm of civil war. The slumbering feelings that found expression in that war, awed, and almost frightened, men from their steadfastness for the truth. Men, otherwise staunch and firm, proved unfaithful and untrue.

The society in St. Louis soon felt it necessary for the protection of Mr. Redfield to publish the following resolutions, which were adopted, and ordered to be published without his knowledge:

"Resolved, 1. That we deem it due to our worthy brother, Rev. Dr. Redfield, to state that amid all the difficulties, as well as the causes, which have resulted in the division of the Methodist Episcopal Church, at Ebenezer, in this city, he has stood aloof, neither advising nor counseling us as to what course to pursue in relation to said division; but like a man of God, full of love for the salvation of souls and the prosperity of our common Zion, he wept over the apparent calamities brought upon us by the unwise conduct of those assuming to have authority over us.

"Resolved, 2. That as our brother is about to leave us, we commend him to all the churches in our beloved land, and pray that the great Head of the church may shield and protect him and his devoted wife, from the persecutions of their enemies, as well as the slanders the ungodly may send after them.

"Resolved, 3. That the *Central Christian*, the *Northwestern*, and the *Western Advocates*, and the *Christian Advocate and Journal*, and those journals favorable to the cause of religion, be requested to publish these resolutions.

"St. Louis, February 28, 1859."

These resolutions were signed by ninety-four members of the society, and taken to the *Central Christian Advocate* for publication. But the editor, Rev. Joseph Brooks, said, "Don't ask us to publish that, but drop all matters, and be still, and we will be still. You publish nothing, and we will publish nothing."

Dr. Williams came to Mr. Redfield, and asked him to use his influence to prevent the publication of it, and promised that they would publish nothing. Mr. Redfield promised to do so, but in a few days the following was published in the *Central Christian Advocate:*

"SPECIAL REQUEST.

"Early in the past winter, a Mr. J. W. Redfield, a local preacher, claiming to be directly from Northern Illinois or Michigan, and more remotely from New York or New England, came to this city. Being properly endorsed by the authority of the church, he was invited to aid in a series of religious services in Ebenezer church. During the time, he succeeded (as I am informed) in sowing dissensions among the members, and at length publicly proposed to take a vote of the congregation, as to whether he should occupy the pulpit. He was kindly invited to desist from further occupancy of the pulpit. This he did; and under a promise of uniting with one of the other city charges, or of going to Illinois, he asked and obtained from the pastor of Ebenezer a certificate of his membership and official standing, giving assurance, at the same time, that he would in no case have anything to do with separate services. In forty-eight hours, I am informed, he was publicly preaching to a company of the members of Ebenezer church, whom he had headed and led off, organizing and establishing separate services in another place, while the protracted services were still in progress in Ebenezer church.

"Three several times has he been officially required to deposit his certificate in some one of the city charges, that he might be held to answer grave charges which are pending against him (and are now in my possession), involving his ecclesiastical and Christian character. He has constantly refused to comply with this requisition, treating the demand with contempt. Various statements have been made by himself and friends as to where he has deposited his certificate of membership. At one time it is said to have been sent to

Illinois; at another to be deposited with some church of another denomination. Thus the case stands.

"With many years' experience in the church, I have never before known a case involving so much evasion, unmitigated duplicity, and contempt of the authority, order, and Discipline of the church.

"This note is to request that any minister or member of the M. E. Church having knowledge of where he holds his membership, and is ecclesiastically amenable, will give me information at once.

"SAMUEL HUFFMAN, P. E.,
"St. Louis District, Missouri Conference."

This was copied in many, if not in all, the church papers. And, strange to say, the minister who had given the church letter which Mr. Redfield presented, and which was publicly read in the Ebenezer church, knew of this published request, and yet never came to his relief with a statement of the facts.

A few days after the publication of that paper, a committee appointed by the new church prepared a reply and took it to the *Central Advocate*, but the editor refused to publish it. It was then taken to the *St. Louis Christian Advocate*, the organ of the Methodist Episcopal Church, South, where it was published in the following form:

"OUR NORTHERN BRETHREN.

"For several weeks past, as we have been informed, our Northern brethren in this city have not been in the most pleasant state of feeling among themselves. Some difficulty occurred in the Ebenezer church—their principal church in the city—which soon resulted in the withdrawal, in form or in fact, of one-half, or more than one-half, of the entire membership. These 'seceders' (we use that word in no offensive sense) organized themselves elsewhere, and have kept up separate services, which are reported to have been interesting and profitable; but the gap between them and 'the old church' (Ebenezer) seems, from what we hear, to be constantly widening. Below, we give place to a communication and explanations, which communication was intended for another paper, but not allowed a place in its columns. We publish it at the earnest solicitation of several persons who are personally friendly to us, and subscribers to our paper, although they never have belonged to the Southern church, and perhaps never will. It seems but just that they should have some medium through which to reply to what they consider unfair and unjust accusations.

"It is not our purpose to meddle with their difficulties, and all we now state is upon information received from others. We have not from the first been any nearer 'the seat of war' than our own legitimate business has called us, but, if reports may be relied on, some strange things have occurred among them.—ED. ADVOCATE.

"Editor St. Louis C. Advocate:

"Dear Sir:—The following was sent to the editor of the *Central Advocate*, with a request that it should be inserted, as a simple act of justice to Dr. Redfield, whom we believe to be an injured man. For reasons of his own, the editor of the *Central* refused to give it a place in his columns. We have, therefore, respectfully to ask that you will do us the favor to give it a place in your paper, as, at present, we have no other available means of reaching that portion of the public whom we most desire should see this, our honest statement of facts.

"The paper was signed by five of those whose names are now appended, as a committee appointed for that purpose. When the editor of the *Central* refused to insert it, it was then reported back to the church by whom the committee had been appointed, and the following resolution was adopted unanimously:

"Resolved, That as the following has been rejected by

the *Central Advocate*, it be forwarded to the editor of the *St. Louis Christian Advocate*, with a request that it be published in that paper, and that it, also, be signed by those holding official position in Ebenezer church, when the separation took place.

"For the Central Christian Advocate.
"[SPECIAL REQUEST.]

"Mr. Editor:—An article bearing the above title, signed Samuel Huffman, P. E., published in your issue of the 16th, contains so many false statements of an injurious character, that we beg permission to correct the most important.

"Mr. Huffman charges the Rev. J. W. Redfield with being unwilling, when he came to this city, to tell definitely where he was from, 'claiming,' he says, 'to be directly from Northern Illinois, or Michigan.'

"The tendency of this is, to excite suspicion that there must be something wrong about him, or he would be able and willing to state 'whence he came.'

"This charge is utterly false. Dr. Redfield brought official letters from the church, which were read publicly in Ebenezer church, stating that he was 'directly' from Elgin, Illinois.

"Mr. Huffman next charges, on 'information,' Dr. Redfield, with 'sowing dissensions among the members' of Ebenezer church. That Dr. Redfield preached the gospel with great plainness and power, we readily admit; and many 'came out from the world' and gave themselves anew to Christ. But for other influences than those excited by Dr. Redfield, we believe no 'dissensions' among the members would have taken place.

" Mr. Huffman charges Dr. Redfield with ' publicly proposing to take a vote of the congregation, as to whether he should occupy the pulpit.' Dr. Redfield *never proposed any such thing*. He had been invited by official members, the pastor concurring, to occupy the pulpit, and hold a series of meetings for three weeks. During the first sermon he preached after this invitation was given, Dr. Redfield proposed to take an expression of the congregation, as to whether they would like to have this searching class of truth presented. The pastor interrupted, and the next night forbade him the further occupancy of the pulpit.

"Again, Mr. Huffman charges him with obtaining, under false pretences, from the pastor of Ebenezer 'a certificate of his membership and official standing.'

"We should like to know what right any 'pastor' has to exact a promise before he will give a certificate of membership?

"The certificate relates to present standing, and not to future conduct. But, as we understand it, the doctor made no 'promise.' He did not buy a 'certificate.' He simply expressed his intention. That intention, expressed honestly at the time, he had a perfect right to change.

"Mr. Huffman charges Dr. Redfield with 'heading and leading off a company of the members of Ebenezer church.' This, also, is utterly untrue. Dr. Redfield never encouraged or advised, so far as we could learn, any one to leave Ebenezer church.

"Those who left, did so of their own accord, and, as they believe, for sufficient reasons.

"With 'organizing and establishing separate services,' he had nothing to do. He even refused to attend their first meetings.

"At the request of those who organized themselves into a separate society, he has preached for them, and, we trust, will continue to do so as his health will permit.

"The Rev. Mr. Huffman, P. E., expresses great anxiety to have the Rev. Dr. Redfield placed in his power. He exhibits an eagerness, totally unbecoming a minister of the gospel, to see his anticipated victim writhing under the tortures of the modern inquisition.

27

"We trust that he may find himself disappointed.

"For the withdrawal from Ebenezer of the large num-bers of members that have left, we do not consider that Dr. Redfield is in the least responsible. We have our own views as to where the blame rests, but, at present, accuse no one.

"There is room enough in this large and wicked city for both the old and new organizations to live and labor for the salvation of souls. Crimination and recriminations can do no good. Let us employ our strength in peace and harmony, in building up the Redeemer's kingdom.

"From our intercourse with Dr. Redfield, we are satis-fied that he is a holy man, devoted entirely to the service of Christ. He preaches with apostolic zeal, eloquence and power, and we most cordially commend him to the confidence and sympathy of the Christian public, wherever he may bestow his evangelical labors.

> "H. WICKERSHAM, · Leader,⎫
> "L. H. CORDRY, L. P.,   ⎪
> "HENRY STEPHENS, L. P.,   ⎬ *Com.*
> "LIBERTY WAITE, Steward, ⎪
> "A. W. HARRISON.   ⎭
> "AD. C. CAUGHLAN, Steward,
> "JOHNSON BROOKS, Leader,
> "RICHARD THORNTON, L. D.,
>   "and one hundred members."

Before Mr. Redfield started for Quincy, a friend handed him a copy of the paper with the article his enemies had published. This induced him to leave his wife, for the present, in St. Louis, as he did not know the reception he might receive in that place. With a heavy heart he started on his journey. The tempter beset him with questioning as to his course. He soliloquized thus: "What am I about? If I am right, why don't God stop this great wrong? Well, I don't know; I cannot see! I am an offense. I cannot help it. I am like a poor hunted animal, dodging the blows of its enemies. But still I'll try to work for God as well as I can."

The next morning, after leaving St. Louis, he arrived at Quincy, and found the paper with that special request had preceded him. He was immediately waited upon, and asked if he would deposit his letter, and come to trial. He replied, "I am not willing to let my case be acted upon by such as know of the fraudulent letter, and connived at it. I can show you papers which will attest the truth of the whole matter. Now you can do as you please, but I do not feel it my duty to suffer all I have for these men, and then to begin a series of meetings here after having been tried for a crime which they have committed."

But the president of the Methodist college, and the agent of the same, said, "We will go to St. Louis and find out all the facts."

They returned in a few days, and said to Mr. Redfield, "We saw only the men who are pursuing you, and we knew from their own mouths that the whole matter of the disturbance is with, and caused by, them. So you have our confidence, and can go to work."

While Mr. Redfield was waiting for their return, the lady with whom he boarded related to him the following experience:

"Brother, I have lived here seventeen years. I have felt it to be my duty to work for God. I have seen one church, among the Germans, built up, and become a Bethel for souls. And we have two American Methodist churches. About five years ago, I got to feeling so bad over the low state of religion, that one night, after meeting, I took a by street to go home, so I could cry aloud, and ask God what was to be done. That night he showed you to me in a dream, and told me you would come and preach the gospel in its power. And as soon as I saw you I knew you, and remembered my dream."

Mr. Redfield remarks in connection with this account, "All this was very consoling to my wounded heart. But for these occasional instances of revelation to God's people, I think I should have given up the struggle."

He now went to work, and God came in glorious power in the salvation of souls. A Baptist clergyman, an honest, earnest seeker after what he called "the higher life," soon entered into the experience. One day, when Mr. Redfield was out visiting, he was sent for by a sister of the church, who was in great distress of mind. Several were with her, and were engaged in prayer, when he arrived. She would walk the floor, throw herself flat upon it, wring her hands, and cry, and whenever the praying would cease, she would scream out, "Oh, do, do pray every moment, for I cannot live." The friends prayed until they were exhausted. Mr. Redfield had been quietly watching her in the meanwhile, and at last said,

"Sister, hold on a moment."

But she cried out, "Why don't you pray?"

He said to her, "You are not ready for prayer. Now, do you say, if the Lord will bless you, any way?"

"Oh," said she, "that is the difficulty. I am not willing to be singular."

"Well, if God will save you, do you say, any way, Lord?"

Soon she broke out, with, "Any way, Lord."

He said, "Say it louder"; and she repeated it at the top of her voice. In a few minutes she was so filled with joy that her shouts of praise aroused the people of the entire block.

In the following letter, written at this time, Mr. Redfield opens his heart and mind to our gaze:

"QUINCY, Ill., March 30, 1859.

"Dear Brother and Sister Foot:—Your letter came to hand this afternoon, re-mailed from St. Louis.

"I have been here two weeks next Saturday. Mattie will come up to-morrow or next day. I send you a paper, the

St. Louis Christian Advocate, a Southern paper, which will set that matter of the *Central Advocate* right. I have likewise papers signed by about one hundred persons, stating the facts concerning the church difficulties. The depths of corruption which have come to light by the acts of the few men who have tried to father on to me the fruits of their own wrong, will put them in a very unenviable light at the next conference. The city of St. Louis, churches and outsiders, seeing the wrong and the persecutions of these men, have offered and are now preparing to build a church at a cost of about $20,000—lot and all. A brother was up here yesterday to negotiate for the brick.

"They are still having salvation power in the new church. Mattie reports, that Sunday before last, six were converted in a single class meeting, and a number sanctified. They have now six classes, and a Sunday-school of more than two hundred, and very flourishing. More or less are joining, at almost every meeting. They say salvation was never in the city before in power like this.

"The first week after the publishing of that article in the *Central,* more than fifty of the subscribers stopped taking it. The city carriers have refused to take it, as, they say, so many refuse to take it longer. That shows what the people in St. Louis think. Two of the first ministers of this conference (the Illinois) have been down to St. Louis, and took the reports from the men who published that article, and they say those men are condemned out of their own mouths; and assure me that I have their confidence and sympathy, and shall have their support. So I feel that I have nothing more to do with the matter. I shall keep on serving God and doing all the good I can amid this persecution. It is hard enough to be without home, and away from friends, and to meet the powers of darkness, of the world, and infidels; but if my track lies amid perils by sea and by land, and false brethren, yet God will not excuse me.

" 'The way may be rough,
But it will not be long.'

"We are having conflicts here, but glorious victories also.

"A goodly number have entered into the rest of perfect love. Two Baptist preachers have attended some of the meetings and are earnestly seeking holiness. They came to my boarding house to talk with me and pray over the matter to-day. They said they would pay the cost. One said, 'By faith I can see men as trees walking, and I never knew anything like this before.' The other says he will not yield until he knows the fullness for himself; and then he will preach it if he is turned away from Quincy. Bless the Lord! The work is spreading all over the place, and into nearly all the churches. Hallelujah to the Branch!

"The dear, good sister where I stay, is a pilgrim indeed. She has stood nearly alone for fourteen years, weeping and praying over this wicked city. Five years ago, she says, God showed her the man whom he would send here to work; and she says, 'When I first saw you, I remembered the dream in which I saw you.' Oh, how this did comfort me amid my fight 'with the beasts of Ephesus.' Right, or not, such things do encourage me.

"The people in St. Louis insisted upon it, that we must not leave them this summer. They think, if the work keeps moving as it now does, they will have at least three churches of a salvation stamp, in two or three years. Next Sabbath they are to have their first general quarterly meeting, after the manner of such meetings in Western New York. One of the preachers from the East is with them now, and they expect another to take his place soon.

"The society goes in strong for Northern Methodism, and organized on the Discipline of 1842. It is said that one of the bishops has said, the society will be recognized, although those men who have fought us say they will leave the conference if that is done. But we shall see.

"I was never more sure that God sent us to that city of sin. It did seem that it would crush me for awhile, and I was laid up sick for two weeks with the burden and trouble. 'But having obtained help of God, I continue to this day,' preaching the same gospel, and having the same Jesus to help me. My dear Mattie has stood by me like an angel of mercy; and when I felt like fainting, she seemed to possess the courage of a hero, and insisted upon it that we should not quit the field, but have victory or die in our tracks. God has given the victory. If Mattie's health permits we shall visit St. Charles this season, the Lord permitting. Then we can give you all the interesting details, which are too tedious to write.

"The people here are urgent that we shall make this place our home this summer, but I don't know. We have two more new places open, as soon as we get through here, where the ministers knew me East, and know all about the St. Louis troubles. They are very urgent that we carry the same word of salvation into their places.

"Oh, how I want to see you all at St. Charles. Please give my love to all; tell them to pray for us. If ever we needed prayers it is now. We are kicked on one side, and patted on the other. We need humility to bear the one, and courage to meet the other,—especially when we get into the unfortunate fix of the poor fellow who went down from Jerusalem to Jericho. We have had the worst squall that we ever got into. But thank the Lord, salvation has got into St. Louis, and I think it will take years for the devil to get it out; and in that time a goodly host will pass safely over.

"Love to all.

"J. W. REDFIELD."

CHAPTER LVIII

SUBSEQUENT events proved the wisdom of Mr. Redfield's refusal to submit to trial by the Ebenezer quarterly conference. The trial of a number of local preachers took place, which developed the policy of the administration. The trials of two were postponed from time to time, until the sickness of one and the business of the other prevented them from attending, and then they were published as having refused to appear. Another was tried, and cleared, and when his character was "passed," he asked for his letter, and united with the new society. Another local preacher, whose drunkenness had been a great scandal to the church, had his license renewed after signing the temperance pledge.

Mr. Redfield had now taken his letter again, and for the time being put it in the keeping of a minister in the church South, thinking the mutual jealousies of the two churches would make that a safe asylum for the time being. But Dr. Williams was constantly on the search for it, finally discovered it, and immediately published Mr. Redfield as having compromised his anti-slavery principles. This drew letters in large numbers from all parts of the country, asking for explanations. But what was painful to him was that some staunch friends for this cause now forsook him. Among these was ex-Bishop Hamline. Down to this time their friendship had been close, and Mr. Redfield had received much encouragement from the good man. Often, fields of labor had opened to him through the bishop's influence. For some reason, probably from the evil reports then in circulation, their fellowship was broken. But a few years elapsed before they both had passed away, and doubtless in heaven mutual explanations have been made, and they have entered into a fellowship to be no more broken.

During the summer following, Mr. Redfield went East,

on a visit, and met with handbills, stating that he and the new society in St. Louis were slaveholders, and belonged to the Southern Methodist church. From this time he found his way in the Methodist Episcopal Church almost entirely closed.

In the autumn of 1858, Rev. Seymour Coleman, a super-annuated preacher of the Troy Conference, settled in Aurora, Illinois. For many years he had been noted for the advocacy of the doctrine and experience of holiness. This was his theme, and his preaching was in great simplicity and power. He has the honor of being the first Methodist preacher who invited seekers of holiness to the altar for prayer. At his next conference his character was arrested by his presiding elder, for so doing.

Mr. Coleman had attended most of the laymen's camp meetings in Western New York, and knew the "pilgrims" well.

In the spring of 1859, a vacancy occurred in the pulpit of the First church, in Aurora, and he was employed to fill it until the ensuing conference. Almost immediately the Spirit of God began to be poured out upon the Aurora church, and large numbers of the membership entered into the experience of perfect love, and a general awakening among the unconverted soon became apparent. His first more public appearance was at the district camp meeting held near Syca-more in De Kalb Co. At this camp meeting were large numbers from Marengo, Woodstock, Elgin and St. Charles, who had been brought into the experience of perfect love through Mr. Redfield's labors. There were visitors also from long distances, who were full of holy fire, and ready for work. Mr. Coleman was invited to preach the opening sermon. In this he pitched the keynote for the entire meeting. Full salvation was the theme, and all the full salvation folks walked out in glorious liberty. Mr. Coleman preached again Friday afternoon, on the Vine and the Branches. In this sermon he handled the timid and the unsound theologians in the church "without gloves." During the sermon he gave expression to the following:

"I understand there are preachers in this country, who are afraid of the Bible terms, sanctification, holiness, perfect love, clean heart, and talk about 'a little more religion,' 'a deeper work of grace,' etc. The Lord pity the poor things. Jesus has said, 'Whosoever shall be ashamed of me, and *my words*, in this adulterous and sinful generation, of him shall the Son of man be ashamed, when he cometh in the glory of the Father with the holy angels.'" Presiding Elder H—— gently pulled Father Coleman's coat, as a check to such severity, but the old man, with a dignity and almost majesty of manner, that thrilled all who observed it, turned and laid his hand upon the elder's head, and said, "It will not hurt you, elder." At the close of the sermon, Father Coleman was about to sit down, when the elder told him to go on. He then turned back to the congregation, and asked to have the whole altar cleared. The altar was one of the old-fashioned kind, with a railing around to keep off the crowd from the seekers and laborers. In a moment, almost, the whole altar was cleared. He then asked for seekers for holiness; and, about as quick, the place was filled again, until only two persons could get in to labor with the seekers. More than 150 were on their knees consecrating all to Christ.

Many of the ministers present were astonished at the power of the truth of a full salvation to move and bless the people. The evidence of the divine approval of preaching the doctrine was apparent to all.

While a group of Christians were talking together of the wondrous scene a little while after, a gentleman approached, and said, "I saw the old man this forenoon far out in the grove stretched flat on the ground, with his coat and vest off, struggling in prayer; and again, since dinner, I went out, and he still was there engaged in prayer." This explained it all.

The next morning the love-feast started off in glorious power. Many were the testimonies to entire sanctification. Some would say, "Thank God, three years ago," or "two years ago," or "one year ago," "I saw the light." This meant when Mr. Redfield came into this section. These testimonies seemed to disturb the presiding elder much. At last, apparently in great indignation, he arose, and said: "Brethren, you are doing us preachers a great wrong. You talk as though this was a new thing. But we have been preaching it all these years. I thank God that three weeks after my conversion I was led to the altar by my mother, though I was only nine years old, and there and then I consecrated myself wholly to God. It has cost me many a struggle to keep all on the altar, but by the grace of God I have been enabled to do so."

A sister Irvine, the wife of one of the conference preachers, a contributor to the *Ladies' Repository*, and an advocate of holiness, was present, and her swift pencil took down the elder's testimony, and the next week it appeared in the *North-western Christian Advocate*.

But there were on the camp ground, a brother Bishop and his brother-in-law, Fairchild, the latter a local preacher, who were differently moved by the testimony than most others who heard it. At noon, when they came together in their tent, the following conversation took place:

"What do you think of the elder's testimony?"

"I don't know what to make of it."

"When he came to our first quarterly meeting in Wood-stock, last fall," said the local preacher, "I asked him at the close of his Saturday afternoon sermon, if he enjoyed the blessing of holiness, and he answered, 'No; but I am seeking it; and I want the friends to pray for me.'"

"But," said Father Bishop, "at our last quarterly meeting at Franklinville, on Sunday morning, he preached against the use of the technical terms, sanctification, etc. Monday morning I felt so badly about it, I went to the parsonage to talk with him about it.   He then told me he had 'been read· ing Mattison on the subject, and had grown skeptical.'"

In the minds of these brethren and those who listened to them, there was great confusion as to what the elder meant by that testimony.

In the city of Aurora, the work of holiness went forward with great power under the labors of Father Coleman. Here were strong men who stood by the doctrine and ex- perience; and whose hearts were loyal to God. Some of these had entered into the experience and others had not.

In August, a camp meeting was held near Aurora, which was largely attended by the lovers and advocates of holiness. Benjamin Pomeroy was there from New York state, but for some reason did not get free, and failed to make much impression. Father Coleman was at his best.   How he preached, and how he prayed!   Dr. T. M. Eddy, editor of the *Northwestern Christian Advocate*, preached Sunday morning.   The only minister who felt free to follow him in the afternoon was Father Coleman, who preached from "Tarry ye at Jerusalem, until ye be endued with power from on high."   It was a characteristic discourse.   There was no comfort in it for an unfaithful and cowardly ministry; there was much that gave offense to the fastidious and time-serv- ing; but God was glorified.

About five o'clock two prayer meetings were started, one in a large Aurora tent, led by Father Coleman, and the other in a St. Charles tent, led by a boy preacher.   God came in great power, and many were saved.   Among the rest who attended this meeting was the Hon. Benjamin Hackney, of Aurora. He had been converted but a short time, and under the preaching of Father Coleman, had come to see the doc- trine of holiness clearly, but had not yet entered into the experience.   Sunday evening, just before the preaching service, he was walking back and forth across the grounds in meditation, when he met Father Coleman, and said, "Father Coleman, I've got everything upon the altar; what shall I do next?"

"Oh, just leave it there," said the old veteran, and passed on.

Mr. Hackney resumed his walk, and his meditations. But to himself he said, "Well; that is a strange way to treat a man! Why did he not try to help me? Perhaps that is the way to do. Well; I'll do that." He continued his walk, thinking and praying, and waiting upon the Lord. Little by little his faith took hold, and little by little came the peace of believing. The assurance began to spring up in his heart, and at last he was enabled to say:

"'Tis done, thou dost this moment save,
  With full salvation bless.
Redemption through thy blood I have,
  And spotless love and peace."

The next day was a busy one with him up town in his office, and on the campground, looking after his own tent, and a number of others he had provided for those who could not provide for themselves, and he had no opportunity to testify in public. It was the same on Tuesday, until the meeting broke up. In the afternoon while quite a company was waiting for a train, and he was superintending the removal of the tents under his care, an impromptu service was held in the altar. After awhile Mr. Hackney arose and testified. He said:

"I have dealt in railroad stocks, and canal stocks, and bank stocks, and state stocks, and in all kinds of stocks, but I never got hold of anything that yields such dividends as the stock I have in Jesus."

In a few days another camp meeting commenced on the old ground near Coral. Here the holiness people were out in force. Elder Crews again had charge, and Mr. Redfield was present to preach and help on the battle. A wonderful spirit of prayer prevailed. At almost every hour of the day, the woods were vocal with the sound of prayer. A Rev. N. P. H—— preached the Sunday morning sermon. It was a strained effort to do a great thing. In the afternoon Mr. Redfield preached, in his characteristic manner. While touching upon the subject of dress, the Rev. H—— was evidently disturbed, and pointing towards Mr. Redfield's back, said, "But he wears buttons on the back of his coat."

These three camp meetings greatly strengthened the holiness people, and as greatly exasperated their enemies. In the city of Aurora lived Rev. A——d, the presiding elder of Chicago District, who held to the development theory of sanctification. He became greatly stirred over the growth of the holiness sentiment, and the spread of the work. The First church desired Father Coleman to supply them another year; but Elder A——, though it was not within his jurisdiction, said, "He shall not supply a pulpit in Aurora, if it shuts every church, store and shop in the city."

Elder Crews, of the Rockford District, took to the conference the recommendations of Edward P. Hart and I. H. Richardson, both from the Marengo Quarterly Conference. Elder H——, of the St. Charles District, opposed both of them, because, as he said, they were tainted with Redfieldism. In his speech against their reception, he said: "Redfieldism has nearly driven me from my district during the year." He was the presiding elder whose testimony created such a sensation at the Sycamore camp meeting in June.

One fact should be borne in mind, namely, that in all these conflicts, East and West, the opposition to these holiness workers came from men who did not hold clearly to the doctrine of entire sanctification as a distinct experience.

But to return to the session of the Illinois Conference. It was argued by some, that as Mr. Hart was a young man, he might be cured of his Redfieldism, but Mr. Richardson was too old for that. Mr. Hart was admitted, and Mr. Richardson was rejected.

Rev. D. D. Buck, a presiding elder of the Minnesota Conference, had been present, listening to all that was said, *pro* and *con*, against Mr. Richardson, and after the adjournment for the day, went to him, and putting his arm around him, invited him to come to Minnesota to his district, for he had a place for him. Mr. Richardson went to Minnesota, and became a useful and successful minister of the gospel.

They were greatly mistaken in Mr. Hart, for they were unable to cure him of Redfieldism, and he is still tainted with it, and spreads it wherever he goes, as one of the general superintendents of the Free Methodist Church.

CHAPTER LIX.

DURING the following August, the writer, then a local preacher, was invited by the local preachers of Mt. Pleasant circuit, to assist them in revival meetings. The invitation was accepted, and immediately after the Coral camp meeting I went to that place. I found the preacher appointed by the conference, had been obliged to resign because of ill health, and the work was being supplied by the local help. The meeting was held in a large country church, in a thickly-settled farming community. From the first the interest was strong, and the meeting increased constantly in power. At the end of the second week the newly-appointed preacher came on, but refused to take part in the meetings until he was moved and settled. Being in poor health and in need of help, and knowing Mr. Redfield, I was requested to write for him to come. A letter was at once forwarded to a friend, inquiring for Mr. Redfield's address. The letter was taken to Mr. Redfield at St. Charles, where he was awaiting the result of an effort to get him an opportunity to hold a meeting in that place. He answered at once, saying he would come on the following conditions:

"1. That the preacher in charge of the circuit requests it.

"2. That I can go straight on the Bible and the Discipline.

"3. That the preacher in charge will take hold of said work with me."

When his letter was received at Mt. Pleasant, it was taken immediately to the preacher in charge, who replied, "I want him to come; I want him to be Dr. Redfield; I will take hold with him and do the best I can."

A letter was now written to Mr. Redfield to come, inclosing the words of the preacher in charge. He arrived on Wednesday.

That night he preached and the preacher in charge sat back in the congregation near the door. The text was, "For he that will save his life shall lose it, but he that will lose his life for my sake, and the gospel's, the same shall save it."

The congregation was large, and very attentive. Many had complained of my preaching, but now they heard what they never had heard before. The truth came with such vividness and strength, and was attended with such an unction of the Holy One, that Christians were compelled to look over their hopes, and sinners were in amazement.

About thirty had been converted, and fifteen had entered the experience of perfect love. One of the latter, then a class-leader, but since a traveling preacher, was put on such a searching of heart that for eight days he dared not profess to be a Christian.

At the close of the sermon Mr. Redfield sat down, and turned the meeting over to me. I arose, and asked for seekers; but none came. There had been fifteen the night before. Then the church members were asked to come forward for a prayer meeting; but not a person came. Opportunity was then given for any to speak; but none embraced it. After offering prayer, I dismissed the meeting. Immediately I was surrounded by members of the church, who asked, "Is this going right?" I replied, "Yes; you look to the Lord."

The next night Mr. Redfield preached more strongly still. The interest was intense. The pure truth in its searching power came upon the mind and heart with marvelous clearness. There was no playing upon the sympathies or passions of the people, but the most honest dealing with the understanding and the conscience. Toward the close of the discourse the feeling of the audience may be described as awful. When he had finished, he said, "While I sing two short-metre

28

verses, if any one will forsake the world and come out on the
Lord's side, come." He sang to the tune "Shawmut," the
words,

> "And can I yet delay,
>   My little all to give?
> To tear myself from earth away,
>   For Jesus to receive?"

At first the congregation attempted to sing with him, but
he desired them to think. To bring this about, he varied the
tune and the words, and repeated both, until every voice but
his own was hushed. He then sang the second verse with
great sweetness and power:

> "Nay, but I yield, I yield,
>   I will hold out no more;
> I sink by dying love compelled,
>   And own Thee conqueror."

Not a person had moved. He then said, "Perhaps some
one has a confession to make." No one responded to this.
He then pronounced the benediction, and the congregation
dispersed in great quietness.

Many came to me and asked, "Is this going right?" to
whom I answered, "Yes; you look to the Lord."

The next night the truth seemed to come with still greater
power than the night before. The house was packed to its
utmost capacity. Every eye was fixed intensely upon the
speaker. The minds of the people were led to the judgment
scene, and made to look over the acts of the life and the feelings of the heart under the light of God. The people began
to lean toward the speaker; here and there one rose to his
feet. A deathly pallor spread over every face. But all was
still, save the preacher's voice, which, in measured tones,
with great clearness and distinctness, pronounced the truth
that arraigned all at the bar of God. At the close of the
sermon, more than twenty were standing on their feet, while
the very hush of the congregation was painful. He closed,

and gave the invitation. The congregation arose, and before a word could be sung, there was a simultaneous rush from all parts of the house toward the altar, with wailing and lamentations, and screams for mercy. There could be no orderly praying, but every one broke out for himself. Christians, and backsliders, and sinners, were mingled. More than eighty had come as penitents. One of the most fastidious of ladies came screaming most disagreeable hallelujahs; and continued them after she reached the altar. It awakened my curiosity, and I watched her with much interest. At last she screamed out, "There; I've said I'd go to hell before I'd shout." In an instant the power of God fell upon her. Her hallelujahs were changed to the sweetest tones. She rose to her feet, and flew about the house, shouting "Hallelujah" as she went.

So great was the feeling among the seekers that it was about impossible to instruct them, or even to gain their attention. Now and then, with shining face, one would spring to his feet to tell what Christ had done for him; but the screaming for mercy by those still seeking, drowned their voices. Thus the meeting went on until a late hour. Finally the seekers, from sheer exhaustion, quieted down, and the service was closed.

Up to this time there had been no opportunity even to introduce the two preachers. Each night the preacher in charge had seated himself in the rear of the congregation, and when the service closed, would immediately leave the house. But now, after the service closed, he came forward and was introduced. It is quite possible that if Mr. Redfield's effort had been a failure, he would not have come forward at all. He said, "I have taken no part in these meetings heretofore, but now I will be on hand every night to assist." Turning to me, he said, "I will take charge of the prayer meeting, before preaching to-morrow night, and you take charge of it after the preaching. Hereafter we will alternate in that manner."

On the way to our lodgings, I remarked to Mr. Redfield, "Doctor, that was glorious."

"Oh, but we must go forty feet deeper yet!" he exclaimed.

The next night, Saturday, the preacher in charge was on hand, and in a very systematic manner took charge of the prayer meeting before preaching.

The scene during the remainder of the evening, the matter and manner of the discourse, and the results, were similar to those of the evening before. It seemed as though the forty feet deeper stratum was reached. On the way home, I again remarked, "Well, that was glorious!"

"We must go ten feet deeper yet," said Mr. Redfield, in a very impulsive manner.

Sunday morning came. A testimony meeting for an hour before preaching gave an opportunity for any to speak freely. Some very humiliating confessions were made, and some very clear experiences related. The sermon was in the same line of those which had preceded it. An altar service lasted until two o'clock. Many were converted, and many entered into the experience of perfect love; among them the invalid preacher of the year before.

In the evening the house was filled, and many could not get in. A deathly stillness pervaded the congregation while Mr. Redfield preached. There was the same rush to the altar as on the preceding nights. The preacher in charge stepped forward to take the management of the prayer meeting. But when he wanted them to pray, somebody wanted to speak, and when he wanted them to speak, somebody wanted to pray. He became greatly excited, hurried from one end of the altar to the other, and at last turned to me and inquired, "How do you *do* it? How shall I manage it?"

"Let it manage itself," I replied.

"Is that the way?" he asked.

He quietly dropped out, and took no active part in the meetings after that.

On Monday night, Mr. Redfield preached on the Way of Faith. But he saw before the service closed, that the subject was premature. He went groaning all the way home. He remarked as we entered the house, "We must go *sixty feet deeper yet.* In such meetings, you must go down, *down*, DOWN, until all is broken up; then the work will go of itself if there is not a preacher within forty miles."

The next night, the plow of truth went in deeper than at any time before. How the power of God came with it! A doctor of medicine by the name of Roe, had been listening to the truth night after night but had made no move. He was a member of the church, but wholly backslidden. During the altar service he was heard screaming for mercy with all his might; and was found rolling upon the floor in great agony. He was a large man, with a powerful voice, which soon drowned all others. He at last began to confess that he had been called to preach the gospel, but had run away from duty. Late in the evening he found peace.

One night, Mr. Redfield preached a discourse of marvelous eloquence. His subject was, the Final Catastrophe of Earth. He drew a vivid picture of the earth with its inhabitants; the various elements of the earth subject to their Maker, performing their offices, men engaged in their various avocations, when, in an instant, at the bidding of Jehovah, the falling rain became drops of fire, the rivers, and the lakes and the oceans, all liquid flame, etc., etc. A student, who was preparing for the law, who sat on the front seat, said afterwards, he found himself looking upward to see the drops fall; and many in the congregation thought the time had come.

Another passage in the sermon was as follows:

"Suppose, that in the judgment, your soul and your body should be remanded to the grave, there to be confined forever, with no want, from cold, or heat, or hunger, or thirst, but only this, 'I want to get out.' And when age after age has gone by, and the confinement has become almost unendurable, you cry out in your anguish, 'How long, O Lord, must I lie here?' and back should come the answer, 'Eternity! eternity!' And age after age again goes by, and you cry out, 'How long, O Lord, how long?' and the answer comes, 'Eternity! eternity!' You would jump into a hell of liquid fire to be free."

Mr. Redfield was with us two weeks and then returned to St. Charles. During this time he had won a permanent place in the affections of every fully consecrated man and woman, and every young convert. With weeping eyes they bade him good-by the last night.

The meeting continued for three weeks longer, ending in a quarterly meeting. The presiding elder took great pains to explain to the saints when they should say amen, and when they should shout, but his motive was so apparent, and his instructions so void of spiritual wisdom, that they failed to make any permanent impression.

We now began to note the permanent fruit of the meeting. More than one hundred had been converted, and about seventy-five had experienced perfect love.

The Sunday night after Mr. Redfield left, Mr. F——, the preacher in charge, preached with unusual liberty for him. When the invitation was being given for seekers, a lady who had lately been converted, and then sanctified a few days after, went to him and asked him to go forward as a seeker; but he repulsed her. With a scream she fell to the floor in great agony. A large number came forward, and the prayer meeting commenced. When the service had closed, as I turned to prepare for leaving the house, the lady referred to, who was still prostrate on the floor, cried out to me, "He says you set me at him." This arrested the attention of the congregation, the greater part of which remained to see what it meant. In the pulpit, on the floor, reclined Mr. F—— and the invalid preacher, in consultation about something. In answer to my inquiry as to what the difficulty was, the latter replied, "Brother F—— is in an awful state if he did but know it." Aware that my name had been mentioned in connection with the case, I refrained from saying anything further. In a few moments Mr. F—— arose, stepped forward to the desk, and began an explanation. The lady, who was still prostrate on the floor, evidently in burden for him, cried out, "You have a confession to make." He then said, "I have been very angry since these meetings have been in progress. One night when passing out of the house, I said in the hearing of several persons, 'It makes me mad to see how these preachers act'; and a sinner near me said, 'If that is so, you had better go forward for prayers.'"

"You have not confessed all," said the burdened sister.

The preacher continued, "I have been in the habit of writing for mere literary papers to piece out my salary; and my articles have not been of a character consistent with my call to the Christian ministry. I see now I have done wrong in this; I must stop it; I will."

"There, that will do," said the burdened sister.

It was now eleven o'clock, and the entire congregation was still waiting to see the end. He now went down into the altar, and asked the prayers of the congregation.

Some of the membership who had stood aloof from the work, and whose character for consistent piety was not the best, now gathered around him, and began to pray for, and to talk to him. I finally interfered, and said, "You had better keep still, and let Sister B—— lead him. She can do more for him than any of us."

Twelve o'clock came, and still his friends and the congregation were waiting for him. He now began to talk out his thoughts and feelings. "It is plain to me," he said, "that if I do not consent to take the track Dr. Redfield does, God will leave me." Some time elapsed, and his ministerial friend asked, "Brother F——, what are you thinking about?"

He replied, "I am thinking of what occupation I shall take up?"

About two o'clock in the morning, he suddenly arose, and said to his wife, "Let us go." Sister B—— and her husband went with them to their place of stopping, and as soon as he came from his room in the morning, she renewed her labors with him. He finally refused to go any further and in a short time became an opposer of the work. A few years after he left the Methodist Episcopal Church, and united with an unorthodox denomination.

CHAPTER LX.

On returning to St. Charles, Mr. Redfield found that the preacher in charge had taken a decided stand against his holding a revival meeting there. Among his reasons for so doing he said, "I have been sent here to guard this pulpit against Redfield and Coleman."

"What have you against them?" was inquired.

"Nothing," said he; "I believe them both to be good men; and they are doing good; but they must be sacrificed for the good of the church."

When it became known that he had refused the pulpit to Mr. Redfield, some of the Baptist people suggested that he could have their pulpit, as their preacher was away. Accordingly, arrangements were made for Mr. Redfield to preach in their church for one Sunday, which he did morning and evening, to the delight of the pilgrims, and many outside the churches. Mr. Redfield was also invited to preach the following Sunday, to which he consented, and arrangements were made for it; but on Saturday, when too late to take up the appointment, his friends were informed that he could not have the pulpit. Mr. Howard, the Methodist pastor, had been to the officers of the church, and had presented the matter in such a light, that they withdrew their invitation. A trustee of the Universalist church, which was unoccupied at the time, overheard the conversation in regard to the Baptist pulpit, and immediately offered theirs. As it was too late to circulate the action of the Baptist people, this offer was accepted, and Mr. Redfield preached morning and evening in the Universalist church. As he would not leave the place for a few days, he also preached there Monday evening.

Monday Mr. Howard went to Chicago to counsel with

Bishop Simpson, who instructed him to call a meeting of the official board, and decide whether in its judgment the members who went to hear Mr. Redfield preach had withdrawn from the church, and if decided in the affirmative, he should read them out as having so withdrawn. He returned, and called together such of the official board as would follow his leadership, and they declared these members withdrawn. A majority of the official board, who were not present, nor knew of the meeting, were declared withdrawn, as well as five out of nine of the trustees of the church. Fourteen persons were thus declared withdrawn, though one of them, a brother's wife, was not a member of the church.

Wednesday evening these persons, with no knowledge of what had occurred, went to the church prayer meeting as usual. But Mr. Howard, contrary to the usual custom in that church, announced that he would call on those he desired to have pray, and the old workers in the church were all left out. Sister Foot, a woman above sixty years of age, and more than ordinarily intelligent and cultivated, when she perceived the object of Mr. Howard, groaned aloud. He sprang to his feet and in a loud voice commanded her to be silent. Thinking she would be unable to control her sorrow, she arose and left the house; when outside the door, her feelings gave way and she cried aloud for God to have mercy.

At the close of the prayer meeting, Mr. Howard read them out of the church. On Sunday morning this was repeated, and when the quarterly meeting came some time after, they were read out as withdrawn the third time.

Under the laws of the state of Illinois, the office of a trustee of a religious corporation becomes vacant only by expiration, death, or resignation. Five of the persons read out were trustees, a majority of the board. Their places had to be declared vacant by resignation, as they were all alive, and their term of office had not expired. These men, none of them, resigned; therefore somebody had to make an affidavit before a magistrate, that they had resigned. But such was the heat of opposition to Mr. Redfield and his friends, that this was done.

I returned to my home near Elgin that same week, and hearing that Mr. Redfield was holding meetings in St. Charles, I went there on Saturday. On the train I found a lay brother from Marengo on the same errand. We got off at Wayne Station, and walked across the fields to the house of John M. Laughlin; and who should open the door at our knock, but Mr. Redfield himself. As soon as he recognized us, he asked, "Are you ready to lose your heads?" We were seated and the matter was explained, as related in this chapter.

A prayer meeting had been appointed at the house of Elisha Foote, a man seventy-five years of age, a Methodist for nearly fifty years, and a brother-in-law of Rev. John Clark, noted in Methodist history, as a missionary among the Indians. A wagon load of pilgrims from Mr. Laughlin's went to that prayer meeting. When we arrived the old man was offering the opening prayer. In it he compared the circumstances of the company to those of the children of Israel at the Red Sea, with the mountain on either hand, the sea before them, and the enemy behind; and he pleaded for divine guidance and help. The crying of the company could be heard out into the street. When he ceased, we opened the door, and to our astonishment, instead of fourteen, there were more than sixty present. This was more than half the membership of the church.

The prayer meeting went on. Some time was spent in testimony, and save one exception, that in the old man's prayer, was the only allusion to the trouble, in the entire meeting. In the evening another prayer meeting was held in the same room. The company was larger than in the morning. Some more of the society, and some from the Baptist and Congregational churches, met with us. The same blessed spirit prevailed. This time there was not an •

allusion to the trouble. The bliss of a present salvation made them blessedly forgetful of it all.

While Mr. Redfield was waiting here, he wrote the following letters which will explain themselves:

"WAYNE STATION, October 20, 1859.

"Dear Brother Rogers:—We had a visit from Brother Coleman and wife yesterday. The conference refused to grant the petition of the First church of Aurora, to supply the pulpit with Brother Coleman. Presiding Elder A——d said he should not go back, if it shut every store, and bank, and church in the city. Presiding Elder H——k also said, 'This stuff has got to be put down.' But the people in Aurora say they will get a hall, or build a church; and Brother C—— says if they do, he'll preach for them.

"We have just heard from the Genesee Conference. They have expelled at least three more, and probably. will expel others before the conference closes. Well, bless the Lord! We expect Brother Roberts out here in a few days, and shall learn more of the particulars about the doings there.

"The pilgrims here are anxious to have us hold a meeting, here this fall. But whether the preacher will allow it or not I cannot tell. I shall not ask him if the way opens.* I shall obey God rather than man. We have good news from St. Louis. God is favoring Zion in the Sixth Street church We shall stay here without doubt two weeks longer.

"We learn that without doubt the Methodist preachers generally are going to follow the Genesee Conference, if they cannot in any other way put down this heresy, as they call it. But while Illinois is a free state for white men, I think I shall obey God rather than men; and keep going on as long as I can.

"Give the pilgrims our love.

"J. W. REDFIELD."

* This was based upon a hope that the Baptists would invite him to hold a meeting.

"St. Charles, Kane county, Ill.
October 24, 1859.

"My dear Sister Kendall:—We have long wondered why the mails did not bring another of your very welcome letters, all of which we preserve with great care, and read over and over again to the precious pilgrims in this western world. But we have learned from Brother Roberts that you have been quite sick.

"We have also learned of the infatuated conduct of the Genesee Conference toward those precious men, whose record of fidelity to God is recorded in the Book of Life. How my heart takes courage to breast the storm when I learn that men are found in this nineteenth century who, like Luther, can suffer, but cannot yield God's rights. These facts are green spots in the Sahara of formalism. A chord has been touched that vibrates to this far West, in many an honest pilgrim's heart. Yes, they feel the blow that struck Roberts and M'Creery, and now has fallen on the heads of Stiles, Cooley, Wells, and Burlingham. And you may confidently believe that hundreds in this region are in sympathy with these men of God. Already quite a number of prominent laymen have taken the stand of the Albion convention, that they will with-hold supplies from ministers who oppose vital godliness. Some say they will use their money to help these proscribed men of God.

"I am not surprised at the developments in the Genesee Conference. But they came sooner than I expected. I think our good and hopeful brethren will soon learn that the Methodist Episcopal Church will never wholly reform. The struggle has at last come. May God help us in love, kindness, and firmness to stand for the right.

"We have just come from a most glorious revival, about sixty miles west of here. We witnessed old Bergen power beyond anything I have seen in the West before. Doors are opening all around, but there are many adversaries. The presiding elder on this district says this work must, and shall be, put down. Father Coleman, whom you know, took work in Aurora last year, as a supply, and God was with him. The church sent a petition to conference to have him returned, but it was refused. Such is the spirit manifested by the authorities of the conference, that the people are thinking of getting a hall for him. The conference granted a similar petition from worldly men of a Universalist stamp for the return of Lyon, the little dandy from Buffalo, against the wishes of many in the society.

"If Mattie's health will permit, we expect to go into one or two more battles in this section before we go South. The motto given Sister Roberts, 'Go thorough, but hurry,' I have adopted. I shall do all I can for Jesus until I am stopped. We shall look for you and Sister Hardy to visit the people in this region before long.

"We desire more full details of the conference proceedings, and Brother Purdy's camp meeting. I learn, in a round-about way, that they have cracked the whip in Brother Purdy's face. I am glad of it, for nothing but that will open his eyes to the fact that he has nothing to hope on the fence. I think, now, he will be likely to herd with the pilgrims, fight their battles, and share their persecutions.

"The Lord bless you forever.

"J. W. REDFIELD."

CHAPTER LXI.

In a short time Mr. Redfield returned to St. Louis. The evening before he started was spent in company with the writer. No one else was present, Mrs. Redfield and the family with whom they were stopping being away at a prayer meeting. Mr. Redfield gave the entire evening to a review of his life work. It was more in the form of soliloquy, or thinking aloud, than a narrative. He dwelt much on the gloomy side. He spoke of place after place where he had labored, places where Methodism was nearly extinct, or struggling for an existence, where by the blessing of God he had been instrumental in increasing the membership until the societies were strong enough to support the other class of ministers, who would then go to work deliberately to destroy their peculiarly Methodistic character. After spending some time in this manner, during which for several minutes at a time the large tears would run down his face, he at last began to look on the brighter side. In Burlington, Vermont, he could name a few who were holding out firm and strong. In Syracuse, Rochester, and Albion, in New York state; in Appleton and Beaver Dam, Wisconsin; in Marengo, Woodstock, Elgin, Mount Pleasant, St. Charles, and Quincy, in Illinois; and St. Louis, Missouri, there were some tried and true. As he talked of them and the probability of their getting through to the skies, he became joyous in the extreme. This singular evening was concluded with prayer, in which he prayed for many of these pilgrims by name, with evidently a keen perception of their peculiarities and difficulties. Could those favored ones have been within hearing of that remarkable prayer, it would have been to them a matter of almost priceless value. It is not every one who has such a friend, or a friend in such communion and power with God.

On their arrival at St. Louis, he found that disaster had overtaken the new society, and its membership reduced from two hundred and seventy-five to about one hundred.   After he left them in the spring, they employed a man by the name of Dunbar to preach for them.   He was the reputed author of the Sunday-school hymn, titled, "A light in the window for thee."   He came, and for a season his sensational style drew large crowds.   He insisted upon the society going into larger quarters, at an expense of $1200.00 per year, and their paying him nearly as much; besides which he rented a theatre for a Sunday afternoon appointment.   Altogether, the financial burden became so great, that soon murmurs began to arise.   Brother Wickersham, a careful, successful financier, in his own business, remonstrated.   He thereby got in the way of this lofty man, and was crowded by him until he could endure it no longer, and he withdrew from the church.   This caused others to do the same.   The enthusiasm was checked; the revival spirit was lost.   The society now refused to be led by this hair-brained fellow; and then he left them, taking what would go with him to the Mariners' Bethel.   In a few months he fled the city, and three or four years after he was arrested and tried on a charge of bigamy, and sent to the penitentiary in Minnesota.

When Mr. Redfield saw the desolation this man had caused, he was nearly heart-broken.   It so wrought upon his mind as to induce a slight stroke of paralysis.   He was now obliged to cease entirely from all public labor for a season, and put himself under medical treatment.   By spring he had so far recovered as to be able to preach again, but the society had lost its prestige, though those who had followed Dunbar returned.

But the work in other parts was prospering.

Three miles south of Elgin, on Fox River, was a village of about fifteen hundred inhabitants, then known as Clinton-ville.   Years before, it had been a Methodist appointment, but long since had been abandoned. There were a few faithful Methodists living in and round about the place. Two local preachers, C. E. Harroun, the one saved in Mr. Redfield's first meeting in St. Charles, and D. F. Shephardson, went into the place and commenced a meeting. Soon the Spirit began to be poured out in great power and many were converted.

The little band in St. Charles, which had been read out of the church, within a fortnight found their number to be about sixty, and that something must be done to provide for them. They rented some rooms on the ground floor of an unoccupied hotel, and by taking out some partitions, prepared and seated a place for worship, which would seat about two hundred people. The first Sunday in which they occupied it, the writer and another local preacher were present, and were invited to preach. At the close of the morning service, the writer was invited by this band to preach for them, and accepted the invitation. By the following March, they numbered one hundred and twelve.

Rev. I. H. Fairchild, a local preacher belonging in Woodstock, invited the family of his brother-in-law, L. H. Bishop, to assist him in holding a protracted meeting at a country school-house, where there had been no preaching for about fifteen years. He was no singer, while they, five in number, were all good singers, and could be of great help to him in the work. In a few weeks about forty had been converted, many of them heads of families.

The question now arose at each one of these places, "What shall we do with the converts?" and Mr. Redfield was sought for advice. What the advice was and his reasons for it, can be best given in his own words. He says, "I well knew that we must now show our hand, if we meant the Methodist Church to see the need of permitting Methodists to enjoy Methodism. So I wrote to them for the first to keep every one, and organize under the Discipline as we

20

had in St. Louis. This was being done in the East also, and I thought that it might lead the General Conference to meet in May of the next year, to correct the abuses from which we had suffered, re-instate the members and ministers who had been excluded, and give us guarantees that the preaching of living Methodism would be sustained."

This advice was accepted, and three societies were organized; and waited the action of the General Conference in May.

But there were some encouragements to Mr. Redfield amid all that he was called to suffer. Some good fruit remained, and some of the saints who had gone through the fire with him were passing away to their reward in clouds of glory that showed that the narrow way he had chosen led to joys immortal.

The following account of the life and death of Mary Ferguson, of St. Louis, furnished by Mrs. T. S. La Due, formerly Mrs. Kendall, relates to one of these. She says:

"Mary Ferguson was a favorite everywhere, welcomed alike by young and old in the church. No church party or sociable was considered complete without her wit and beauty. Pastors and presiding elders made her welcome to their families, the more as she was the only daughter of a widowed mother, and refined and very intelligent as a companion. Not one of them, she told me had ever treated her otherwise than as a perfect creature ready for heaven at any hour.

"Her beauty was uncommon, and her brothers and friends were anxious to see it set off in ornaments and gay apparel as the world judges of beauty. She needed none. Her graceful form, intellectual head, large, lustrious black eyes, with tender drooping lashes, glossy raven hair, parted smoothly back from a high, white forehead, delicately molded features, which usually wore a very thoughtful expression, needed no setting by human arts.

"No minister or class-leader had ever intimated to her that the ornaments she wore were not in keeping with her profession—their own families wore them.

"She had been taken into the church without a change of heart, or even conviction, which to all real Methodists means a putting off the old man so completely that by the power of the Holy Ghost the new man is put on, and as an evidence that Christ is within the fruits are seen. Up to the time she heard Dr. Redfield's searching sermons on the new birth, the crucifixion of self, the strait gate and the narrow way, Mary never had dreamed of such experiences as the right of the believer in Jesus. With other formalists, she gaily looked on, full of caviling and doubt.

"She ventured in one day, however, to a social meeting with other church members. Se was drawn by a love for the honesty and earnestness of the doctor's appeals. That day he was lead very clearly, he said, to pray for her as one who was stabbing Jesus to the heart, by giving the lie to her profession—living, dressing, acting like a child of the devil, while solemnly pretending to be a child of God.

"She was shocked, mortified, outraged that a minister should so dare to insult her before such a company. She declared she would never be found in his presence again; and when, after a few evenings, she was persuaded to hear him once more in the Sixth street church, near her mother's house, she was still so indignant that as he arose in the pulpit, she resolutely turned her back to the end of the pew that she might not see his face.

"He had not proceeded far, however, when the truth came with such power that she said she was seized as by an invisible hand and wrenched around in her seat till she found herself gazing into his face, and felt the tears rolling down her cheeks, with neither power nor disposition to turn away. That night she was converted—born again—and, for the first time in her life, tasted rest and everlasting joy. Oh, how she praised God that one minister had dared to deal faithfully with her soul. That prayer, which had roused all the slumbering rebellion in her heart, had revealed her real condition and constrained her to fly to Christ and be saved. She hastened home, and told her mother. Stepping to the glass, she caught a glimpse of the long, white plume upon her hat. 'Slowly and solemnly,' her mother told me, she laid aside the hat, took off the plume, stripped the heavy gold rings from her fingers, unfastened the brooch at her throat, and the glittering pendants from her ears; then stepping to the grate, where a bright fire was burning, laid the costly plume upon the glowing coals, and stood and watched it burn with evident satisfaction, saying to her mother, 'Oh, how light I feel! *The world is gone!*'

"Her mother, for a moment, feared she did not realize all she was doing, but was very soon reassured by her account of what the Holy Spirit had that evening written upon her heart.

"She talked with members and ministers of her former inconsistent course of life, living like a mere butterfly of fashion, going the round of pleasure, sociable, party, ride, concert, etc., like a very child of the world, an utter stranger to the joys of everlasting life.

"She told me she wrote very plain letters to those ministers who had been foremost in leading her into these gay scenes, expostulating with them for their lack of faithfulness, and warning them that unless they repented as she had, they must expect to wake up in the world of woe! These letters were never answered. One by one, old friends and flatterers forsook her, even ministers and presiding elders that ought to have rejoiced with her.

"She had turned her back upon the world, and the world turned its back upon her. This gave her a fresh evidence that she was a child of God, and all alone in her chamber she settled it with the Lord, again, and again, that she would *endure unto the end.* As her consecration was tested and she did not waver, immortal joys were poured into her heart, such as she had never dreamed a mortal could know!

* * * * * * * * * * *

"But consumption brought her to an early grave. Yet— oh! the glory that was let down into that sick-chamber! I used to love to sit by her bedside and hear her tell of the visits from Jesus she was permitted to enjoy, in the long night-watches. As pain increased and she was confined to her room, and only now and then one came in, to whom she could confide the joys and conflicts of her heart, Satan pressed her sore to complain, but she looked to Jesus, and power came to *rejoice!* There were times she said, when heavenly music was given to quiet her restless nerves. I think it was even so, for at times such an unearthly beauty would gather on her fair face, and the eyes glow with such spiritual depth and beauty as we talked of the things of God, and she tried to describe to me the strains of melody that floated down into her soul from the upper choir, that I felt like one entranced, such was the heavenly hush of sacred awe!

"She said to Dr. Redfield one day, as he was leaving the city for a short time, and he was telling her of the many temptations he had to discouragement, on account of the murderous spirit that was roused in the M. E. Church, ministers and presiding elders publishing and threatening to arrest him, official members declaring if they could meet him on the street anywhere they would horsewhip him, etc., etc. 'Doctor, you ought to praise God that you ever came to St. Louis, if only *my* soul is saved! I mean to endure to the end, and I may go soon—I think I shall, and I want you to preach my funeral sermon. Tell them what I was *saved from*; and remember if I go first, and I am permitted, I will stand on the battlements of glory and be the first to hail you as you come up!' The Doctor promised to remember her request, and wept for joy to see such fidelity to God in one so young and so lately separated from all the world calls promising.

"A few weeks after this, she fell asleep in Jesus, witnessing to the last, that she had no regrets in leaving the world. Jesus' image was so reflected, from her very countenance lit up with glory, and her calm, joyful messages to the brothers away, that no one ever doubted for a moment, but that she was ready, when Jesus called her to the mansions above.

"She gave directions to her mother for the funeral, requesting as a favor, that there be no display beyond the presence of her Bible class as pall-bearers.

"She desired to be laid out in a simple white mull, without flowers, except in her hand; and as was the custom for young people, in a plain white velvet coffin. Dr. Redfield was in the city, and preached as she had desired, dwelling much on the rich reward of those who are to 'come up through great tribulation, having washed their robes and made them white in the blood of the Lamb.'

"To me it was the most glorious funeral I ever attended! Sorrow seemed to flee away, as the white coffin was borne down the aisle of the church to the front, and those twelve young ladies dressed in pure white, were seated around it, bearing a faint resemblance to the purity of her who had gone, and to the home where she was now safely housed *forever and ever!*

"A large concourse of people were present. The brothers from a distance were there, who had been very proud of their sister while she was gay, and when they heard the account of her glorious conversion and happy death, and messages to them, trembled like stricken men, and were forced to acknowledge there was a reality in the religion of Jesus Christ. The Doctor was deeply affected as he gave the closing scenes of her life, and her last exhortation to him, to praise God if only *she was saved* as fruit of all his toil and suffering in spirit in *St. Louis.* Perhaps he remembered the counsels of his own sister Mary, who had so often encouraged him to endure unto the end! As the saints were singing at the close the favorite hymns of the pilgrims in those days, 'We're going home to die no more,' and the 'Beautiful world,' when they came to the chorus, 'Palms of victory, crowns of glory, we shall wear in that beautiful world on high,' the glory of God filled the place, and many who had been saved in the Sunday-school were greatly blessed. The relatives kindly furnished a number of carriages, so that several of us could accompany the remains to their resting place in the cemetery six miles south of the city of St. Louis.

"We gathered about her after she was tenderly laid away, and sang as a band of pilgrims traveling to the same home, that song again, over her grave, 'Beautiful world'; and as often as we came to the refrain, 'Palms of victory, crowns of glory, we shall wear in that beautiful world on high,' waves of joy rolled over us as we thought that one more was added to 'the innumerable company,' 'redeemed through the blood of the Lamb!' As we returned to the city, some of us were so blessed as we sang on our way, that several lost their strength in the carriages, and shouted loud hallelujahs! Never have I known of such a glorious funeral as that was, the first fruits unto God of Dr. Redfield's labors in the city of St. Louis. By several, it was thought to be a remarkable coincidence, that when Dr. Redfield received his final stroke of paralysis, that those in the room with him as he breathed his last, felt a strong and clear impression that Mary's spirit was indeed hovering near. Who knows but that she did come to the battlements, and looking over, send a salute down to hail the one who had dared to tear off the bandage from her eyes when closed by sin, and cause her so to see herself that she flew to the foot of the cross, gave *up all forever*, and was saved!"

On February 14, 1860, Mr. Redfield wrote the following letter referring to events then occurring in various quarters:

"Dear Brother and Sister Foot:—"So greatly does my large correspondence press me that I am compelled to make one letter do for a place, or I should have written to you before. I learn by way of Brother Tyler of your prosperity. I am learning from various quarters where they have heard of the stand you have taken that the same thing for the same cause is contemplated. I feel deeply burdened at the melancholy sight of the Methodist Episcopal Church in arms against effective Methodism; and putting fidelity to Methodism down as a capital offense, and rending the church in an effort to rid it of soul-saving piety. I have long seen the tendency to this, and trembled at the threatening division, which must come if one party or the other would not abandon its position. But I saw clearly that if the pilgrim party compromised God's rights, and lowered the standard of piety at the demand of the other, all efficiency for soul-saving would be at an end, and our church would sink into a powerless formalism.

"February 27.

"You see by my dates that I have been interrupted. The fact is, we have been passing through a squall. Our preacher here proved to be well calculated to stir up strife, by going from one to another and retailing the stuff that our enemies invented. Both he and one of our leading men have been, and still are, trying to rend us in pieces. That man is bent on ruling or ruining us. But God is still with us, and though they have left and taken as many as they could persuade to go with them, trusting in God, we expect to live and enlarge our borders. We have a good and reliable membership, who are now engaged in planning for a new church. We expect that our late preacher will soon run his race and leave the city.

"I have just received a call from Mt. Vernon, Iowa, to come, or send some one to preach the salvation that saves. The writer, a stranger to me, saw the report given of my connection with your affairs at St. Charles, and wrote to me for explanations. I answered, giving a full account of the matter. I have now received another letter stating that the same opposition had developed there, and for the same cause; and the faithful are now threatened with expulsion if they persist in praying for and exhorting the church. The spirit of the letter seems to be right, and as well as I can judge from its tone, and the manner of reporting the facts, that it is not a fault-finding spirit, but an honest desire to see the cause of God prosper.

"I write this much to prepare the way to ask if Brother T—— cannot go to their relief. At all events I wish he would write and learn the state of things, and get what items of information as may be needed to form an opinion as to what is best to be done. Please communicate with Brother T—— about it.

"Has Brother Cooley come yet? Brother Roberts wrote me that he would hasten him on, although he was greatly needed there. But they are careful to do nothing, more than · they can help, to prejudice their case before the coming General Conference. After that, if nothing is done to make things right, a conference will be organized, and then your place will be provided for regularly.

"Love to all.

"J. W. REDFIELD."

On March 26th, he wrote to Brother Rogers as follows:

"I long to hear from you, and learn of the state of religion among you. We have been having a trying time here, but the Lord has conquered for us. We expect to go to work to build a new church at once.

"This mighty work is rapidly spreading, and my calls are far more than I can accept. I expect from present appearances, that after the General Conference, we shall have another conference organized, which will carry the battle to the gates, and we shall see a great and glorious revival of genuine Methodism, carried on by local preachers. If the conference preachers will not go the way, in the name of the Lord, the local preachers will.

"J. W. REDFIELD."

April 6th, 1860, he writes again to Brother and Sister Foot, as follows:

"Your welcome letter was duly received; but my large correspondence prevented me from answering until now. Every sentiment of my heart is enlisted in your behalf. God is raising up a great people, and you in St. Charles have the honor and disgrace of standing foremost. I have written Brother Roberts to hold on, and not send a preacher to you until after the General Conference. It begins to look as though we will have to organize immediately after that, in a permanent form. I am greatly rejoiced that God has raised up a preacher for you. Please send a statement of your wants and condition to Brother Roberts.

"I send you a number of circulars, and desire that all the pilgrims will give us at least ten cents each towards building a church here. The lot will cost $10,000. We want to build two more to meet the wants of this great city. But we are poor, and need help.

"Yours,

"J. W. REDFIELD."

CHAPTER LXII.

A LAYMEN's Convention was called to meet in Olean, February 1 and 2, 1860. As the principal members of the church in that place were in sympathy with the convention, it was designed to hold it in the Methodist church; but upon an application by a member of the church, Judge Green granted an injunction upon the trustees restraining them from, and forbidding them to, open the edifice for that purpose. With commendable liberality, the trustees of the Presbyterian church tendered the use of their house, which was accepted.

At 10:00 o'clock, on Wednesday morning, Abner I. Wood, president of the convention held at Albion, December 1 and 2, 1858, called the convention to order, and S. K. J. Chesbro, secretary, assumed the duties of his office. After prayer, the call for the convention was read. The first action of the convention was to provide for the administration of the Lord's Supper, by requesting Rev. Loren Stiles to officiate in the evening.

When the names of delegates were handed in, it was found that every charge in the Genesee Conference was represented.

A "Free Methodist Church" had been organized, and a delegate from that organization was invited to a seat in the convention.

The following petition to the General Conference was adopted, and a committee of five was appointed to circulate it through the conference for signatures.

"To the Bishops and Members of the General Conference of the Methodist Episcopal Church, to be held in Buffalo, N. Y., May 1, 1860.

"Reverend Fathers and Brethren:—We, the undersigned,

members of the Methodist Episcopal Church, in the bounds of the Genesee Conference, respectfully represent to your reverend body, that a very unpleasant state of things prevails in the church throughout this conference. This difficulty has grown out of the action of the conference. Many honestly believe this action to have been wrong and oppressive. We, therefore, ask your reverend body to give to the judicial action of the Genesee Conference, by which six of the ministers, to wit: B. T. Roberts, J. M'Creery, J. A. Wells, William Cooley, L. Stiles, and C. D. Burlingham, have been expelled from the conference and the church, a full and careful investigation, trusting you will come to such decision as righteousness demands. We also ask your reverend body so to amend the judicial law of the church, as to secure to the ministers and members the right of trial by an impartial committee."

A petition to the General Conference asking for the insertion of an anti-slavery chapter in the Discipline was also adopted by the convention. The following is a copy of that petition:

"Reverend Fathers and Brethren:—Inasmuch as there are now known to be, in the slave states, many members of the Methodist Episcopal Church, who hold their fellow beings, and even their brethren in Christ, as slaves, contrary to natural justice and the gospel of Christ; and whereas, we believe the buying, selling, or holding of a human being as property, is a sin against God, and should in no wise be tolerated in the church of Christ: therefore,

"We, the undersigned, members of the Methodist Episcopal Church in the —— charge, Genesee Conference, would earnestly petition your reverend body to place a chapter in the Discipline of the M. E. Church, that will exclude all persons from the M. E. Church or her communion, who shall be guilty of holding, buying, or selling, or in any way using a human being as a slave."

With the new year, Mr. Roberts had commenced to publish a monthly magazine, called the *Earnest Christian*, which called forth the following resolution, which was adopted by the convention:

"Resolved, That we are highly pleased with the appearance of the *Earnest Christian*. The articles, thus far, prove it to be just what is needed at this time, when a conforming and superficial Christianity is prevailing everywhere. We hail it with delight among us; and we pledge ourselves to use our exertions to extend its circulation."

The committee on resolutions reported as follows:

"God deals with us as individuals. No man or body of men can take the responsibility of our actions. It is a Bible doctrine, very clearly taught, that 'every one must give account of himself to God.'

"Ministers cannot take into their hands the keeping of our consciences. The right of private judgment lies at the foundation of the great Protestant Reformation. It forms the basis of all true religion. No person who does not act and think for himself can enjoy either the sanctifying or justifying grace of God. When John Wesley was told that he could 'not continue in the Church of England, because he could not in principle submit to her determinations,' he replied: 'If that were necessary, I could not be a member of any church under heaven; for I must still insist upon the right of private judgment. I cannot yield either implicit faith or obedience to any man or number of men under heaven.'

"This is equally true of every honest man. In our church, the government is vested exclusively in the ministry; the bishops appointing the preachers to whatever charge they please, and thus having the power to influence them to a great extent, if not absolutely to control them, by the hope of obtaining preferment, if they are submissive, and the fear of being placed in an obscure position if they do not carry out the will of their superiors. They are elected by the ministers, and are responsible alone to the men who are thus completely dependent upon them for their position in the church. The General Conference, possessing all the power to make laws for the churches, is composed exclusively of ministers, elected by ministers. The annual conference, which says who shall preach and who shall not, is made up of ministers. The book agents, wielding a mighty pecuniary influence, are ministers. The official editors, controlling the public sentiment of the church, are ministers. The same principle is carried out in the administration upon our circuits and stations. The preacher sent on—it may be in opposition to the wishes of a large majority of the members—appoints all the leaders, nominates the stewards, and licenses the exhorters. If he wishes to expel a member, he selects the committee, and presides over the trial as judge. He goes out with them, and sees that they make up their verdict as he desires.

"The only check to this immense clerical power—without a parallel, unless it is in the Church of Rome—consists in the right of the laity to refuse to support those ministers who abuse their trust, and show themselves unworthy of confidence. This only remedy in our power against clerical oppression we have felt bound to apply.

"The course of those members of the Genesee Conference, known as the 'Regency party,' in screening one another when lying under the imputation of gross and flagrant immoralities; and in expelling from the conference and the church devoted ministers of the gospel, whose only crime consisted in the ability and success with which they taught and enforced the doctrine of holiness, and the fidelity with which they labored to secure the exclusion of slave holders from the church—this course, so contrary to the spirit of the gospel, as honest men going to judgment, we felt called upon to discountenance. We dare not give these ministers Godspeed in their bloody work, lest we be partakers in their evil deeds. We accordingly voted, in our conventions, that we could not sustain these preachers who were putting down the work of God.

"These efforts of ours to correct great evils have been met by persecutions worthy of the priests of Rome in her darkest days. Men of approved piety, of long standing, whose prayers and efforts and money have been freely given to promote the interests of the church, have been expelled from the communion of their choice for having dared to act according to their convictions. Therefore,

"Resolved, 1. That we heartily endorse the sentiments contained in the preambles and resolutions passed at the Albion conventions (December, 1858 and November, 1859). The position then taken we this day unhesitatingly affirm, in our estimation, to be right. Convinced more than ever, that we need to act as one body in this matter, we hereby pledge ourselves unflinchingly and uncompromisingly to stand by the principles then laid down; and to sustain by our sympathy and our aid our brethren in the ministry who have been the subjects of a heartless and wicked proscription.

"Resolved, 2. That we heartily condemn the practice pursued by many of the Regency preachers, in reading out members as withdrawn from the church without even the form of a trial, or without laboring with them. We deem it an act of outrage upon our rights as members of the church, contrary to the Discipline, and in direct opposition to the Spirit of Christ. We truly extend to our brethren and sisters who have thus been illegally read out from our beloved Zion, the right hand of fellowship. We rejoice that the Lamb's Book of Life is beyond the reach of human hands. And while they continue faithful followers of Jesus, whether in or out of the church, we hail them as members of the body of Christ."

The report of the committee, after remarks made by several persons, all on the affirmative, was unanimously adopted. The following resolution, concerning the adherence to the M. E. Church, was also adopted:

"Resolved, That we reiterate our unfaltering attachment to the Methodist Episcopal Church; while we protest against and repudiate its abuses and iniquitous administration, by which we have been aggrieved and the church scandalized. Our controversy is in favor of the doctrines and discipline of the church, and against temporary mal-administration. And we exhort our brethren everywhere not to secede, or withdraw from the church, or be persuaded into any other ecclesiastical organization; but to form themselves into bands, after the example of early Methodism, and remain in the church until expelled."

On this resolution the following remarks were made:

Rev. J. M'Creery said:—"Four years ago when we commenced this war, we sought to bring back Methodism to its pristine purity, and throw out these innovations which had crept in. We can spare all the preachers if the Lord and the people will be with us. We intend to stick to the church. We are where we stood years ago, and intend to stay there. We must stand on the Discipline, which is the constitution of the church. We are not secessionists, and they cannot drive us out, unless they expel us. We purpose to stay in the church. I am in favor of that resolution."

T. B. Catton said:—"We can organize bands and still be in the church, as it is in the Discipline. I am opposed to secession always. We have organized bands in Wyoming, and have met with good success, for the Lord has been with us."

William Hart contended that the constitution of the church discountenanced slavery. He argued that the Discipline granted every member a fair trial. But all those who had been expelled had been denied that privilege. We have no

need to secede, but to keep right on for God, and not be persuaded into any other ecclesiastical organization. Four were
read out in my section on mere suspicion. He was in favor
of the resolution.

B. T. Roberts contended that bands were no new things,
but were being organized all over the country, and in
Europe, for the salvation of souls; and said that Orville
Gardner was the leader of one in New York. He hoped
these bands would be organized everywhere. If the ministers will help, all right; if not, go right on without them.

S. K. J. Chesbro said, that the bands in his place had
been prosperous, and many had been converted. He gave a
history of their organization, which started with only ten
members, but now it had thirty. He was strongly in favor
of bands, and urged the brethren to do likewise.

J. M'Creery did not want to follow the plan of Orville
Gardner's band, but the plan contained in the Methodist Discipline. The resolution defines itself. The members of the
band in this section had not yet been turned out, and the
authorities will not dare to do it.

J. W. Reddy said, that the Regency preachers held the
opinion that these bands were unconstitutional; but he denied it, and argued that we have as good a right to do so as
they have to join the Odd-Fellows or Masons. He believed
in standing by the church, but contended for the right of
religious liberty. He hoped the brethren would go to work
with energy and organize these bands.

These are characteristic remarks, and show the temper of
the convention. The resolution was unanimously adopted.

Several other resolutions, were adopted, committees, etc.,
were appointed, and the convention adjourned *sine die.*

Mr. Redfield was watching these proceedings from St.
Louis with deep interest. His letters and his labors in the
West, including the proscription used by the church authori-
ties there, show that the work East and West was one.

30

The following letter will show another phase that was beginning to be manifested, and was destined to become a prominent feature of evangelistic work. It will also show a philosophical vein in his thinking upon a subject that gets but little attention.

"ST. LOUIS, Feb. 1, 1860.

"My very dear Sister Roberts:—Your very interesting letter came to hand last night. I most deeply sympathize with you in your trying circumstances, and feel refreshed by the recital of your daring to obey God when I am so full of haltings in view of public opinion. I have long seen that our church must come to the exact state we now occupy, and that some one must take the stand and meet the conflict. I have shrunk and run from all responsibility I could, and yet preserve anything like peace with God. But I see God has thrust you out into the front rank, and I feel deeply ashamed that I have been so tardy in my labors for the cause of Jesus. Could I see you I could open my mind freely, and tell you my views relating to the matters of which you inquire.

"I will say, however, I am more than ever convinced that God is about to perform a work in this land which is to tell in the salvation of myriads, and to stimulate sister churches to a higher tone of religion. And I am equally sure that God will open this era by means and instrumentalities quite out of the old stereotyped forms. Among these instrumentalities I believe woman is to take a very prominent part. But aside from all theorizing, I shall ask but two questions: (1) Does God bless them? (2) Are souls converted and sanctified under their labors? If these questions are answered in the affirmative, no man can say nay.

"As to the polish of rhetoric and philosophy to embellish the cross of Jesus, we have enough of it. As to great learning, to give the pedigree of Christianity and to illumine the dark sayings of the fathers in theology, we have it in abundance. But the world is not saved. Science, metaphysics, eloquence, and divinity have marched in solemn grandeur over Christendom, and yet the world is not saved. What we want, what we must have, is a type of religion that will bring God back to the world; that is, God in the moral phase of his character. And how can this be done except through the emotions of mankind? Men are bound too much by conventional rules, and strive to recommend the moral nature of God by his mental qualities or physical powers. We need to have manifested the love, justice, and purity of God, and this in the out-gushings of a heart that dares to be moved as God moves it. Man fears to betray such 'weakness.' Women are more willing to let God bless them, and this seems to be their calling.

"Had any one told me six months before I came to St. Louis that ministers in the Methodist Episcopal Church (North) would abet the vile system of slavery, and not only that, but oppose the doctrines of Methodism, I should have regarded it as a slander. But I am compelled to own the humiliating fact, and that if some one is not raised up to re-establish the broken foundations of Methodism, she has run her race, and must soon be reckoned among the things that were. But whoever undertakes the task must take the consequences of his effort.

* * * * * * * * * * *

"J. W. REDFIELD."

CHAPTER LXIII

THE venerable Elias Bowen, D. D., in his history of the Origin of the Free Methodist Church, says:

"The General Conference—upon which so many anxious eyes were turned, on account of the Genesee difficulties, in the hope that all there would be made right—commenced its session May 1st, 1860, in the city of Buffalo, and continued its deliberations during the entire month. It was soon apparent, however, that the spirit of early Methodism had departed from that venerable body, and another spirit than that of the fathers—the spirit of a worldly, ambitious, temporizing policy—ruled the hour. The delegates belonging to secret societies, and those of a pro-slavery type, making common cause of it, refused by a majority vote which they contrived to command, to entertain Mr. Roberts' appeal, though in barefaced opposition to one of our strictest rules; and, of course, this ambassador of the Lord Jesus Christ, in accordance with the action of the Genesee Conference in his case, stood expelled from the church."

Rev. William Hosmer, editor of the *Northern Independent*, in that paper, said:

'Methodism has taught us to live in the presence of God, and to shape all our acts under the inspection of his eye. Whatsoever cannot abide this test, must be discarded and abhorred, because it will surely be condemned in 'the eternal judgment' to which we are hastening. That the Court of Appeals, constituted by the last General Conference, did not do its work so as to secure either divine or human respect, is a conclusion forced upon us from every view we have been able to take of the subject. Gladly would we pass by these judicial proceedings without further notice if it were allowable. But they are of too serious a character, and will be found too far-reaching in their consequences, to admit of silent acquiescence. Ecclesiastical courts are not famous for liberality and justice; but we believe the courts of Methodism have not generally sunk to the level indicated by the trial of these appeals.

"First in order was the case of Rev. C. D. Burlingham. He was expelled from the Genesee Conference and the Methodist Episcopal Church for doing three things:

"1st. Admitting B. T. Roberts into the church on trial.

"2nd. Licensing him to exhort.

"3rd. Officiating with expelled preachers at a general quarterly meeting held in a Wesleyan church, at the same time that his presiding elder was holding a regular quarterly meeting in the same charge, about three miles distant.

"Mr. Burlingham admitted the facts, but pleaded in justification:

"1st. That he received B. T. Roberts, and licensed him to exhort, on the unanimous recommendation of the society meeting of the church with which Mr. Roberts had last labored. In this action he believed he was covered by Bishop Baker, who says, in his work on the Discipline, page 159, 'If, however, the society become convinced of the innocence of the expelled member, he may again be received on trial, without confession.'

"2nd. That when engaged to attend the general quarterly meeting, he supposed that Mr. Roberts had a right as an exhorter to hold meetings.

"3rd. That he did not know that the Methodist Episcopal Church had a society, or an appointment, in the place where the general quarterly meeting was held. He supposed the ground was occupied exclusively by the Wesleyans.

"These were the only offenses with which Mr. Burlingham was charged.

"After his expulsion he waited patiently for the General Conference. He did not preach, nor lecture, nor exhort— did not attend meetings held by expelled preachers—but did

penance up to the session of the General Conference. He
should have been restored on the ground of having expiated
his guilt, if he was guilty of any ordinary offense, if on no
other. When his appeal came up, Mr. Fuller, * who had
been chief prosecutor in all those trials, challenged several of
the committee who had manifested a desire to have Genesee
Conference matters fairly investigated. Though the General Conference, in constituting the committee, or Court of
Appeals, had given to parties the right to challenge *for cause*,
yet Mr. Fuller, after the first instance, was not required to
give cause, but challenged as many as he chose, and they
were set aside. He simply said of the challenged, 'he considered them prejudiced.'   •

"Mr. Olin, of the Oneida Conference, managed the case
for Mr. Burlingham with consummate tact and great ability.
His plea was a masterly effort, and carried conviction to the
minds, we believe, of all who heard it, except the committee.
They sent the case back to the conference for a new trial.
This we regard as a remarkable decision. Neither party
asked for it. We never heard before of a case being remanded for a new trial, unless there was some alleged informality
in the court below, or defect in the record, or unless one or
the other of the parties claimed to have new testimony which
could not be introduced into the first trial. But nothing of
the kind was intimated in this case. There can be no new
testimony, for Mr. Burlingham admitted all the facts with
which he was charged.

"Do these facts, mentioned above, constitute a crime, for
which an able minister, of spotless reputation, who has
served the church for over twenty years, devoting the vigor
of his manhood's prime in self-sacrificing efforts to promote
her interests, should be expelled? Then let the General
Conference say so, that all who henceforth enter the Methodist ministry may understand that they are expected to lay

---

* The same man mentioned in the chapter on the revival in Albion —T.

their manhood in the dust, part with the right of private judgment, and yield a servile, unquestioning obedience to all behests of their ecclesiastical superiors.

"Was Mr. Burlingham, through party malignity, treated unjustly? Was he wrongfully deposed from the ministry, and excluded from the church? Then the General Conference should have restored him. This was due to him; it was due to outraged justice; it was due to the Methodist Episcopal Church, whose Discipline—confessedly more susceptible of abuse than any other church in this country—has been used for the purpose of inflicting ecclesiastical oppression without a parallel in the nineteenth century.

"But the General Conference, through its committee, or Court of Appeals, after gravely listening to the testimony and pleadings, sent the case back for a new trial, without a motion to that effect from either party. What, we ask, is there to try? There can be no issue on the facts—these are admitted.

"But Mr. Burlingham contends that these facts do not constitute a crime for which he should be deposed from the church.

"The Genesee Conference has said they do. Here is the issue—who shall decide? The Discipline vests the power in the General Conference—the body to try appeals. The case was properly brought before them; they have sent it back for the Genesee Conference to decide over again. What an absurd decision! What an insult to Mr. Burlingham, and to common sense! Suppose the views of law and justice entertained by the Genesee Conference remain unchanged, and the same sentence be again pronounced against Mr. Burlingham, and he again appeals. After waiting four years for another General Conference, if he still survive, there will not only be the same reason for sending the case back for a new trial as now, but the additional one of precedent. Thus, this mockery of justice may continue *ad infinitum*.

"This looks more like the tiger playing with the victim he intends to devour, than like a body of Christian ministers bound by every consideration that can influence to right action, to judge righteous judgment.

"Another fact is worthy of especial notice. Though the decision in the case was not asked for *in court* by either party, yet it is precisely what partisans of the Regency party of the Genesee Conference have been endeavoring for months to persuade Mr. Burlingham to consent to. These efforts were continued up to the morning of the day on which the appeal was heard. Yet neither in their pleadings, nor at any time while the appeal was being heard, did the counsel for the conference signify their wish that the case might be remanded for a new trial. At whose suggestion was it done? When was the suggestion made? Was there any collusion in the matter? It is impossible for us to answer these questions. View it in whatever light you may, the whole case has a dark and suspicious aspect.

"Perhaps some clue to an explanation of the strange proceedings in relation to the Genesee Conference appeal cases may be found in the action had upon the slavery question.

"The Genesee Conference has heretofore been one of the strongest anti-slavery conferences in the connection. The proscribed party have been from the first uncompromising in their hostility to slavery in the church and in the state.

"The Genesee delegates were once regarded as antislavery; what they are now their votes will show. We asserted last fall that the conference had become pro-slavery, and gave as proof the fact that while it condemned this paper, it refused to take any action against slavery. The truth of our inference was denied by some; but the recent course of their delegates has made our words good. When the important question was decided in the General Conference upon a change of the constitution, so as to prohibit slave-holding in the church, the delegates of the Genesee

Conference voted against a change, *and their vote turned the scale.* And when the Genesee Conference matters came up, the border pro-slavery delegates voted solid with the representatives of the majority of the Genesee Conference. This may be all fair. It may be that men who, four years ago, took the stump to keep slavery out of the territories, have suddenly become convinced that it should be nestled and fostered in the bosom of the church! We should like to know by what arguments they were converted, and when it was done! Was this a part of a scheme to keep slave-holders in the church? Did the border delegates understand that if they voted as desired by the Genesee delegates, they would reciprocate the favor and assist them in their extremity? Or did this strange coincidence come about by chance? '*

There were exciting scenes in the West about this time. In March, of this same year, after a three-months' continuous meeting in St. Charles, the writer went to visit those converted the fall before. On arriving at the place he learned that the church trustees, by a majority vote, had adopted a resolution that neither Mr. Redfield nor himself should preach in the church again. Some of these men were also school trustees, and they had adopted a similar resolution as to preaching in the school-house.

But few knew of this action of the trustees until we met in church the next morning. A large number of the young converts came together in the afternoon, at a private house, for prayer and testimony.

While we were singing the hymn,

"Jesus, lover of my soul,"

the power of God came upon us in a wonderful manner. But so great and so intense was the opposition here where we had formerly experienced such a signal victory that our

*As a resu't the church was put to the sorry extremity of changing the Discipline on slavery in 1864, when there was not a slave left in the country.--T.

enemies went from this meeting and reported that Mr. T——
had the young converts get on their knees and swear that
they would follow Mr. Redfield and himself.

At the close of the meeting the writer was asked when
he would preach to them; and it was then that it became
known that the trustees both of the church and school-house
had taken the action already referred to. J. W. Dake, now
a Free Methodist preacher in Iowa (1888), and who was
present, said, "I know of a school-house where he can
preach"; and agreement was made to have service in the
one alluded to about two miles distant on Monday evening.
This was announced at the church that evening in a private
way. The next evening a large congregation gathered, and
the power of the Lord was present to heal. Indications of
a revival were so strong that we could not hold back from
announcing a service for the next night. This was the occasion of the setting in of a severe persecution. Young people
were forbidden to attend the meetings. Falsehood and
slander began to do their best. The timid were frightened
from their steadfastness, and the brave rapidly developed as
soldiers for Jesus.

The second Sunday morning, the pastor of the church,
instead of the usual Scripture lesson, read a long original
paper, in which he accused the writer of being in league
with Mr. Redfield to divide the church; and concluded with
the proposition that, if he would confess the wrong, and
promise to do so no more, they (the church at Mt. Pleasant)
would take him to their hearts and to the church. Three
weeks later he handed in his church letter, and was immediately given a regular appointment to preach in that church.

The meeting in the Union school-house, as it was called,
lasted but a fortnight, but quite a number were converted,
some of whom became noted for piety and triumphant
death.

At the close of this meeting the writer visited Marengo,

in McHenry county, the scene of one of Mr. Redfield's greatest victories. Here it was learned that the Bishop family, in whose country home the noted Monday-night holiness meeting had been held so long, were now cited to trial on a charge of disobedience to the order and Discipline of the church. The first specification was, non-attendance of public worship in the church where they belonged. The second was, non-attendance of class.

The facts were they had spent the most of the winter in a revival in a country school-house, six miles from home—at great inconvenience to themselves—where more than forty persons had been converted. What had made it more easy for them to do this was the fact that they could neither attend preaching or class meeting without being made a target for sharp speeches, both by the pastor and the members of the church. It was also a fact that there were members of the church who not only did not attend worship, but they did not profess to be Christians at all. And more, there were more than one-half of the membership who never attended class. It was evident from these facts that the trial was persecution, and not a sincere attempt to bring the church to discipline. The family of five—father, mother, two sons, and a daughter—were all expelled. In his hot haste the pastor had forgotten that he had given a letter to the oldest son who was a Garrett Biblical Institute student.

A large company had gathered, as witnesses for the accused, many of them the fruits of the revival described, while some, like the writer, had come from sympathy. The minister at first ordered us all out of the church, but as it was a severe March day, this was impracticable, and while we were deliberating what to do, he adjourned the trial to his dwelling, and left us in peaceable possession of the church. An impromptu love-feast was inaugurated, and for several hours the time was fully occupied. During this time there was but one allusion to the trouble; save that, it was forgotten in the enjoyment of the hour.

Sunday the writer visited the young converts at the Brick
school-house, where the Bishop family had spent their winter, and found them giants in experience. Many of them
were heads of families.

Monday evening there was a great gathering at Father
Bishop's for the holiness meeting. Father Coleman was
present, and led the meeting. His was the only allusion to
the trouble. He said, "Don't pound your troubles; if you
do, they'll pound you, and you will get the worst of it. If
they turn me out of the fold, I'll go bleating around until
they take me back in again."

The General Conference came and went, but there was
no redress of the grievances complained of. Mr. Roberts'
case was left as the Genesee Conference left it. Nearly
every law-point, under which these wrongs had been perpetrated, was decided against the presiding bishops.

The conference declared that the interpretations of law
by a bishop in the interim of conference did not have the
force of law; that is, they were authoritative only when the
bishop was presiding in a judicial capacity. This was aimed
at Bishop Simpson's interpretation of the law, that with the
consent of the official board a preacher might declare a
member withdrawn who did not attend the service of his
own church. On this opinion, many had been excluded
from the church in that summary way. But though it is,
and was, a maxim of Methodism, that a member shall not
suffer from the maladministration of a preacher in charge,
there was not a single instance, so far as is known, where
there was an attempt to re-instate a member who had thus
been excluded.

In view of taking such action as might be necessary after
the General Conference, a Laymen's Convention had been
called to meet July 1, 1860, in connection with a camp meeting to be held on the grounds of J. M. Laughlin, near St.
Charles, Illinois. A similar convention had been called in
Western New York. The object of both was the same.

Mr. Redfield had charge of the religious services at St. Charles, assisted by Revs. B. T. Roberts, Seymour Coleman, G. H. Fox, and E. P. Hart, besides a large number of local preachers from various parts of the Northwest. St. Louis, Mo., Southern Iowa, and Wisconsin, and Marengo, Woodstock, Queen Anne, Garden Prairie, Brick School-house, Elgin, Coral, Clintonville, Geneva, Aurora, Wheaton, and Mt. Pleasant, within the state of Illinois, were represented by laymen. The camp meeting was one of great power. . God was there, and many were saved.

The following are the minutes of the Laymen's Convention:

"After devotional exercises, B. T. Roberts was chosen president, and C. E. McCollister, secretary.

"Members of the convention:

"St. Louis:—Richard Thornton, local elder; Daniel Lloyd, Ad. C. Coughlin, Charles R. Townsend (local preacher), J. W. Redfield (local preacher), C. E. McCollister, L. E. Benedict.

"St. Charles: — Elisha Foote, Warren Tyler, John Laughlin.

"Clintonville:—Joseph Corron, Benjamin Peaslee, C. E. Harroun (local preacher).

"Coral:—J. M. White.

"Union:—Joseph Deitz, L. H. Bishop, Wm. D. Bishop (local preacher), I. H. Fairchild (local deacon).

"Woodstock:—S. Wilson, Warren Stanard, William Wright, M. Best.

"Queen Anne:—G. N. Fairchild.

"Mt. Pleasant:—Melville Beach, J. W. Dake, U. C. Rowe, J. G. Terrill (local preacher).

" A camp meeting was ordered to be held at Coral, McHenry county, Ill., commencing September 5, and holding one week.

"It was also ordered to hold another on the same grounds about the same time next year.

"President Roberts wrote and presented the following resolution, which was unanimously adopted:

' 'Resolved, That our attachment to the doctrines, usages, spirit, and discipline of Methodism, is hearty and sincere. It is with the most profound grief that we have witnessed the departure of many of the ministers from the God-honored usages of Methodism. We feel bound to adhere to them, and to labor all we can, and to the best possible advantage, to promote the life and power of godliness. We recommend that those in sympathy with the doctrine of holiness, as taught by Wesley, should labor in harmony with the respective churches to which they belong. But when this cannot be done, without continual strife and contention, we recommend the formation of Free Methodist churches, as contemplated by the convention held in the Genesee Conference, in New York.'

"I. H. Fairchild was recommended to take work in the itinerary of the convention.

"U. C. Rowe was licensed to preach.

"C. E. McCollister was appointed to missionary work in Michigan.

"A committee of five was appointed as a standing stationing committee, consisting of three ministers and two laymen, to hold their position until the next convention. I. H. Fairchild, C. E. Harroun, J. W. Redfield, E. Foote, and O. Joslyn, were made said committee.

"J. W. Redfield's character was passed, and he was appointed superintendent of the Western work.

"President Roberts and J. W. Redfield were requested to appoint a preacher for St. Louis.

"The committee on stationing preachers was instructed to employ all local preachers under their charge.

"A motion was passed to recognize the ordinations of those ministers who have come among us.

"A. B. Burdick, a local preacher of St. Louis, was made a member of the convention.

"B. T. Roberts was unanimously elected general superintendent of the work.

"The stationing committee made the following appointments:

"Ogle Circuit, J. G. Terrill; St. Charles, C. R. Townsend; Clintonville, C. E. Harroun; Coral, I. H. Fairchild, and W. D. Bishop; Queen Anne, R. M. Hooker; Big Rock, D. F. Shephardson; Elgin, A. B. Burdick; Iowa Mission, P. C. Armstrong; St. Louis Mission, Ad. C. Coughlin, and Robt. Jamison; St. Louis Circuit, Joseph Travis; Michigan Mission, C. E. McCollister."

The broken style of these minutes indicate that these men were new to the work of such assemblies, and that their action was unpremeditated. The General Conference was just over. In almost all of these places to which ministers were appointed there were members of the Methodist Episcopal Church who had either been read out, or expelled, or were suffering from some form of proscription. Some of these local preachers were still members of that church.

In the month of August a general convention was held in Pekin, N. Y., in connection with a camp meeting. Isaac M. Chesbrough, of Pekin, was chairman, and A. A. Phelps secretary. This was a delegated body, and was composed of sixty members—fifteen preachers, and forty-five laymen. The deliberations of the convention resulted in the organization of the Free Methodist Church, and the formation of their Discipline.

In September a convention was held on a campground at Aurora, Illinois, by which the new Discipline was adopted. The preachers who had taken work in June now went forth to organize Free Methodist churches wherever opportunity could be found.

The writer has thought it best to give this history of the

rise and organization of the Free Methodist Churc:, first, because Mr. Redfield was so closely identified wit.: it; and, secondly, to vindicate his course. It seems clear that he could do no other way. Necessity was laid upon him, as it was also upon others who were identified with the movement.

CHAPTER LXIV.

AFTER the Pekin Convention, Mr. Redfield returned to the West, and commenced his labors for the winter with great zeal and encouragement. He undertook the visitation of all the points where societies had already been organized, and where there was a desire to organize.

Rev. E. P. Hart, about this time, withdrew from the Methodist Episcopal Church, and took work under Mr. Redfield; and an opening occurring in Belvidere, Illinois, he went there and labored with great success. A society had been organized in Aurora, Illinois. Calls were coming from every direction, and about twenty laborers were already in the field. Mr. Redfield in his visits reached Aurora the first of November. He preached for the new society on Sunday, met the official board Monday night, and while sitting in the rooms of a friend, Tuesday morning, was suddenly smitten to the floor with paralysis. He was taken to the house of Rev. Judah Mead, a local preacher, where he lay for weeks in terrible physical and mental anguish. The latter arose from his inability to understand this peculiar providence. He knew he had overtaxed himself. He knew that the severe mental strain through which he had gone during the troubles in St. Louis, and his care and anxiety for the new organization, had induced this. But he had been of the opinion that, if one was honestly seeking the divine glory, and doing his best to advance the kingdom of God in the earth, that God would not allow him to fail. This notion now afforded the ground for severe mental conflicts. Again, his physical pain was such, and so intense was every sense of sight, of hearing, of smelling, of tasting, and feeling, and so excruciating was the pain inflicted by the simplest offenses to the organs of these senses, that it

31   (453

was almost unendurable. Then temptation would assault him in regard to his conduct during these seasons of distress, that he had behaved like anything but a Christian.

A Christian brother, who had been converted under his ministry, was impressed while praying at home, that Mr. Redfield was in great trouble, and that he must go to his assistance. He immediately went to Aurora, and found him in the condition described above. From this time for three years this brother, with all the fidelity and sympathy of a son for a father, nursed, and traveled with, and cared for, this afflicted man of God, until he saw his remains laid away in the tomb.

As spring approached, Mr. Redfield was so much better that he was removed from Aurora, and finally became able to travel quite extensively. He visited the East, and held meetings a few weeks in Buffalo, in the Free Methodist Church. From there he wrote the following letter to Samuel Huntington, of Burlington, Vt., which describes his health, his feelings, and, to some extent, his financial circumstances:

"BUFFALO, N. Y., April 17, 1861.

"Dear Brother Huntington:—Your letter, dated the 12th, was received last evening. My health is gradually improving. I can walk about the house a little by using a cane, but I still have to be lifted in and out of a carriage. We are now holding meetings in the Second Free Methodist church, in this city. I have been able to preach three or four times a week. At the rate I am improving, I hope to be able to get in and out of a carriage during the summer.

"I wish you could see it in your way to come to our camp meeting at St. Charles, Illinois, on the 12th of June. We shall probably have a good representation at that time. If you have the time to spare, you could go by the way of the lakes, from Buffalo to Chicago, for from six to nine dollars. From Chicago to the camp ground, by rail, it is only about thirty miles.

"I would like to have you get acquainted with our Western pilgrims. A more noble, whole-hearted and red-hot set of pilgrims you never saw. The work of salvation in the West is spreading rapidly. So large is the demand that we can hardly find men enough to man the walls of our Zion.

"I hope you will not permit the true interests of the cause to suffer for want of independence in yourself, even to stand alone if need be. If the conference does not send you the right kind of a man, 'go it on your own hook,' and if the worse comes, I think we could find a preacher among the Free Methodists that would suit you.

"I hardly know what to say about Dr. W——'s proposal. I fear I cannot make an offer that will seem to him perfectly right. I took this view of the matter: first, that I am in need of what he owes me; second, I cannot think it wrong for me to ask him to return to me what he is unable to pay for. Yet if I felt able to lose it, I would say nothing. But in thinking the matter over, I do not see what he will be able to do for a library and medicines if I take mine back.

"If he can pay ten dollars a month, and not fail, I will try and get along with that. But I would like to have things so secured that no one else can take them away from him.

"If he does not wish to do this I will take the books, if in as good order as when I let him have them, at the same price I charged him; and the same with the medicine chest.

"I do not want him to think that I would distress him.

"Love to Dr. W—— and all good pilgrims.

"Yours affectionately,

"J. W. REDFIELD."

He returned to Illinois, and the last of May came to Ogle Station, now Ashton, near Mt. Pleasant, to attend a quarterly meeting on my new circuit. This had been organized in part out of the fruits of the great revival at Mt. Pleasant, which has already been described.

On Sunday morning he preached from the text, "It is finished." His wife was obliged to sit by his side, and prop him up by holding her hands under his left elbow, while he held on to the pulpit with his right hand. During the opening prayer, he seemed to talk face to face with God. I was impressed with the thought, we shall see wondrous things to-day. While attempting to read the second hymn emotions overcame him, and he requested us to sing without further reading.

The outline of his sermon was somewhat as follows:

1. Man's condition before the fall.
2. His condition after the fall.
3. None among men or angels who are qualified to redeem him.
4. The finding of "the Lamb slain from the foundation of the world."
5. Man redeemed.

After the first few introductory remarks, probably not one-half dozen of the large congregation had a thought outside of the theme of the sermon. One could read the separate divisions of the discourse upon the countenances of his listeners. While portraying in the most graphic manner, his conception of man's physical, mental and spiritual state before the fall, every face seemed beaming with admiration. When he introduced the Tempter amid this scene of loveliness, consternation seemed to take the place; and when at last the sin was finished, and all the dire results were ushered in, an expression of indignation spread over every face. When he portrayed the disabilities of sin, and the helplessness of humanity, Christians, for the time, forgot they were Christians, and both they and sinners simultaneously wailed out their anguish, and every face took on a look of fearful despair. When he at last found a ransom in the person of

the Son of God, and, in a few sentences, made plain the
reasonableness of the atonement of Christ, sinners forgot
they were sinners and joined in the rejoicings of the saints.
Before he was through with his last point, the benefits of redemption, more than twenty persons were on their feet,
with eyes closed, clasped hands, and streaming faces, gazing
by faith upon the wonderful provisions of grace. For some
moments I expected to see a group of very wicked men back
by the door on their feet, uniting in this demonstration of
joy.

Several times, I now recollect, I was lost with the rest.
But at this point there came to my mind, with great clearness and power, William Wirt's story of "The Blind Preacher," which I had read in my boyhood. Mr. Wirt, after
describing the man, the circumstances, the occasion, and the
wonderful eloquence of the preacher, and its effect upon his
congregation, spoke of his fears, that when the congregation came to realize where they were, and what they were,
that the mental shock would destroy the good effect of the
discourse. And I now found myself wondering in like manner. But while I wondered, Mr. Redfield began to let
them down so gradually and perfectly that the good effects
were saved. He said:

"When the great Erie Canal was completed, a line of
cannon was stationed along its banks its entire length. When
the water was let in at Buffalo, cannon number one was
fired, and cannon number two took up the report, and
passed it on to number three, and number three to number four, and so on, until the report reached Albany; and
whoever heard the report of the cannon understood it to
mean, *it is finished.* And so when God had prepared the
way and let in the tide of salvation on which man was to
come back to his Maker, the first report was heard in the
song of the angels—'Glory to God in the highest; on earth
peace, good-will to men'; and the last dying echoes of it

came from the cross in the words of the text, 'It is finished.'"

He then let go of the desk and allowed himself to fall back upon the pulpit sofa.

The next day the writer accompanied him and his wife to St. Charles, and in a few days to a general quarterly meeting at Crystal Lake, and the next week to Belvidere, and at last to the camp meeting at St. Charles. At all these places we had meetings of great power and success.

The St. Charles camp meeting was largely attended. It was led by Superintendent Roberts. Mr. Redfield did not attempt to preach but once, and that was spoiled by a fanatical Congregationalist who was determined to have him healed on the spot.

Soon after this Mr. Redfield began to entertain hopes that God would restore him. His knowledge of his case, as a physician, gave him no hope from the arts or skill of men. He knew none but God could do the work. His mental conflicts were most severe. He saw so much to do, so few to do it, and himself willing to do his best, and he wondered why God did not set him free. For twenty-six years he had longed for the time to come when he could work untrammeled. Now the time had come, and he was mysteriously laid by. He would ask the feeblest saints to account for it, and would listen to them with the profoundest attention. It was pitiful at times to see him, when some unwise believer would publicly condemn him with the philosophy that if he was right he would not be thus afflicted. At such times he would receive their idle vaporings as the most solemn truth, because it coincided with his oppressive temptations on the subject. At times he would rise above it all, and would triumph gloriously.

He visited the quarterly and camp meetings, gave advice, counseled with the young preachers, and did what he could in the public services. He sometimes tried to preach, but his thinking powers seemed paralyzed; and at last he gave up trying altogether.

The following letter will show his state of mind at this time. Some of it evidently tokens the breaking down of his magnificent mind.

"MARENGO, Ill., Feb. 10, 1862.

"My dear Sister Roberts:—I have felt drawn to write to you and have begun and then abandoned it for the time, and thought it best to wait till I had something of more importance to write. I have been learning lessons through my whole affliction that nothing but this very severe stroke could teach me. Astronomers, who wish to gaze at the heavens in daylight, go into deep wells, and from those dark places can see what they cannot see above ground. I, too, have been making this dark valley my observatory for about fifteen months, and some of the views I have had, and still have, are not lawful to describe. I see a deep meaning in my case that must have a bearing upon the cause of Free Methodism, all over the land. I had been learning fact after fact till a few weeks ago in St. Charles, when I saw the wonderful cure of Sister M—— from a state of disease which under the best of treatment must have taken weeks if not months, and yet it was done instantly. I saw great light, and was rejoicing in it, and my heart was deeply agitated, when I asked the Lord, 'Why may I not also receive the healing touch?' I began a thorough search to find out where there might be any deficiency in my moral state, and the first thing I ran against was, my undue care and anxiety for the Free Methodist Church, and preachers. While I was giving up the church it seemed that it would almost take my life. After the church came the preachers, and I had to give them all up. I had not once suspected that it was wrong to love the dear boys, or to feel an interest in them; but I found that unsuspectingly I was assuming the place of the Lord, and I was regarding them above all other gospel ministers. I now learned that I must not value the Free Methodist Church or its preachers, above any other. Uni-

versal charity was the lesson I was here taught. Next came
the most gentle and sweet intimations that I must soon go to
Syracuse. I gave way to reasoning about the propriety of
this, when I was seized with strangling spasms, and it seemed
I must yield to go or die. Four or five were present who were
in a great struggle of prayer for me. But as soon as I gave
up to go, reason or no reason, I was instantly at perfect
peace and rest. I had no idea that I would be made to suffer so intensely for simply a conscientious hesitancy about
going until I felt clear that it was the voice of the Lord.

"To-day I had another down spell, little dreaming that
anything was affecting me except the usual depression which
affects me on account of my feeble condition; when the most
mild and gentle influence turned my eye back to about ten
years ago when God gave me a commission to preach redemption, * and the question came, 'Will you go back to
that?' When I said, 'I will,' I was all light again. I am
now holding myself in readiness for marching orders. I
may not be mustered out for some time to come; but I say,
'Anytime and anywhere.'

   *   *   *   *   *   *   *   *   *   *   *

"I have much to say that I cannot put on paper. I have
learned much I never could have known had I not been afflicted.

"I am now writing my life, and shall bring it with me,
to see about getting it published.

"My love to Brother Roberts.

"J. W. REDFIELD."

During this summer Mr. Redfield gathered together
what means he had, and purchased forty acres of unimproved
land near Geneva, the county seat of Kane county, and about
three miles from St. Charles. A letter before me in which
he ordered small fruits from a nurseryman, is a curiosity.

---

* Mr. Redfield held to the idea of a redemption of the mental faculties, to be
experienced by the faithful in this life.

When asked what he intended to do with his land, he divulged a plan to make it a pilgrims' home. His house and out-buildings would have cost many thousands of dollars. When asked where the income of the home was to come from, he did not know.

In the fall of 1862 he attended a camp meeting in Ogle county, Illinois. Here an incident occurred that drew him out, and for a few moments he seemed himself again. At half-past ten o'clock Monday morning Mr. Roberts commenced a sacramental service. A table was spread with the bread and wine, in front of the desk; the love-feast had closed, and Mr. Roberts gave out the hymn commencing,

"What! never speak one idle word?"

when one of the preachers interrupted him with the question, "Is that hymn a just test of entire sanctification?"

"It is," was the answer.

"Then I have not got it," replied the questioner. "Nor I," "nor I," said several. Immediately commenced a spirit of confession, of being without the experience, first on the part of many who had lost it; then others threw away their confidence as they listened to those confessions, until it resulted in a panic. Mr. Roberts was unable to preach because of it until ten o'clock at night. There was scarcely any partaking of food, and no cessation of the meeting during the day. The scene was indescribable. The gloom of despair seemed to settle upon almost all. About four o'clock in the afternoon, Mr. Redfield arose, and, after considerable effort, secured the attention of the despairing ones, and when all was quiet, he asked, in his inimitable manner, "Is there not a short way out of the woods?" and then proceeded to clear away the confusion of thought which prevailed. In a very short time, those who had unnecessarily cast away their confidence began to take it back, at first tremblingly, and at last joyously. Then those who had need to confess their backslidings and to seek for salvation, did so, and a glorious victory was the result.

During the winter of '62 and '63, a visit was made to Buffalo, and then to Syracuse, where were pilgrims of mighty faith, and he hoped for restoration in answer to their prayers. Here he began to show evidences of the breaking down of his mind; which led many of his friends to distrust his personal convictions of duty. This caused him great pain. At last he turned his face toward the West again, weeping as he went. He said but little now in public gatherings. He attended the annual session of the Illinois Conference. The love-feast Sunday morning was truly blessed, and none enjoyed it more than Mr. Redfield. When the bread and water were passed, he tried several times to drink from the cup, such were his overflowing tears, and the convulsive joy of his heart. Little did some of us think that it was the last we should see him alive. He returned to the home of Brother Joslyn, who had so long cared for him. The last letter he ever wrote was the following. It shows the ruling spirit of his life. It was to a Wesleyan minister.

"MARENGO, Ill., Oct. 29, 1863.

"Dear Brother F——:—Your kind favor of the 17th came duly to hand. We have often wondered why you left here so soon, and why you did not write. We see by your letter that the devil is neither dead nor converted, and that you are beginning to learn that to take sides with God is equivalent to a declaration of war against the world of formalism. But while we were sympathizing with you in your conflicts for God and truth, our hearts were made glad last week, at our conference, to see an old man, a postmaster, who had come about eighty miles to see the Free Methodists, and to learn the way of holiness. He said he saw a report in the *American Wesleyan* from a Brother F——, giving an account of his experience, and now he wanted to know how to get what Brother F—— had got. He began in good earnest,

and soon was hopping and shouting in a glorious manner, and
went to his home to show what great things the Lord had
done for him.

"I think if you could have seen him, you would have
taken courage to stand for God and the truth. We will
pray God to make you a power in the earth; and I think he
will look to you to spread holiness in your church. God will
stand by you. Shall the Almighty find in you one who
dares to stand for the right? Some one must' assert the
rights of God, and stand in defense of the gospel. The
commission is to you; will you honor the call, or let God's
cause go by default? True, you will be often misunderstood,
often slandered, and will pass a stormy life, and possibly die in
obscurity. Your epitaph from mouth to mouth may be, 'Poor,
mistaken man;' he might have passed through the world like a
comet, leaving a luminous path behind; but he disregarded
the judgment and opinions of men, and died unhonored by
the masses.' Can you stand thus to be unappreciated, and
even depreciated for God and truth's sake? Oh, take
courage, brother. Don't make it necessary for God to scrape
the truth in pronouncing on you, 'Well done, good and faithful servant.' The great battle has begun. God and the
devil are in combat. War, war, is everywhere. The spirit
land is in commotion. The world has caught the spirit conflict. Armageddon has sounded the war cry, and the closing
struggle is upon us. As a sentinel for the truth you, yes you,
Brother F——, must stand. God has ratified your authority
by your success, and he now demands, and will hold you responsible for, fidelity. God help you, is my prayer.

"Yours in Jesus,

"J. W. REDFIELD."

The delay in answering the letter was caused by his
attending the conference.

November 1st, the next day after writing this letter, another stroke of paralysis came, and he was laid upon his bed

in an apparently unconscious state. Friends watched over him with more than filial solicitude; but his eyes were darkened, and his eloquent lips were hushed. A few minutes before eight o'clock, November 2, 1863, his right leg drew up and straightened out again in the same manner in which he was accustomed to stamp at the turning point of his great spiritual battles.

A hush came upon all in the room. The place seemed filled with the hosts of God, and JOHN WESLEY REDFIELD was at rest.

Two days later his funeral was held in the Free Methodist church in Marengo, Illinois, conducted by his friend and beloved brother in the Lord, Rev. B. T. Roberts. Six young ministers, who loved him as their lives, bore him to his last resting-place in the beautiful cemetery near by. Above his grave stands a small marble shaft, and inscribed upon it is this fitting tribute:

"HE WAS TRUE TO HIS MOTTO,—FIDELITY TO GOD."

THE CONQUEROR CROWNED.

"Servant of God, well done!
   Thy glorious warfare's past;
The battle's fought, the race is won,
   And thou art crowned at last;—

"Of all thy heart's desire
   Triumphantly possessed;
Lodged by the ministerial choir
   In thy Redeemer's breast.

"In condescending love,
   Thy ceaseless prayer he heard,
And bade thee suddenly remove,
   To thy complete reward.

"With saints enthroned on high,
   Thou dost thy Lord proclaim,
And still to God salvation cry,—
   Salvation to the Lamb!

"O happy, happy soul!
   In ecstasies of praise,
Long as eternal ages roll,
   Thou seest thy Saviour's face.

"Redeemed from earth and pain,
   Ah! when shall we ascend,
And all in Jesus' presence reign
   With our translated friend?"